STARTORN

A Starstruck Novel

BRENDA HIATT

dolphin star
PRESS

StarTorn

A Starstruck Novel

Copyright 2025 by Brenda Hiatt
Cover art by Ravven Kitsune

All rights reserved
This is a work of fiction. Any resemblance between actual events or persons, living or
dead, are purely coincidental.

License Notes

Dolphin Star Press

ISBN: 978-1-947205-45-1

DEDICATION

For everyone who wonders if they really matter...
You do!

✦

THE STARSTRUCK SERIES BY BRENDA HIATT

Starstruck
Starcrossed
Starbound
Starfall

✦

Fractured Jewel: A Starstruck Novella
The Girl From Mars
The Handmaid's Secret
Convergent
Yuletide Perils: A Starstruck Novella
Unraveling the Stars
Mindbound
StarTorn

DHIRFURACHA

(dji-FUR-uh-sha): sisters

M

"I'm sorry, but you did agree to spend a year in your current community before requesting a change," I repeat to the distraught woman facing Molly and me in our recently designated audience chamber at NuAgra. "You're by no means the first to ask for an exception, and we simply can't grant all of them."

The woman's pretty face reflects her disappointment. "I...I suppose not. I really thought living close to my sister in the Chicago suburbs would make our transition easier, but lately she and I don't get along nearly as well as we used to. My husband and I now feel our family may do better in a purely *Echtran* community, at least until our daughter is older."

"How old is she?" Molly asks. She usually stays quiet during these audiences, even though I've encouraged her to speak up more so she can get a better feel for the process.

"Fifteen," the woman answers.

The same age I was when I learned the truth about myself, and Martians, and, well, everything. "Fifteen isn't an easy age," I concede, "but your message indicated she's doing quite well in school."

"Well, yes, in terms of her grades. Not that we expected otherwise, given how relatively simple the *Duchas* curriculum is. It's just—" Breaking off, the woman darts an almost furtive glance at me, then at

Molly. "It's the other students that are the problem. The *Duchas* students. The, ah, *Duchas* boys, in particular. I'm...we're...afraid our daughter might—" She stops again, now clearly embarrassed.

"That she might become *too* friendly with one of them?" I prompt.

Head lowered, not meeting my eyes, she nods. "There...there are no *Echtran* boys in her high school, you see. And her classes unfortunately aren't challenging enough to distract her from—" She swallows. "No offense, Excellency. I know you grew up here, and you spoke in such glowing terms about what life in a *Duchas* town could be like, but in our case..."

"No offense taken," I assure her. "This transition has been difficult for most of our people. If Nuath's energy shortage were not so critical, I never would have urged so many to make the sacrifice of relocating to Earth. The majority are adjusting remarkably well, however, based on all reports. Your family will, too, I'm sure. In fifteen months, another launch window will open, bringing another influx of Martian colonists to Earth. We very much hope that by then the first, brave wave that included your family will be settled in well enough to ease their transitions. I'd very much like your family to hold out until then, if possible."

Sighing, the woman nods again. "We'll try, Excellency, though I do wish my sister would stop with her unnecessary advice. She thinks that just because she's lived on Earth for five years already, she knows everything, but her sons already had wives when they moved here. She's never —" She stops abruptly, looking stricken. "Forgive me, Excellencies! I should not have— That is, I'm sure Aliana means well. I, ah, thank you for allowing me this opportunity to speak." She bows deeply to us both, right fist over heart, then hurries out of the room.

Molly waits until she's gone to say, "Poor thing. She probably thinks she got her sister in trouble by criticizing her to you."

I grin at her. "Hardly, but it does make me appreciate how well I get along with *my* sister."

"Same." She smiles back at me. "Was that our last one for this week?"

By mutual agreement, we only hold these audiences once a week on Monday afternoons after school, at least for now.

Glancing at the schedule on my omni's holo-screen, I nod. "Once we have enough local magistrates in place, people won't have to travel all the way to Jewel to have their petitions heard in person. We still need to appoint a bunch more temporary ones."

"Aye, I thought we'd be done with that by now, but the new *Echtran* immigrants are more widely scattered than I realized. But there are only a few small communities left now, right?"

I nod. "Less than a dozen, I think. You've helped speed up this process a lot—and made it less boring, too."

"I've only been helping for a few days," she protests. "Maybe it's more the thought of having help at all that's making the difference?"

"Maybe. Either way, I appreciate it. And once Kyna winds up this research project of hers, she can take over a lot of the boring admin stuff —though you and I should probably be involved in some of the final vetting of election candidates."

Molly stands up. "Not today, though, right? I still have homework to do."

"So do I. Besides, Rigel and Tristan will be here any minute to take us home."

⁺⁺

Tuesday morning at school, I'm briefly bemused—again—by the contrast between the person I am at NuAgra, where I have to assume the role of Sovereign Emileia, and at school, where I'm still plain Marsha Truitt. Maybe not the total loser I was a year and a half ago, before Rigel arrived in Jewel and I learned about my true heritage, but definitely nobody special.

Of course, just being Rigel's girlfriend feels pretty special all by itself, what with him being our star quarterback and all. But nobody except the other dozen or so *Echtran* students, plus Bri and Deb, have any idea who I really am. It absolutely needs to be that way for now, but sometimes I wish I could clue in a *few* other people.

Like Trina.

"One of these days, maybe you'll develop a sense of style, Marsha," she snarks when I walk into third period Chemistry class, hand-in-hand with Rigel. "Dressing better might make you look a *little* less like a deranged homeless person. Though I wouldn't count on it, since the deranged part is totally true."

I walk past her without so much as making eye contact. She's determined to make sure no one, including me, forgets I attacked her last week. No matter how much she deserved it, I did go way overboard—in fact, I might have killed her if Molly and Tristan hadn't stopped me. Maybe losing control like that wasn't *entirely* my fault while I was still messed up from Faxon's memories, but I still feel guilty about it.

You okay? Rigel thinks to me as we sit down at our lab table, well away from Trina.

Yeah. Thanks to you. I smile over at him. If not for his "intervention" last week, I'd be in the *Echtran* equivalent of a psychiatric lockdown facility right now.

His answering smile is accompanied by a wash of love that makes me warm all over. *Anytime. You know that.*

I do. I send a return blast of love to reinforce my silent words. I'm so beyond lucky to have him!

At lunch, I'm pleasantly surprised when Erin, one of our two *Echtran* sophomores, shyly approaches me as I leave the cashier.

"Er, M?" She only bobs her head slightly, a definite improvement. She's come close to bowing a few times in the past. "Can I talk to you for a sec?"

"Of course!" I smile as invitingly as I can. The younger *Echtran* students, in particular, still have trouble treating me like just another classmate. "What's up?"

Though she returns my smile, she hesitates for a long moment before answering. "Is it...I mean...are there any rules we should know about, um, accepting an invitation from a *Duchas?* A boy, I mean?"

"No, of course not. I've encouraged you all from the start to make friends with them."

"I know. But...even if it's sort of like a date? I mean, I know Liam and Lucas are dating *Duchas* girls now, but they're your special friends."

Without even focusing, I can sense her nervousness—but also no small degree of hopeful eagerness.

"Do you like him?"

Her face goes nearly as red as her hair as she nods. "We have Geometry together and he's...really nice. This morning he asked if I want to meet him at Dream Cream one afternoon this week and I sort of said yes. Then realized I should probably check with you first?"

"I appreciate you being cautious, but you definitely don't need my approval for something like that. Though if things get really serious, to the point you're tempted to break secrecy—"

"Oh! No, no, nothing like that, I promise! I just...thought it might be nice to get to know him a little better. Outside of class. That's all."

"Which is totally fine," I assure her. "In fact, it sounds like a great idea."

She lets out a relieved breath. "Oh. Good. Thank you! Probably nothing will come of it, but—"

"Just see where things go before worrying about that, okay? And have fun!"

Grinning, she nods enthusiastically, then scurries off to join the other younger *Echtran* students at their usual table. I go to mine, where Molly, Tristan and Rigel are already sitting.

"What are you smiling about?" Molly asks when I reach them.

I shrug. "Just glad the newer students are finally getting more comfortable with me. Erin, especially, has acted almost afraid to talk to me, but I think maybe she's over it now."

"That's good to hear," Molly agrees. "It was super weird when they all treated me so formally right after the news about us being sisters broke, but they got over it pretty quickly. I guess with you actually being Sovereign and all, it's a little different."

"It shouldn't be, not here. I'd much rather they see me as just another high school junior and not someone...special."

At school, anyway. Much as I'd like to, I don't dare encourage that degree of informality at "official" *Echtran* gatherings, like the monthly NuAgra meetings. At those, I have to project enough authority to ensure the adult *Echtrans* take me seriously.

"Sorry, man," I hear Tristan saying to Sean when Rigel and I approach the other members of our "Bond Squad" in the parking lot after school. "I wish the Council wasn't so—"

"Yeah. Me, too." Sean sounds more resigned than upset. "It would be easier if everyone hadn't assumed all along we'd go to State again this year. I know Liam is especially bummed we won't."

Kira's already leaning comfortingly against Sean's side and now Molly puts a sympathetic hand on his arm, too. "At least he didn't go overboard last night, trying to win after all. I was afraid he might."

Sean shakes his head. "Alan and I talked to him—drummed it into him, really. He gets it. But none of us liked it."

The *Echtran* Council laid down the law a couple weeks ago that if Jewel High's boys' basketball team went to State again this year, they'd forbid *any Echtran* students, anywhere, from playing on sports teams. It can't have been easy to comply. With three *Echtrans* on the team, the Jewel Jaguars could probably beat most NBA teams, much less other 2-A high school teams.

I feel bad for our guys...but not enough to countermand the Council's decision. Because they're right that it's way too soon for our people to risk discovery. Earth humans simply aren't ready for that yet. Which reminds me.

"Molly, you still plan to sit in on our meeting with world leaders next month, right?"

Her spike of alarm is impossible to ignore. "*Our* meeting? I thought I was just going to watch, off-camera!"

"You don't have to actually participate if you don't want to, but I should at least introduce you to them. If not next month, then soon."

"Soon, maybe. But not *that* soon, okay? And don't say anything about it to Mum if you can avoid it. Please?"

I chuckle. "I always try to avoid giving her extra reasons to push—not that it stops her."

Mrs. O'Gara is just dying for Molly to take a more active leadership role. She was beyond delighted to learn I'm now mentoring Molly so she can help with some of my duties, but it's clear she'd like her to do way more. Like become a second Sovereign.

Tristan pats Molly reassuringly on the arm. "Remember, she can't force you to do anything you don't want to. But I should probably get you home, huh?" He pulls out his omni-phone to check the time. "Ah, looks like this week's *Echtran Enquirer* just dropped. Let's see what—Oh, crap!"

"What?" the other five of us ask at once.

"Let me guess," I say. "Gwendolyn Gannett?"

He nods. "Yeah, but this time her column has the headline for the whole issue." He holds the screen so we can all see the bolded words.

"BREAKING: Our Sovereign a murderer?"

Molly and I both groan and Rigel curses aloud, then we all lean in close to read the article.

⁺˙✦

BREAKING: Our Sovereign a murderer?
An exclusive story by Gwendolyn Gannett

Last week we all learned that a group of protesters was arrested outside the entrance to NuAgra, our new government center in Jewel, Indiana, just as the escaped dictator, Faxon, was recaptured on Mars. Your intrepid reporter has now uncovered all kinds of juicy details connected with the nature of that protest, as well as the extremely disturbing incident immediately preceding those arrests.

As you'll recall, many of us were deservedly worried by Faxon's threats while he was still eluding his captors, not to mention his so-called demonstrations, which caused significant damage in Nuath. Fearing for the fates of their friends and families back home, a coalition of *Echtrans* gathered at NuAgra to petition our *Echtran* Council and Sovereign to take stronger action to safeguard our people on Mars.

"Petition?" Tristan repeats disbelievingly. "Those radicals were demanding Molly and M's execution!"

"Shh," Molly soothes him. "We're fine now. Let's keep reading."

For reasons never fully explained, our Sovereign and Princess Malena, along with their teen Bodyguard boyfriends, were allowed by the Council to go outside the NuAgra gates to speak with the protesters without the precaution of a NuAgra security force. Had that precaution been taken, could the outrage that followed have been avoided? Sadly, we'll never know.

I spoke with several of those arrested, who told me that when negotiations for a solution broke down, our Sovereign and her Bodyguard used some sort of enhanced offensive weapon to fatally electrocute Murgh Gall, the protest leader. A member of NuAgra's security team testified to investigators that the protest had turned violent by that point, though I've heard no reports of the Sovereign, Princess Malena or their Bodyguards sustaining any physical injuries. It is therefore difficult to imagine such lethal measures could possibly have been justified.

With the publication of this report, I expect to hear renewed calls for Sovereign Emileia and Rigel Stuart to be kept apart for the safety of everyone, both *Echtran* and *Duchas*. In addition, it may be prudent for Princess Malena to take a more active leadership role while her sister is evaluated for mental stability. I'm told no criminal charges are currently being considered, but as more details about the nature of that fatal attack emerge, we should not be surprised if that changes.

A source with close ties to the *Echtran* Council has promised me an interview later today that should shed more light on precisely what occurred, and how. I'll be sharing what I learn from that interview during my program this evening, so be sure to tune in!

✦

There's a long moment of silence before Rigel starts cursing again. It's something he rarely does, but this time I'm tempted to join him.

"I wonder who her source is?" Tristan says then. "And what they'll tell her?"

Sean's frown deepens. "Surely not someone on the actual Council?"

"Close ties, she said," Molly points to that line in the article. "So probably not. You don't think—?" She glances at Sean.

He shakes his head. "No. No way it's Dad. He'd never talk to Gwendolyn Gannett about stuff like that."

"My father might, though." Tristan looks—and feels—troubled. "Or it could even be Devyn Kane himself. Father was telling him everything for a while."

"Bet she won't say," Kira predicts. "Whoever it is, they're probably not authorized to speak to the press, since the investigation is still going on. You watch, she'll just say 'an anonymous source' when she spills whatever new dirt she gets."

"Maybe she won't get any?" Molly, ever the optimist, suggests. "I mean, the whole truth about what happened would only prove what M did was totally justified. Right?"

Nobody answers right away.

"Except it wasn't, not really," I force myself to say. "You all know as well as I do we could have just stunned the guy. Honestly, if the justices in Dun Cloch decide to bring charges against me, I can't claim they'd be wrong."

"We've been over this." Rigel gives my hand, clasped in his, a little shake. "You weren't yourself. Faxon was majorly messing with your head when that happened. You're fine now."

I still have a hard time completely accepting that excuse. "Faxon's *memories* were messing with my head," I correct him. "Not Faxon himself, not directly. And it was my choice to open myself to those memories, which does make it my fault."

"If you hadn't, he'd probably still be on the loose, might even have destroyed all of Nuath by now," Molly reminds me. "You took a huge personal risk and it paid off. The guy you accidentally killed was already a murderer, Kyna said so. You saved thousands, maybe hundreds of thousands of lives. If they try to bring charges, I'll testify to that, and so will everyone else who knows the truth."

"Accidentally?" I raise an eyebrow. "When I let loose that lightning bolt, I totally meant to kill him for what he'd done."

Molly stubbornly shakes her head. "Only because of what Faxon's memories did to you. Less than a minute later, you were as horrified by what you'd done as anyone. More, actually."

She's right, but I'm not at all sure that should let me off the hook. I doubt I can win an argument with Molly, though, given her *graell*-enhanced persuasive ability.

"Let's just wait and see what happens," I finally say. "You and Rigel are always telling me not to borrow trouble, so I'll do my best not to."

"Good. Don't." Molly pats my shoulder. "How about you all come over to our house tonight so we can watch her stupid show together? See if she really does find out any more than she's already spilled?"

Rigel glances at me, then at Molly. "Okay if I invite my folks to come, too? They'll also want to hear whatever she says, and between the O'Garas and my dad, maybe we can figure out who her source is, even if she doesn't say."

"Sure," she says.

"Thanks." *Though if she learns too much and shares it with the world, who told her will hardly matter,* Rigel adds silently, just to me. *The two of us will still be royally screwed.*

BEIDAN

(BID-den): gossip; scandal

Molly

That evening after dinner, everyone gathers at our house, as planned. Much as we all hate Gwendolyn's weekly broadcast, there's no way we *can't* watch after the buildup in her dumb column. With Rigel's parents both here along with all six members of our "Bond Squad," our little living room is every bit as crowded as when we hosted the weekly *Echtran* Council meetings. Especially since two Council members usually attend holographically.

"Honestly, Van, I wish you hadn't felt obligated to give that woman regular airtime," Mum says, fussing with cups and saucers as she sets out tea and almond cookies for the group. "She's always gone out of her way to stir up trouble, and this gives her an even wider platform."

"I had no real input on programming," Mr. Stuart explains, not for the first time. "Once the network itself was up and running, my only involvement has been troubleshooting. Unfortunately, like it or not, hers is now the ENN's most highly-rated show."

Tristan scoffs indignantly. "More popular than Molly and M's? No way!"

Mr. Stuart lifts a shoulder. "Their weekly broadcasts run a close second in viewership, but...yes, I'm afraid so."

"Scandal sells," Dad reminds us all. "Always has, probably always will.

It's how her columns in the *Enquirer* became so widely read in the first place. If there's scandal to be found, she'll find it."

"And if there's not, she'll make it up," Mum adds with a snort.

No one disagrees. I can think of at least three times she's done exactly that over the past year and a half. M can probably think of more.

Dad sets his omni on the coffee table and activates the big holo-screen while Mum pours out tea for everyone. A moment later, the red-and-blue *Echtran* News Network logo is replaced by Gwendolyn Gannett's overly-made-up face. I brace myself.

"Good evening, everyone!" she gushes, wearing a huge, fake smile. "Based on the calls and messages I've received over the past few hours, you're all beyond eager to hear what I learned today, so I won't keep you in suspense. I should warn you, however, to prepare yourselves to be shocked." She stops and titters. "No pun intended."

Pausing for dramatic effect, she schools her expression to one of grave concern, though I can tell she's barely reining in her glee at having explosive news to share.

"As I mentioned in today's *Echtran Enquirer* column, I was granted an interview with a source who provided convincing proof of his—or her —" she punctuates that with a wink— "access to confidential *Echtran* Council information. This person only spoke to me on the condition I would not reveal their identity. Indeed, I couldn't if I wanted to, as they masked both their face and voice for our whole video call. I can assure you, however, that I *have* been able to validate this person's credentials.

"You will recall our scare early last fall, when an alien menace threat-ened to release an electromagnetic pulse powerful enough to disrupt all technology on Earth. That potential catastrophe was supposedly averted by our Scientists, with the help of Sovereign Emileia and Rigel Stuart. However, precisely what help those two young people provided was never explained. Desiring to bring you the full truth, I requested more details at the time, but was told that information was classified. When you hear what I learned today, you'll understand why."

As she pauses again, allowing anticipation to build, M and Rigel exchange a worried glance. "Do you think she—?" M starts to ask, but then Gwendolyn continues.

"My source was privy to *all* the reports from our Scientists, both before and after that incident, as they researched possible ways to prevent the alien attack. Among other things, they re-tested the electrical charges our Sovereign and her Bodyguard are able to produce, which were only hinted at in the earlier paper detailing their supposed *graell* abilities. The reason for lack of full disclosure is now obvious. Believe it or not, those tests revealed that together, those two teens can generate what amounts to a significant lightning strike capable of vaporizing solid matter!"

She looks gravely at the camera for a moment to let that sink in, and all ten of us watching groan aloud.

"Who would have told her—?" Dr. Stuart begins, when Gwendolyn starts talking again.

"According to my source, the massive electrical charge the pair produced was what boosted the power of our Scientists' existing equipment enough to avert the alien EMP. I, ah, suppose that means we have more to thank our Sovereign and her Bodyguard for than we realized.

"At the same time, I'm sure I'm not the only one alarmed by learning two teenagers have the ability to create such an incredibly destructive force. Especially as it's now reported that the pair recently used exactly that ability to *kill* one of our own people. Some witnesses to the events outside NuAgra assumed an enhanced *Echtran* weapon was used for that attack, but apparently not. My persistent questioning of a forensic expert in Dun Cloch got him to admit the deceased man's injuries were far more consistent with a lightning strike than even the maximum one of our energy weapons can inflict. As children may be watching, I'll spare you the grisly details from his autopsy report.

"One woman I spoke with, who was among those protesting that night, claims that our Sovereign turned on her immediately after murdering her compatriot and likely would have killed her, too, had others not intervened. Given this new information, I hope you'll join me in demanding the *Echtran* Council conduct a full evaluation of Sovereign Emileia's mental and emotional fitness for the important position she occupies. After the horrors of Faxon's regime, the last thing our people need is another dangerously unbalanced leader.

"According to their own broadcasts and the Sovereign's articles, Princess Malena has recently begun assisting with her sister's duties. This is all to the good, as the better prepared our Princess is to step into a primary governing role, the less our people risk being left without a competent leader. The fact that Princess Malena seems to be moving toward a far more traditional pairing than her sister should be an additional comfort to you all.

"In a moment, I'll be speaking with a few candidates who have put their names forward for our upcoming mayoral elections. But first, here's a message from Dun Cloch about some exciting new omni apps they've been developing."

Dad mutes the sound as the video feed shifts to a commercial.

After an awkward silence, M is the first to comment. "Okay, that was...even worse than I expected."

"Who would have shared such sensitive information with her?" Dr. Stuart finishes the question she started to ask earlier. "One of our Scientists? I can't imagine anyone on the Council would do so." She looks at her husband, who's frowning, then at my parents.

"Certainly not," Mum affirms, though she looks a little uncomfortable. Because she's been pushing all along for me to take a bigger leadership role, just like Gwendolyn suggested?

Tristan's even more uneasy. I clearly feel his discomfort through our clasped hands but before I can ask, even silently, he speaks up. "Maybe not someone *currently* on the Council. But my father was still a member when those tests were done."

I squeeze his hand. "We don't know it was him." *And even if it was, you had nothing to do with it,* I add silently.

"Do you think you can get him to tell you if he's the person Gannett interviewed?" Sean asks, clearly remembering how Tristan got his dad to spill a ton of info about Devyn by using his persuasive ability.

"At this point, it hardly matters who told her," Rigel says. "The result will be the same. People will start demanding—again—that M and I be kept away from each other."

M swallows visibly. "I had a ton going on, but I still should have made the time to write my own column for this week's *Enquirer*, saying *something* about what happened before Gwendolyn could beat me to the punch. It was too much to hope that none of those people would talk about what they saw that night."

"Yeah, but it sounds like most of them thought you guys used one of our energy weapons," Sean points out. "Nobody would have known about the lightning thing you and Rigel can do if someone in the know hadn't blabbed to that busybody." He darts a glance at Tristan, who tenses again.

I glare at my brother. "Let's not go flinging accusations when we don't actually know anything, okay?"

Tristan responds to the unspoken implication anyway. "Like I said, Father was still on the Council when the Scientists did those tests. He didn't say anything to Mother or me about them at the time, but he could totally have told Devyn Kane. We know they were in touch back then. So even if Father didn't talk to Gwendolyn Gannett himself, Devyn could have. Or somebody Devyn put up to it."

Several of us nod at that reasoning. Considering that Devyn tried to have me killed, then tried to take control of the whole Council with an Ossian Sphere, he definitely wouldn't be above sharing secrets with a muckraking reporter to make M look bad.

"You're right, that does make the most sense," M agrees. "But Rigel's also right that figuring out who told her isn't nearly as important as dealing with the fallout."

"Maybe there won't actually be that much," I suggest hopefully. "I mean, people already knew about you guys talking telepathically and that you could generate electrical charges, those were in the Scientists' original report and Shim's write-up about your *graell* bond, way last fall."

The look M gives me is almost pitying. "But now they know I actually killed somebody using that power. Somehow I don't see that being just glossed over. I need to address it head on, like I should have already."

"What will you say?" Kira asks before I can.

"I'm not sure yet," M admits, "but I'll come up with something before Thursday's broadcast."

"And I'll help," I emphatically assure her. "Tomorrow you and I can work on exactly what to tell people to minimize any blowback. Okay?"

That gets a smile from her, which was half my goal. "Thanks, Molly. If anybody can come up with a way to spin things so they sound less awful, it'll be you."

⁺✦₊

At school the next day, we get our first inklings of how people—our people, anyway—are reacting to yesterday's *EE* article and last night's broadcast.

First period Pre-Cal isn't too bad, since Liam is the only other

Echtran in the class and he's dating M's good *Duchas* friend, Deb. It's clear from the way they both act that they either saw or heard about yesterday's news, but they seem more concerned and sympathetic than scared.

Kira, M and I are the only *Echtrans* in second period French, so no worries there, either. But when we get to third period, I don't need M's emotion-sensing ability to notice how jittery Mr. Abbot, our *Echtran* Chemistry teacher, is. He keeps sending worried glances M and Rigel's way as he explains today's lab, and actually gets another student to pass them the worksheet. Coward.

I consider reassuring him—or maybe telling him off—after class, but Tristan discourages me from doing either one.

M and Rigel have to have noticed, he silently points out when the bell rings. *They're the ones who should say something—or not. Either way, it should be up to them, right?*

Irritated, I frown at him. *How can I not defend her? She's my sister AND my Sovereign! I'm not going to let anyone—*

He takes my hand and tugs me toward the hallway, sending soothing vibes through his touch. *I know, but give her first crack at defending herself, okay? But yeah, if anybody criticizes her to your face, have at 'em!*

That gets a reluctant grin from me. Because I totally will.

I get my chance to do just that at lunch, when freshman Jana and sophomore Erin approach me as I'm leaving the cashier.

"Hey, Molly," Jana says. "We, uh, wanted to invite you and Tristan to sit at our table today if you want. You'll be...safer there."

"Safer?" I stare at them. "What are you talking about? Gwendolyn Gannett's stupid crap? She has no idea what she's talking about."

Erin blushes scarlet and stares at the floor, but Jana raises her brows at me. "Are you saying she made it all up? That none of what she said is true?"

I don't miss a beat. "I'm saying she got her facts all twisted up—or whoever she talked to did. I was there during those tests last fall *and* when that violent mob at NuAgra tried to kill us all, so I know exactly what happened both times. M's no more dangerous today than she ever was. In other words, not at all."

But Jana's not backing down either. "What about last week, when she went after Trina right here in the cafeteria? She sounded pretty out of control, I heard her."

"That was—" I hesitate, but only for a second. "You obviously didn't hear what Trina said right before that, or what she did to M earlier. If M hadn't gone after her, I'd have done it myself. Trina's the menace, not M."

Okay, M really *was* out of control at the time, but it wasn't her fault, since she was still under Faxon's influence. But Rigel cured her of that just a couple hours later, and she's been totally fine since then.

Jana shrugs. "If you say so." Clearly unconvinced, she heads back to her usual table. Erin, following after one last, uncertain glance over her shoulder at me.

Sighing, I continue to our table, the last of our group to sit down.

Tristan, who was obviously listening in to the exchange, leans over to whisper, "Good job."

I shake my head. "Not good enough, obviously. Maybe I should have used some 'push.'"

"You still can, if necessary," he says. "But I think you already convinced Erin, at least."

I'm not sure even of that, but don't argue. I just pick up my fork.

"Everything okay?" M asks from across the table. "You seem a little tense. And no, I didn't probe."

I've asked her to please not "read" my emotions all the time, since it feels a little weird and intrusive...though of course Tristan can do it, too, especially when we're touching. M assured me she has to focus to identify emotions, which I guess is good. I imagine it would drive her nuts to be bombarded by them from all sides, all the time.

"Jana and Erin got a little freaked out by the crap GG said, that's all," I tell her. "I talked them down. I think."

M winces a little. "It's not just them, unfortunately. Tristan was just telling us what he overheard Mr. Abbot saying to Cormac on his way to lunch."

I turn to Tristan. "What?"

"You saw how he acted in Chem class. A few minutes ago, I heard him asking Cormac whether M and Rigel should be kept separate during school hours. For everyone's safety."

"Seriously?" I huff out a disgusted breath. "What did Cormac say?"

Tristan grins. "That they don't pose any danger to anyone at school, but if Mr. Abbot fears for his own safety, he can request someone else take over his class for the rest of the semester. He didn't exactly call him a coward to his face, but it was kind of implied."

That gets a chuckle from all of us.

M's *Duchas* friend Bri, sitting a little further down the table, leans forward then. "Can you clue us in on what's going on? Liam and Lucas told us about that article and broadcast, but—"

"But we don't really know all the background," Liam finishes.

Deb nods. "We're guessing there's a lot more to the story? Lucas says that reporter is always trying to create scandal out of nothing."

"I wouldn't say it's *nothing*, exactly," M tells her friends, "but she definitely made it sound way scarier than necessary. I already told you guys about what those aliens tried to do back in September, and how Rigel and I helped stop them, remember?"

Her *Duchas* friends exchange a glance. "The thing the TV news claimed was solar storms, right?" Bri asks.

"Right. Rigel and I *can* create pretty powerful electrical charges, but only if we feel really threatened. It's not something we can just randomly do by accident, like she implied."

"So...that protester who died?" Lucas ventures.

M tenses, but I jump in. "He was way worse than a protester! He'd already kidnapped Tristan and Rigel and we barely stopped him from murdering them both. The mob he was leading wanted M and me executed, too, because that's what Faxon demanded. We were all *super* lucky to get away from them alive."

"Then that reporter had it backwards?" Deb asks hopefully. "M and Rigel didn't actually...kill anybody, right?"

I suck in a panicked breath and look at M, realizing I probably said too much. No way is it my place to explain how M dug into Faxon's memories and how doing that made her a little crazy.

M's return glance is startled but not angry. Then she gives a resigned little shrug before turning to her *Duchas* friends.

"*We* didn't," she says. Then, before they can relax she adds, "But I did. Even though Rigel tried to stop me."

"But there were extenuating circumstances," I quickly insist, determined to undo the damage, if possible. "M—"

She cuts me off. "I wasn't exactly myself. The reason is a little complicated and there isn't time to explain right now." She glances off to our right, where I see a couple of *Duchas* guys from the basketball team heading our way. "Or enough privacy. I'll tell you after school, okay?"

Though both Bri and Deb—and their boyfriends—look kind of freaked, they all nod. The two basketball players reach us then, so we change the subject to regular school stuff for the rest of the lunch period.

While I privately beat myself up for forcing M into this situation.

3

COSC DAMASTE

(kosk DAHM-uh-stay): damage control

M

On our way to fifth period Government class, I try to reassure Molly that I'm not mad at her. From the guilt she's broadcasting, she obviously thinks she messed up, though I know she was only trying to help. Moving closer, I put a hand on her arm.

It's okay. Really, I silently assure her. This new ability we've discovered, to talk telepathically when touching, can be pretty handy sometimes. *We had to tell them something, and you did the best you could.*

I didn't mean to back you into a corner, though! Anguish comes through in her response. *I should have thought ahead before opening my big mouth.*

What else could you, or any of us, have said? I'm not going to deny the truth, especially to close friends. I feel guilty enough as it is. I don't need you feeling guilty, too, when you didn't do anything wrong!

We reach the classroom then, so I let go of Molly's arm, but I can tell my words helped.

I still need to decide exactly what to tell Bri and Deb later today, though. And what to tell *everyone* tomorrow night, during Molly's and my regular Thursday broadcast. *Echtran* Council leader Kyna contacted me an hour after that article appeared and I promised I'd do everything possible to counter what Gwendolyn Gannett said about me. As Kyna pointed out, after their recent scare with Faxon, the last thing we need is for all Martians, everywhere, to be terrified of their legitimate Sovereign!

Yeah, and the last thing we need is everyone insisting all over again that we need to be kept apart, Rigel thinks to me as we go to our seats. *You heard what Tristan said about Mr. Abbot—and he's one of the good guys.*

All the more reason Molly and I need to come up with exactly the right approach for when we're on the air tomorrow night. If that's even possible?

That afternoon I get a trial run when Rigel and I get to the parking lot after school and find Bri, Deb and their *Echtran* boyfriends waiting by Rigel's car.

"You said you could finish telling us what really happened that night once school was over," Bri reminds me as we reach them. "That it's kind of complicated?"

Deb nods. I can tell they're both hoping for an explanation that will be a lot less scary than the sensationalized version Gwendolyn Gannett put out there.

"It is complicated," I confirm. "And I'm still not sure how much of it should be generally known, even to other Martians. But you guys are close friends, so I think you deserve the whole story."

Where to start, though? I look over at Rigel for guidance and see Molly and Tristan heading our way. Eager for any extra support I can get, I wait till they join us before I continue.

"Okay. Remember at my birthday party, how upset everyone was by the news that Faxon escaped?"

The other four all nod. "Also about Rigel's granddad's surgery complications," Deb says. "Was it really sabotage?"

"Yes. A Faxon supporter messed with the equipment to take Shim out of commission, right when he'd be needed most to help catch Faxon."

"Then Faxon killed the guy, the moment he wasn't any more use," Tristan adds. "That's the kind of monster he is."

The others shudder. "Ugh," Bri and Deb say together.

"A couple days later, he tapped into the broadcast networks on Mars and started making demands and threats and blowing stuff up," Lucas tells Deb and Bri. "We didn't tell you that part at the time, figured there was no point scaring you when there was nothing any of us could do from here."

"What kinds of demands?" Deb looks at me. "Molly said something at lunch about wanting the two of you executed? Why? Other than him just being evil, I mean."

Molly answers her. "To wipe out the last of the ruling Royal line. His whole crusade from the start was to get rid of all the Royals so the people could take over...except that just meant Faxon himself taking over. He never gave any kind of power to anyone else. So once he was imprisoned, of course he blamed us—Royals in general, but especially M—for his downfall. He'd dedicated his whole life to revenge, so this was just more of the same."

"How *did* they finally catch him?" Liam asks then. "And what was the real story with the guy that got killed out at NuAgra that night? Were they connected?"

"Sort of." I hesitate for a second, then plunge on. "I was actually the one who figured out where Faxon was hiding. But to do that, I had to... to go into his memories. *All* his memories."

The others stare at me. "Huh?" Liam says. "How?"

"That's the complicated part, and the part I'm not sure should be made public," I tell them. "It might be too scary. Liam, Lucas, do you remember those power outages last spring, right around the time I was trying to get Acclaimed?"

Both boys nod. "Problems with the power grid, the acting governor said," Lucas recalls.

"He only said that so people wouldn't panic. Those outages were actually caused by the Grentl."

Immediately, I sense a spike in anxiety from the *Echtran* twins. "Wait!" Liam exclaims. "Those same aliens who tried to release an EMP at Earth last fall?"

"Yep. They were making Nuath's power glitch because nobody had responded to their last attempt at contact. What I didn't tell everyone in my big announcement last fall was that the Sovereigns have known about the Grentl since early in Sovereign Aerlis's reign, nearly three hundred years ago."

"What?" both boys practically shout.

I glance around the parking lot. "Sshh! Maybe we should continue this someplace more private. Because there's kind of a lot more. Let's go to my house. Aunt Theresa shouldn't be home for at least another hour." Even though she knows the truth about me now, hearing this story would be bound to freak her out all over again.

Everyone agrees to that, and we separate to our cars—Bri, Deb and their boyfriends to the beat-up old Honda the Walsh twins got last month for their seventeenth birthday.

"Maybe don't tell them *all* about digging into Faxon's memories?" Rigel suggests on the way to my house. "Just knowing you accessed them should be enough, right? I...don't want you to have to relive any of that."

I smile at his concern. "No, I shouldn't have to go into all the details. I don't want to relive any of it either, believe me." In fact, the very idea makes me nervous, remembering how badly those memories messed me up.

Liam pulls up in front of my house just as we get there, and Tristan parks his black Porsche right behind them, even though Molly lives right around the corner. There's obviously no time for our usual after-school makeout session. Shooting Rigel a wistful smile that he echoes, I get out of the car and lead the way up the front porch steps.

As everyone arranges themselves around the dining room table, Molly and I get cookies and milk for everyone from the kitchen. Once we're all seated, I begin again.

"Okay, so where was I?"

"Telling us how the Sovereigns found out about those aliens centuries ago, but never told anybody," Liam immediately responds. "Which seems crazy! Why didn't they—?"

Lucas answers his brother before I do. "Because of the panic it would have caused, obviously. But that was an awfully big secret to keep all that time."

I nod. "It was. Shim didn't tell me about them until after Faxon was toppled. Most of the *Echtran* Council didn't find out until then, either. He made me promise not to tell *anybody*, not even Rigel—which was awfully tricky, considering he can read my mind."

He and I exchange a glance, remembering what a rough time that was for both of us.

"Anyway, it turns out the Grentl had been demanding regular updates on the colony of Nuath over the years, but they would *only* communicate with the Sovereign...or a direct blood descendant. So the last time they called, there was no one on Mars who could answer them, thanks to Faxon. That meant I had to get to Nuath as soon as possible, then get Acclaimed, so I could get into the Royal Palace, where their secret communication device was hidden. Because of my screwup on the trip to Mars—you know, getting caught on camera kissing Rigel—I almost didn't get there in time."

Molly swallows, pale with remembered terror. "She cut it awfully close, like with less than an hour to spare before they would have totally destroyed Nuath. But it wasn't her fault!" she quickly adds. "There was this super old Engineer, and he—"

"I don't think we need to tell that part now," I interrupt her. "Maybe later. The important part is that I had to, um, interface with the Grentl's device to answer them. When I did, it bombarded me with all the memories of everyone who'd ever touched it before...including Faxon. He'd tried to use it toward the end of his regime. It didn't work, but the Grentl still sucked out all his memories...and then zapped him. That's actually how he was overthrown. Though with the way the Resistance was growing by then, he might have been ousted soon anyway."

Lucas and Liam both stare at me, clearly boggled by having so much they thought they knew completely rewritten.

"I know. It's a lot." I try to smile sympathetically, but I know the hardest part of my story is yet to come.

"No kidding," Liam agrees. "You're telling us those aliens can...can pull the plug on Nuath's power anytime they want? That sounds way worse than anything Faxon could have done!"

I cringe a little. "See? This is why I can't see making all of this public. It's pretty scary stuff. I honestly don't think the Grentl *will* mess with Nuath's power again, but yeah, they could if they wanted to. Those outages they caused were just to get our—my—attention. I don't think they were *necessarily* planning to destroy the whole colony."

The twins don't look particularly reassured.

"Anyway, the point of telling you all this was so you'd understand how I was able to access Faxon's memory, to figure out where he was hiding after he escaped."

I don't mention that I didn't even realize that was possible until I was clued in by Sovereign Leontine in my Scepter Archive. That's one secret I don't *ever* plan to make public.

"How did that work, exactly?" Curiosity seems to be crowding out Lucas's worry. "Was there a file or something you could search?"

"Nope. It was all locked in here." I tap my forehead. "I needed a little help from a Mind Healer to dig them up, then comb through them. But spending time in Faxon's mind was...kind of awful."

Molly nods. "It really messed her up for a few days. Regent Shim—and Rigel and I—all warned her that might happen, but she decided catching Faxon before he could cause any more destruction was worth the risk. And it worked."

Deb leans forward, her expression more concerned than scared now. "So when you killed that guy, you were still messed up?"

"Very. By the time I found Faxon's secret hideout, I'd spent nearly two whole days in his memories and...had a hard time getting back out. It wasn't until a few days later—last Wednesday, actually—that I finally shook off the last of his influence. With a lot of help from Rigel." I reach over and squeeze his hand.

"I would have helped sooner, if you hadn't been so stubborn," he reminds me. "But like you said, you weren't yourself. At all. It was such a huge relief to get you back, M."

To me, too! I think to him before turning back to the others.

"Before that, I was still infected by Faxon's personality. I'd get furious over the littlest things, the way he did. So when I thought that mob leader had killed Tristan and was about to kill Rigel and me, I...just reacted without thinking. But that doesn't change the fact that I really did murder him. Even if he deserved it."

"It wasn't murder, it was self-defense," Molly insists. "And we found out later that guy was a murderer himself, several times over! Kyna herself said if he'd been captured alive, they'd have given him the *tabula rasa*. A complete memory wipe," she explains to Bri and Deb. "It's our ultimate penalty. Most of our people consider it way worse than death."

All of which is true, but— "Even so, I can't claim Gwendolyn Gannett, or the people she talked to, lied about me killing that man. I did. Full stop."

Molly stubbornly shakes her head. "She made it sound so much worse, though! If people knew that you'd just saved thousands, maybe tens of thousands of Martian lives, they'd look at it differently."

"For sure," Lucas agrees, regarding me with something like awe.

Liam nods, too. "We still have lots of friends back in Nuath. Our whole family was terrified for them when Faxon started blowing things up and threatening to do way worse. But you saved them all! Taking out a known murderer is practically nothing compared to that."

"See?" Molly says to me. "Like I've been telling you, M, you're a hero. Again. Even if most people don't know it yet."

I shrug. "Even if that's true, I don't see how I can take credit without scaring people all over again. Which I definitely don't want to do."

"Let me think about that." Molly furrows her brow. "I've got until our broadcast tomorrow night to come up with something."

That gets a reluctant smile from me. "If anybody can, you will."

Privately, though, I wonder if there's anything either of us can say to restore our people's faith in me to lead them.

✦

"Are you sure you don't want me to do most of the talking?" Molly asks when we're about to go live the following evening.

I smooth the front of my conservative blouse and sit up straighter on the silvery-blue chair that's part of our broadcast set. "No, I'm the one everyone needs to hear from, if I'm going to reassure them I'm still fit to be Sovereign."

"Just don't go all apologetic, okay? We've planned out what you're going to say. Stick to the script and you should be fine. And if you do want me to jump in at some point, just give the word."

"I will. Thanks, Molly."

The two of us spent all afternoon in Molly's room working out how I can tell the truth without revealing the scariest parts. Like she so often does, Molly came up with a way to word things that should be perfect, as long as I don't go off on any tangents. I turn to face Carleen, the show's producer, and nod for them to start the cameras.

When the red "broadcasting" light comes on, I summon a serious sort of smile and start talking.

"Hello, everyone. Due to unsettling reports about me that most of you have probably heard by now, we've preempted our pre-recorded interviews with this live broadcast, to clear up some misconceptions about what occurred. While those reports did get some of the facts right, enough of the truth was omitted—we *assume* unintentionally—to give a false and much more frightening impression than is warranted. Tonight, I'd like to fill in some of those gaps with information not previously made public. You'll understand why when you hear the details. Afterward, if we have time, we will address some of the questions we've received.

"I'm sure you all remember the events of last September, when Earth was menaced by the aliens who originally founded Nuath. Also, that my communication with those aliens ultimately helped us to avert the worst effects of their attack. What I did not tell you at the time, was that my very first contact with the Grentl was quite...dramatic.

"Before true communication was established, the Grentl accessed all of my memories, back to childhood. They then bombarded me with the memories of everyone with whom they'd ever been in contact. These included the Nuathan Scientist who first discovered the Grentl's device, and Faxon, who tried—unsuccessfully—to use it for his own ends. All of this happened in the space of minutes, far too quickly for me to process or recall any specifics afterward. Not until Faxon's escape did it occur to me that if I still possessed his memories, they might assist in his recapture.

"Unfortunately, recovering those buried memories proved far more involved and traumatic than I anticipated. Prior to beginning that effort, I was warned by Regent Shim and others that the process could negatively affect my own mental health. However, when Faxon began destroying sections of Nuath's infrastructure and threatening worse to come, I decided the importance of quickly finding and stopping him outweighed any potential risk to myself.

"With the assistance of a skilled Mind Healer, I was able to access, then sift through Faxon's memories. I experienced them in order, starting from before he came to power, not knowing when he might have created or discovered his hideout. As it happened, he constructed his secret bunker in the final months of his regime. That meant I was forced to spend the better part of two days essentially inside Faxon's twisted mind before I could locate it.

"Needless to say, the whole experience was unpleasant in the extreme, and affected my mental state even more profoundly than I'd expected. Thankfully, the effect proved temporary, but when my sister and I confronted the mob outside NuAgra on the night of Faxon's capture, I'd only been free of his memories for a couple of hours.

Because I was still heavily influenced by his vicious mindset, I behaved in ways completely opposed to how I would normally think and act."

I pause, steeling myself for what I need to say next. Though Molly and Rigel—and others—have repeatedly assured me that what I did wasn't completely my fault, I still feel compelled to take responsibility. It's what a leader should do.

"Mitigating factors aside," I continue, "I deeply regret causing the death of a fellow *Echtran*, no matter what crimes he might have committed. My...my actions that night—"

Stop! Molly's urgent thought and sudden grip on my forearm startle me into breaking off.

I turn to see her gray eyes beseeching me, reinforcing her silent command. *Not another word!* she thinks to me. *I'll take it from here.*

Though I can tell she's using her enhanced "push," I don't push back. Instead, I give her a tiny nod.

4

BRU

(BROO): pressure; insistence

Molly

Even though I can't sense emotions—other than Tristan's—the way M can, it's totally obvious to me when she starts getting overcome by guilt again. Luckily, I'm able to stop her before she says too much... which I was afraid from the start she might do. The second she gives me a silent go-ahead, I turn to the camera.

"Since becoming Sovereign, my sister has had to make several difficult decisions on behalf of her people," I solemnly tell our viewers. "It's the sort of thing good leaders do, even at the risk of great personal sacrifice. On *every* occasion, our Sovereign has nobly stepped up to the task. Her actions leading up to the events sensationalized in the press this week were only the latest example of that.

"The earlier example you heard mentioned on this network two nights ago involved even greater risk to our Sovereign than her exploration of Faxon's memories. In fact, she and Rigel Stuart were warned beforehand that they almost certainly would not survive the effort to turn the Grentl's electromagnetic pulse back on itself, even if they were successful. They both heroically elected to proceed anyway. Fortunately —miraculously—they lived through that desperate, last-ditch attempt, though the resulting blast knocked both of them unconscious. I have to say, I've never been prouder of my sister than when she willingly risked

33

her life to save us all—even though I had no idea at the time she *was* my sister.

"What she did last week to keep Faxon from blowing up more of Nuath was equally heroic. Instead of her life, this time she knew going in that she'd be risking her sanity, which was even scarier. Nobody could have blamed her if she'd decided not to try. In fact, I did my best to talk her out of it. Rigel did, too. Of course, being Emileia, she chose to proceed anyway. The experience was even more mentally devastating for her than we feared, but it saved thousands—probably tens of thousands —of lives. Possibly even Nuath itself. Every single one of you with loved ones still in Nuath owes her an enormous debt of gratitude."

I reach over and squeeze M's hand to underscore my own thanks.

"As she said, it took her nearly two full days to find the memory that included the location of Faxon's hideout. What she didn't say is that she had to keep putting herself into a trance to search for it. Every time she came back out, we could tell she was getting more and more messed up by the awful stuff she had to witness, but she refused to stop until she found what she needed.

"I was with my sister when she emerged from her final trance after locating Faxon's secret hideout. She was so deeply immersed in his memories, I had an incredibly hard time waking her up. By then she was exhausted, dehydrated and practically starving. Even so, her very first action was to contact Regent Shim with the information his security forces needed to find and stop Faxon. Then, bare moments after she sent her message to Mars, we learned that the leaders of those so-called protesters outside NuAgra had kidnapped both Rigel Stuart and Tristan Roark. They were holding them hostage, threatening to kill them unless Emileia and I turned ourselves over to the mob so they could execute us, like Faxon had demanded.

"She and I wanted to go out and negotiate with them, but the *Echtran* Council refused to let us do that. We were certain Tristan and Rigel would be killed if they sent security people out instead, so my sister and I eluded the Council and snuck out of NuAgra to rescue them. As it turned out, it's a good thing we did. The mob's deranged leader was just about to murder them when we got there and overpowered him. Because they'd been drugged, Tristan and Rigel were pretty wobbly. We were trying to get them back to NuAgra when the protest mob spotted us and attacked. They outnumbered us at least twenty to one, and hard as we fought, we were afraid we were all going to end up dead after all.

"Then things got even worse. We thought their leader was down for the count, but he suddenly showed up again and started shooting at us, trying to finish what he'd started. With our lives on the line, M— Emileia, I mean—used the electrical power she and Rigel can produce to stop him and...went a little overboard.

"What she did was totally justified. Not only was he attempting to kill us all, we found out later he was a known murderer and Faxon supporter. So if he *had* been captured alive, he definitely would have received the *tabula rasa* mind wipe for his crimes. That was confirmed by Council Leader Kyna Nuallan.

"Even so, my sister felt horrible about what she'd done. The very next morning, she begged NuAgra's Mind Healer to help her purge Faxon's influence from her mind. She also kept her distance from Rigel, to make sure nothing like that could ever happen again. As it turned out, though, that wasn't the best idea. Because of their *graell* bond, staying apart from him made her worse instead of better.

"When those of us closest to her realized that, we convinced her to let Rigel help—and he did. Last year, their bond healed his erased memory and last week, the *graell* healed M's mind—completely. Afterward, she was thoroughly tested by our Mind Healers. They've pronounced her perfectly sane, and as capable of leading as she ever was. They are confident neither she, nor she and Rigel together, pose any further danger to anyone. Our people remain in good hands."

Still touching her arm, I smile over at M, who smiles back.

Thank you, she thinks to me. *You did that so much better than I could have.*

Then we both turn back to camera. "You've sent hundreds of questions over the past two days," I tell the viewers. "I hope we've now answered most of them, but as Emileia said earlier, we can spend our remaining time tonight addressing a few others."

M nods. "Thank you, Malena. I know some of you expressed concerns about whether it's safe for Rigel and me to continue going to school now that you know the extent of the electrical charges we can produce. As my sister just told you, it's really not an issue. Last fall, Rigel and I underwent extensive testing by our Scientists. They proved conclusively that we can *only* do that when threatened.

"Creating the equivalent of a lightning bolt not only takes focus, it's very draining for both of us. In other words, not something that can just randomly happen. The types of petty annoyances we encounter in daily life, like at school, are nowhere near enough to provoke that sort of response. In fact, over time we've learned to exert more and more precise control over the power we generate, both for safety's sake, and to make it more generally useful in situations where only a tiny bit of electricity is called for. We've even figured out how to create a dampening field, should we ever need to neutralize a potential explosion."

I'm glad she doesn't reveal the two times they *did* have to do that, since the whole point of tonight's broadcast is to reassure everyone after GG's scare tactics. As we agreed earlier, I address the final issue—the one that matters most to me.

"The *Echtran* Council tells us that multiple people have suggested they ask or even force my sister to step down as leader, and for me to take over her duties," I say to the camera. "I can tell you right now, that's never going to happen. Not only has Emileia already been formally Acclaimed Sovereign by the entire population of Nuath, I feel in no way prepared to take on such a role at this time. Nor is it the least bit necessary. As I said, our Mind Healers have thoroughly examined her and certified Emileia fully capable of continuing as Sovereign—particularly now that Council Leader Kyna is transitioning to a more active role as Emileia's Earth Regent. She'll take over some of the Sovereign's more time-consuming tasks so she can focus on the ones truly requiring her personal attention. Meanwhile, I've reduced some of my own school commitments to learn more about my sister's duties. Eventually, we hope to split some of her responsibilities between us."

"That's right," M agrees. "Malena is already turning out to be a great help. The Mind Healers believe one reason I was so badly affected by my exposure to Faxon's memories was the stress I'd been under during the months leading up to his escape. There's no question that without an Earth Regent, I was trying to spread myself too thin, skimping on sleep and cutting out nearly all leisure activities. Going forward, I'll be more careful about that sort of thing. I know Kyna taking over some of my administrative duties will help enormously, and already having Malena assist me with others is reducing my stress levels. Some of you may not like to hear this, but spending more time with Rigel is also hugely beneficial for both my mental and physical health, thanks to our *graell* bond. Yet another reason staying apart from him, as some of you have demanded, is *not* a viable option."

At the rear of the studio, Carlyn gives us the wrapping-up motion to indicate we're nearly out of time, so I launch into the closing spiel we rehearsed.

"We hope everything we've shared with you tonight has allayed the fears generated by the partial—and rather sensationalized—version of events you heard earlier this week. My sister and I can both assure you that we plan to continue doing everything in our power to benefit our people going forward."

"Absolutely," M confirms, now exuding confidence. "From the moment I embraced my role, first as your Princess, then later as your Sovereign, my main goal has always been to exert every effort to bring about the best possible future for all Martians everywhere. Thank you for joining us this evening, and for your continuing support. Good night."

The red light on the camera goes off and Carlyn gives us a thumbs-up. "That's a wrap, Excellencies," she says. "I must say, you both did an absolutely admirable job with this broadcast. I'm certain all of our people will sleep better tonight. Thank you."

M and I grin at each other. "And thank *you*, Carlyn," M tells her, still smiling. "You're such a great asset to our people. It's a shame most of what you do is invisible to them."

"Believe me, Excellency, I prefer it that way," she replies wryly. "You surely know better than anyone the downside of high visibility."

That gets a chuckle from M, though I think it sounds a little strained.

"Point taken," M concedes. "Have a nice weekend."

✦

Tristan and Rigel greet us as soon as we emerge from the recording studio with much-appreciated kisses.

"You guys did great!" Tristan crows. "We were both a little worried, though we didn't want to say anything before you went on."

M and I both laugh. "We could tell," I say and M nods.

"I think we'd have been able to tell even if we couldn't read your emotions," M adds. "But since I was pretty worried myself, I didn't try to reassure you. Of course Molly saved the day. Again." Her smile is both grateful and proud.

"Seriously, thanks for stepping in when you did, Molly," Rigel says to me. "Even from out here, I could tell M was getting close to guilt-tripping on the air. Glad you kept her from doing that."

M nods. "So am I. Even if—"

Rigel places a finger against her lips. "No. You don't deserve anyone's condemnation, you deserve their gratitude. Just like Molly told them. I wish you'd stop beating yourself up over what happened. It's done. It's over. It won't ever happen again. And I love you."

Of course, she melts at that. "Ditto. What would I do without you?"

He smiles crookedly. "Let's not ever find out, okay?"

"So, um, we should probably head back," Tristan says before they can start kissing again, right in the open NuAgra lobby. "Especially if we want to, y'know, stop along the way."

We all know he means parking to make out before dropping M and me off at our houses, a plan I heartily approve.

Fifteen minutes later, Tristan pulls his Porsche into the back lot of the little office park that's become our favorite makeout spot and we spend a blissful ten minutes recharging each other by kissing. And kissing. Finally, with a happy sigh, I sit back and reluctantly re-buckle my seatbelt.

"I should get home, if I don't want Mum asking too many questions. She'll know we finished broadcasting a full half hour ago."

Tristan shrugs. "Tell her we stopped for ice cream or something. You're great at coming up with plausible excuses." He reaches out to start the car, then pauses. "I'm glad you said that bit tonight about eventually sharing M's role as Sovereign. Because I think you're way more prepared for that than you claimed."

I glance at him in alarm. "I didn't say I'd share being Sovereign! Just that I'm trying to learn enough to lighten M's load a little. Did it really sound like I meant that?"

He shrugs again. "Maybe not exactly, but I don't think M would have a problem with it. Do you?"

"That's not the point, Tristan! Didn't you promise not to pressure me into taking on any more leadership duties than I'm comfortable with? I get enough of that from Mum, believe me!"

"I know, I know." He holds up both hands. "And I'm not. Pressuring you, I mean. I just don't like to see you underestimating yourself. Because I think you do."

I frown at him but don't reply, even silently, though I know he can sense the conflict—and betrayal—I'm feeling. Instead of reminding him yet again how much I *don't* want to assume even an iota of M's power, I just say, "It's late. I'd better get home."

Tristan doesn't say anything else until we pull up in front of my house, when he looks over at me in concern. "I'm sorry, Molly. I did promise not to nudge anymore about the leadership thing. I'll try not to do it again. But I had a thought. No! Not about that." He holds up his hands again. "I was thinking maybe I should talk to my father—in person—and see if he'll admit to being Gwendolyn Gannett's source. Even if he wasn't, maybe he knows who is."

"Like Devyn?" He *is* the most obvious next choice.

"Yeah. Or someone Devyn put up to it. Since Father was the security leak on the Council before—and Devyn knows they know that—he might have used someone else this time to do his dirty work. He seems awfully good with the plausible deniability thing."

I snort. "Except when he outed himself to the whole Council with his coup attempt in December. I can't believe Malcolm *still* makes excuses for him after that."

"Devyn obviously didn't expect us to spoil his plan—or for the Council to remember what he did afterward. It did take them a while."

That's true. When we blew up Devyn's Ossian Sphere, the blast knocked most of them briefly unconscious. It was more than a week later before they started remembering exactly what they'd seen and heard that night. When they did, M and I were forced to come clean about the rest of our *graell* bonds...though Mum still has trouble accepting the idea of Sean and Kira being bonded.

"Do you think you can arrange to talk face-to-face with your dad without him getting suspicious?"

"That part'll be easy—Mother said he's coming to visit this weekend. He...really does still seem to be trying. With the counseling and with us."

That makes me smile. "That may be the best thing yet to come out of your *graell*-enhanced charm. I really hope it lasts."

"So do I." There's no missing the longing that accompanies his words.

After a lifetime of working, mostly in vain, to win his father's approval, it took a lot of courage for Tristan to speak out against him to the Council, even knowing how wrong Connor's actions were. If the rift that created is starting to heal, I'm really happy, both for Tristan's sake and his mom's. I lean over to give him one last, lingering kiss.

I get out of the car then and go inside...only to find my mum waiting at the foot of the stairs, looking royally pissed.

"What kept you?" she demands as I shut the front door behind me. "Nothing *else* that could reflect badly on you as a possible leader, I hope?"

"Else?" I repeat. "What do you mean? M and Rigel and Tristan and I stopped for ice cream on the way home. It's not even ten yet." That's my curfew on school nights, unless I'm helping M with official business.

Mum focuses on me and I realize too late I didn't think to block her lie-detector probe. Her expression makes clear she knows I was fibbing about the ice cream but she doesn't call me on it.

Instead, she says, "After what you said during that broadcast, I'm sure you know why I want to talk to you."

"Um..." I think back over everything I said, wondering which part upset her. "No, not really."

She raises a skeptical brow, though she must be able to tell I'm not lying now. "Insisting that you'll *never* step into a true leadership role? That's never been decided, certainly not permanently. I can't believe you would diminish yourself like that on the air! Especially after Emileia's recent...issues, we can't possibly know what you could be called upon to do next week, much less in years to come."

I take two deep breaths to stop myself from snapping at her. "Mum, we've been over and over this. M is *fine* now. What happened to her last week was purely temporary—because of what she did to save all of Nuath. You sure acted grateful to her at the time, but now—"

"Of course I'm grateful," she interrupts. "We all are. But the Council would be remiss not to consider all possibilities, with an eye to the future. The reason your true identity remained a mystery for so long was to safeguard that future, should our people ever need an alternative.

Uncomfortable as that idea may make you, you have a duty to prepare yourself for that eventuality."

"I'm learning all I can," I protest. "But that's so I can *help* M, not replace her!"

Sometimes I almost wish we'd never found out who I really am. Life sure was a lot less complicated when I and everyone else thought I was just an Ag orphan. But then I never would have gotten to know my real parents, through their holographic archive...or that M and I are sisters.

"Yes. Well." Mum's not done, unfortunately. "I spoke with a few other Council members after your broadcast. At this Saturday's meeting, we'll be addressing this and other things that were said on the air tonight."

"I can hardly wait." I don't even try to hide my sarcasm.

Mum sucks in a breath like she's about to lambast me for it, but then seems to remember who I am—or who she wants me to be—and controls herself. Barely. "I suppose that will do for tonight. Do you still have homework?"

"A little. G'night, Mum."

I swing by the kitchen for a glass of milk and head upstairs, where I immediately contact M to give her fair warning of what we can expect at Saturday's *Echtran* Council meeting. I have a feeling it'll be a long one.

5

CRUINHU

(KRIN-hyu): meeting; gathering, as of a committee

M

"Great job last night," Kira whispers to Molly and me in French class Friday. Liam said the same thing in first period.

"Thanks," I whisper back. "Here's hoping it made a difference."

At lunch, it's obvious it did help some. Erin, the sophomore *Echtran* whose parents are Healers, makes a point of apologizing to me for believing everything Gwendolyn Gannett said.

I thank her, but Molly's not as gracious. "What about Jana?" she asks. "She's the one who was making cracks about M yesterday."

Erin's cheeks go pink. "She seems relieved and a little sorry, but she's too embarrassed to say so. You know how she is."

Molly and I exchange a glance. Jana may be Kira's sister's best friend, but she has a tendency to look for the worst and stir up trouble. Of all the new *Echtran* students at Jewel High, she and Alan Dempsey are the only ones still resistant to fitting in.

I sigh to myself. "I'm glad she's not still scared of me, at least. If she wants to talk about it, tell her I'm happy to answer any questions she still has."

Clearly embarrassed as well, Erin nods and heads back to her lunch table—and Jana.

"Hey, it's progress," Tristan says when she's gone. "Mr. Abbott didn't

42

act as afraid of you in Chem class today, either. Didn't we tell you last night you guys did a great job?"

Molly's smile is slightly cynical. "Not everyone agrees. I told you what Mum said. Tomorrow night's meeting will probably suck."

"Not if we don't let it," I say bracingly, though I suspect she's right. "You're supposed to be the one who always looks on the bright side, remember?"

Those within earshot chuckle.

I turn to Tristan, ready to change the subject. "Molly said your father's coming for a visit? When does he get here?"

"Tonight. Should be interesting." Even without trying, I pick up on his conflicted emotions.

Molly reaches over and takes his hand. "His last visit wasn't bad at all, you said."

"Yeah, it went way better than I expected. But now, well... We'll see."

I can understand Tristan not wanting to assume anything before finding out whether Connor was Gwendolyn Gannett's source.

"Tristan plans to talk to his dad tomorrow night after his mother leaves for the meeting," Molly quietly tells Rigel and me on the way to Government class after lunch.

"I figure that'll be my best chance to get info out of him, since we'll be alone for a couple of hours," Tristan confirms.

His mother took her husband's place on the Council after he was booted off for sharing sensitive information with Devyn Kane—and lying about it. Teara Roark has proved a *much* more valuable Council member than Connor ever was.

"If he knows anything, I'm sure you'll find out, as strong as your persuasive abilities are these days," I tell Tristan. "Why don't we all meet up sometime Sunday, so you can fill us in on whatever you learn?"

We all agree to that as we reach the classroom.

⁺₊✦

The next evening, before I can head over to the O'Garas' for my usual ride to the meeting when Molly rings my doorbell. Behind her, I see her mother pulling into my driveway.

"I wanted to let you know I haven't said anything to my parents about Tristan questioning Connor tonight," she says as I join her outside.

"Probably just as well. No point mentioning that plan to anyone until we know how it'll pan out."

Molly nods her agreement, sliding open the side panel of the O'Garas' maroon van. Mrs. O'Gara is driving. Like always, I climb in back with Molly.

"Excellency, are you sure—?" Mr. O asks from the passenger seat, his hand on the door handle.

"Yes, yes, it's fine," I assure him. Every week he asks if I'd rather sit up front, and every week I decline. "Your legs are a lot longer than mine. You'd be uncomfortable back here and I don't mind a bit."

He lets it go—like always—but looks uncertain about it. Like always.

I wonder what it will take for him to finally stop sucking up to me. What he did last year *was* pretty bad, plotting and then erasing Rigel's memory and convincing me it was Rigel's idea. No matter how much he tries to make up for it, I don't know if I'll ever fully forgive him for that —or if he'll ever forgive himself.

The drive to NuAgra takes nearly fifteen minutes, since it's on the outskirts of Jewel, even more in the middle of nowhere than the town itself. A few Council members are already in NuAgra's big lobby area when we arrive. Exchanging greetings, we all move to the conference room where we now hold our Saturday night meetings. By the time everyone physically present is seated, Council leader Kyna and little Nara have joined us holographically from Washington, DC.

"Thank you, everyone, for being so prompt," Kyna says to open the meeting. "As you might imagine, my time right now is limited as I work to wrap up all of my ongoing projects as quickly as possible. Therefore, I'd like to move right to the main item on tonight's agenda—damage control from that *Echtran Enquirer* article—as well as Thursday night's revelations from our Sovereign and Princess."

Molly and I exchange a glance. Apparently Mrs. O was right.

I speak up before anyone else can. "After what Gwendolyn Gannet wrote and then said publicly, we didn't have any choice but to set the record straight. And yes, I know most of you agreed the details of what happened that weekend should be kept private. We tried, but it was never realistic. With that many witnesses, it was inevitable that some would talk to the press."

"Most of our people know better than to take anything Gwendolyn Gannett says at face value," Breann, one of the Council Royals, protests. "Had you categorically denied—"

"No." I cut her off. "I've always avoided lying to our people, even when there were things I couldn't disclose. I'm not going to start now. This is only the latest example of how keeping secrets can backfire and do more harm than good. If we'd been more upfront from the start, Gwendolyn couldn't have scooped us like that or accused us of hiding things—again."

Kyna frowns. "Perhaps you're right, Excellency, but we didn't want to risk frightening people. Of course it's important that our people trust their Sovereign and this Council, but I don't see how having them *afraid* of you will help with that."

"Gwendolyn's sensationalistic reporting scared them a lot more than the simple truth would have," I point out. "By trying to hush things up, we gave her the opportunity to make everything sound even worse than it was."

"I noticed during your broadcast you never directly addressed the massive electrical charges you and young Stuart can generate together," Malcolm, another Royal, comments. "That was probably wise, but doesn't it rather undercut your supposed goal of openness?"

Molly gives a tiny snort. "We may not have said exactly how many gigajoules it took to stop the Grentl, but M was absolutely clear that there's no risk she and Rigel can just fire off lightning bolts any time they happen to get mad about something. You know as well as I do that they can't—and wouldn't if they could."

"I'm sure we all want to believe that," Mrs. O'Gara says, "but now everyone knows they did create and use a lethal bolt against that mob leader. How can our people trust it will never happen again? Faxon may have ruled by fear, but our legitimate Sovereigns never have."

I stifle a gasp. "Are you implying I want to do that? That I ever would?"

She sniffs, avoiding my eye. "Perhaps not intentionally. No disrespect intended, Excellency, but as Kyna said, our people must have *complete* faith in their Sovereign if she is to rule effectively."

Teara, Tristan's mom, speaks up then. "Surely last night's broadcast has largely restored any faith that might have been shaken due to that reporter and her biased presentation of the facts?"

Nara nods eagerly. "Absolutely, it did! Some of the people who contacted me previously contacted me again to apologize for their earlier overreactions and to express their relief."

"Yes, I'm sure it did help at least a bit," Malcolm concedes. "Though it would have been much better if those mob members could have been prevented from speaking to the woman in the first place."

"Our laws don't allow for us to censor people who haven't been found guilty of a crime," I remind him, "and most of those protesters weren't. The majority were just swept up in the moment, driven by the fear Faxon intentionally spread, which was amplified by the leaders of that mob. Only a handful committed actual crimes, or proved to have criminal backgrounds."

Molly chimes in then. "Besides, Gwendolyn wasn't the only reporter they talked to. She put the worst spin on everything, like she always does, but several other journalists spoke with them as well. Their stories just didn't get the same attention, since they weren't nearly as explosive. But they basically corroborated the main facts."

In other words, that it really was me who killed that man. I swallow.

"True," Mrs. O agrees. "Which is why simply refuting the more sensationalistic bits of the story may not be enough. Our people need a leader they can rely on to rule with a steady hand, with no whiff of doubt that she could—"

"Don't even go there, Mum!" Molly glares at her mother. "I've promised to do all I can to help M with her Sovereign stuff, but I don't ever plan to stand for Acclamation myself. Not only do I not want to, even a little, it's totally unnecessary." She pauses to look around at the whole rest of the Council. "Does anyone other than my mum think it is?"

There's a brief silence, during which I sense a strong spike of anxiety from Molly, but then every other head at the table shakes no. Mrs. O grimaces slightly, but doesn't try to argue the point further. Yet. I doubt she'll ever truly abandon her aspirations for Molly. It was hard enough for her to relinquish her dream of Sean becoming Royal Consort.

"I suppose we can at least be grateful you didn't feel compelled to share the true history of our Sovereigns' contact with the Grentl," Breann says after a moment. "That could have tarnished our people's faith in the entire Sovereign line."

"We did consider it," Molly admits, "but decided that would be *too* scary. It also wasn't needed to refute the worst of what Gwendolyn said. Thank goodness whoever blabbed to her didn't tell her that part."

Malcolm raises his brows. "So much for complete honesty. You say, Excellency, you try never to lie to our people, but didn't you do just that when you said you first learned of the Grentl last fall?"

"I didn't actually say that, though I might have implied it," I reply. "It was Molly's idea to be vague about exactly *when* my first contact with them occurred. Not just to avoid exposing how the Sovereigns kept it secret all this time, but because of how much it would frighten people, especially those still living in Nuath, to find out how much control those aliens have over their power supply. Though I suppose if Gwendolyn Gannett's source really is privy to all Council business, we can't be sure they won't leak that, too."

As I speak, I scan the emotions of everyone present. I sense suspicion, annoyance, even some outrage, but nothing that feels like guilt. That reassures me Gwendolyn's anonymous source isn't still sitting in on our meetings...but makes it even more likely it was Connor. Poor Tristan.

Then Teara puts my thought into words. "Though no one has come out and said so, most of you are probably wondering whether my husband was that source. So am I. When he arrived in Jewel last night, I asked him directly whether he'd spoken with her. He denied it, but quickly deflected before I could follow up. He's...very good at that, I'm afraid."

"Yes, I remember," Kyna says gently. "But even if he was her source, you can't be held responsible for your husband's failings, Teara. We've been clear about that since voting you onto this Council."

Mrs. Roark swallows. "Thank you. I'll of course let you know immediately if I learn more from him while he's here."

She clearly considers that unlikely, but I'm hopeful Tristan might even now be persuading Connor to be more forthcoming.

"Now," Kyna says, "I propose we move on to the topic of our upcoming elections. I assume you've all read the report I forwarded from the Sovereign about the interviews she and Princess Malena have been conducting with some of the candidates?"

The rest of the meeting is devoted to dissecting those reports and going over—again—the schedule and procedures for the first election of that sort ever to be held on Earth. Previously, only Dun Cloch, Bailerealta and Fiarway, in Colorado, had local magistrates and were able to handle those elections themselves. Now, with so many more *Echtrans* scattered around the country and more coming in the next launch window, we need a more centralized system.

Malcolm, Breann and Mrs. O all push for Royals having precedence for judicial appointments, rather than relying solely on the recommendations of various regional representatives.

"All of our current justices are Royal for good reason," Breann insists. "Our *fine* is genetically predisposed to render fair judgments. In fact, I don't believe there has ever been a non-Royal adjudicator in all our history."

"But is that because Royals are the best qualified, or just because it's always been that way?" I ask. "An awful lot of Nuath's government structure is based on tradition. Isn't that right?" I look to Teara, our expert on such things.

She nods. "That's true, Excellency. I suppose without any historical examples of non-Royal justices, we oughtn't assume members of other *fines* can't be equally competent. The idea may be somewhat unsettling to our people, however."

"Exactly," Malcolm quickly agrees. "I realize one of your goals, Excellency, is a more equal distribution of power across *fines*, but there is something to be said for tradition, as well. Particularly during this time of upheaval for our people. They are still adjusting to the restoration of a proper legislature in Nuath, not to mention a true Sovereign. On top of that, they're under pressure to emigrate to Earth, to ease the power shortage on Mars."

"I realize that," I tell him. "I'm not suggesting we change the way things are done in Nuath." Not yet, anyway, though I'd eventually like to. "But Martians on Earth are less steeped in Nuathan traditions. Many have told me one reason they chose to relocate was a hope that their own *fine* might have more advantages here than seemed possible on Mars. Limiting judicial appointments to Royals could undermine that hope."

The wrangling goes on for some time. Not until Kyna's ready to adjourn the meeting do we reach a compromise—potential justices will have to pass some sort of suitability test, which we'll now have to create. Contentious as the discussion gets, I much prefer it to another debate over the safety of Rigel and me spending time together. Not that I don't expect it to be brought up again at some point.

Sure enough, Kyna's hologram has barely winked out after adjourning the meeting when Mrs. O speaks up.

"I still feel it would reassure our people if the Council were to issue a statement saying we'll be monitoring the Sovereign's interactions with her younger Bodyguard going forward," she mutters to those still in the room.

"Monitoring how?" My voice is sharp. "I won't consent to being spied on any time I happen to be with Rigel. We pose zero risk to other people now—*especially* when we're alone together. Then, there's nobody around we could hurt even if we wanted to. Which of course we don't. And won't."

Molly backs me up. "C'mon, Mum. The very last thing any of us should want is to keep M and Rigel apart again. When you—and M—tried that before, it only made things worse. Anyone with half an eye can see how great they are together."

I shoot her a grateful glance, then look at the remaining Council members. "It should be obvious to all of you by now that I'm a much better leader because of my bond with Rigel. Our Scientists have already proved how it strengthens us both. Do you really want to weaken your Sovereign by taking away that source of strength?"

"Not...take away," Mrs. O protests as most shake their heads. "Merely limit it a bit, while providing more oversight. But as this week's meeting is already adjourned, I suppose that discussion can wait."

By which time Rigel and I will surely have demonstrated even to the most skeptical that we're not dangerous. That *I'm* not dangerous.

I hope.

6

MHINHU

(MIN-hyu): explanation; clarification

Molly

"Wait till you hear what Tristan found out last night," I whisper to M before church the next morning, after Mum, M's Aunt Theresa and Tristan's mother all head to the choir room. "Can you guys meet at the arboretum this afternoon?"

M exchanges a glance with Rigel and nods. Then, looking past me to where Dad is sitting, she scoots a little closer and rests her arm against mine.

Can you give us the basics now? she asks silently.

Since my other arm is touching Tristan's—my parents don't like us to hold hands in church—he hears and answers, using the group telepathy we discovered in December.

Bottom line is, Devyn was almost certainly Gannett's source, though Father doesn't know for sure. I tried to get him to tell me everything he's ever told Devyn from when he was still on the Council. Unfortunately, it was a lot. More than—

He breaks off as the choir files back in, dressed in their blue robes.

I'll give you all the deets this afternoon, he promises then. *Two o'clock sound good?*

M, Rigel and I all agree to that as the pastor motions the congregation to stand and join in the opening hymn.

As we're leaving the service later, we clue in Sean and Kira, who always sit in the back with her family.

50

"We were going to shoot hoops at the school, but this sounds a lot more important," Sean says.

Kira nods. "Maybe we'll still have time for some hoops after."

They both miss playing basketball now that the boys' and girls' teams have been knocked out of the playoffs—on the Council's orders.

"Have you two given any more thought to starting a *caidpel* club out at NuAgra?" I ask as we all leave the church together.

"A little," Kira admits. "We still need to figure out all the logistics, but now that our seasons are over, we're going to work on that."

An icy drizzle is falling when Tristan rings my doorbell at a quarter to two that afternoon. We'd been planning to walk to the arboretum, but the weather's not exactly conducive.

"Tristan and I are going to Dream Cream, if that's okay?" I call over my shoulder after greeting him with a quick kiss.

"That'll be fine," Mum says, wiping her hands on a dishtowel as she comes out of the kitchen. "Mind you come straight back after, though."

I roll my eyes, more out of habit than real annoyance. Any time Tristan drives me somewhere, she's suspicious we'll use the opportunity to make out somewhere. Which we often do, though we try to be discreet about it.

"Of course, Mum. Anyway, I think Sean and Kira, and maybe M and Rigel are going to meet us there, so you don't have to worry we'll be alone for long."

"That's not what I—" she starts to protest, then smiles. "Very well. Have fun."

Since we're not scheduled to meet the others for another ten minutes, we put that time to good use in the arboretum parking lot, only breaking apart when Rigel's car pulls in next to us. A moment later, Sean and Kira show up in Sean's little blue Toyota.

"Sucky weather for this," Sean comments as we all approach the entrance. "Let's hurry and get out of sight, so one of us can put up a rain shield."

We do. As soon as we're well away from the archway at the corner of Diamond and Coral Street, Sean pulls out his omni. He's now the only one among the six of us who doesn't have one of the cool new ones that look just like a regular cellphone. But since he's had an omni longer than any of us, he doesn't seem bitter about it.

"There, that's better," he says as the umbrella app activates, making the rain shear away—though we have to be touching for it to work for all of us.

"I'll do mine, too," M says, pulling out her omni-phone.

Tristan does the same, and then we only have to stay connected to our own bond-mate to stay dry. Much less awkward.

We all move to the far corner of the arboretum, where we'll have plenty of warning if any *Duchas* are foolish enough to brave this weather, then turn to Tristan.

"Well?" Rigel asks. "What did you find out?"

Tristan takes a deep breath, his hand tightening around mine. For support? I can clearly sense his tension and conflict, both extreme.

"Kind of a lot," he begins. "Mother probably mentioned at last night's meeting that she asked Father point-blank if he was GG's source and he denied it."

M and I both nod. "Do you think he was lying?" I ask.

"No. He wasn't the one who gave her that interview." A bit of relief seeps through our connection. "But back when he was still on the Council, he *did* tell Devyn everything she's spilled so far. In that sense, I guess he *was* the source, though not directly and not this past week. From what he told me last night, the person she interviewed was either Devyn or someone Devyn briefed on all that stuff."

"I'm guessing Devyn himself," M says, "since Gwendolyn said the person masked both face and voice to the point she couldn't even tell what gender they were. And I doubt he'd trust anyone else to spin the facts exactly how he wants them spun."

Tristan nods. "You're probably right."

"So...how much did you get him to tell you?" Rigel's clearly impatient to hear the whole story. "And how? I mean, obviously you used your persuasive ability, but how did you approach the subject? What kinds of questions did you ask and how did he react?"

"I waited till we finished dinner and Mother left for the meeting, like I told Molly I would. He started to head to his old office—not sure what he planned to do in there—but I asked if we could talk first. He tried to brush me off, which I kind of expected. I mean, the last time we talked just the two of us, I forced him to face up to how he'd treated Mother all these years, along with the other stuff he'd done, then convinced him to get anger management therapy. Of course, the very fact he didn't want to talk convinced me he had info we need to know about. So I...pushed. It didn't take much, honestly.

"Anyway, after waffling for a few seconds, he agreed to a talk and we sat down in the living room together. I started by asking innocent stuff like how he was getting along in Denver without us, how his therapy was going, what he was doing to stay busy, stuff like that. Among other things, he's managed to land a pretty decent job in Fiarway as Resettlement Liaison. That lets him keep tabs on the local *Echtran* immigrants and their issues, plus earns him a nice salary. It's probably been a little galling for him to be dependent on Mother's income from her Council and NuAgra work, after being our main support all this time.

"I let him ramble a bit about how essential he's become there, then brought the conversation around to GG's most recent column and show. Before I could even ask, he repeated—emphatically—that he hadn't spoken to her. As he put it, 'I've never trusted that woman. I may no longer be on the *Echtran* Council, but your mother is, and I respect the others. The last thing I'd do is undermine them—or the Sovereign—to that muckraker.' Since I was laying the charm on pretty thick by then, I'm sure he was telling the truth."

M frowns. "Did he come out and say it was Devyn, though?"

Tristan shakes his head. "That was the next question I asked, but I don't think he knows for sure one way or the other. So I asked him exactly what he told Devyn, and when. That's when he admitted that while he was still on the Council, he pretty much passed along everything from the weekly meetings to Devyn. I pushed him to be as specific as possible, so we'd have an idea what other bombshells GG might still have up her sleeve, but he insisted he couldn't remember absolutely everything. Which might be true. It's been months since he's had access to anything confidential. Still, we should probably assume anything the Council discussed before Father was removed, Devyn knows, too."

"Hm. That's not good." M states the obvious. "Though honestly, I think Gwendolyn's already publicized the worst of it. I guess she could expose how long the Sovereigns have known about the Grentl, or that they can still control Nuath's power grid, but I'm not sure most people would believe her. Actually, I kind of doubt Devyn would have shared that with her. In his own twisted way, he seems to believe everything he does is for the good of our people. Last spring, at least, he definitely didn't want them to learn the Grentl have the ability to destroy Nuath on a whim. Trust me, he was as scared by that idea as anyone. He just hid it better than most."

"He's always been super slick," Tristan agrees. "Anyway, when I asked Father if he thought Devyn might be GG's main source, he admitted—reluctantly—that he probably was. That he—"

Tristan breaks off with an almost furtive glance at me.

"What?" I demand, puzzled by the tinge of guilt I'm now sensing from him.

He swallows, then shrugs. "Father told me, when I pushed, that he still talks with Devyn occasionally, hoping to learn about anything else Devyn's planning, so he can tell the Council. I doubt Devyn trusts Father far enough now to give away much, but he does like to remind Father that it could really benefit our family if...if you took a stronger leadership position."

Outraged, I yank my hand out of his—and get a face full of rain, which has picked up without me noticing. Sputtering, I grab his hand again, though I'm already soaking wet. "I hope you set him straight on that?"

I can tell Tristan's trying not to laugh at my self-inflicted drenching, which almost makes me pull away from him again. Instead, I just glare until he sobers.

"Yes, though you made that pretty clear yourself in Thursday night's broadcast. Father did ask if you meant what you said and I told him you did, that you have zero desire to ever become Sovereign yourself."

That mollifies me somewhat, though I'm still irritated. "Then why —?" I break off and finish my question silently. *Why did you feel so guilty just now?*

I dunno. Maybe because I've sometimes thought— But like I've said all along, that's totally your decision and always will be. I'm on your side no matter what. You know that, right?

I don't reply for a long moment. Part of me wants to push harder for his real thoughts on the matter, but another part of me isn't sure I want to know. Though he always frames it as confidence in my ability to do anything I set my mind to, this isn't the first time I've wondered if he secretly wishes...

Thanks, Tristan. I know you're on my side. It's just—

"Um, guys?" Rigel's words interrupt me. "You always give *us* a hard time for doing that."

I belatedly realize the others are all watching us. "Sorry. You're right."

M grins. "See? Not always as easy as you think. Anything else we should know, Tristan? How long is Connor staying in Jewel?"

"Till at least tomorrow, but I got the impression he's keeping his return date flexible until he sees how things go. With Mother, I mean... or mostly with Mother. But I think I've told you everything important I got out of him last night. The biggie is that Devyn's almost certainly the one trying to make you look bad."

"And I can trust Gwendolyn Gannett to take full advantage." M's smile is more of a grimace. "Especially after the way we practically called her a liar in our broadcast Thursday. I guess time will tell if she has more dirt to throw at me. I'd better finish up my own column for this week so I can get it off to the *Enquirer* editors."

Sean and Kira exchange a glance. "Are we done here, then?" Sean asks. "We'd still like to spend some time shooting hoops today."

M looks at us, then Rigel, and nods. "Sure. I can't think of anything else we need to talk about until we know more. Go have fun."

The two of them practically sprint off, which makes the rest of us chuckle.

"They really should start a *caidpel* league," Rigel comments. "Shoot, I might try learning *caidpel* myself, if the Council decides Tristan and I can't play football next season."

"Same," Tristan agrees. "You guys want to hit Dream Cream before we go home? That's where Molly told her mom we were going."

M and Rigel both agree, so the four of us head out to the little parking lot.

As soon as we're in his car, Tristan turns to me. "You're not mad at me, are you?"

Smiling, I take his hand so he can feel the love I'm sending his way. "No, of course not. You were just reporting what your dad said...and what Devyn's pushing on him. I just get pissed every time somebody brings it up. I'm afraid I'm going to hear it more and more after the crap GG put out there. What I said Thursday night obviously wasn't enough to keep your dad from mentioning it. Again."

Tristan starts the car. "He might not have, if I hadn't been pumping him for every scrap of info about Devyn I could get out of him. And I did tell him, in no uncertain terms, that you're not the least bit interested in taking M's place."

"Good. Thank you. Okay, let's go get some ice cream—or maybe hot chocolate." I'm still shivering a little from getting soaked.

Of course, Tristan notices. "You have an omni app that'll dry you off and warm you up," he reminds me. "Maybe you haven't used it yet?"

I haven't. I didn't get my cool new omni-phone until after Thanksgiving, and still haven't explored everything it can do. Now, I go into its holo menu and locate the app he mentioned. By the time we park in front of Dream Cream a couple minutes later, it's like I never got wet or cold at all.

"You take such good care of me." I lean over to give Tristan a lingering kiss. "Thank you."

"Part of my job description as a Bodyguard-boyfriend," he replies with a grin. "I love you, Molly."

That obviously calls for another kiss before we get out to join M and Rigel inside.

We spend the next hour talking about everything from school to contingency plans for any future bombshells. None involve me taking on more responsibility or authority, thank goodness. I'm sorry when this nice interlude ends, already dreading my next argument with Mum about things I don't even want to think about, much less talk about.

Well before I've been away long enough to make Mum suspicious, Tristan drives me back to my house. Rounding the corner onto Opal, I see an unfamiliar white car out front. "Huh. I wonder who's visiting?"

A spike of alarm from Tristan startles me, but it dissipates almost immediately.

"What—?" I start to ask, but he shakes his head.

"Sorry. For a second I thought it might be my father's rental car— just because it's also white."

I stifle a snort. "No way. He knows my parents—especially my mum —can't stand him, after all the stuff he said and did last fall. I doubt they'd even let him in the house!" When Tristan doesn't reply, I'm immediately contrite. "I'm sorry. I know he's your dad and all, but—"

"No, you're right. They have every reason to mistrust him, even hate him, for what he did and tried to do. Sometimes so do I."

I wait till he parks his Porsche behind the nondescript white sedan at the curb to put a hand on his arm. "I was never actually hurt, thanks to you. And Mum confirmed your dad didn't know about the assassination attempt in advance. It's not like he actually sent that guy after me."

"No, he just blabbed confidential information to Devyn so *he* could. I doubt I'll ever forgive him for that. Even if Mother—"

"Connor's getting the help he needs to get past his issues," I remind him. "If they can eventually patch things up, won't that be good?"

Tristan shrugs. "I guess. Though if she does eventually take him back, I kind of hope it's not till after I leave home for...whatever I do after graduation next year. I'd rather not live under the same roof with him again. I can't believe she'd ever want to, either. Speaking of, I really can't stay. I don't like leaving them alone together too long. He asked an awful lot of questions about the Council meeting when she got home last night. She didn't tell him much, but I was right there. Now, though—"

"No, I get it," I say, opening my car door. "His charm may not be as powerful as yours, but it might be enough to worm info out of her."

He nods, clearly glad I understand. We hurry through the still-falling drizzle to my front porch, where we indulge in one last, long kiss before Tristan goes back to his car.

I wave as he drives off, then, still smiling, I go inside...only to find Connor Roark sitting in our living room, having tea and cookies with my mum and dad like it's no big deal.

AVHRAS

(AHV-ruhs): suspicion; doubt; misgiving

Molly

"What are you doing here?" I demand before I realize how rude that sounds.

Mum admonishes me with a glance. "Connor stopped by to apologize for his earlier behavior."

Smiling, he stands and bows deeply to me. "Yes, something I should have done long before. But as they say, better late than never. Don't you agree, Excellency?"

It's jarring to be called that when it's just me, without M by my side. Before I can reply, he continues.

"Given how close you and Tristan are becoming, it seems only fitting that your respective parents get along well. Particularly as we'll likely all become family in the future."

His words produce a rush of conflicting emotions in me. Though Tristan and I have never actually discussed a whole future together, the idea sends a definite thrill through me...though I still completely mistrust Connor and his motives.

"In any event, I really should be going," he says when my only response is a frown. "I told Teara I wouldn't be gone long. I, ah, hope to see you again while I'm in Jewel." That's directed mostly to my parents.

"I hope so, too," Mum surprises me by saying. She's made no secret of how much she detests Connor, after everything he did last fall. How can a simple apology have changed that?

If anything, I'm even more suspicious now. "How long will you be in town?" I ask, since Tristan said he'd been vague about that.

"For a few days, perhaps longer, depending...well, on a few things. Have a nice evening, everyone. Excellency." Again, he bows deeply to me —way deeper than he ever did last fall.

The moment he's gone, I turn to Mum. "I can't believe you even let him in the house. What did you talk about before I got here?"

She doesn't quite meet my eye. "He apologized, as he said. More nicely than I expected, given his previous behavior."

"What else did you talk about? He was obviously here a while, since you had time to serve him tea and cookies." I gesture at the remains on the coffee table.

After a slightly awkward pause, Dad answers. "He mentioned that he's getting counseling out in Colorado, in Fiarway. Judging by his behavior today, I'd say it's helping."

Mum nods, her smile looking a little forced. "Yes, he was surprisingly charming. He's clearly trying to turn over a new leaf and make up for his past actions."

"So...what else did you talk about? Did he tell you he's still in contact with Devyn Kane?"

"Why, yes." She's clearly startled I already knew about that. "He believes Devyn may still be up to something, though he doesn't know what. He promised to find out more, if possible."

She still seems a little evasive, and I think I might know why. "What about that bit he said about our two families?" I ask, sternly telling myself not to blush. "Did that come up?"

"Only in the most general sense." Again, she doesn't quite meet my eye. But then she does look at me, her gaze sharp. "Didn't you say you still have homework to do before tomorrow?"

Though her non-response only confirms my suspicion, I nod. "Yeah, some. I guess I should get to it."

But as I head upstairs, I'm not thinking about homework. I need to give both Tristan and M a heads-up about Connor being here. Because I still don't trust him at all. At this point, I'm not sure I completely trust my mum and dad, either.

"So that really was his rental car?" Tristan says when I call to tell him about his father being here. "That was pretty gutsy of him to just show up at your house. Or did your parents invite him over?"

"It didn't sound that way, though Mum was kind of evasive when I asked what they talked about. They both claimed he just wanted to apologize for everything he said and did last fall...but he sure seemed eager to leave the moment I got home."

Tristan hesitates for a moment before asking, "What do *you* think they talked about?"

"I obviously don't know for sure. I mean, it's possible he only wants to mend some fences before going back to Denver, but especially after what you said earlier, I worry he's as gung-ho as my mum for me to grab more power. They could start tag-teaming the two of us, trying to sway us to their way of thinking."

"We won't let them," Tristan assures me. "Neither one is nearly as persuasive as we are, especially together. There's no way they can force you to do anything you don't want to."

His words help allay the worst of my fears, though I still plan to be on my guard. "Mum did say your dad thinks Devyn may still be up to something, and that he'll try to find out what."

"Yeah, he said basically the same to me last night, but— Oops, sounds like he just got back. I'll see if I can get any more out of him... unless you'd rather not know?"

That gets a reluctant chuckle from me. "No, forewarned is forearmed. You should find out everything you can. I'll let you go, so I can tell M about this, too. Love you, Tristan."

"Love you, Mol. See you tomorrow."

The second he disconnects, I call M and tell her about Connor's strange and unexpected visit. Somewhat to my irritation, she doesn't seem to find it nearly as suspicious as I do.

"You have to admit, it does make sense," she says. "It's reasonable Connor would want to be on friendly terms with your folks, now that you and Tristan are *graell* bonded and all. He knows about that, right?"

"Yes, Tristan's mother told him last month. But—"

"Do you have any actual evidence they're plotting something?" she interrupts.

Now I'm even more irritated. "Not *hard* evidence, but why else would Mum be so evasive?"

"Probably because they'd both like to see you take a stronger leadership role—which you already knew. Considering how resistant you've been to that idea, it's no surprise your mother wouldn't want to bring it up again."

I huff out a not-quite-laugh. "She will anyway. Count on it. Probably over dinner tonight. Tristan says even if they do team up to push the idea, they can't make me do anything I don't want, but—"

"And he's right. Please, Molly, try to relax. If Connor is up to something, Tristan's sure to find out. You said you already gave him a head's up."

"Yeah. He's also going to ask his dad more questions. You're right. Sorry I'm so paranoid."

Her laugh is more genuine than mine was. "I think we're both pretty paranoid right now. I mean, we *did* have people wanting our heads just a couple weeks ago. We're entitled. But there's no point spinning wild theories."

"No, you're right. Thanks, M. If Tristan learns more—which he will, if there's more to learn—he'll let us know. See you tomorrow."

After that, I turn my attention to homework, though it's hard to focus with this niggling worry about what Mum and Connor might be plotting. I've just finished my creative writing assignment—which took twice as long as it should have—when Tristan messages me.

> Can you come over for dinner tonight? Father suggested inviting you, probably to make nice again. But I'm thinking if he held any info back last night, together we should definitely be able to get it out of him.

> I'll ask my parents. Do you think he's talked to Devyn again?

Tristan messages back,

> I guess he could have. He spent a good half hour shut in his office after he got home, so he must have been doing something.

Okay, just a sec.

I run downstairs to tell Mum and Dad about Tristan's—Connor's—invitation. They immediately agree I can go, acting suspiciously pleased about it.

"It's nice that they've invited you, particularly as you were rather rude to Connor earlier," Mum says. "This must mean he doesn't hold it against you."

My eyebrows go up. "I've got a whole lot more to hold against him after what he did last fall, don't you think?"

"I suppose that's true," Mum allows, with a glance at Dad. "But he's right that as things stand between you and Tristan, it only makes sense we all get along as well as possible. Would you like me to drive you, or will Tristan pick you up?"

M and I will finally have a chance to take Drivers Ed after spring break, so I obviously don't have a license yet. Or a car.

"He'll probably come get me." I fire off a quick message asking that and he quickly replies in the affirmative.

I can be there in about fifteen minutes, if you think you'll be ready?

I relay that to Mum, then run upstairs to change into something a little nicer than the jeans I wore to the arboretum. Not that Connor deserves that consideration, but Tristan and his mother do.

On the way to his house a short time later, Tristan detours into the little business park—closed, of course, since it's Sunday—that's become our favorite weekend makeout spot.

"I'll just say I hung around to chat with your folks for a few minutes, if Mother or Father ask questions," he tells me with a wink as he parks around back.

The five minutes or so we spend kissing wipes away the last of my lingering unease from those earlier confrontations with Connor and Mum. By the time we reach the Roark's mini-mansion, I feel fully fortified to get every possible scrap of useful information out of Connor over dinner.

Tristan's parents greet me at the door with bows—Connor's deeper than Teara's, probably because I've asked her multiple times not to bow at all. I guess she figures it would look weird if she didn't now, with her husband observing the formalities right next to her.

"Come in and sit down, Excellency, please," Connor says with an ingratiating smile that gives me the creeps. "Teara will have dinner ready in just a few minutes, I believe."

Mrs. Roark nods, her smile just the slightest bit strained. "Yes, I just need to finish up the potatoes and plate everything. In the meantime, a few snacks are laid out on the coffee table. Would you care for some raspberry sparkling water?"

That's been my new favorite the last few times I've visited here. "Thanks, that would be great," I tell her, following Connor to the living room, Tristan at my side.

"I must apologize for startling you earlier, Excellency," Connor says as we all sit down. "I imagine it was quite a surprise to find me at your home after the conclusion of my last visit there."

"Er, yeah. It was." No point elaborating. He's as aware as I am that when he left that time, he was basically under arrest for spilling Council secrets to Devyn, then lying about it.

Tristan, beside me on the loveseat, takes my hand, silently signaling his intention before turning to his father. "Have you by any chance heard from Devyn today?"

Connor frowns, looking a little pissed at such an abrupt question. Taking a firmer grip on Tristan's hand, I add my persuasive ability to his. Almost immediately, Connor's frown smooths out.

"In fact I did, shortly after I got home this afternoon," he slowly replies. "He, ah, sounded happy to hear I'm making progress in repairing our family relations and wished me success in that."

"Did you tell him you'd visited my parents, too?" I ask.

Connor nods. "He was pleased by that as well, though perhaps for less than altruistic reasons. Needless to say, I don't trust Devyn as I used to. I rather suspect he hopes, through me, to reestablish a line of communication with the *Echtran* Council."

"So you can pass along more information to him?" Tristan's voice is sharp.

"Probably," Connor admits. "Though I rather hope the reverse might prove true instead. If I maintain a cordial relationship with Devyn, he may let slip hints about anything he's planning. In fact, just this afternoon he—"

"Dinner's ready," Tristan's mother calls from the dining room.

I hide a grimace at her poor timing. As we all stand up, Tristan thinks to me, *Whatever it is, we'll get it out of him over dinner, or after.*

Once we're all seated around the table, though, Connor brings up something completely different.

"Your mother and I have talked it over, Tristan, and I'd like to invite you to spend your spring break with me in Fiarway. She feels it may help us to reestablish a healthier father-son relationship."

Even as I feel Tristan's spike of alarm—which I share—Connor adds, "Princess Malena is welcome to come as well. Teara tells me that the two of you can suffer unpleasant physical symptoms from being too long apart, as a result of your *graell* bond."

Tristan looks questioningly at his mother, who smiles back.

"It's your decision, of course," she tells him, "but I haven't liked seeing how estranged you and your father have become over these past few months. Repairing that rift would be definite progress toward eventually healing our family."

As she speaks, I try to decipher Tristan's emotions. Surprise and alarm seem to be giving way to something else. Hope? Maybe even a hint of eagerness?

"You needn't decide on the spot," Connor says when Tristan hesitates. "Think it over, discuss it with your mother and with Princess Malena, then let me know. Your break begins next weekend, correct?"

Tristan nods. "Friday afternoon. Counting the weekends, we have nine days off. I'll, um, think about it." He shoots me a quick glance and I know he's trying to gauge my feelings, too.

I'll go along with whatever you decide, I silently assure him, taking a bite of my chicken so it won't be obvious we're communicating. *You've been so supportive of me, I'm more than willing to return the favor.*

I'm rewarded by a small smile. *Thanks.* He picks up his own fork and starts eating. "This is really good, Mother," he comments aloud. "New recipe?"

"Yes, thank you for noticing." Clearly relieved to move on to a completely safe topic, she describes how the meal was prepared.

When we're all finished, she starts clearing the table. I immediately jump up to help, but she won't let me. "No, Excellency, please sit down.

I realize you became used to doing this sort of thing before learning your true identity, but now it seems rather...unseemly. I'd much prefer to do this myself. I'll have dessert out in a moment."

It's not the first time she's refused to let me help with anything the slightest bit servant-like. The only reason I usually give in is to spare her distress, but now I realize it also gives Tristan and me a chance to get more info out of Connor.

Tristan clearly has the same thought, because the moment his mother leaves the room, he turns to his father. "Earlier you started to tell us about something Devyn said this afternoon?"

Again Connor hesitates, and again I feel Tristan applying his charm. I quickly add mine to it.

"Er, yes." Connor nods, relaxing once more. "I vaguely referenced his earlier plans having apparently been delayed, hoping to hear he's now abandoned them entirely. Instead he laughed and admitted there'd been a slight setback that required scaling back his original goal. He implied, however, that he still has the means to pursue a more limited version, which he's confident he can ultimately achieve. Before I could inquire further, he abruptly changed the subject, asking how my work in Fiarway is going and when I expected to return there."

Ask where Devyn's living these days, I quickly think to Tristan, who proceeds to do just that.

Unfortunately, Connor shrugs. "I'm afraid I don't know, not exactly. He's aware the Council still wants to question him and may fear I would pass along any address he might give me. A reasonable fear, as he's encouraged me to continue in my efforts to reconcile with your mother and to reestablish friendly relations with Council members."

So Devyn can again have an inside source of information, I assume. "Do you at least have an idea of the general area where he's staying?" I add a bit of extra "push" to my question.

"He, ah, must live somewhat near Fiarway, as he visits there quite regularly—though discreetly. The Council never put out any public call for his apprehension, so no one there considers that unusual."

I'm trying to think of a good follow-up question when Mrs. Roark reappears with a pie and a small tub of ice cream.

"It's been a while since I've taken the time to make a proper apple pie but it's a favorite of Tristan's. I hope you like it too, Princess."

"I'm sure I will," I tell her, our questioning of Connor effectively at an end—not that it sounds like there's much more to get out of him.

That's enough to share with M and maybe the Council, though, Tristan thinks to me as he helps his mother serve dishes of pie a la mode to all of us.

He's right, I realize. Coming to dinner was apparently the right decision after all.

8

AETIGH HAR

(AY-teeg-ur): convince; persuade

M

"Have you guys decided yet if you're going to Colorado for spring break?" I ask Molly and Tristan at lunch Monday.

Before school this morning, the two of them filled Rigel and me in on everything they learned from Connor last night. While I'm pleased we finally have a solid lead on Devyn's likely whereabouts, that bit about him reviving his earlier plans is worrisome.

"I think we will," Molly replies with a quick smile at Tristan. "Staying with Connor might be kind of awkward, but I'd get to see where Tristan grew up and meet some of his old friends."

He nods. "That part should make up for spending time with my father. I hope. It might also give us a chance to find out more, especially if he hears from Devyn again."

"I messaged Kyna after the text you sent me last night," I tell Molly. "She got back to me just before lunch and wants a quick Council meeting tonight to discuss—probably just a virtual one."

Molly grimaces. "We already have to spend this afternoon hearing more petitions. At some point I need to catch up on homework. The teachers have really piled it on and everything's due before spring break starts."

"Yeah, I'm in the same boat. We'll manage, though," I say with more confidence than I feel.

"You will." Rigel assures me. "I'll help where I can. The last thing we want is you getting burned out again—either one of you," he adds to Molly.

"I'll help, too," Tristan promises her. "Especially in the classes we have together."

After that we turn our attention to eating before the lunch period's over—and to the non-Martian conversations going on around us. We probably spend more time than is wise whispering together in school as it is. Some of the *Duchas* students are already suspicious enough of anyone with NuAgra connections.

✦

That afternoon, Mrs. O drives Molly and me to NuAgra, where we hold our weekly audience session. There seem to be fewer petitioners than usual this time—maybe because of last week's revelations about me?

That suspicion is strengthened when our third petitioner, a man from the Chicago suburbs, glances nervously around the room as he enters. "Your—ah—young Bodyguard isn't here?" he asks me.

"Rigel? No." The man visibly relaxes at my reply. "He and Tristan, Princess Malena's student Bodyguard, don't sit in on these audiences. The Council feels having our adult Bodyguards present provides us suffi-cient security."

The man flushes at the implication that *that* should have been his reason for asking, though we all know it wasn't. I don't mention that Rigel will be here later to drive me home. No point scaring the guy out of his wits.

"You have a request?" I prompt, stifling a silent sigh.

Nodding, he launches into a rehearsed speech about the potential benefits of establishing an apartment complex in or near Chicago solely for *Echtrans*. "Among other things, we could more easily socialize together without raising *Duchas* suspicions," he concludes.

"You may tell the group of people you represent that we'll have someone look into the possibility," I respond. "It may not prove to be feasible, however."

"I understand. Thank you, Excellency. Excellencies." Stepping back, he bows jerkily to me, then to Molly, before scurrying out of the room.

As soon as the door closes behind him, Molly comments, "Guess our broadcast didn't do quite as much damage control as we hoped, huh?"

"Maybe my column in tomorrow's *Enquirer* will do more." I hope so.

The next person on our schedule is a judicial candidate for Ohio. She impresses both of us with her thoughtful and informed answers to our questions. Molly and I smile at each other after she leaves.

"She seems like a good one to have on our team, don't you think?" Molly asks.

"Yes, let's go ahead and confirm her. That'll give us one less district to worry about."

Slowly but surely, we're filling all the appointed positions and approving enough qualified candidates for the elected ones.

An hour later, the final petitioner leaves, seeming satisfied with our assurance that more housing will be available in Jewel in time for the next launch window.

Rigel and Tristan are waiting for us in the lobby when we leave the audience chamber. I greet Rigel with a discreet kiss and Molly does the same with Tristan—we both try to refrain from too-obvious displays of affection in public. Martian public, anyway.

"Oh," I say to Molly as we turn toward the exit, "I asked Kyna if we can just do a holo meeting from your house tonight, so we don't have to come all the way back out here. She said she's fine with that."

Molly nods. "When I get home, I'll type up some notes about last night's conversation and send them to the whole Council," she offers. "That may keep things shorter."

"Good idea," I agree and turn back to Rigel.

Done with shop talk for now? he thinks to me teasingly.

Yes. Sorry. Let's go.

We link hands and head out of the building, more than eager for a few minutes of makeout time on the way home.

⁺⁺

After dinner that evening, I go over to the O'Garas' house, where most of the *Echtran* Council members will holo in. Kyna has promised to keep the meeting brief, but wanted the full Council's advice and approval for any plan we propose.

"Hello, Excellency," Mrs. O greets me. "Teara called a few minutes ago to say she'd prefer to attend in person. I told her that would be fine." I sense a trace of confusion from her.

"Connor doesn't leave until tomorrow," Molly explains to both of us. "Tristan suggested she come here so there's no chance of him listening in."

If anything, Mrs. O's confusion increases. "Does she still believe he could be a security threat?"

"Maybe not intentionally," I say, "but we know he's still in contact with Devyn Kane so it seems safer not to risk it. Especially considering what this meeting will be about."

Tristan's also hoping to use this as another chance to get info out of Connor, if there's any more info to get. But since we haven't yet shared the extra-persuasive ability he and Molly now have outside our Bond Squad, I don't mention that additional advantage of Teara attending in person.

The doorbell rings then, heralding Mrs. Roark's arrival. It's nearly eight, the time set for the meeting, so we all go into the O'Garas' living room to await the others' holos.

Within moments they begin arriving. First Kyna, then everyone else —Nara, Mr. Stuart, Breann and Malcolm. Before Kyna calls the meeting to order, Mrs. O asks if it will be all right for her husband to sit in.

"Molly tells me she and Tristan have been invited to visit Connor in Fiarway over spring break and I know he'll want to hear about any potential risks ahead of deciding about that," she explains.

Kyna nods. "That will be fine."

Then Mr. Stuart speaks up. "Perhaps Rigel can listen in as well? I told him I'd ask."

"That's a good idea," I say before Kyna, clearly startled, can reply, "since the plan I want to discuss tonight will involve him, too."

Rigel *could* "listen in" through our telepathic link, but no one here except Molly knows the extent of our range and we'd prefer to keep it that way. Just in case.

"I suppose that makes sense, then, Excellency. Van, you may tell your son it's all right."

A moment later Rigel's hologram appears next to his father's.

"If there are no other last-minute additions, I'd like to begin." Kyna's tone becomes brisk. "Last night the Sovereign relayed to me some rather concerning information involving Devyn Kane that I feel I should share with you all. While we'd all hoped that the destruction of his antimatter-enhanced Ossian Sphere forced him to abandon his plot to seize leadership, it now appears that may not be the case. Excellency?"

"It actually makes more sense to let Molly explain, since she heard this from Connor firsthand and I didn't."

Though I didn't warn her in advance, Molly only hesitates for a second before beginning. "Er, right. I had dinner at the Roarks' house last night and Tristan and I spent some time talking with Connor. He admitted he still occasionally hears from Devyn, so we asked what kinds of things they'd talked about, where Devyn lives, things like that. And Connor told us he doesn't believe Devyn's given up on his plan, from stuff he's let drop in their conversations."

"Does he also know where Devyn is?" Breann asks then.

"Not exactly," Molly says, "but he thinks it must be pretty close to Fiarway, because he visits there pretty often."

There's a startled pause.

"Openly?" Malcolm demands. "If so, why hasn't he been apprehended?"

"Why would he be?" Mr. Stuart asks. "We've never put out a general call for his arrest, for fear of driving him further underground and making him even harder to locate."

That decision was the subject of a lot of argument within the Council around the first of the year.

"This is the best lead we've had on his location since his attempted coup in December," I point out to everyone. "That's why I propose Rigel and I also go to Fiarway for spring break, so we can finally track him down, once and for all."

That provokes a lot of murmuring from the other Council members.

"Do you really believe you can?" Nara asks, regarding me wonderingly.

"Yes, I do," I tell her. "If we can get within a few miles of him, our combined ability to locate someone specific should be able to do the rest. That's how we found Gordon Nolan in Elwood, two towns away from Jewel—just before accidentally finding the Grentl in orbit."

Rigel nods. "We've tried scanning the whole western United States for Devyn a couple of times, since that was the best info we've had on where he might be, but it's way too big an area for us to search effectively from here. But if he really is living somewhere near Fiarway, it should be—well, maybe not a piece of cake, but totally doable."

There's another moment of silence while that sinks in. Then Breann turns to Molly. "If it's true he still hopes to take over the *Echtran* leadership by force, do you think that means he has another Ossian Sphere?"

"No idea," she replies with a shrug. "If so, he didn't tell Connor about it. Of course, he never told Connor about the last one, either, so who knows? He must have *something* if he thinks he still has a chance to take over."

"Then I should say finding him—and neutralizing whatever weapon he has—is a definite priority," Kyna declares. "Excellency, what resources would you like us to put at your disposal? Your safety, and Princess Malena's, are of prime importance. No matter how high your chances of finding Devyn may be, I'm not willing to put either of you at undue risk."

She's obviously remembering how Molly and I gave my Bodyguard Cormac the slip a couple weeks back, to sneak out of NuAgra so we could rescue Rigel and Tristan. It *was* risky—in fact, we both could have died. Which, okay, would have been a huge blow for our people. But both boys almost certainly *would* have died if we hadn't, which was absolutely not an option for either of us.

"Rigel and Tristan are both trained Bodyguards, and they'll be with us," I remind her. "Normal protocol would have Cormac and Gilda accompany us, too, so that shouldn't raise any suspicions. Bringing along a full security force could send Devyn into hiding, though."

Mrs. O'Gara clears her throat. "They really should have proper Handmaids, as well. Both girls have insisted there's no need here in Jewel, but—"

Molly rolls her eyes. "And there totally isn't. I won't need anyone to help me dress in Fiarway, either."

"That discussion can wait," Kyna says firmly. "Right now I'd prefer to make certain we have sufficient precautions in place to ensure their safety."

I glance over at Mr. Stuart. "We do have these trackers you insisted on, after what happened." I hold up my left wrist, where the microscopic chip was inserted just under the skin. "Can we use them to send an alert if we suddenly need the troops sent in?"

A feature like that would have been awfully useful when that mob attacked us—though if we'd already had these trackers then, we probably would have been caught before rescuing Rigel and Tristan.

"I can tweak the programming to make that possible, yes," Rigel's dad replies. "Once done, a simple series of taps on the tracker site would activate a signal we can pick up."

"Perfect!" I look back at Kyna.

She ponders that for a moment, then nods. "I suppose that will do to start. I'll also discreetly ask Fiarway's own security to be on standby—a reasonable enough request, given recent events. Shall I make your travel arrangements, Excellency?"

I agree to that, since my Aunt Theresa is better off knowing as little as possible.

"If there's nothing else, we can adjourn for this evening," Kyna says once that's settled. "Excellency, do you still plan to hold a town hall meeting at NuAgra this week, to further reassure people about your status?"

"Yes, Thursday evening, instead of our usual broadcast. The announcement will be in tomorrow's *Echtran Enquirer*. I can say I'm going to Fiarway to do another one there, so my tagging along with Molly won't seem weird. And hey, if we find Devyn quickly enough, maybe I can even squeeze in a visit to Dun Cloch, too, before the end of spring break—though we probably shouldn't announce that yet."

"Very well," Kyna says. "Let's plan our next meeting for a week from Saturday, or as soon as possible after the Sovereign and Princess return to Jewel. I'll of course keep you all apprised of developments in the meantime."

With that, she adjourns the meeting and those here holographically wink out.

⁺✦

"Have you two booked your flight to Denver yet?" I ask Molly and Tristan the next morning as we walk from the parking lot to the school.

Tristan nods. "Father bought our plane tickets less than ten minutes after Mother got back from the meeting last night. How about you guys?"

"Kyna's handling Rigel's as well as mine," I tell him. "I should give her your flight info so she can put us on the same plane, with seats close together."

"I'll text it to both of you," Molly offers, pulling out her omni phone.

By the time I reach Pre-Cal, Kyna has already responded that she's on it. *Everything's going smoothly so far,* I think to Rigel as we go to our desks.

He quirks an eyebrow at me. *I doubt finding Devyn will be as smooth, but we can hope. I'll feel a lot better once he's under lock and key.*

So will I, considering Devyn's been behind every recent threat to my life—and Molly's.

When I check my omni at lunch, I have a confirmation from Kyna that our plane tickets are bought. Looking at the attachment, I see we'll be across the aisle from Molly and Tristan—in business class. Nice! Cormac and Gilda will be in coach, but just a couple rows behind us.

That afternoon, all six members of the Bond Squad gather in the school parking lot again to read the *Echtran Enquirer*.

"Not as bad as I expected," I comment as I finish Gwendolyn Gannett's latest column. "No more bombshells anyway. Just her usual dose of snark at the end."

I quietly reread that bit aloud.

"Though the Sovereign's actions earlier this month *may* have been justi-fied, the risk posed by her continued close association with Rigel Stuart remains. If those forced to spend time in their proximity are willing to take their chances, I suppose that's their prerogative. One does hope, however, that Princess Malena is taking proper safeguards as it still seems likely she will need to step into a primary leadership role at some point, if not immediately."

The last line makes Molly shudder. "Not ever, if I can help it," she declares, clicking away from the article.

I don't argue, since assuring Molly—again—that I'm fine with her sharing power would just upset her more.

She'll be fine once she gets used to the idea, Rigel thinks to me. *She's getting more and more practice helping with all the stuff you have to do. Maybe soon she'll be willing to take point on a few things.*

I can't ignore his suppressed eagerness for that to happen. Though he's careful not to say so directly, I know Rigel would be thrilled if Molly became co-Sovereign...or even Sovereign in her own right. Then I'd have a real life again, which would include a lot more time for him. Shouldn't I want that, too? It's not like I ever *asked* for all this power—or responsibility.

"M's column is way better than hers," Molly loyally insists. "You stuck to facts. She's just trying to spin up new conspiracy theories, with nothing to support them. You also ended on a really upbeat note, the polar opposite of her doom and gloom crap."

The others chorus their agreement, warming me with their support.

"Thanks, guys. Too bad so many people enjoy getting outraged over the least little thing, even if it's mostly imaginary. You'd think *our* people would be above that, but—"

"They're definitely not," Kira says. "How do you think Faxon gathered his following? He figured out how to tap into people's appetite for outrage more than twenty years ago. Guess that particular aspect of human nature couldn't be bred out of us."

My laugh is a little forced. "Devyn knows how to put it to good use, too. Even before this more recent stuff, he proved that a year ago, when he was trying to get Acclaimed. With luck, by the end of next week he'll never have a chance to do that again."

Remembering all the ugly anti-Rigel rhetoric on the Nuathan feeds last year, largely due to Devyn's innuendoes, I'm more determined than ever to neutralize him once and for all.

● 9

SHILCLOAS

(shil-CLO-ahs): hearing another's thoughts; telepathy

Molly

During the Thursday evening assembly at NuAgra, M does an incredible job of reassuring any people who were still worried about her ability to lead—to my massive relief. I'm glad her remarks are being live-streamed to all *Echtrans* on Earth as well as on delay to Mars.

"Yes, I now feel completely recovered from my experience, thank you for asking," she responds to the final question. "Unpleasant as it was, it taught me a lot about myself, and about the potential pitfalls of leadership. I plan to use that knowledge in my ongoing quest to bring about the best possible future for our people."

Applause breaks out, many people rising to their feet to bow in her direction. Once the clamor dies down, M finishes up.

"Thank you all for coming." Her smile doesn't look forced at all, though I suspect it is. "If you have any questions I didn't address this evening, please feel free to send them via the Council link. I'll reply as quickly as I can. Good night, everyone."

She shuts off her tiny button mic and leaves the podium. Tristan, Rigel and I, who watched from the front row, hurry forward to meet her.

"You were awesome, M. Seriously," I tell her. "I was never even tempted to jump up and help you out."

Not *quite* true, but the one time she stumbled when mentioning the incident that brought all this on, she recovered way faster than she did during last week's broadcast. I was worried about her allowing questions, but she handled them beautifully. I'm sure all our rehearsing helped.

"She's right," Rigel says, putting an arm around her. "I'm proud of you. We all are."

The way she leans into him, I can tell this town hall format took more out of her than she wants to admit. "Thanks, guys. Your support helped a lot."

I'm about to suggest stopping for ice cream on the way home when an all-too-familiar voice speaks up from behind me.

"Skillfully handled, Excellency." Gwendolyn Gannett steps forward with a toothy smile. "I imagine your performance tonight was quite reassuring to those in attendance, though time will tell how it played to those watching at home. Perhaps now I can ask my follow-up questions you didn't allow earlier?"

M's wince is barely discernable as she turns to the reporter. "I made it clear at the start that I'd be limiting everyone to a single question to allow as many people as possible to voice their concerns. I'm sure you agree that was only fair?"

"Of course, of course!" Gwendolyn's smile gets bigger and faker. "But now I'd very much like to know what efforts have been made to contact the family of the deceased man. Will some sort of reparations be made to them?"

I notice a small crowd has gathered behind the muckraker, eagerly listening to the exchange. Fans of GG's, I assume.

"He was one of several people who intentionally disappeared shortly after arriving on Earth last summer," M informs her. "Even before the incident in question, extensive efforts were made to discover any connections they might have here or on Mars. Most had no close family, and those who did had become estranged from them. Perhaps not surprising, as they'd all left Nuath to escape prosecution for crimes they committed under Faxon."

Gwendolyn's heavily-made-up eyes narrow. "Do you have any actual proof the man you killed was a Faxon supporter? I spoke with some who took part in the protest who insisted that wasn't the case."

"Those people were misled." Though her voice is firm, M is clinging more tightly than ever to Rigel's arm. "Our investigators were able to positively confirm Murgh Gall was one of Faxon's *bullochts* on Mars and organized various pro-Faxon activities here on Earth. He was also responsible for several murders—four in Nuath and one here on Earth."

That results in a startled murmur from the group behind Gwendolyn, but she seems undeterred.

"Even if true, surely that did not justify you appointing yourself his jury and executioner?"

Her insinuating tone pushes me over the edge. *Let me,* I think to M, then let go of Tristan's hand to get right in the reporter's face.

"The Sovereign has already explained how her judgment was impaired that night," I snap before M can reply. "You and everyone else should be bowing down to her in gratitude for risking her own life and health for the sake of all Nuathans. If that murderous Faxon supporter did have any family, they'd be thanking her, too. Not only for preventing what could have been the complete destruction of Nuath, but for sparing him the *tabula rasa* he absolutely would have received if he'd been brought to trial. Would any of *you* choose to have your minds wiped instead of a quick execution?"

I'm not trying to use any "push," so I'm startled when every single head—including Gwendolyn Gannett's—emphatically shakes *no.*

"I...I see your point, Princess," Gwendolyn says after a moment, her tone uncharacteristically subdued. "I was...merely trying to do my job, you know."

"Of course." M's smile is only the tiniest bit condescending. "As I'm sure you know, I have always fully supported a free—and accurate—press. Thank you again for coming."

She turns away. As the small crowd disperses, I join Rigel, Tristan and our adult Bodyguards in blocking anyone else from approaching her. No one tries, though.

Our small group exits through the door near the podium, into the passageway behind the auditorium.

"Thanks, Molly." M smiles at me. "Again."

"You were handling her just fine on your own," I assure her, "but I really needed to vent. She pisses me off so much."

M chuckles. "What else is new?" But then she frowns. "Actually, this might be." She puts a hand on my arm. *I heard your thought back there, when you said, 'let me,'* she sends silently. *Even though we weren't touching.*

I blink. *You're right, we weren't! I was so mad, I didn't even think to grab you first. I just launched into her.*

"I wonder—" she begins aloud, then lets go of me and continues, *can we both do this now?*

I heard that! I think back excitedly. *Cool! I wonder what our range is?*

By now, Gilda and Cormac are looking confused and I realize this isn't the best time to experiment further. So far, only our boyfriends know we can do this. Considering this ability helped us give Cormac the slip the night we rescued our guys, we may want to keep it that way.

"So, um, do you think it's too late to stop at Dream Cream on the way home?" I say to break the apparent silence.

Rigel glances at his phone. "Yeah, I think they close in about ten minutes. Maybe we can get ice cream in the airport tomorrow."

"Oops, that reminds me, I still need to pack. We're leaving for Indy right after school?"

Tristan nods. "Our flight's at six-thirty and we're supposed to be there two hours ahead."

"Okay, home it is, then." *Though maybe not straight home,* I add silently, just to Tristan.

Even with a week's packing still to do, I'm more than happy to delay it long enough to squeeze in some alone time to make out. Who knows how many chances we'll get in Colorado?

++

M and I don't get another chance to experiment with this potential enhancement to our newest ability until we're on the plane to Colorado the following evening.

I thought we'd be able to try at school today, but between midterm exams and the frenetic atmosphere of the last day before spring break, it was too hard to focus. Then, on the drive to Indy, my mum kept up a steady stream of advice on how we—especially I—should conduct ourselves in Fiarway. With M in the car, she didn't directly say I should be positioning myself to take over leadership, but I know full well she still has that in mind.

· · ·

Can you hear me? I think to M before takeoff, when we're settled in our comfy business class seats, Tristan and me directly across the aisle from M and Rigel. When I get no response, I grab Tristan's hand and repeat my question.

I can! she sends back this time.

Glancing over, I see she and Rigel are already holding hands. Maybe that's necessary? If so, we won't be able to use it much at school.

Let's try without touching our guys, I suggest.

M nods and we both let go of our boyfriends' hands.

I don't hear anything from her for several seconds, so I try thinking to her. *I guess this isn't working?*

After a minute or so, she shakes her head and shrugs—not a direct response to my silent question, but the answer's just as clear. Hm. I take Tristan's hand again while M's are still in her lap.

How about now?

No response. Watching M, I can tell she's trying to send to me, too, but I can't hear anything.

Finally, she grabs Rigel's hand again. *Guess we do need them for this— must be a* graell *thing.*

Probably. Still pretty cool, though.

Releasing Tristan's hand, I attempt another silent message. So does M. Still nothing. We keep playing with it as the plane taxis, then takes off. Our telepathy does get easier as long as we're both touching our boyfriends, but no matter how hard we focus, we can't make it work otherwise. Oh, well.

After the flight attendant comes by to take our drink orders, I swap seats with Tristan and M does the same with Rigel so she and I are right across the aisle from each other.

Anything? I think to her from only two feet away. Apparently not. We frown across at each other, concentrating as hard as we can, but we can't make it work. By now, I can tell Tristan's getting a little bored. Probably Rigel is, too.

"Sorry," I mutter.

"No, it's cool," he insists. "There's no knowing when this could come in handy, and it's a more useful way to pass time than watching some dumb movie."

I grin. *Making out would be even better.*

Absolutely! But not really an option right now.

Even so, we indulge in one lingering kiss, long enough to make me realize I needed the recharging after all that mental work. Rejuvenated, I silently suggest M and Rigel do the same—a suggestion they're only too happy to take.

Now, I think to M, a thought both Tristan and Rigel can hear since we're both still touching our bond-mates, *let's see if that helped.*

A good bit, it turns out. Not only is our telepathy while in contact with our guys noticeably easier, for the first time I can hear M—barely —when just she and Rigel are touching. It still doesn't work if only Tristan and I are, though. Still, it's progress!

I'll bet with enough practice—and enough recharging from guys—we'll eventually be able to do this just the two of us, I think to M a little while later.

Here's hoping, she sends back with a grin. *Because Tristan's right that might turn out really handy someday.*

We're among the first off the plane after landing, since we're in business class. Gilda and Cormac asked us to wait for them before leaving the gate area, so we do. Several minutes later, the six of us head to baggage claim.

We've only just made it past the secure area of the airport when we're greeted by Connor.

"Welcome!" he exclaims with a big smile that *looks* genuine. His fist comes halfway to his chest but before he can bow, he apparently realizes how inappropriate that would be in the middle of a *Duchas* airport.

After an awkward pause, he continues, "I, ah, trust your flight was uneventful?" We all nod. "Good, good! Do you have luggage to claim?"

Neither of the guys checked bags, but M and I needed enough outfits for any official functions we attend while we're here.

"Two suitcases," Cormac informs him. "I'll retrieve them."

The Bodyguard's chilly tone reminds me that Cormac's the one who hauled Connor out of the Council meeting in November, when he was caught leaking classified info to Devyn. I doubt they've seen each other since.

As soon as M and I have our bags, Connor conducts us all out to the curb, where a stretch limo is waiting. I try not to stare.

"You'll receive a more official welcome in Fiarway," Connor says as we all climb into a spacious interior that would accommodate twice this many people. "Here in public, it seemed wiser to keep things low key."

A stretch limo is low key? I think to Tristan.

He lifts a shoulder. *Father's always been obsessed with appearances.*

Like my mum, I respond sourly.

"I wish I could invite all of you to stay with me this week," Connor continues as we leave the airport. "Unfortunately, I simply don't have room. I've arranged for Sovereign Emileia and her attendants to stay in Fiarway's most prestigious accommodation instead."

M tells him that will be fine. She's probably just as glad not to be around Connor any more than she has to. I can't help wishing I wouldn't have to, either.

Soon, though, I'm distracted by the scenery. As we head west, majestic mountains rise ahead of us, silhouetted by the fading sunset. They're gorgeous.

I've only been here once before, when M visited briefly after our return from Mars last summer. But M was so stressed then, all my focus was on her and on performing my role as her Handmaid as flawlessly as possible, not admiring our surroundings.

It takes us over an hour to reach Fiarway, first skirting the Denver suburbs, then winding our way up into the mountains, following progressively smaller roads until we seem to be on a rutted track only fit for off-road vehicles. That's an illusion, though. The ride is still as smooth as ever, reminding me a little of the approach to Bailerealta, in Ireland.

Finally, we round one last outcropping into a narrow pass blocked by the gate into Fiarway proper. The gate guard bows us through and I eagerly look around me as we proceed into the town.

"It looks bigger than I remember," I comment.

"That's because it is," Tristan tells me. "Something like six hundred more people moved here last summer, once they finished their Orientations in Dun Cloch and Bailerealta. They were still building here like crazy when I left for Jewel last fall."

Full darkness has fallen but the streets are well lit as the limo makes its way past Fiarway's little downtown, where a fair number of bystanders wave as we drive by. Leaving downtown, we pass a few dozen houses before halting in front of the same small mansion I remember from last time. Several people are waiting in front of the house.

"Here we are," Connor exclaims, opening the limo's double doors. "I imagine your Bodyguards will want to secure the area before the reception committee greets you?"

Gilda and Cormac jump out, followed by Rigel and Tristan, all with omnis in hand to scan our surroundings. A few moments later, they indicate that M and I can follow.

Once we're out of the limo, a tall man I recognize as Fiarway's mayor comes forward, flanked by a few other official-looking people.

"Excellencies!" he booms, sweeping us a formal bow. The five men behind him do the same. "I am delighted to welcome you both to Fiarway again, this time with Princess Malena in her proper role." He bows again to me.

"It's nice to see you again, Mayor Alban," M replies with none of the hesitation I'd have had. She's become really good at this sort of thing.

His answering smile looks a little strained. "I do hope you will both enjoy your visit here. Though…" He glances back at the men behind him, who I notice are keeping a very respectful distance. "I believe it would make everyone feel a bit, ah, safer if the Sovereign and her younger *Costanta* will agree to separate lodgings for the duration of your stay?"

"That won't be necessary, Mayor Alban," M replies pleasantly but firmly. "Nor could Rigel serve as an effective Bodyguard from somewhere else. I promise you that we pose no danger whatsoever to you or your populace."

Mayor Alban apparently doesn't have it in him to argue with M. "Of course, of course, Excellency. I didn't mean to imply that *I* am in any way afraid, I was simply thinking about some of our more timid townsfolk."

"Very thoughtful of you." I detect only the slightest trace of sarcasm in M's voice.

Clearing his throat, the mayor quickly continues. "I'd have prepared a larger welcome for your arrival, but I assumed you'd be tired after traveling—particularly as it is two hours later in Jewel. Tomorrow, however, there will be an assembly in your honor in the town square. I know everyone would be honored if you could speak a few words?"

"Of course." M's smile seems to reassure him she's not offended. "I look forward to it."

"Lovely. Lovely. Now, please let me present the members of our

Town Council, all of whom wished to join me in welcoming you tonight."

None of them venture very close as they take turns murmuring their names and bowing again. I wish again I had M's ability to read emotions, so I'd know how all these guys really feel toward each of us. I'll ask M later.

As those introductions conclude, the mayor beckons to two women hovering near one of the cars parked along the curb. They hurry forward and he turns back to us both with another ingratiating smile.

"Excellencies, I have taken the liberty of assigning each of you a temporary Handmaid to see to your comfort during your time with us."

I blink. *Handmaids?* I wonder if Mum had something to do with this.

Both women are a good bit older than we are. The taller, fairer one bows to me. "It will be my honor to serve as your *Chomsereich,* this week, Excellency. My name is Sorcha."

The other woman, shorter and darker, bows to M, identifying herself as Morag—a name with unpleasant associations, especially for M and Rigel. Both women wear severe expressions that make me suspect they plan to take their chaperoning duties very seriously—probably way more seriously than we'd like.

I'm still struggling with the weirdness of *having* a Handmaid just a few months after *being* one when the mayor says, "I imagine you'll wish to retire soon, though I understand Princess Malena will be staying with Connor Roark?"

"Yes," Connor confirms. "My son and the Princess will be my guests this week. Only the Sovereign and her attendants will need this residence." He then motions Tristan and me toward a smaller but still ritzy car further along the street. "Let's get you two home, shall we? I'm sure the Sovereign is eager to settle into her quarters as well."

I send a slightly alarmed glance M's way, but when she gives a little shrug, I swallow my protest at such a quick separation.

"Here, Princess, you sit up front." Connor opens the passenger door for me. "Tristan can share the back with your Handmaid and Bodyguard. I quite look forward to showing you both the house."

Forcing down my uneasiness—hopefully unwarranted?—I give him a polite smile. "We're looking forward to it, too," I lie.

10

FIARWAY

**(fee-AHR-way) (pop. 1,032): Echtran compound near Denver,
Colorado, founded 1948**

M

The encouraging smile I give Molly helps to calm the nervousness I sense from her as she leaves with Connor. I'm not thrilled about us being separated, either, but staying here should make it easier for Rigel and me to discreetly search for Devyn.

"I'll take my leave of you also, Excellency, if you have no objection?" Mayor Alban says then. "Unless you'd like me to escort you into the residence prepared for you?"

"No need," I tell him. "I became familiar with it during my visit last summer. Thank you for your warm welcome." I'm careful to keep all irony out of my tone.

From the moment he approached us, I've sensed a fair bit of negativity from him—and outright fear from two of his councilmen. Clearly none of them are huge fans of mine. I'm also picking up a trace of hostility from my assigned Handmaid. The fact that she happens to have the same name as Rigel's nasty grandmother back in Nuath doesn't help.

Got it, Rigel sends silently, as we turn toward the house. *I'll keep an eye on all of them and give Cormac a heads-up, too.*

Thanks.

"Excellency?" Morag the Handmaid interrupts our silent conversa-

85

tion. "Shall I escort you to your rooms? Your two *Costanta* can follow with your things."

Rigel grabs my backpack as well as his, while Cormac picks up my suitcase. After giving Cormac his contact info, the limo driver leaves and we all head up the walk to the house.

Nice, Rigel thinks to me as we approach the mansion's imposing front entrance.

Oh, that's right. You've never been to Fiarway before, have you?

When I was here last, he'd only just arrived back in Jewel from the healing facility in Bailerealta, Ireland, with his memory still missing the whole previous year.

I think I visited with my parents once when I was little, but we definitely didn't stay in this place!

The front door is already keyed to my touch. Opening it, I lead the way inside. The opulent entryway looks exactly as I remember. So does the fancy reception area directly ahead, with a big formal dining room off to one side and a well-appointed office on the other. Further back, I recall, are the kitchen and breakfast room, a somewhat smaller, more informal option for meals.

I consider giving Rigel a tour right now, but Morag is already heading toward the ornate, curving staircase.

"Your rooms are up here, Excellency. I hope you'll find them to your liking," she says.

"I'm sure I will." Determined to win her over, at least a little, I accompany my words with a smile. Which she doesn't return. Ah, well.

We follow her upstairs, where she opens the door to a large suite boasting a tastefully decorated living area with three doors leading off of it. Like it did last summer, the layout reminds me of my quarters on the *Quintessence,* during our trip to Mars.

"Your bedroom is through there, Excellency." She points to the door standing open at the rear of the suite. "The smaller ones are traditionally assigned to your *Chomseireach*—me—and your *Costanta.* Your younger Bodyguard will stay in the room we passed at the top of the stairs."

I frown, not liking that arrangement at all—an opinion Rigel clearly shares.

"I'd prefer to sleep on one of the couches here." He indicates the longer of the two sofas in the living room. "I can better safeguard the Sovereign's security from inside her suite."

Morag shakes her head, her expression uncompromising. "My instructions were clear. As your personal relationship with the Sovereign is well known, Mayor Alban insists on the strictest protocols while you are both in Fiarway. He wishes to avoid even the slightest appearance of impropriety."

Yikes. *This is going to make finding Devyn trickier than we expected,* I think to Rigel, remembering how impossible it was to get any privacy when we were on the *Quintessence.*

Rigel must be remembering the same thing, because he immediately glances up at the corners of my living area. I look, too, but don't see anything like the tiny cameras that monitored my quarters on the ship.

Still, let's not take any chances, he thinks to me. "Before you settle in, Excellency," he says aloud, "We should do a standard sweep for surveillance devices."

He and Cormac both pull out their omnis and activate the apps they have for that purpose. Rigel walks around the main area while Cormac scans my private bedroom and bathroom. They both get alerts from their apps, discovering a listening device in the living room and another in my bedroom.

Cormac then asks if I'd like them disabled, which their omnis can also do, fortunately.

"Please," I reply with mock politeness. "I'd like to believe those bugs weren't installed specifically for *my* stay, as that could be construed as an insult—or worse. But whatever their intended purpose, they constitute a security risk. It's entirely possible I'll need to discuss confidential matters with the Council while I'm here."

Out of the corner of my eye, I see Morag twitch slightly. Focusing, I sense both alarm and outrage, barely concealed.

I share the emotions I'm perceiving with Rigel. *So they probably were installed just for you, and she knows it. I bet she's supposed to spy on you, too. In fact—* He does another broad sweep around the room. *Yep, she's also bugged. Want me to—?*

No, leave it and let her think she's doing her job. It's not like I'd say anything in front of her that I don't want Alban or even Devyn to hear about.

Rigel quirks a half-smile, though I can tell he's pissed. *I'd rather call her out on it, but if that's what you want, I'll let Cormac know, too, in case he also notices it. Who knows, maybe you can win her over.*

I manage not to laugh out loud. *I'll try, but I have a feeling it won't be easy.*

It's not. When Morag begins unpacking my things in the oversized bedroom shortly afterward, I attempt to make small talk.

"Have you always lived in Fiarway, Morag?" I ask, pulling my cosmetic case out of the suitcase to carry to my private bathroom.

"No, Excellency." She practically snatches my makeup kit out of my hands and takes it to the bathroom herself. Returning, she continues hanging up my dresses. "I was born in Nuath and lived briefly in Dun Cloch before relocating here several years ago."

I reach for the next dress but she's too quick for me, whisking it away and deftly fitting it on a hanger before I can touch it.

Giving up on my unappreciated attempts to help, I ask another question. "Do you like living here?"

"I've found Fiarway quite acceptable," she responds without emotion.

When it's clear she won't elaborate, I try again. "I take it you've never lived in a *Duchas* community, then?"

"Certainly not." I sense a spurt of indignation at the idea. "Shall I show you how to operate the ionic shower?"

"Um, no thanks. I've used it before."

I remember being surprised they use those in Fiarway, until someone mentioned that Colorado has to deal with water shortages. Not as severe as on Mars, of course, but it makes sense they'd want to conserve wherever possible.

"Of course. Apologies, Excellency."

I smile warmly, hoping to prompt at least a slight thawing of her manner. "No apology necessary, Morag. You've been very helpful. I'd like to get to know you a little better, though, since we'll be spending a fair bit of time together while I'm here."

Far from returning my smile, she stiffens. "No offense, Excellency, but if you don't mind, I would prefer to keep our association strictly professional to avoid any distraction from my duties."

Wow. So much for winning her over. "Er, of course, if that will make you more comfortable."

"Thank you. Is there anything else I can do for you this evening? A light meal, perhaps?"

It's after eleven in Indiana, but just past nine here—and that dinner on the plane was kind of a long time ago. "A snack would be good, thanks. The kitchen has a recombinator, as I recall?"

"Yes," she confirms. "If you'd care to come to the dining room, I can acquaint you with the selections available."

"Great." I'm sure Rigel's hungrier than I am—he usually is. "Let me freshen up in the bathroom and I'll be down in a few minutes. Oh, and I'd prefer to eat in the breakfast room."

Though I still sense some hostility from her, she bows respectfully before leaving. The moment she's gone, I reach out mentally to Rigel.

Did you listen in on any of that?

Yeah. She's a real cold fish, isn't she? Sounds like her name's not the only thing she has in common with my grandmother.

That gets a chuckle from me. *I was thinking the same thing! We may have to get creative to arrange the kind of alone time we'll need to search for Devyn.*

We'll manage, he assures me. *We've had to deal with a lot worse than a starchy Handmaid.*

True, I reply, still grinning. *Let Cormac know we'll be heading down to the breakfast room and I'll see you in a few minutes.*

Going into the bathroom, I use the toilet—also a Martian-style waterless design—then sterilize my hands and brush my hair. I consider changing clothes but decide it's not worth bothering this late.

Cormac and Rigel are waiting in my sitting area when I come out. Morag's nowhere to be seen, presumably already downstairs. I take advantage of her absence to hurry to Rigel's side, tilting my face up for a quick kiss.

"Let's not waste this opportunity," I murmur. "We may not get many."

Rigel obliges with a delicious, if all-too-brief kiss while Cormac discreetly looks away. I'm glad *he* understands our need for frequent alone time, even if nearly everyone else around me disapproves.

We all go downstairs, where Morag presents me with a tablet displaying an impressive array of food choices.

"Wow. I'm not super hungry and it's late, at least for us. I'll just have a half-portion of the broccoli salad and some chamomile tea. What would you two like?"

I hand Rigel the tablet and see Morag's eyebrows go up in obvious disapproval. Tough. I won't make Rigel taste my broccoli, either, since he hates it.

Rigel requests a cheeseburger, fries and a root beer, then hands Cormac the tablet. He takes it more tentatively, aware of Morag's scandalized glare, but asks for a grilled cheese sandwich.

With a sniff, Morag takes the tablet back and heads to the kitchen.

"Get yourself something, too, if you want," I call after her, though that'll probably only irk her more.

Predictably, when she returns two minutes later, she only brings my meal out, no one else's. Protocol dictates my Bodyguards and Handmaid stand while I eat, then have their own meals in the kitchen after I'm done—a stupid custom, in my opinion.

"Please bring the rest of the food out, too," I tell her as she sets my plate and cup on the table. "I'm surprised no one informed you that I prefer to dispense with the formalities whenever possible, as I believe that's fairly well known by now. Rigel will sit on my left, as my presumptive Royal Consort and secondary Bodyguard. You and Cormac can sit anywhere you like."

The simmering resentment I've sensed from her all along intensifies. For a second I think she'll flat-out refuse, but after what appears to be a brief internal struggle she manages a terse nod. "If that is your wish, Excellency."

Back ramrod straight, she marches to the kitchen and returns a moment later with a tray bearing two more plates. Rigel takes his seat next to me and Cormac takes the chair two places to my right, leaving open the one next to me, for Morag. She ignores it, instead standing behind my right shoulder in the traditional Handmaid position.

Maybe I really should taste your food before you eat it, Rigel silently suggests. *I wouldn't put it past her to have poisoned it.*

I manage not to chuckle aloud. *I don't think she hates me quite that much, but she might have spit in it. I'll take my chances. Besides, it's broccoli.*

Then Cormac surprises me by taking the initiative. "Excellency, if I may?" he asks, reaching for my plate. He's obviously noticed Morag's hostility toward me, too.

Though I'm sure it's not necessary, I hand him the plate. "If you insist."

"Thank you, Excellency." He keeps his expression grave, though I detect a twinkle in his eyes.

Dutifully, he puts a tiny bite of my broccoli salad on his own plate before handing mine back. After tasting it, he nods to me and I'm free to start eating. At least there aren't any stupid finger bowls.

With Morag's attitude casting a pall over the meal, we eat in near silence. I'm just finishing when my omni pings with a message from Mayor Alban.

Good evening, Excellency. I hope you are happy with your accommodations and have settled in by now. Do let me know if you require anything else, either by return message or via your Chomseireach.

As a quick reminder, tomorrow morning's assembly is scheduled for ten o'clock in the town square, followed by your tour of the Healing facility at eleven. Sunday evening at seven, there will be a special dinner in the banquet room of our Town Hall, preceded by a procession through the town, to honor you and Princess Malena. The rest of your weekend has been left free, as you requested. Your visits to our school and Planning Commission have been scheduled for Monday.

Wishing you a pleasant night,

Alban, Mayor of Fiarway

I respond with a quick message saying I'm perfectly happy with my lodgings and confirming my attendance at Sunday's dinner. I'm still peeved about Rigel being forced to stay in a separate room, presumably on his orders, but I don't mention that—yet.

Message sent, I stand up. "I should probably get to bed. It's close to midnight my time, and I have a speech to give in the morning."

Rigel and Cormac get to their feet as well. Morag whisks the empty plates into the kitchen, where I assume there's an ionic sterilizer cabinet. I head toward the stairs, hoping for another brief moment with Rigel outside his room. She's too quick for me, though, and we all go up together.

Want to try the same thing I talked you into on the Quintessence? I think to Rigel as we reach the upper hallway. *Come to my room once Morag's asleep?*

Oh, right, because that ended so well, is his wry response, referring to the disastrous aftermath of that tryst. *I've disabled their bugs, at least, but my bedroom's not inside your suite like it was then.*

As if to underscore that reminder, just then Morag opens the door to Rigel's room, well away from mine. "The Sovereign should not need your protection overnight, young man. Her other *Costanta* and I will see she gets to bed safely."

I open my mouth to protest, then realize I don't have any plausible reason, since I did say I wanted to turn in soon. Still, I refuse to let this temporary Handmaid bully Rigel—or me.

"I'll see you in the morning," I tell him, stepping close for a good-night kiss. Brief as it is, it provokes an indignant hiss from Morag that she can't quite suppress.

If you're not careful, she really might poison your food—or mine, he jokes as he kisses me back. It's way less than both of us need, but much better than nothing.

Rigel goes into his room and the rest of us continue down the hall to my suite. Once inside, Morag closes my door and rather pointedly locks it. Sheesh.

Though I obviously don't need any help getting ready for bed, I let Morag turn down the covers and set out my nightgown, like Molly always did in the Royal Palace when we were in Nuath.

"Thank you, Morag, that will be all." I absolutely don't want her helping me undress or shower.

To my relief, she doesn't argue, just bows and leaves. I brush my teeth, then take a super quick ionic "shower." As I put on my night-gown, I mentally touch base with Rigel.

Oh, you might want to listen in to this. His response is laced with amusement.

Curious, I do—and "hear" Morag lecturing him.

"—will behave with proper decorum toward the Sovereign while staying in this house," she's saying. "I may not have any authority to dictate her actions, but you, young man, would be well advised to keep the traditional protocols in mind."

"Um, our *graell* bond—" Rigel starts to say, but she cuts him off.

"Yes, yes, I've kept up with the news reports and realize you expect to become Royal Consort in the future as a result of those claims—something else I cannot control. While here, however, I expect you to comport yourself more formally than is apparently demanded of you in Jewel."

I can sense him suppressing a laugh and visualize his expression as he tries to keep a straight face. "I'll...try to keep that in mind. Good night, Morag."

A few minutes later, Rigel reaches out to me again as I'm getting into bed. *So, any ideas on how to give Morag the slip tomorrow?*

I doubt I can do it before my speech, but maybe afterward we can plan something with Molly and Tristan. If I'm with Molly, Morag won't have anything to chaperone, so I can give her the afternoon off.

Clever, Rigel sends back. *That can be Plan A. Do we need a Plan B?*

I think for a moment. *If that doesn't work, maybe I can get Cormac on board to distract her. He knows the real reason we're here.*

He agrees that's a reasonable backup plan. *Do you know what you're going to say in the town square tomorrow?*

More or less the same stuff I said at NuAgra last night. I don't see any point coming up with a whole new speech.

We briefly discuss whether or not I should take questions. Then, as we often do at home, we spend the next half hour or so just sending loving thoughts back and forth as we both drift off to sleep.

11

MIHUINAS

(mee-HOY-nus): discomfort; embarrassment; apprehension

Molly

I feel super awkward sitting up front next to Connor as he drives to his house, with Tristan, Gilda and Handmaid Sorcha relegated to the back seat. The only other time Connor drove me anywhere, I was still M's Handmaid and he treated me like dirt. My, how times have changed.

That amusing thought distracts me from my awkwardness until Connor pulls into a driveway a couple of minutes later.

"Here we are, Excellency. Shall we go in?"

The house looks nice enough, but is nowhere near as big as the mini-mansion Tristan and his mom live in back in Jewel. A house Connor obviously picked out when they moved there last fall, since he's all about appearances. Like my mum.

Tristan jumps out and opens my car door before I can—and I suddenly remember him doing that the first time his dad drove me. Proof that even then he wasn't nearly as stuck up as his father. After helping me out, he grabs my suitcase out of the trunk, while Sorcha takes my backpack.

As we head up the walk to the front door, Tristan takes my hand in his free one, which gets a throat-clearing from Sorcha, behind us.

"Excellency, I realize young Mr. Roark is likely to become your Royal Consort in the future, but as he currently serves as your *Costanta,* such familiarity should properly be avoided. Particularly in public."

I glance around. "Does this count as public? I don't see anyone watching us."

She sniffs. "Mayor Alban was quite clear about my duties when he appointed me your *Chomseireach*. Morag and I were instructed to—"

"Aye, I know the drill," I interrupt without letting go of Tristan's hand. "I was the Sovereign's *Chomseireach* myself for nearly a year, so I imagine I got a lot more training—and practice—than you've had. Enough to know your duties definitely don't include telling me what to do."

"N-no, Excellency," she replies, clearly abashed. "Apologies. I only meant—"

Now I feel mean. "No, that's okay. I realize it's your first day on the job. But in case no one's told you, Tristan and I are *graell*-bonded. He's my boyfriend as well as my Bodyguard, so the usual rules have had to be modified a little."

"That's understandable when you're in Jewel, Excellency," Connor remarks as he unlocks the front door. "Here in Fiarway, however, I should advise you—both of you—to observe the usual formalities whenever possible. Here at home we can be a bit more relaxed, but maintaining tradition elsewhere can only improve your standing in everyone's eyes."

My standing? I think to Tristan. He responds with the mental equivalent of a shrug.

"Welcome to my home, Excellency." Connor throws the door open with a flourish and steps back to let me go in ahead of everyone else.

Swallowing my automatic retort that I don't care beans about "standing," I step into his impeccably decorated foyer.

"This house is of course much smaller than your position deserves, Princess, nothing on the order of the one your sister will occupy while here." Though Connor's words are apologetic, his tone borders on smug. "To compensate, I have vacated the master suite for your comfort. I hope you will find it acceptable."

I nearly apologize for putting him to that trouble, especially since my room at home is nothing special, but some instinct tells me not to.

"I'm sure it will be fine," I reply instead, privately hoping Tristan's room will be close enough to mine for telepathy. This will be our first time sleeping under the same roof.

Tristan picks up on that thought. *Unless he sticks me in the garage, we should be able to talk like this.* He gives my hand a little squeeze.

Connor leads us all upstairs, where he indicates who'll be sleeping where. "As I said, I've given you the master suite, Excellency." He points to the large corner bedroom. "Tristan and I will share the guest room at the other end of the hall and your *Costanta* and *Chomseireach* will share the smaller one next to yours. If that meets with your approval?"

"Yes, it should be fine," I reply, though it occurs to me it's a good thing my adult Bodyguard is female, or sleeping arrangements would be awkward.

The others all nod, though I can tell Tristan isn't thrilled about sharing a room with his father.

"May I assume your house has some sort of security system?" Gilda asks then.

"Of course."

Connor proceeds to describe it in great detail, which seems to satisfy her. He then turns back to me.

"And now, Excellency, I imagine you'd like to get settled and perhaps freshen up a bit before dinner? I realize it's quite late in Indiana, but I thought you might appreciate something light before bed."

Reluctantly letting go of Tristan's hand, I open the door to my room for the next week. Rather than go to theirs, Sorcha and Gilda follow me inside.

"I'd like to do a quick security scan of the room, Excellency, if you don't mind," Gilda tells me.

Sorcha, meanwhile, begins unpacking my suitcase and putting away my things. I feel like I should help, but remembering how seriously I took my own Handmaid duties in the beginning, I just let her get on with it.

"Thank you, Sorcha," I say when she's done.

She looks almost startled. "You're very welcome, Excellency. I...apologize again for speaking out of turn earlier. I was so incredibly honored to be chosen for this position, I'm anxious to do everything correctly."

"You're doing just fine." Smiling, I project confidence and approval her way. "I was nervous during my first few days as a Handmaid, too. Try to relax a little if you can. We'll get along better that way."

A wide smile breaks across her face, making her look much prettier. "Thank you! Thank you, Excellency. I'm so glad— That is—"

"What?" I prompt, with just the tiniest bit of "push." The better I understand her, the better chance Tristan and I will have of convincing her to occasionally look the other way when we're together.

"You see…" She hesitates, then quickly goes on. "Morag also petitioned Mayor Alban to be assigned to you, when the two of us were selected to assist you and the Sovereign during your visit. She was quite disappointed I was chosen for this job."

I frown in confusion. "Why? Surely being Handmaid to the Sovereign is the higher honor?"

Sorcha shakes her head. "Most no longer see it that way, Excellency. Not after—" She breaks off, clearly horrified. "I'm sorry! I've spoken out of turn again. It's not my place to disparage your sister."

Disparage?

"What *are* people saying about my sister?" I demand, again putting some "push" behind my words to force an answer. Because this is important.

She gasps and gives her head a little shake like she's trying to snatch back her last words—and maybe resist my "push." I intensify it and she capitulates.

"Some people…maybe most people….feel Sovereign Emileia should step aside for you, Excellency. Not only since the recent unfortunate incident you've both explained, but because of her continued determination to pursue a completely unorthodox pairing. I…I realize she's done some good for our people, but—"

"A lot more than *some* good," I exclaim, despite a sinking sensation in my stomach. I had no idea this opinion was so widespread! "Emileia is a true heroine several times over to all of our people, both on Mars and here on Earth. She singlehandedly located Faxon before he could destroy Nuath. Not to mention how she and Rigel saved *this* whole planet last fall, when the Grentl attacked. How can people have already forgotten that?" I'm nearly shouting in my indignation.

Sorcha backs away from me, wide-eyed. "I'm…I'm so sorry, Excellency," she gasps. "I don't know what made me say such a thing! I have no right to speak ill of our Sovereign, none at all. If…if you wish to dismiss me from my post, I will quite understand." She's nearly crying now.

"No. I'm not angry at you, Sorcha." Especially since I basically forced her to spill the truth, much as I hated hearing it. "I'd rather know what people are saying than not. But I promise you, my sister is every bit as capable of leading now as she ever was. More, in fact, after so much experience this past year. Way, *way* more capable than I'll ever be."

It's clear she doesn't agree with my final declaration, but doesn't dare say so. Not that I'd want to hear it anyway.

"I think Gilda's done with her security check." I nod toward my Bodyguard, who's now standing by the door. "Why don't you two stop by your room to put away whatever you need to. I'm going to hit the bathroom, then we can all go downstairs together."

Tristan and his father are waiting in the dining room when we get there. Connor stands and bows to me while Tristan pulls out my chair. His *brath* when I step close seems to surround me, something I noticed way last fall, before we were even dating. Back then, it freaked me out—freaked both of us out. Now it feels...great.

Missed you, he says silently as I sit down. He takes the seat to my left and Connor sits on my other side. Sorcha and Gilda stand behind me, like it's a formal state dinner or something. I'm about to wave them both to chairs when I notice a finger bowl in front of my plate, adorned with a pale green orchid.

Frowning, I look over at Connor. "Why is this here?" I point at the orchid. "I'm not the Sovereign."

He smiles ingratiatingly. "Simply a show of respect, Excellency. I realize many of our traditions cannot easily be observed in Jewel, but here in Fiarway they are expected. Emileia occupied the Sovereign's place at formal functions prior to being Acclaimed, to include that mark of honor, if you recall. As your bloodline is identical to hers, it seems only fitting to accord you the same."

I regard him suspiciously, but decide not to make an issue of it on our first night here. Later, though...

"May I?" Tristan murmurs, picking up my finger bowl and holding it out to me with an apologetic smile. *Just humor him for now,* he thinks to me when I hesitate.

Since everyone's waiting, I reluctantly dip my fingers three times in the bowl like I remember M doing, then dry them on the tiny towel next to my plate. Tristan offers the bowl to Gilda next, who dips and dries her fingers on the cloth and then holds the bowl out to Sorcha, who does the same and then hands the silly little bowl back to Tristan.

He sets the bowl and cloth back down at my place, then dips his fingers into his own bowl, which I hadn't even noticed till now.

Connor uses his own little finger bowl, then nods to Sorcha. She scurries into the kitchen and returns with a tray full of food. While she spoons a tiny bite of each thing onto a small plate, Gilda serves Tristan and his father. Then Sorcha offers the little plate to Gilda, who goes through the stupid ceremony of tasting each item. Finally, Sorcha loads my real plate with some kind of cheesy casserole, green beans and applesauce.

"I guess this is safe to eat," I can't resist commenting to Connor, "since you probably wouldn't poison your own son."

He quickly conceals his grimace at my snark with an insincere smile. "There seemed no harm in letting you both practice the dinner ceremony tonight. Tristan confirmed to me that neither of you have had a chance to do so in your current roles."

That's true, but doesn't make me any more comfortable with it. I notice he only assigned Tristan the part of Consort, not Bodyguard.

"So, can we all eat now?" I know I sound ungracious but don't much care. I was looking forward to a break from Mum's constant hints about taking my role more seriously, but apparently Connor's going to be even worse.

Connor's smile sours slightly as he nods. "Of course. You must be tired after traveling much of the day."

I accept the excuse he's offering for my rudeness. "Yes, sorry, I am. I'm sure I'll be in a better mood tomorrow, after a good night's sleep."

As we eat, Connor tells us about everything he's scheduled for our visit.

"We'll attend your sister's speech tomorrow morning, of course. Later, I believe Tristan would like to show you the house where he grew up, as well as the schools he attended. Denver itself is also well worth seeing, so I thought we'd spend one day this week sightseeing in and around the city. I imagine Tristan may want to take you to a few of his favorite hiking trails, too, at some point."

Since Tristan and I have no agenda this week beyond getting more info out of Connor, if there's any to get, I don't object. Neither does Tristan. I can tell he really is looking forward to showing me around his old haunts.

Since it's late, we don't linger over dinner. After I'm upstairs and ready for bed, I reach out mentally for Tristan.

Are you still awake? Can you hear me?

Yep, loud and clear! I think Father's already asleep. How are you holding up? Sorry for all that formal crap at dinner. I know you weren't expecting it.

I smile. *I won't say I liked it, but at least I didn't do anything stupid. I sure hope your dad won't insist on that at every meal!*

Nope. I specifically asked him not to and I don't think he will. Are you okay otherwise?

His concern warms me. *I'm fine. Especially this part, being able to talk to you from bed. I hope our range keeps increasing until we can do this back home, like M and Rigel can.*

Same here! The burst of love and longing that accompanies his thought warms me further. *Sleep well tonight sweet stuff. I love you!*

Love you, too!

I fall asleep still smiling.

The next morning, I reluctantly let Sorcha help me dress even though I'd rather do it myself. Gilda is waiting outside my bedroom door when I open it and I do a double-take when I see she's wearing the traditional Bodyguard uniform. She's never worn it in Jewel as far as I know, but the short black pants over form-fitting dark blue body suit definitely flatter her ultra-fit body. And the leather strap crossing her chest with her energy weapon holstered at her hip makes her look like a total badass.

When we reach the dining room, Tristan greets me wearing an identical outfit that on *him* makes me practically hyperventilate, he looks so gorgeous.

He grins as my eyes go wide. "What do you think?" He turns in place so I can see him from all angles.

I remember being struck by how handsome Rigel looked in this uniform when he wore it in Bailerealta last year—and I wasn't in love with him. Seeing it on Tristan makes me want to drag him upstairs to my bedroom and...

"Um, you look great. Really great." Only then do I realize Connor is also in the room. *Like, impossibly hot,* I add silently to Tristan.

That gets an even bigger grin from him. "I'm glad you like it. Father said I should wear it for the event at the square this morning, but I can change before we go sightseeing after."

"Actually, I'd prefer you either wear this or a traditional Consort ensemble, at least in public," Connor tells him before bowing to me. "That will help to maintain the proper impression while you're here."

Ugh. Appearances again. At least there are no finger bowls on the table this morning, thank goodness. Jumping through all those formal hoops at breakfast would be ridiculous.

With some cajoling, I even convince Sorcha and Gilda to sit down and eat with the rest of us. Definite progress.

After breakfast, Connor drives us all to the town square, though it's close enough we could have walked. Not till we're out of the car do I realize we're a tiny bit late. M is already moving toward the raised platform and podium at one corner of the square, Rigel, Cormac and Morag close behind her. What must be nearly all of Fiarway throngs the space in front of her.

I wave to M from the opposite side of the square. She spots me and waves back, which makes a lot of heads turn our way. An explosion of cheers break out, startling me. The cheering continues as I make my way along the edge of the square toward M.

"*Faoda byo Banfriansa Malena!*" people start yelling as I pass (long live Princess Malena). I also hear occasional shouts of, "*Faoda byo Thiarna Malena!*" which isn't appropriate at all, since I'm not the Sovereign.

I try hard to hide my discomfort when I reach M, not wanting another lecture from her on how I need to get used to this sort of thing.

"Wow," I exclaim, forcing an extra-broad smile like it doesn't bother me at all. "They really seem to love us!" Maybe M won't have to do much to win them over after all? "Sorry we didn't get here sooner. Guess we should have coordinated, so we could have come into the square together."

Her return smile also looks a tiny bit strained. She's never been a fan of this kind of over-the-top adulation, either.

"You made it, that's all that matters. I really appreciate you being here, Molly." She gives me a quick hug. "Okay, guess I'd better get on with it."

Squaring her shoulders, M steps onto the platform with Rigel, Cormac and her dour-faced Handmaid ranged behind it. She doesn't show the least trace of nervousness as she affixes a tiny microphone to her neckline.

I'm sure I'd be too jittery to speak if it were me up there, facing this adoring crowd. But not M. She totally has it together, just like a Sovereign should. I'm proud of her.

12

CHORIDIGH

(KOR-digh): search; seek; investigate

M

"Hello, everyone, and thank you for coming." My voice booms across the square, sounding much more confident than I feel.

The boisterous welcome Molly just got compared to the lukewarm one I received on my arrival wasn't exactly confidence-inspiring. Nor are the dramatic differences I've sensed in the emotions of the crowd—from respect with some resentment toward me, to exuberant joy at Molly's arrival, and now back to less-than-admiring respect for me. Molly's excitement at receiving such a welcome didn't help, though I'm sure she didn't *mean* to rub it in.

"It's nice to be here in Fiarway again. It's been far too long. From all I've heard, those of you who arrived during the last launch window are adjusting very well, which makes me extremely happy. It was my hope for you from the beginning.

"That said, please do feel free to let me know if you have ideas to make the transition even smoother. I understand a few of you have settled in the surrounding *Duchas* communities, which I know can be a bit challenging. Since quite a lot of our people have done exactly that in Jewel, you may want to reach out to some of them for tips, as well."

I pause to take a deep breath, then plunge into the real reason—or at least the purported reason—I'm here.

"Recent disclosures in the news about certain events earlier this month may have caused some of you to doubt my fitness to continue serving as your Sovereign. I hope my broadcasts and columns since then have allayed most of your worries on that score. While visiting Fiarway, I hope to lay to rest any lingering concerns you might have about my leadership.

"As Princess Malena and I have both explained, the regrettable incident in question occurred under extreme conditions that no longer exist. While my judgment was temporarily impaired due to my effort—my successful effort—to locate Faxon after his escape, I am now fully myself again and as able to lead as I was prior to that crisis. In addition, I'm now receiving welcome assistance in my duties from Princess Malena and Regent Kyna here on Earth, as well as Regent Shim on Mars, who has fully recovered from his temporary incapacitation."

I pause again, mostly to gauge how they're reacting to my speech so far. The initial resentment has largely subsided, though I still sense pockets of doubt here and there. Also a distinct sense of relief from some people, which is what I primarily hoped for.

"Even prior to Faxon's escape, I was warned by Regent Shim and others that I was spreading myself too thin. They were right, and that likely contributed to the devastating mental toll I suffered from spending hours and hours exploring Faxon's memories. It's an experience I wouldn't wish on anyone, no matter how successful the final result proved. Fortunately, with the help of our skilled Mind Healers as well as my friends, I was able to escape the darkness and return to full mental health, which I have every reason to believe will be permanent. I'm particularly grateful for the support from my bond-mate, Rigel—" I turn to smile back at him— "and from Princess Malena."

Scattered cheers break out again at her name. I suppose I should be glad that *one* of us is popular here. I'd planned to say more, but abruptly decide to end on that up note instead.

"I'm sure you all have weekend plans, so I won't keep you from them any longer. Again, do feel free to let me know if you still have concerns, so that I can do my best to address them completely. Meanwhile, I hope to continue in my goal of leading Martians everywhere into our best possible future. Thank you."

Nearly everyone cheers as I step away from the podium, though I can't help wondering if that's partly because I kept my speech short.

You okay? Rigel sends to me. *I think you did great!*

Thanks.

I send a rush of love his way, then turn to Molly, standing off to the side with Tristan. Connor and Gilda are behind them, along with her temporary Handmaid. I wonder if she's wearing a wire, too? I'll ask Rigel to give Gilda a heads-up.

The moment I step off the platform, Molly hurries forward with a smile. "You were great," she exclaims, though her expression is a little wary. "Everyone seemed to like it."

"As long as they're no longer afraid of me or worried I'm unfit, I'll take it," I reply with a shrug. Then, before the throng of people clearly hoping to talk to one or both of us can interrupt, I whisper, "Any chance we can spend some time with you guys today?"

When Molly glances uncertainly at Tristan, I put a hand on her arm. *I need an excuse to get away from Morag so we can do a proper search for Devyn.*

Before she can respond, Connor steps forward. "Princess, there are a few people here who've asked to meet you. Then I believe Tristan would like to show you around a bit before we join Mayor Alban for luncheon."

I blink. "Luncheon? Was I supposed to—?"

Connor shakes his head apologetically. "I'm sorry, Excellency, no. Mayor Alban and I are old friends, so he suggested the three of us join him for an informal meal so that he can get to know...Tristan's girlfriend."

Though it's obvious he almost said something else, I don't push. "Oh, um, sure. That's fine. You all go on. I'll call you later, Molly, okay?"

She nods emphatically, a question in her eyes that I'm not sure how to answer right now. So I just smile, trying not to let my inner disquiet show.

"Have fun today," I tell her and Tristan.

Other people demand her attention then, with Connor making introductions. His smug expression weirdly reminds me of my Aunt Theresa practically lording it over her friends, reveling in reflected glory after I was named Homecoming Princess last fall.

After a moment, people are coming up to me, too. Aware that this is a chance to cement the impressions I tried to convey with my speech, I greet each one warmly, gauging their emotions, then spend the next half hour patiently answering questions. Several of them thank me on behalf of relatives in Nuath, their relief evident. As they finally disperse, I hope

I've shored up my standing with at least some of the doubters, though I still sense more nervousness than I'd like.

Rigel stayed discreetly in the background while I interacted with the townsfolk, though still close enough to intervene if necessary. Cormac and Morag did likewise, on my other side. As we leave the square, they all move to flank me more closely as we head to our waiting car for my visit to the Healing center.

I guess we go to plan B now? Rigel silently asks on the way there.

Guess so.

I'm trying hard not to be bothered by the way I was brushed off not only by Connor, but by Molly's lack of protest at his high-handed ordering of her schedule.

Of course, Rigel picks up on my discomfort immediately. *You know Connor. He's probably been making a big deal in Fiarway about hosting the Princess and about her relationship with Tristan, so he's dying to show her off to all his bigwig friends. And it makes sense Tristan would want her to see where he grew up. Their family dynamics have been messed up for a while. No surprise if things are a little awkward there.*

You're right, I admit. *Again. I need to remember that not everything is about me, Sovereign or not. It's good Molly's getting a chance to learn more about Tristan's background and friends and all. And if Connor has some ulterior motive other than looking important to his friends, we can trust Molly and Tristan to find out about it and tell us.*

Five minutes later we arrive at Fiarway's small Healing center, where I again do my best to reassure everyone that I don't pose any danger, even with Rigel by my side. Even so, as I tour the facility, I sense a lot more nervousness from the Healers and researchers than I'd like—more than I expected, to be honest. I try not to let it bother me *too* much, but it's worrisome.

"I'm impressed by the expansions you've made since my visit last summer," I tell the head Healer as we conclude the tour.

"As you suggested, Excellency," she says with a deferential dip of her head. "There is still work to be done, but we have more than a year to complete it before the next launch window. When finished, we'll be able to support almost twice Fiarway's current population."

I smile, but it doesn't do much to lessen the anxiety I sense from her. Her eyes keep darting behind me to Rigel, who's staying a discreet distance away.

"Thank you again for taking the time to give me a tour. We'll let you get back to work," I say, inclining my head in response to her bow before turning to the exit. It's obviously going to be harder than I thought to undo the damage Gwendolyn Gannett caused with her fear mongering.

We pull up to the guesthouse a couple of minutes later. Before getting out of the limo, while Morag's still in the back seat, I tap out a quick message to Cormac on my omni-phone.

I've asked Cormac to help us distract Morag long enough for us to do some Devyn-searching this afternoon, I think to Rigel as we all walk from the car to the house.

Hope he can manage it, Rigel sends back. *She's awfully stubborn about her so-called duty.*

I hope he can, too. I've never asked Cormac to do anything quite like this before, nor is it the sort of thing he's been trained for.

Going up to my bedroom, I change into a more casual outfit of slacks and a lightweight sweater, then check my omni for any reply from Cormac—which hasn't come yet. There are, however, a few messages forwarded from Kyna. A couple are fairly time-sensitive matters requiring a response, so I deal with those, then suggest we all have lunch.

The four of us descend the elegant staircase and take our same places at the dining room table as last night and this morning—Rigel on my left, Cormac two places to my right. Again, despite my invitation, Morag doesn't sit, just impassively hands me a menu tablet.

After I select a salad with grilled shrimp, I pass the tablet to Rigel, then Cormac. Cormac orders his meal with a little less reluctance this time, making me wonder if he's begun to secretly enjoy needling my joyless Handmaid—not that he'd ever admit it.

Morag serves us, her disapproval evident as she sets down Cormac's and Rigel's plates. Then, at my insistence, she disappears into the kitchen to have her own lunch. Rigel and I both eat quickly, eager to begin our search for Devyn, and are nearly done when Morag returns.

When we all go back upstairs a few minutes later, Cormac clears his throat.

"Though I did a security sweep of this building last night, perhaps you can show me where the primary control panels are located, for power as well as security?" he says to Morag. "After that, I would appreciate a thorough accounting of where the ingredients for the Sovereign's recombinator originate. As her safety is my prime concern, I'd like to trace the source of all food coming into this residence."

While he's talking, I go sit on the couch and start messing with my omni. Rigel stands attentively near the door, several feet away. Morag regards the two of us suspiciously for a moment before responding to Cormac.

"Mayor Alban's instructions were clear that I not leave the Sovereign and her younger *Costanta* without chaperonage, even briefly. I recommend you contact Fiarway's Comptroller for the specs of this residence and message our Chief Provisioner for any information you require on our recombinator ingredients."

So much for that ploy. I send Cormac a look that I hope conveys, *Sorry, I appreciate the effort.*

After replying to one more official message, dutifully screened by Kyna, I decide it's time to try a more direct approach.

"Rigel, will you come over here a moment?" *Let's see what we can accomplish with her in the room,* I add silently.

Hiding a smile, he comes over to join me on the couch.

Morag instantly stiffens. "Excellency, I must protest this level of familiarity. My instructions—"

"Yes, so you've said." This time I don't bother to sweeten my words with a smile. What's the point, when she's determined to dislike me? "But due to the *graell* bond Rigel and I share, we require frequent physical contact to keep both of us at peak health. In public, I'm willing to observe the protocol Mayor Alban has requested, in return for his hospitality. Here, however, we must take advantage of our relative privacy to strengthen each other. We'll do our best not to offend your sensibilities or sense of duty any more than necessary."

She swallows visibly. Though she doesn't dare say anything else, I sense her resentful outrage as I take Rigel's hand and pull him closer.

We're not really going to make out with her watching, are we? Rigel's clearly uncomfortable at the idea.

No. Much as we both need it, she's one heck of a mood-killer. Let's see if we can locate Devyn by just holding hands. That was enough to let us find Bri and Deb after they were kidnapped.

Not that we had much choice, since Rigel was driving at the time.

Knowing them both so well made it easier, he points out. *Plus knowing the general area to search. But okay, let's try this.*

I tighten my grip on his hand and close my eyes, then deliberately recall the last time I was in the same room with Devyn to remind myself of the exact vibe I'm looking for. It was in the Royal Palace in Nuath, when I laid down my ultimatum after discovering Devyn, Mr. O and Nels Murdoch had lied to me about Rigel's memory erasure. I bring up a memory of Devyn's face and superior expression as he haughtily insisted they'd acted for the best.

Weirdly, Devyn never gave off the "bad-guy-vibe" I can usually detect from anyone with a sinister agenda. Projecting trustworthiness is apparently part of his particular brand of "push." I fell for it myself until I discovered he was anything but trustworthy. Still, I'm able to bring to mind the way he "felt" when I was near him.

Ready, I think to Rigel. I start stretching out with my senses, searching for that particular vibe.

The distraction of having Morag and Cormac in the room does make it harder to focus, but after a few minutes I'm able to push past the room, then the house, widening my scope. When Rigel puts his free hand on top of our clasped ones, it gets a little easier.

I begin to sense emotions from inside the closest houses and buildings, then those from the next street over, scanning in an ever-widening circle. Soon I pick up Molly's distinctive vibe, then Tristan's—at Mayor Alban's for lunch, I presume. Yep, there's Connor, too. All three seem strangely uncomfortable, but I don't linger long enough to figure out why. Connor no longer gives off the faint bad-guy vibe I got from him last fall, but Mayor Alban's makes me flinch.

Yeah, he's absolutely someone to watch, Rigel comments, picking up what I feel. *Any chance he's hiding Devyn right in his house?*

I carefully check the whole area around them but don't find any sign of Devyn's vibe. *No such luck. I'll keep looking.*

I keep broadening my search until I reach, then pass, the outer perimeter of Fiarway. Wherever Devyn is, it's not right in town. I put my own free hand on top of our clasped ones and Rigel obligingly turns his palm to mine, further increasing our contact.

Strengthened, I push harder.

I sense no humans at all within a mile or two of Fiarway, consistent with what we saw while driving in last night. Soon, though, I reach the closest suburban area and spend some time probing around it.

Nope, not here, either. Should I try downtown Denver? I cringe inwardly at the thought, having learned the hard way that big cities generally contain an overwhelming amount of negative emotion. To search it properly, I'll have to experience every one.

Let's save that for last, Rigel replies. *Try the outlying areas first. If he's amassing any kind of army, it would have to be out in the boonies.*

Relieved, I start scanning up into the mountains west of the city, pausing at each small neighborhood I encounter to make a more thorough search. Along the way, I also discover several widely scattered pairs and small groups of people—probably hikers and isolated mountain cabins.

Ugh. This could take a while, I think to Rigel. *Want to take a break and try again later?*

Why don't we give it ten more minutes? he suggests. *Getting started always seems to take the longest.*

He's right, so I keep sweeping the mountainous area around and above the city, trying not to get too discouraged. Maybe Connor was wrong that Devyn lives in this area? Or he could—

Ah! I mentally exclaim. *That felt familiar. Definitely worth checking out.*

Backtracking slightly, I start tightening my focus instead of broadening it, zeroing in on the vibe I just sensed. The closer I get, the more sure I am it's Devyn. *Yes! Found him!* I declare in silent triumph.

Excellent! I knew you could do it. Now let's figure out exactly where he is, so we can send a security force to nab him.

Devyn's vibe now firmly pinpointed, I start widening my focus again, looking for landmarks we can relay to Cormac. He's almost due west of us, roughly six miles out. A cluster of other emotions surround him, most with definite "bad guy" vibes, but aside from those, I don't sense anyone else within two miles of him.

Okay, Rigel thinks, *let's triangulate. You know how far he is from Fiarway and in what direction. Now let's figure out where he is in relation to Denver.*

I may be the one with this special power, but Rigel's much better than I am at refining its uses, as he's proved on other occasions. Following his mental instructions, I'm able to convey to him two imaginary lines leading to Devyn—one from Denver and one from here.

Perfect! he silently tells me. *The spot they intersect should be Devyn's precise location.*

Sending a grateful wash of love Rigel's way, I loosen my grip on his hands, open my eyes and grin at him. *We did it! With luck, Devyn will be under arrest by dinnertime. This really was a piece of cake!*

●
13

ATEAMH RIOGA

(ah-TEV ree-OH-gah): a persuasive ability shared by some of Royal blood

Molly

As we leave the town square, Connor points out a few landmarks of interest, then drives us through the streets of Fiarway before taking us back to his house so Tristan can change clothes.

"As the Princess already has a Council-appointed Bodyguard, there's no need for both of you to fill that role this afternoon, particularly as this is to be a friendly visit," he explains. "We wouldn't want the mayor to infer we expect any sort of threat to your safety while at his home, would we?"

Tristan obligingly trades his sexy Bodyguard uniform for a gold-embroidered green tunic and darker green leggings—exactly the sort of thing a presumptive Royal Consort would wear. I remember Sean wearing similar ensembles in Nuath, when escorting M around before and after she was Acclaimed.

Not as over-the-top hot as your other outfit, but you're gorgeous in this, too, I silently assure him when he joins us in the living room with a questioning look.

"Yes, that's far more appropriate," Connor approves. "Shall we go?"

Lunch at Mayor Alban's house is even more awkward than I expected. Though Connor told M it was going to be an informal get-together, the mayor and his wife are dressed as formally as Tristan is, and greet me with bows and what amount to oaths of allegiance. In other words, all the traditional deference a fully Acclaimed Sovereign would receive. More than M usually allows, in fact.

When we get to the dining room, I see they've pulled out all the stops there, too, including the stupid finger bowls. When I try to protest, Connor quietly suggests I play along rather than embarrass them. I don't want to do that, so I stay quiet as we go through all the ridiculous pomp.

Tristan hesitates at first, not sure whether he should act as my Bodyguard or future Consort, but both Connor and Alban insist he sit at the table, on my left.

Father's still not super happy about the Bodyguard thing, in case you hadn't figured that out, he thinks to me as he takes the indicated chair. *He claims he's fine with it now, but he originally insisted it was demeaning.*

I don't say much during the meal other than responding politely to direct questions. Connor and our hosts obviously go way back, so they carry the bulk of the conversation, reminiscing about the old days and discussing current local matters Tristan and I know nothing about.

Gilda and Sorcha retire to the kitchen for their own belated lunches after serving dessert, at which point the mayor's wife turns to Tristan with a smile. "I must say, Tristan, though I never doubted you'd turn out well, you've quite exceeded my expectations. You've grown up into an exceptional young man. Of course, you already showed great promise when I last saw you. How many years has it been?"

"Nearly three, I'd guess." Connor regards his son proudly. "Tristan rarely visited Fiarway after we moved closer to Denver and he began attending the *Duchas* high school there. I had some misgivings about that, though it turned out to be excellent preparation for his transition to Jewel, where I understand he's become very popular."

Tristan smiles, though he's clearly embarrassed. "Now that I've settled in there, I'm really happy in Jewel." He brushes my hand and gives me a ghost of a wink.

"I'm sure you're happy to have him there as well, Excellency." Alban's wife gives us both a sappy smile. "Such an attractive young couple you make. Why, everyone has been saying so."

"Er, thanks?" I respond to her uncertainly, hoping we can leave soon.

Just as I think that, she gets to her feet. "If you'll excuse me, Excellency, I'm scheduled to attend a ladies' tea this afternoon, so I need to get going." With another deep bow to me, she leaves the room.

After a slightly uncomfortable pause, Alban turns to me. "I, ah, do hope your sister the Sovereign was not offended that she wasn't invited to lunch here today? Tomorrow night's formal dinner will be a more appropriate setting in which to honor you both together."

"Please don't worry. Emileia isn't easily offended," I assure him—though I do hope her feelings weren't hurt.

"That's very good to hear," he replies with evident relief, "considering how dangerous she can be. I felt certain my wife would be more comfortable without her here, though I imagine her little speech this morning helped to allay some of her concern."

I manage, with difficulty, not to roll my eyes. "Emileia is no more dangerous than I am under normal circumstances, Mayor Alban. Seriously. Right, Tristan?"

"She's right," he confirms. "The incident that freaked everybody out —especially after Gwendolyn Gannett put such a scary spin on it—was a completely unique situation that won't ever happen again."

The mayor's smile is disbelieving. "Your loyalty is commendable, both of you. And perhaps in time the rest of our people will come to believe as you do." Both his expression and tone make it totally clear he doubts that.

Sitting right next to me at the table, Tristan has no trouble sensing my growing irritation. Probably hoping to stave off a full-scale argument, he changes the subject.

"Do you and Father get together often, now that he's living in Fiarway again? I remember when I was growing up, the two of you—and Devyn Kane—used to spend a lot of time together."

"Our duties don't allow for much socializing, but we meet when we can," Connor replies. "As you say, we've been friends a long time." He ignores the mention of Devyn.

That doesn't surprise me, but now I'm curious. "Does Devyn still visit here in town?" I ask Mayor Alban. Connor already told us he does, but I want to see what the mayor will say.

He hesitates, which probably means Connor—or Devyn himself?— warned him not to mention that. I clasp Tristan's hand under the table and focus on him, letting my question hang in the air.

"Er, yes," Alban finally says. "In fact, I speak with him rather frequently." A sudden frown suggests he hadn't intended to say that.

Tristan catches on and joins in, adding his "push" to mine. "Then you're still close friends with Devyn?"

Alban darts a quick glance at Connor, then nods, unable to resist us. "Yes, I would say so. He was instrumental in securing my election to this position, so I have cause to be grateful to him, as well."

"Wow, that was nice of him." I try not to let my cynicism show. "What sorts of things do you talk about when you get together?" I include Connor in that question.

Tristan's dad shifts uncomfortably. "I, ah, haven't been privy to their most *recent* conversations."

He looks to Alban, who now answers without hesitation, fully under the influence of Tristan's and my combined persuasive power.

"When we spoke yesterday morning, our primary topic was the Sovereign's and your impending visit, as you may imagine. He shares my concerns about potentially putting my townspeople at risk by allowing Rigel Stuart to remain by her side while here. You must agree that their joint destructive capability—"

"Poses zero risk to anyone in this town," I snap, making him blink. "Did Devyn suggest a solution to this nonexistent problem?"

Mayor Alban swallows, then nods jerkily. "He—we—agreed it would be wisest to separate them for the duration. For everyone's safety."

I narrow my eyes at him. "Yes, you suggested that last night when we first arrived, but didn't insist on it."

"Er, no. Devyn and I felt that attempting to separate them by force would be far too risky."

"So...did you give up on the idea when the Sovereign refused?" Tristan asks.

Again, Alban hesitates before answering. "Not...not necessarily."

"What exactly *do* you plan to do?" I demand, amping my "push" almost to the max. "And when?" This sounds important.

He swallows twice, making a little motion like he's trying to throw off our influence—but failing. "I don't know exactly. When I told him the Sovereign rejected my suggestion last night, Devyn mentioned watching for other opportunities to separate them. At some point, I could have men standing by to seize young Stuart when he's too far from the Sovereign to touch. Then he could be removed and securely held. But not hurt, of course. Devyn did assure me of that." His expression is apologetic.

"And then what?" Tristan bores into him with his gaze. "Where would he be taken, and how do you plan to explain what you've done?"

"It would be presented as a simple security precaution," he answers. "I believe Devyn may have a location in mind, but he did not share that with me. Of course, Princess, if your sister could be similarly removed from the public eye, it would create an excellent opportunity for you to demonstrate your own leadership abilities," he tells me ingratiatingly. I can tell he's now trying to use "push" of his own. "Already, nearly everyone in Fiarway feels you would make a better Sovereign than your sister, quite apart from her crime and the danger we now know she poses."

I suck in an indignant breath at his phrasing but Tristan silently warns me not to interrupt. *Not till we get every last scrap of info out of him!*

He's right, of course, so I force myself to relax. "Are you saying they felt that way even before that news came out?" I ask.

"Oh, absolutely," he affirms. "Almost as soon as your identity was revealed and it became known you intend to pair with Tristan, public sentiment began swinging strongly your way. Not surprising, as Connor's family has always been very well regarded here. Particularly as your sister's intended pairing is...unorthodox, to say the least. Unorthodox enough to be completely unacceptable to many people. You must have noticed how much more enthusiastically this morning's crowd greeted you, in comparison to her."

I exchange an alarmed glance with Tristan. "I...no. We got there a little late, but I assumed they cheered just as loudly for my sister when she arrived."

Alban actually chuckles at that. "Oh, my, no, not nearly. I'm sure *she* noticed the difference. I do hope she won't hold it against you, Princess," he adds in sudden concern.

But I'm way more concerned with how it must have made M feel. I cringe, remembering how pleased I acted about all the cheering when I arrived just before her speech. It must have seemed to her like I was gloating! I'm too upset to reply, but fortunately Tristan has the presence of mind to continue the questioning.

Haltingly, Alban outlines everything he and Devyn had hoped to achieve during our visit—I'm guessing they started strategizing as soon as they learned we'd all be coming. Ideally, M would remain in the VIP quarters, incommunicado, while Rigel is securely held elsewhere. Once they've explained the whole thing away as a security precaution, I'd be asked to take over any remaining Sovereign functions M would have been performing.

"What about when our week here is over?" Tristan asks at that point. "Would you have let the Sovereign and Rigel go then?"

Mayor Alban shrugs. "I don't recall discussing that with Devyn in any detail, but I believe that would largely be up to you, Princess. He believes that once given the opportunity, you will most likely wish to retain leadership of our people...permanently."

14

DANGHAN

(DANG-un): fortress; stronghold

M

Still side by side with Rigel on the couch in my sitting room, I reluctantly let go of his hands and look around. Neither Cormac nor Morag have moved, as far as I can tell—Cormac still stationed by the door leading to the hall, Morag standing stiffly (and disapprovingly) near the opposite wall. A glance at my omni-phone shows we spent a solid forty-five minutes searching, a long time for them to just stand there doing nothing.

"Sorry," I say to them. More than one Council member has admonished me that a Sovereign should never apologize, but I ignore that advice regularly. "I should have told you both you could sit down, at least. But...we really did need that. Thanks for being so patient."

Cormac gives me the ghost of a smile but there's no sign of unbending from Morag. I sigh inwardly. What will it take?

"If you're finished with that...whatever that was, Excellency," she says coldly, "perhaps we can all go downstairs for the extra security checks your *Costanta* requested?"

Even knowing it won't be returned, I smile at her. "Thank you, Morag, that's a good idea. Just let me hit the bathroom first and I'll join you down there."

Unlike last night, when I emerge from my bathroom and bedroom a couple minutes later, Morag's unfortunately still with Rigel and Cormac in my living room.

Darn, I think to Rigel. *I was hoping to sneak in another quick kiss before going down. I feel like I could use it.*

His only response is a surge of longing that matches my own.

We all go downstairs together, where Morag dutifully shows Cormac all the house's systems' controls. Then I silently suggest to Rigel that he and Cormac go somewhere well away from Morag's prying eyes, so he can bring Cormac up to speed on what we accomplished.

After a quick inventory of the recombinator in the kitchen, Rigel suggests he and Cormac go to the ground floor office, ostensibly to further discuss security, but really so Rigel can tell Cormac we found Devyn and give him the location. To make extra sure Morag can't eavesdrop on them, I have her get me a glass of water, then motion her to follow me upstairs, where I make a play of asking her to help me select which outfits to wear to my upcoming engagements. Then I deal with more accumulated Sovereign business while she stands practically at attention.

There was another bug in this office—I disabled it before telling Cormac anything, Rigel sends up to me several minutes later. *I'd better do a thorough sweep of the rest of this building. Anyway, Cormac has the coordinates now and will head out in a few minutes to do a recon.*

Great! I send back. *If he can manage to arrest Devyn this afternoon, we'll be able to relax and actually enjoy some of our spring break.*

I'm sure Morag will do her best to prevent that, he wryly reminds me. *Maybe tomorrow we really can go someplace with Molly and Tristan and ditch her for a few hours.*

While waiting for Cormac to scope out Devyn's residence—and hopefully arrest him on the spot—Rigel conducts his promised detailed sweep of the VIP residence and I try to distract myself with more Sovereign business. The more of it I can get out of the way, the more down time I can enjoy later. Pulling up the latest list of petitions that have come in, I transfer them to the sitting room vidscreen so I can go through them one by one.

Nearly an hour passes before Rigel's satisfied with his super-thorough sweep of the house. Then he comes up to my suite to stand guard near the door while he silently reports everything he discovered.

I found at least one bug in every single room downstairs, even the kitchen, but no cameras. There's also a signal booster in a corner of that big reception room to amplify what the bugs send to whoever's listening. Every listening device except the one your Handmaid's wearing is now disabled, but I think we have another problem.

What? I think back, scrolling to the next petition on my screen for the benefit of the watchful Morag.

I'm pretty sure all communications coming in and going out are being monitored, and I can't find any way to prevent that from inside the house. You haven't called or texted anyone mentioning what we're really doing here since we arrived, have you?

Yikes. *No, not yet, but I was planning to as soon as Cormac gets back.*

Well, try to avoid regular texts or voice calls—those would be the easiest to pick up and decipher. Holo or video calls should be safer—they're more securely encrypted. If you also activate your sound-canceling app, anything you say should *be virtually impossible to intercept.*

Interesting. *I can't imagine this level of surveillance is a standard feature of the VIP guest house,* I think to Rigel. *Mayor Alban or Devyn or both must want to keep super close tabs on everything I say and do while here. But why?*

Because they feel threatened by your visit? Rigel suggests.

Probably.

There's a long pause before Rigel silently says, *If Devyn's feeling cornered, there's no knowing what he might try to do. You need to be extra, EXTRA careful until he's in custody, M. Let's sit tight in here until Cormac reports back.*

With luck, he'll come back with the news he's already taken Devyn out of commission, I think back. *I should be safe enough after that, right?*

Let's hope so. We're both remembering the bad-guy vibe I sensed from Alban earlier.

Ten minutes later, the front door security chime heralds Cormac's return. Abandoning my list of petitions, which I'd only been pretending to read anyway, I jump up and accompany Rigel downstairs to meet him. Morag follows a couple of steps behind, of course, but when we reach Cormac in the front hall, I turn to her.

"I need to confer with my *Costantas* about sensitive security matters, Morag, so you'll need to either wait out here or go back upstairs."

She immediately starts to protest. "Excellency, my instructions—"

I cut her off. "Sorry, this is not up for discussion. You do not have the necessary security clearance to be privy to all Sovereign business. As

I won't be alone with Rigel in the office, your chaperonage won't be necessary anyway."

With that, I usher my two Bodyguards into the office and close the door in Morag's indignant face. Holding up a hand to forestall anything Cormac might say, I pull out my omni and engage my silencing app to make absolutely sure nothing can be heard outside this room.

"Okay, that should work even if Morag has her ear to the door," I say once I'm sure it's active. "What did you find out, Cormac?"

"I discovered Devyn Kane's residence exactly where I was told it would be," he informs us. "Clearly, your ability to locate specific individuals is as accurate as it is useful. Taking him into custody may not be an easy matter, however."

I exchange a concerned glance with Rigel. "Oh? Why?"

"The building I found at your coordinates is not a typical residence. It appears to be composed primarily of stone and steel, and is partially embedded in the mountainside. To attempt entry, I would need substantial reinforcements."

My spirits sink. So much for having Devyn under lock and key before dinner tonight! "How substantial? What exactly do you have in mind?"

"With your permission, Excellency, I would like to assemble a strike force of at least twenty, using as many local security officers as we can press into service and perhaps calling in at least one other trained unit from Dun Cloch or elsewhere."

"Wow. It's really that much of a fortress?"

Cormac nods. "The facility is not only physically impregnable, it is also heavily guarded. I observed no fewer than four armed men atop the structure itself, and at least two more patrolling at ground level. I was unable to get a completely accurate count while remaining out of sight myself."

"Guess you were right that Devyn's feeling threatened by your visit," Rigel comments with a wry smile. He then informs Cormac about all the extra bugs he found in the house, and his belief that all our communications are being monitored, based on his omni readings.

My older Bodyguard frowns. "That level of surveillance directed at the Sovereign goes beyond insult to possible treason. Excellency, I recommend you notify the *Echtran* Council about this security breach. Someone should be held accountable for this."

"Hopefully they will be, once we take Devyn out of commission," I tell him. "But I'm not sure a strike force is the way to go. Won't going in with guns—well, energy weapons—blazing, result in casualties on both sides?"

He considers for a moment, then says, "Without knowing what sort of armaments those inside may have, or how they might have been modified, I can't know for certain, Excellency, but yes, some injuries or even fatalities are probable. If apprehending this man is a priority, however, a certain acceptable level of losses may—"

"No," I interrupt. "I won't authorize any kind of attack that's likely to end in loss of life. Not even of Devyn's people, who I'm sure have been fooled into thinking they're doing the right thing. We need to find another way."

"You know he wouldn't hesitate to take you out if he had the chance," Rigel reminds me. "Or Molly, either—he already tried that once."

"We never got proof he was behind that attack," I point out. "But even if he was, it doesn't justify putting both our security force and his at risk. We need a way to *only* target Devyn. That, I'd go along with." I turn to Cormac. "Can we somehow lure him out of his stronghold, so he can be taken without a firefight?"

After another moment's thought, Cormac shakes his head. "If so, I'm not sure how, Excellency. Meanwhile, we musn't overlook the possibility that he may attempt to harm you or your sister while you are in Fiarway, perhaps by proxy. If you will not allow me to send in a sufficient force to overpower his defenses, I recommend that you and the Princess return to Jewel as soon as possible, where you can be properly protected."

"That would make our whole trip here pointless," I point out. "Mine, anyway. The whole reason Rigel and I came here was to find Devyn. He needs to be neutralized before he can cause any more problems. Not to mention that Molly and Tristan, especially, would need some excuse for leaving early that wouldn't tip Devyn off. We know where he is right now. That's huge progress. But it'll be useless if he gets spooked and leaves to hide someplace else."

"But your safety—" Cormac begins.

Again, I cut him off. "No one's threatened either of us, and Devyn can't know we've located him. Let's give it another day or two while we explore our options. Molly and Tristan were having lunch with Mayor Alban today. Maybe they'll hear something that will offer some kind of opportunity to nab Devyn without risking a bunch of other people."

Neither Rigel nor Cormac seem happy with that idea, but neither of them argue. Yet.

I need to let Molly know what we've found out, but I don't dare call or text her after what Rigel learned about the level of surveillance here. Besides, she might still be at Mayor Alban's—and there's a good chance he's in cahoots with Devyn. Safer to wait until Molly tries to contact me, then try to manage a secure holo or vidchat. As I decide that, I glance over at Rigel, who gives me one of his crooked grins.

So much for this being a piece of cake.

THRAIS

(thrās): treason

Molly

After lunch, we move to Mayor Alban's living room, where we spend another half hour asking questions, trying to get every last bit of info possible out of him. As he expands on Devyn's grandiose plans for me to become Sovereign and name Devyn my Regent, I get more and more outraged.

Several times I'm right on the point of telling him how ridiculous, how *treasonous* their plotting is. But every time I open my mouth, Tristan stops me before I can blast him, so we can keep milking Alban for details.

If you say what you really think, he'll report back to Devyn that their plan won't work, he points out after my third near-interruption. *Then they might come up with a whole different approach that we won't know about. This way we can warn M and Rigel so they can keep this coup from happening.*

He's right, of course. So, frustrating as it is, I keep my mouth shut and let the mayor think I'm being persuaded by his lame attempt at "push" instead of horrified by this whole horrible scheme.

⁺⁺

"We're getting a later start than I'd hoped," Connor says when we finally leave the mayor's mansion.

He was oddly quiet throughout our conversation with Alban, making me wonder where he stands on all this. Here on the front walk probably isn't the best place to ask, though.

"Still, there's plenty of time for Tristan to show you around more of his old haunts, Excellency," he continues. "Dinner tonight will be more informal, as Tristan tells me you prefer that…for now."

For now? Is he obliquely implying that my status will soon be changing? Scarily soon, if Devyn and Mayor Alban get their way! But I intend to make absolutely sure they *won't*.

"We should probably change clothes first," I suggest. "We're all pretty dressed up for sightseeing." That'll give me a chance to warn M right away about what Alban and Devyn are plotting.

Connor glances at me, then at Tristan. I'm wearing one of my semi-formal Princess ensembles, a flowing tunic and swishy leggings in varying shades of blue, and Tristan's decked out in his fancy gold-embroidered Consort outfit.

"I see no need for that," Connor says with a shrug. "Your clothing is perfectly acceptable for Fiarway, which is all we'll have time to show you today, given the hour. We'll save your tour of the *Duchas* neighborhood where we lived more recently for tomorrow or Monday. Unless you're finding your traditional Royal Consort attire uncomfortable, Tristan?"

"No, I guess it's fine," Tristan responds before I can protest. "My middle school isn't far from here, so why don't we swing by there?" Then, clearly sensing my impatience, he adds silently, *Don't worry, Mol. M and Rigel are probably busy tracking Devyn down now anyway. Assuming they find him, there's a good chance he'll be arrested tonight or tomorrow, and without him, that coup they're planning can't happen.*

I sure hope you're right, I think back. I hadn't considered the risk of interrupting M in the middle of their mental search for Devyn. She's told me how much focus that sort of thing requires.

Tristan's confidence in the outcome helps me relax—a little—but I'm still fidgety as Connor drives us to Fiarway's middle school. At least I can use this time to find out what *he* thinks about Devyn and Alban's treasonous plot.

"What Mayor Alban talked about this afternoon was pretty, um, interesting, don't you think?" I keep my tone conversational—for now.

Connor darts a quick look at me before replying. "Interesting. Yes. I, ah, suppose you could say that. Unexpected, certainly."

I wait for him to elaborate. When he doesn't, I try again. "You hardly said anything while he was outlining the scheme he and Devyn have cooked up. I guess you were as surprised by it as we were?"

Another quick glance at me, then he cautiously nods. "Indeed. Neither of them had mentioned such an idea to me previously."

Sounds like he hasn't been conspiring with them, at least, Tristan thinks from behind me.

Assuming he's telling the truth. I'm about to apply some "push" and ask Connor directly what he thinks of their plan, when he stops the car.

"Here we are, Fiarway's middle school. Tristan, why don't you show the Princess around a bit? This being a Saturday, no classes will be in session." He seems eager to abandon the previous topic, already opening his car door.

Though frustrated to have my probing delayed, I don't protest when Tristan hops out and opens my door for me.

Together, we wander through the little middle school, less than half the size of Jewel's. As Tristan points out his old classrooms and the sports field where he played both soccer and football in his early teens, I can tell he's enjoying his walk down memory lane.

We then walk across the street to the tiny elementary school, containing only three classrooms—though still bigger than the one in Bailerealta.

"Kindergarten through second grade were in that one," Tristan recalls, pointing, "with third and fourth in the middle one and fifth and sixth there. I remember my fourth grade teacher was always encouraging us to try new things rather than stick only to activities considered *fine*-appropriate."

Connor sniffs. "Yes, I believe she was dismissed shortly after you began fifth grade for employing such unorthodox methods."

"Unorthodox?" I echo. "It sounds to me like a really good idea for kids growing up on Earth, where our people are often required to expand out of their traditional roles."

I can tell Connor doesn't agree, but he merely inclines his head respectfully. "I, ah, suppose there might be some wisdom in that, Excellency."

"I really liked her." Tristan sends an irritated glace at his father. "A lot of us did. We were sorry to see her go."

"So, what's next?" I ask before they can start arguing. After all, the reason Tristan's mother wanted us to come here was to improve their strained father-son relationship.

Connor accepts the change of topic. "Given how you were raised for much of your life, Excellency, I thought you might like to visit Fiarway's greenhouses. I'm told we produce the majority of our own food here in town, importing as little as necessary from outside."

Despite my impatience, my interest is piqued. Before discovering I was never an Ag to begin with, I spent a fair bit of time in NuAgra's greenhouses, working hard to improve my nonexistent skill with plants. I'm a little curious to see how Fiarway's compare.

We spend over half an hour wandering through two large greenhouses—nowhere near as big as NuAgra's, of course—and the adjoining livestock barns containing chickens, pigs and a few milk cows.

"Most of the animal protein in Fiarway's recombinators is synthetic," Tristan explains to me, "so the animals are mainly to provide the necessary cells for cloning. Plus milk and eggs, of course."

After that, Connor proposes driving me around the remainder of the small town, so I can get a sense of Fiarway as a whole. I know that won't take long, so I don't waste time before getting back to questioning him.

"So, um, you said you were surprised by the stuff Mayor Alban told us after lunch, but what did you think of it? Do you agree with him and Devyn that I should replace my sister as Sovereign?" This time I do use some "push."

Connor hesitates, swallowing, but then shakes his head. "Not by using the sort of methods Alban described, certainly. Attempting to detain young Stuart or the Sovereign herself while they are here in town strikes me as dangerous, not to mention potentially treasonous. While he and I do share a certain, ah, distaste for your sister's choice for presumptive Royal Consort, I would never encourage the use of force against either of them."

That's probably true, Tristan silently comments. *And we've known all along how he feels about Rigel. The whole point of making me move to Jewel last fall was so I could convince M I should be Consort instead.*

Fortunately it didn't work, I think back, suppressing a grin.

So fortunate! Especially for me, he agrees, sending me a surge of love, which I return.

Satisfied that Connor isn't directly involved in the plot to get M and Rigel out of the way so I can take over, I relax my "push" and ask about some of the buildings we're passing in the small commercial district. Again, Connor seems happy to forget about all the stuff Alban said earlier.

Leaving the central part of town, we meander through the more residential areas of Fiarway. The town's thousand or so inhabitants live in three slightly distinct "neighborhoods," each boasting roughly a hundred houses of varying size and ritziness. Connor points out the homes of some of their more prominent citizens.

I pretend to be interested, but keep sneaking glances at my omniphone. We're nearly finished with this last part of my tour when I see a missed holo call from M a few minutes earlier. She didn't leave a message, so I'm massively relieved when Connor drives us back to his house a few minutes later.

The moment I'm inside, I head for the stairs. "Sorry, I just really need to use the loo. I'll be back down in a few minutes."

It's past four o'clock when I shut myself into the master suite's posh bathroom and activate the secure mode on my omni. Sitting down on the closed commode, I call M.

Several seconds pass before she picks up. "Hey, Molly, I tried to call you earlier, but—"

"Yeah, I saw, but we were still out with Connor. Have you guys—?"

"Can you do a holo call from where you are?" she interrupts before I can ask about Devyn.

I glance around me and shrug. "Sure, I guess so. I'm in the bathroom, though." I stand up so it won't look like I'm sitting on the toilet.

She laughs. "Believe it or not, so am I. Okay, activating holo-mode." A second later, M's image appears in front of me. "I wanted to get someplace private, too—that's why I didn't answer right away. Rigel says this is the safest way to talk right now."

That startles me. "It is? Why?"

"I haven't had a chance to tell you, but this whole house was full of bugs—and I don't mean the insect kind. Rigel was able to deactivate them all, except whatever device Morag is wearing. You may want to have Gilda check if Sorcha is bugged, too. Not only that, Rigel thinks they might be monitoring all our communications, in and out. Did you activate secure mode before answering?"

"Aye, I did, yeah. But...wow, that's some nerve. Aren't there rules against spying like that on the Sovereign? This plot they've hatched must be further along than I thought."

M's eyebrows go up. "Plot?"

"Yeah, that's why I rushed to the bathroom as soon as we got back, so I could call and warn you. But first, did you guys find Devyn?" M's worried expression answers me before she can reply. "I guess not?"

"Actually, we did." She attempts a smile but it isn't very successful. "Quicker than we expected, in fact. Capturing him will be the problem. After we located him, Rigel showed Cormac the coordinates on a map and he did a recon. What he found there is basically a fortress, with a whole squad of heavily-armed guards stationed around it. Cormac obviously couldn't storm the place alone."

"Yikes, I guess not! Now what?"

M bites her lip. "Cormac wants to assemble a strike force, but that's really risky. Any locals he recruits probably won't be very well trained, and he admitted any assault would probably lead to casualties on both sides, which I'm not okay with."

"No, definitely don't use locals!" I exclaim. "We found out, well, kind of a lot while we were at Mayor Alban's house, most of it not good. That's the plot I wanted to tell you about."

She regards me worriedly. "So what's going on? Did Alban threaten you or something?"

"Not me, you. And Rigel. Alban and Devyn plan to grab Rigel and haul him off, the first chance they get, then keep you locked up, so you can't communicate with anyone. Alban will claim they're keeping the two of you apart for 'everyone's safety,' but the real reason is to get you both out of the way. Maybe for good. So you two should probably leave Fiarway as soon as you can."

"Wow. I guess you and Tristan used your special 'push' to make him tell you all that?"

I nod.

"I'm not surprised Devyn and Alban are in cahoots," M continues, "but is this plan something they just came up with on the fly? They can't have found out I was even coming here until just a couple of days ago. I didn't know myself until Monday night."

She's right, I realize. "They do seem awfully tight. I got the impression they talk together all the time. Maybe with Connor, too, though he swears—and we believe him—he didn't know anything about this plot.

He hardly said anything at lunch, but we got him talking afterward. The thing is, Devyn's apparently pretty popular in Fiarway. Nobody here knows he's a wanted criminal."

"I *told* the Council we should—" she begins.

"I know. But they didn't, which let Devyn build up a following here. That's why you can't let Cormac use any local security forces to arrest him. They'd probably turn on Cormac instead."

Frowning in concern, M nods her agreement.

"There's more," I make myself say. Because much as I hate to tell her the rest of their plan, she needs to know. "The *main* reason Devyn and the mayor want to get you out of the way is so I can take over as Sovereign. I didn't find out till later, when Alban mentioned it, but I guess the crowd this morning cheered more for me than they did for you?"

She huffs out a humorless laugh. "Definitely. It was...pretty noticeable. I figured you—"

"No, I had no idea, I swear! We didn't get to the town square until you'd already arrived, so I totally missed how they greeted you. I'm sorry, M, that must have felt, well, not great."

Her smile is more of a wince. "No. In fact, it reminded me of how I mostly got treated at school, before Rigel showed up."

Knowing her now, it's easy to forget that until her sophomore year, M was apparently really unpopular at school, though several people have confirmed that. Especially Trina. Now I feel even worse about being so bubbly about all the cheering when I joined her by the podium.

"If it helps, the only reason they acted so much happier to see me than you is because Mayor Alban, and especially Devyn, have been deliberately swaying public opinion in Fiarway against you, and in favor of me, ever since the news about me, and especially me and Tristan, broke. Then, after this more recent news about what happened at NuAgra, they went even further, saying stuff to make people afraid of you and Rigel. You heard what Alban said when we dropped you off at the guest house last night."

M nods, but looks thoughtful. "Actually, it makes total sense that Devyn would want you to replace me as Sovereign. He knows he'll never, ever win *me* over, after what he did to Rigel. But he doesn't have that baggage with you, so probably assumes you'd be a whole lot easier to influence. Especially since Devyn and Connor have been close friends for years, and now you and Tristan, Connor's son, are a couple."

She's right, of course. It does make sense. Ugh.

"From what Alban said, Devyn thinks I'll jump at the chance to seize power," I tell her. "Probably because he would. Even though I've been making it crystal clear, every chance I get, that that's the *last* thing I want! I nearly said so to Alban's face, more than once, but Tristan kept stopping me. He wanted to make sure we got every scrap of info out of him first, then insisted if they knew I wouldn't play along, they'd just come up with some other plot."

"He was probably right," M agrees. "So, did you get any more details about how they plan to arrange this coup of theirs?"

I grimace. "Not really. They were originally hoping you'd agree to let Rigel stay someplace else when you first got here. When you didn't, I guess they started working on a backup plan to just grab Rigel when they can. Even though they're definitely working together, I kind of doubt Devyn tells Alban everything."

"I doubt it, too. Wheels within wheels, that's always been Devyn's MO. Keep the right hand from knowing what the left hand's doing. Unfortunately, he's scary good at making things sound both plausible and reasonable, even when he's talking about treason."

That's true. He came awfully close to convincing the whole *Echtran* Council to name him Regent and head of the Council. And back in Nuath last spring, he nearly convinced everyone to Acclaim him Sovereign, instead of M.

"I felt awful that I didn't lambast Alban before we left," I tell M earnestly. "I *hated* leaving him with the impression I was okay with all this!" I still feel guilty about it.

"Hm." M frowns, clearly thinking hard.

I start to stammer another apology, but she waves it away with a sudden smile—a real one this time.

"No, I'm actually really glad you didn't speak up, Molly. Because everything you just told me has given me an idea."

16

PLEANAL

(plenn-UHL): advance planning; scheming

M

"A n idea to keep Devyn and Mayor Alban from separating you and Rigel, and maybe sway public opinion back your way?" Molly's holo image looks hopeful.

"Even better, a way to beat Devyn at his own game and smoke him out of that fortress so he can be captured." I'm still smiling as the details of this new idea start unfolding in my mind.

Are you okay? Rigel's thought interrupts me before I can tell Molly what I have in mind. *You've been in there a while now, after acting like it was an emergency. You're not sick, are you?*

"Just a sec," I say to Molly. Then, to Rigel, *No, I'm fine, just talking with Molly. I figured this was where I could be most private...but you may want to start listening in.*

"Sorry, that was Rigel, wondering what's taking me so long. He got worried. I told him to tap in while I explain what I think we should do. You can loop Tristan in, too, if you want. Mentally, I mean."

She chuckles, though her expression is still puzzled and worried. "Aye, it would be a little weird for him to join me in the loo. Give me a mo." Her eyes unfocus briefly, then she looks at me again. "Okay, he's going into the downstairs bathroom so he won't be interrupted either."

Incredibly grateful that we can all securely communicate this way by combining Martian technology with *graell* telepathy, I begin outlining the plan I've just come up with.

As soon as she grasps what I have in mind, Molly starts shaking her head. "No way. This'll never work, M. What makes you think they'll believe I really do want to take your place when I've been telling everyone for months that I absolutely don't?"

"You can claim you were afraid of what I might do, otherwise. If Alban and Devyn have been playing up how dangerous Rigel and I are, that should be believable. Make up whatever reasons you want, so long as word gets back to Devyn that you're on board. Maybe let Mayor Alban think he talked you into it."

She's clearly not convinced. "Sorry, M, but I think this is a terrible idea. What if they take my agreement to replace you as permission to —" she swallows— "to have you and Rigel *killed*? There's no way on Earth I'll risk that!"

"If you play your part the way I'm describing, it won't come to that," I assure her, pretending more confidence than I feel—though I *do* think my idea will work. "Maybe Devyn's eventual plan *is* to get rid of me completely, so nobody can question you being Sovereign. But if he wants to become the power behind your throne, he'll need you to trust *him* personally. Not just Connor and Tristan."

She still looks skeptical—and stubborn. Rigel's also silently expressing his doubts and I suspect Tristan is, too.

"Seriously, I think this will work!" I tell her—tell them all. "Just be totally clear that killing me or Rigel would wreck any chance of you ever trusting Devyn to advise you. Otherwise, say whatever you need to. The important thing is to convince him to come to you, here in Fiarway, away from that fortress he's built. Then he can be neutralized without endangering two whole security forces. Much as I want to remove him as a threat, I won't risk having more blood on my hands. This way I won't have to."

Molly and Rigel—and Tristan, through Molly—continue to argue against my idea as too dangerous.

"Look," I finally say, "Devyn's ultimate goal is to become our people's supreme ruler, right? Play on that. If you can persuade him that coming to you is his best path to get what he wants, he'll do it. He's so arrogant, he'll assume he's the one pulling your strings instead of the other way around. You only have to play along until he can be arrested—then we'll *all* be out of danger."

For the first time, Molly looks like she might be considering it, though I can't decipher her actual feelings via hologram. But then she shakes her head again. "I still don't like it. At the very least, I think you should run your idea past Kyna first."

Crap. "You know she won't agree to this! And any time I spend trying to talk her into it will be time they can use to come up with a Plan B. Persuading Devyn you're on his side—as long as he does things your way—should give us a chance to catch him while keeping both Rigel and me safe."

Molly glares at me. "You're asking me to deliberately put you at risk. It's one thing for you to risk yourself, you've done it lots of times, but think how I'd feel if I agree to this and it gets you killed! I bet you wouldn't do it, if our roles were reversed."

I open my mouth to deny that, then shut it. Because she's right. I wouldn't. Of course, I don't have Molly's persuasive talent, so if our roles were reversed I'd have a way bigger chance of screwing things up.

"Okay, fine. I'll try to contact Kyna securely and let you know what she says. If I can get her to agree to this idea, will you do it?"

Slowly, Molly nods. "I guess so. But if Devyn refuses to talk to me, you guys have to get the heck out of Fiarway ASAP. If necessary, you can hang out in Denver till you get a flight. Promise?"

"Yeah, all right. I promise. But I have total faith you can do this, Molly. Then we can have Devyn taken into custody without putting anyone else in danger—including me and Rigel."

I still don't like it, he sends from my sitting room, *but if it means averting a bigger threat from Devyn later, I guess it could be worth the risk.*

"We should probably wind this up before everyone at both ends gets too suspicious," I say then. "If Devyn finds out we've been communicating, it'll torpedo the whole thing and we've both been in the bathroom a really long time."

"I'll just say I got sucked into reading email on my omni," Molly says with a grin. "You and Tristan can say the same thing. But you're right. Go call Kyna if you can, and while I'm waiting to hear back from you, I'll at least try to get the ball rolling here."

She's obviously hoping Kyna will totally veto my plan, but I can be fairly convincing myself, when I have to be.

Because I assume Alban or Devyn will find out about anything I say in front of Morag, I apologize to her, Rigel and Cormac when I finally emerge into the sitting area.

"Sorry, you guys! I started reading the huge backlog of messages on my omni while I was in the bathroom and totally lost track of time. I hope you weren't all getting worried."

Morag just sniffs, but Cormac says, "I'm relieved to hear all is well, Excellency. I'll admit I was becoming a bit concerned."

In response to the question in his eyes, I give a tiny nod. "Everything is fine."

I glance over at Rigel, who's apparently been pretending to read stuff off his own omni this whole time. "Yeah, we're all glad you're okay. I was getting kind of worried, too." Only the tightness around his answering smile reveals how worried he still is, apart from what I pick up loud and clear from his feelings.

What's my most secure way to contact Kyna? I think to him. *Holo again?*

Or a vid call, as long as you use your silencing app. They might be able to tell you made a call, maybe even to who, but shouldn't be able to pick up anything you actually say.

That'll work. The Sovereign calling the leader of the *Echtran* Council shouldn't make anyone suspicious, since I have to do that all the time.

Here, I'll give you Devyn's coordinates, so you can pass them along to her in case she shoots down your idea. Rigel reels off the numbers to me and I automatically commit them to memory—not that I plan to let Kyna say no.

"I still have a phone call to make, so why don't you guys go downstairs for an afternoon snack?" I suggest aloud to break the apparent silence. "I'm sure Rigel's hungry, at least."

Knowing what I have in mind, he nods. "You're not?"

"Not really, though you can bring me back one of those chocolate brownies. I just want to check in with Kyna on some Council business before it gets any later there."

The three of them leave to go downstairs, Morag displaying no trace of suspicion, and I shut myself in my bedroom. Before calling Kyna, I spend a few minutes thinking through what I can say that might keep her from totally rejecting my idea. Though even if she does, I just might go ahead with it anyway.

I figure the worst that can happen is Alban and the others don't believe Molly's had a change of heart. In that case, they'd assume she warned me about their plot to separate Rigel and me, which should keep them from trying it. We'd lose our best chance to catch Devyn out of his fortress, but it shouldn't put us in any particular danger.

With that decided, I sit in the chair near the foot of my bed—much more comfortable than the bathroom—and take out my omni. Switching on its "cone of silence" so Morag can't possibly overhear me if she returns before I'm done, I place a vid call to Kyna.

When she answers, I make sure she also has privacy enabled and tell her the good news that we've located Devyn. Before she can congratulate me, I go on to describe the fortress Cormac discovered, along with its coordinates.

"Since storming the place, even if we had the manpower, would risk a lot of casualties I came up with a plan." Quickly, I outline my proposal for capturing Devyn without endangering anyone else.

As I feared, Kyna immediately vetoes the idea. "Absolutely not, Excellency. Such a scheme could put both you and your sister at extreme risk. Even supposing Devyn can be deceived into believing the Princess wishes to change allegiances, he may seize on it as an opportunity to eliminate you both, as he's attempted to do already."

I give Kyna the same answer I gave the others earlier. "Devyn's ultimate goal is to become the supreme Martian leader, right? He's smart enough to know our people won't put up with another Faxon-style coup, so he'll want to make it at least *look* legit. That's why he tried to convince me and the whole *Echtran* Council to appoint him Regent and Council leader back in December. He could have just used that Ossian Sphere to blow us all up, but he didn't."

"That may be true, but I still don't think—"

Before she can finish, I hurry on. "That's why if Molly asks for his help getting me out of the way so she can become Sovereign, it'll sound like a perfect path to his goal. He'll probably figure if he can win her trust, he'll be able to call the shots from the shadows while he gradually assumes a more visible role. Then, by the time he really does take over, people will be used to the idea of him being in charge."

"You make it sound very plausible, Excellency," Kyna says drily, clearly not convinced. "But what if Devyn is able to influence your sister rather than the reverse? He has long been friends with Connor Roark, with whom she's staying, and who is himself ambitious—it's why he attempted last fall to have his son become Royal Consort. Some still believe that was Tristan's motivation for transferring his romantic interest to Malena after her identity was revealed."

"That's not what happened and you know it! Tristan fell in love with Molly a solid week before anyone learned who she really is. Remember how upset Connor was when he thought his son was dating an Ag? There's no way on Earth Tristan would ever betray Molly—or me. I don't think Connor would, either, but if this goes the way I hope, he won't get a chance."

Kyna's still frowning. "Devyn Kane has proven himself devoid of conscience as well as ruthless," she reminds me. "If it's true that he's taken refuge in some sort of stronghold, our better course is to ensure he can't leave it or communicate with anyone outside it. Electronic jamming until an armed force can arrive should—"

"Are you forgetting he may still have Ossian Spheres in there?" I interrupt. "Maybe even antimatter—we can't know for sure. If we make him desperate, he might blow all of Fiarway off the map, just to take out Molly and me."

"We would of course wait until the two of you leave to send in our forces," Kyna assures me. "In fact, given this new information on how he's influenced the populace there, I would prefer you both return to Jewel as soon as possible."

I stare at her incredulously. "Are you saying you're okay with him maybe killing everyone in Fiarway once we're gone?"

That stops her, but only for a moment. "Of course not. With the two of you gone, however, he'd have no reason to do such a thing."

"Maybe not, but my plan is a chance to neutralize him once and for all, without putting *anyone* else at risk. If you send in a force, even after we've left, there'll definitely be a battle between them and Devyn's armed guards. People could get killed, maybe a lot of people, and I refuse to be responsible for that."

Kyna looks almost as stubborn as Molly did earlier. "You wouldn't be responsible, Excellency, I would. Creative as your idea is, I find it very hard to believe Malena can convince Devyn of something so implausible. For months, she's been publicly vocal about *not* wanting to share in your power. A man as smart as Devyn will never believe she suddenly wants to turn on you, her sister, and displace you as Sovereign."

"You don't know how convincing Molly can be," I insist. "We, ah, may not have been completely open with the Council about it, but she and Tristan have become incredibly persuasive since *graell* bonding. When they work together, they can convince someone to believe almost anything. I've seen them do it."

Fortunately, she doesn't ask for examples, since I'd rather not provide them. Instead, she says, "*You* certainly seem convinced, Excellency. If she's as persuasive as you say, how can you be sure Malena hasn't—?"

"What? No! This is totally my idea. Molly and I haven't even spoken in person since she learned about Devyn's connection to Mayor Alban at lunch today. She called to warn me about their plot, which is what gave me this idea. Trust me, when I first explained it, she was even more against it than you were. In fact, she's the one who insisted I run it past you first—it's the main reason I called. I think she's hoping you'll talk me out of it."

"As I've been trying to do." But now Kyna looks thoughtful. "If what you say about your sister's persuasive power is true, and if you feel certain Devyn can be lured out of hiding without putting either of you at undue risk..."

I nod vigorously. "Yes, to both of those! If she can't convince Devyn in the next few days, Rigel and I will leave Fiarway—I already promised Molly we would. I can claim I want to visit Dun Cloch, too, during spring break. And if anything goes *badly* wrong, one or both of us can activate our tracking chips and you can send in the cavalry. Honestly, Kyna, this should be almost foolproof."

She sighs heavily. "Very well, Excellency. I've had to trust you against my better judgment more than once in the past, and you've proved right every time. We must hope this will be another. However, as it appears we can't count on Fiarway's security personnel to act on your behalf, I'll send a force we *can* trust to Colorado. I should be able to have a trained security contingent from Dun Cloch there by early tomorrow."

"Deal!" I try not to grin too widely. Because, for all my brave words, I can't deny my plan *is* risky. If anyone can pull it off, though, Molly can —even if she'd rather not. "Just make sure no one in Fiarway knows they're here until they're needed."

"Of course. I'll also make arrangements for you to fly to Dun Cloch Monday evening," Kyna says then. "If all goes as you hope, we should have Devyn in custody by then. If not, the sooner you leave Fiarway, the better. I'd prefer Malena leave as well, in that case."

I frown, then nod. "Okay, you can go ahead and book the flight, but I'm not promising to take it. If I think sticking around here will help Molly make this plan work, that's what I'll do. Meanwhile, I'll let Molly know you've agreed, so she can get started. I'll report back when I can... or she will, if I can't for some reason."

Though her eyebrows go up at that addendum, she looks more resigned than alarmed. "Let's hope that won't be necessary. Please do be careful, Excellency. We can't afford to lose either of you."

"Maybe don't tell the rest of the Council about this just yet?" I suggest, imagining the pushback.

"No, the fewer people who know about this, the less chance Devyn could inadvertently hear of it. I wish you and Malena luck."

Disconnecting the video call, I reach out to Rigel, on his way back upstairs with the others. *I got her to agree!*

Yeah, I heard. His worry comes through as clearly as his response. *Guess it's all on Molly now. Might be good to let her know that.*

He's right. Reluctant as she was, Molly will probably drag her heels on implementing my plan if she thinks there's a chance Kyna will nix it.

What's safest? I ask Rigel. *They can't pick up anything if I leave the house, right?*

No, they don't have your actual omni bugged. But Morag—

Leave her to me.

When I hear Rigel, Cormac and Morag reenter my suite, I exit my bedroom, making a show of stretching my arms and rolling my neck and shoulders.

"Wow, my muscles are really tight after all that time hunched over a screen. I think I'll take a little walk, get some fresh air."

Instantly, Morag is on alert. "You'll want a wrap, Excellency. I'll get one for each of us, so I may accompany you."

"Thanks, Morag, but you don't need to come along. I'll just go down the block and back and Cormac can trail behind me, like he does in Jewel when I'm out walking. I should be as safe here as there, right? Maybe safer, since Fiarway is all *Echtran*. Rigel, why don't you stay back, too? Then I won't have any need at all for a chaperone."

Apparently unable to think of a plausible objection, Morag goes into my bedroom and returns with my suede jacket. "If you're certain—?"

"I am. I've found walking alone is good for clearing my head."

Once outside, I go far enough down the street to be out of sight from the windows before taking out my omni.

> Can you talk for a minute?

I text to Molly.

> Just a sec,

she messages back.

> Holo again?

> No, a regular call is fine unless you're being monitored at your end. I'm outside right now.

A second later my omni pings.

"Good idea, getting out of the house to call," Molly says. "It's all good at my end, or mostly. After we talked, Tristan and Gilda checked Connor's house for bugs. They found one Connor didn't know about, and he had them disable it. He seemed pissed it was there. Sorcha was wearing one, too. She was super apologetic, though, said it was Mayor Alban's idea. Did you talk to Kyna?"

"Yes, that's why I wanted to touch base."

Molly's quiet as I relate our entire conversation. Then, "Seriously? You got her to say yes?" She sounds appalled.

"It took some doing, but I finally convinced her this is our best chance to take out Devyn without extra casualties. She did insist on sending a strike force from Dun Cloch to be standing by, so we can summon them with our tracker implants if necessary. They're supposed to be here tomorrow, so you may as well start laying the necessary groundwork today."

"You don't think Devyn will hear about a bunch of troops showing up in Fiarway?" Molly demands. "Mayor Alban's bound to tell him."

"She'll have them stationed somewhere nearby, not in Fiarway itself.

If all else fails, she can give them the coordinates of Devyn's hideout. But I'd way rather catch him without getting anybody killed."

Molly groans. "I still don't like this, you know."

"Yeah, I know. But you said you'd try," I remind her.

"And I will. But I think you and Rigel should take that flight Kyna's booking anyway, to be extra safe."

I grimace. "And leave you to carry out this plan you hate on your own? Only if there's no other choice. You'd have to call in Kyna's troops yourself—" I stop myself before I can undermine her confidence. "—which you can totally do, if necessary," I finish. "You've got this, Molly. I believe that with my whole heart."

She heaves an audible sigh. "I'm glad one of us does. Okay. I guess I'd better get started."

17

CAMASTALL

(KAM-uh-stahl): deception; deceit; falsification

Molly

I stare at my omni for a long moment after M disconnects.

You can do this, I silently tell myself.

You're right. You can, comes Tristan's confident thought. He was listening in to the whole exchange, just as I'm sure Rigel was, at M's end.

So you really think it's the right thing to do? I'll need your help, you know.

I don't sense any wavering from him. *I know. I also know that together we can do whatever we need to. Because M's right that if we don't take Devyn out now, he'll keep trying to get rid of you both one way or another and we might not get any warning next time. Especially if he has a weapon even worse than that Ossian Sphere.*

He's right. I know he's right. But I still hate the idea of pretending I want to take M's place, even for a couple of days. I told M I would, though—which means I need to start now.

But how?

I've always been so publicly supportive of M, no one will ever believe I've secretly hated her all this time, no matter how well I pretend. Maybe if I instead act like I'm so worried about her, I might consider taking over for *her* sake?

That could work. Especially if I let Mayor Alban, and at some point Devyn, believe they're the ones talking me into this, like M suggested. First, though, I have to plant a seed that will prompt them to do that.

Tucking my omni away, I take one last deep breath and open the door from Connor's master bedroom. Sorcha is hovering in the hall just outside, so I invite her in.

"Can you help me change into something a little more comfortable?" I ask, even though I can do it perfectly well myself.

"Of course, Princess!" she responds eagerly, going to the closet. "Perhaps a tunic and slacks?"

I plan out my words as she helps me out of my formal-ish gown and into a more casual outfit. Then, sending a quick heads-up to Tristan to listen in again, I turn to her with a worried frown.

"I guess you heard most of the stuff Mayor Alban said at lunch today?"

Her expression suddenly wary, she nods.

"What did you think of it all?"

She hesitates for a second or two before answering. "I...well... I do agree you would likely be a better choice for Sovereign than your sister, if only because you've selected a much more appropriate Royal Consort. Some of what the mayor said, however..." She trails off.

"Yes, a few of the ideas he suggested did seem a bit extreme." Massive understatement! "But he still got me thinking. It's...possible my sister's not *quite* as capable these days as I've been telling myself. The thing is, ever since since she went digging into Faxon's memories, she's been...different. She *claims* the Mind Healers completely cured her, but I can tell she's not the same person she was before."

Her eyes go wide and fearful. "Then...you think she might still be dangerous?"

Oops! Did I go too far?

Run with it, Tristan mentally encourages me. *If Alban's listening in, he'll probably take it from there.*

"Maybe not dangerous, exactly," I reply, desperately hoping I'm doing the right thing. "But she *has* made me nervous a few times. Enough I've sometimes wondered if I should offer to take over for just a little while, so she can spend more time with the Mind Healers to really get past everything Faxon's memories did to her."

Sorcha regards me uncertainly and I wish—not for the first time!—I could read emotions like M does.

Hoping I've already said enough to plant the necessary seed, I shrug and smile. "Sorry, I probably shouldn't be telling you this stuff. It's not your problem, after all. Anyway, I should get back downstairs. By now I'm sure Tristan and his father are wondering where I disappeared to."

With a tentative smile, Sorcha opens the door for me so I can precede her down the stairs.

"Sorry for being so antisocial," I say when I reach the living room, going over to sit next to Tristan on the loveseat. "I just needed some alone time. All the stuff Mayor Alban said at lunch today got me thinking I should maybe warn my sister."

Connor's eyebrows go up. "Then I take it you haven't spoken with her yet?"

"I was going to, but then I thought maybe I should talk with the mayor again first, in case I didn't fully understand what he has in mind. I'd hate to get him in trouble if he's already given up on that plan he shared with us. Especially since he's a friend of yours."

Looking uncertain now, Connor replies, "I, ah, appreciate your restraint, Excellency. I confess I was rather surprised you said so little this afternoon, given how outspoken you've been on the subject in the past."

"I know." I bite my lip like I'm embarrassed. "I've been downright rude to anyone, including my parents, who so much as hinted at me sharing M's power. To be honest, the idea scares me." Totally true! "It's a huge job, one I don't feel remotely prepared for."

Tristan takes my hand. "You're a lot more prepared than you think you are. Haven't I been telling you that for a while?"

I nod sheepishly. "You have. I just wasn't willing to listen. I guess it took our conversation at lunch to make me realize how far I've come since I first learned about my heritage."

"Your parents told me how much assistance you've been giving the Sovereign lately," Connor cautiously volunteers. "They seem to feel you're ready for a larger leadership role."

I knew it! I was sure that's what they were talking about, but they wouldn't admit it, I think indignantly to Tristan, though I'm careful to keep my outrage from showing.

Shh! Just stay the course, he warns me. *Alban's the one we need to convince you might go along with their plan. So he'll tell Devyn.*

Right, I think back.

"I'm not sure if they're right about that," I tell Connor, "but I would like talk with the mayor again. If you think he'd be okay with that?"

Though still looking slightly uneasy, Connor smiles. "I'm sure he'd be delighted, Excellency. Shall I invite him for dinner tonight?"

Tonight? I try not to panic.

Hey, in for a penny, in for a pound, right? Tristan sends a burst of confidence my way.

In response, I force a delighted smile to my face. "Will you? That would be great! I'd love to have both his advice and yours. At the very least, I'd like to give my sister a break after all the stress she's been under lately."

"A...commendable idea, Princess," Connor responds. "I'll give Alban a call."

✦

While Connor calls Alban, I again retreat upstairs, feeling slightly queasy about what I'm doing. After asking Sorcha to bring me a cup of tea, I go into the master bath to run a washcloth under cold water.

I've spent several minutes decompressing—sipping hot tea with the cold washcloth on the back of my neck—when Tristan reaches out mentally.

Mayor Alban accepted Father's invitation. With luck, over dinner we can convince Alban to convince Devyn to meet with you.

I sure hope M knows what she's doing, I send back. *Or rather, what I'm doing. I hate this!*

I know. I'm sorry. But if it means nabbing Devyn...

Yeah, I think back with a sigh. *You're right. I'll be back down in a little bit. I need to psych myself up first.*

Up till now, I still had the option of backing out. But meeting again with Alban will commit me to following through. I'm desperate to ask M if she's having second thoughts like I am, but calling her is way too risky. Nope, I'm on my own now.

A few minutes later, my tea finished and the washcloth no longer cold, I again invite Sorcha into the bedroom to help me dress for dinner. I remember how much I appreciated M letting me do that when I was her Handmaid, so hopefully Sorcha will, too. I'd like to keep her in my corner, if possible.

"Yes, Excellency, this will be perfect," she exclaims when I show her the royal blue leggings and flowing, pale-blue top I have in mind. Nice to know I haven't completely lost my touch.

She helps me into the ensemble and I glance in the mirror at the tunic swirling beautifully around my knees. Because Connor promised this meal would be informal, I wave away the little tiara Sorcha offers, though I manage not to recoil.

"I'll save that for tomorrow night's dinner at the Town Hall. But thanks."

All too soon, I'm again sitting down to a meal with Mayor Alban. He and Connor are across from me, with Tristan on my left. There are no silly finger bowls, but Sorcha and Gilda insist on going through the whole food-tasting rigamarole.

Maybe not a bad idea, considering? comes Tristan's wry thought. *Let them think you're afraid M might have you poisoned?*

I don't necessarily want to go that far, but now that Alban's here, I might as well hint at it.

"It's amazing how safe I feel in Fiarway." I smile up at Sorcha as she puts the rest of my meal on my plate at the end of the ritual.

"I suppose that's not surprising, Excellency," Mayor Alban responds. "From all I hear, your sister enjoys far greater support in Jewel, likely due to her claiming it as her hometown."

Claiming? She grew up there! I think but don't say. "That's true. Especially since Jewel's *Echtrans* were specially chosen for their loyalty to her."

"Then I imagine you're very careful not to criticize her in public there?" Alban suggests.

I force a little laugh. "In public? Definitely not!" Not that I've ever been tempted to—or worried about any consequences if I did.

"Or perhaps even in private?" Alban prompts. "Connor tells me your house is quite close to hers. Is it possible she's able to eavesdrop on the O'Garas' conversations?"

That's ridiculous, but I try to look concerned. "I hadn't thought about it, but I suppose it's *possible*. A lot of security equipment was installed in our house while we were gone over Thanksgiving."

"Installed by Rigel Stuart's father," Tristan reminds me. "He's probably a lot more concerned with Emileia's safety than yours, so it makes sense he'd want to know if someone at your place sounds like they don't support her."

I have to fight to keep a straight face, since my mum *constantly* hints I'd be a better Sovereign than M. If what Tristan's implying were true, Mum would have have been arrested months ago!

"Here in Fiarway, you can speak with perfect freedom, Excellency," Mayor Alban assures me, applying the same, lame "push" he used at lunch. "Dare I hope you may not be totally averse to the idea of taking on a primary leadership role?"

I hesitate, then say, "I still don't like the idea of taking on a larger role, but lately—" Breaking off, I give the two men a pleading look. "I probably shouldn't say this."

"You can trust us to keep it in confidence, Excellency," Alban promises.

Though I kind of hope that's not true, it's exactly the encouragement I was angling for.

"Well, it's just...I'm worried about my sister."

"Oh? In what way?" Alban asks.

When I hesitate, Tristan gives my hand an encouraging squeeze. "Go on. Tell them."

Swallowing, I plunge on. "Ever since becoming Sovereign, she's been under an awful lot of stress. We think that's why she sort of...cracked, after spending days in Faxon's twisted mind. The Mind Healers helped her a lot, but..." I let my words trail off.

"But not enough?" Connor says gently, as Alban looks on with what I'm sure is mock concern.

I lift a shoulder in a half-shrug. "Maybe not quite? I'm pretty sure she needs more treatment but I'm afraid if I say so, she'll take it the wrong way. Anyway, it's not like I can just...push my sister out of the way. Or like I'd want to. The last thing I want to do is hurt her."

Not even by doing what she told me to, I silently add to Tristan.

Connor summons a fatherly smile and I can tell he's trying to use his own brand of charm on me—similar to Tristan's, though not nearly as powerful.

"Your concern for your sister is admirable, Princess. Family ties can be strong, as I've recently realized." The fond look he turns on Tristan seems genuine. "In your case, of course, you've only known about the blood relationship for a few months."

"True, though M and I were friends for nearly a year before learning we're sisters," I remind him.

Alban raises a skeptical brow. "Friends? I recall reading an article where you admitted it was a relief to no longer be at her beck and call."

Last fall, Gwendolyn Gannett badgered me into an interview after the news about me broke, then totally twisted my words out of context. I was furious at the time, I can now use that article to my advantage.

"Well...sure," I lie, trying to recall exactly what she claimed I said. "Being ordered around kind of sucked, but M was never *mean* to me. She even let me sit down at formal dinners." I'm pretty sure that's common knowledge by now.

Alban's smile becomes brittle. "Yes, just one of the many ways she's always flouted tradition—though I suppose that one worked to your benefit. I imagine *you* have far more respect for our traditions, as you were brought up with them."

"I *am* sometimes a little shocked by the way M ignores our traditions," I admit untruthfully. "But then I remind myself she spent nearly her whole life as a *Duchas,* so can't be expected to understand why they matter so much to our people."

"Very insightful of you, Princess, not to mention charitable." Alban exchanges a glance with Connor. "Does this mean you might be amenable to what I suggested at lunch?"

I bite my lip as though uncertain while exerting some "push" of my own to make what I'm saying seem more believable. "I still don't *like* the idea of taking over my sister's duties, but these past few weeks she's acted so strangely, I've started wondering if I should. Temporarily, I mean. Just until she can be restored to the person she used to be before Faxon escaped."

Tristan touches my hand under the table. "She's actually scared you a couple of times lately, hasn't she?"

I reluctantly nod, though I hate to let them think that.

"Scared you?" Alban leans forward with barely-concealed eagerness. "What has she done, exactly?"

So he'll think his "push" is working, I blurt out, "Emileia won't admit it, but spending all that time in Faxon's memories changed her a lot. She used to be really easygoing, but now she sometimes gets mad at the least little thing. She's also made a few irrational decisions lately, though I've talked her out of most of them," I improvise.

"Concerning traits in a Sovereign, to be sure," Connor comments with a frown.

Alban nods his agreement. "Indeed. Anything else?" He amps up his feeble attempt at "push."

"Well...she also has trouble concentrating these days. She can hold it together long enough to deliver a rehearsed speech, like she did this morning, or for one of our broadcasts, but..."

"But not for long enough stretches to be truly effective as Sovereign?" Alban suggests.

"That's what I'm afraid of. It's obvious now she should have spent a lot more time with the Mind Healers after Faxon was captured. But... what can I do? Emileia's our Acclaimed Sovereign. It's not like I can *make* her step aside, even to get the treatment she needs."

Mayor Alban nods sympathetically. "Not without help, certainly. Particularly given the potentially dire consequences of angering your sister."

"Dire?" I'm afraid to risk confirming M's truly dangerous. They might use that to justify something worse than helping me take her place. "It's not as though Emileia's ever *physically* hurt me."

"But you worry she might one day?" Alban presses. "You said she becomes angry much more easily now."

Because he's clearly still using "push," I feel obliged to nod. "Maybe a little." As the awful, untrue admission leaves my mouth, I want to snatch it back.

Sensing my distress, Tristan tightens his grip on my hand. *It was her idea for you to pretend you're afraid of her, remember?*

I know, but that doesn't make it easier.

"In that case, we must get her back under a Mind Healer's care before that can happen." Connor looks positively alarmed.

"Indeed!" Alban nods vigorously. "As for taking her place without being formally Acclaimed, I doubt you'll face as much resistance as you anticipate. You've seen how the people of Fiarway adore you already. Not only is your bloodline identical to Emileia's, giving you just as strong a claim to the throne, many feel you would be a better Sovereign than your sister—especially now."

Connor smiles his agreement. "You do have the advantage of being raised Nuathan, with a proper respect for our traditions. I imagine she still thinks like a *Duchas* most of the time."

I don't see much point in denying that. "It's logical she would, since she was raised as one. She's only known about her heritage for a year and a half, so she's still adjusting to our ways."

"Logical or not," Alban says, "I find it hard to believe she can be a truly effective leader to a people she'll never fully understand or identify with."

"An excellent point," Connor agrees. "That alone would tend to make Princess Malena a better choice, even setting apart the Sovereign's recent mental instability."

Alban's smile now borders on smug. "Absolutely. Princess, for the good of our people, I hereby pledge to help you in any way possible."

Trying not to freak out at how well this plan is already working, I take a bite of my dinner to give myself time to think.

You're doing great, Tristan thinks to me. *Keep acting like they're the ones convincing you, so they'll think they're the ones in control. Alban mentioned Devyn at lunch, see if you can get him to do it again.*

I take a few more bites, oblivious to what I'm eating, then finally, plaintively, say, "I appreciate your offer, Mayor Alban, but I don't know if I'm ready. It's not like I grew up with the training a future Sovereign would normally get, since everyone assumed I was an Ag."

"Nor did your sister," the mayor points out. "As you said, she learned of her Martian heritage a mere year and a half ago and never had the benefit of instruction by the previous Sovereign, as most throughout our history have."

"I...I guess you're right. But even so, I can't see taking over her duties, even temporarily, without a whole lot of advice from people way more experienced at being Royal, and using the power that goes with it. Before this Faxon thing, Emileia was the one teaching me the ropes, showing me how things should be done. My parents have given me lots of useful reading material, but they don't know half as much about being Sovereign as she does."

Alban leans forward, making me suspect he's increasing his "push" to the max, though it still has no effect on me. "If I might suggest, Excellency, I believe Devyn Kane would be an obvious choice to serve as your primary advisor. You may not be aware, but before Faxon disrupted everything in Nuath, Devyn was on track to become our youngest High Chancellor in history. He consistently impressed everyone in the legislature with the depth and breadth of his understanding on almost every issue. I recall he was one of the first to warn us of the potential danger Faxon posed, which, alas, proved all too true."

"He's right," Connor confirms. "Then, upon relocating to Earth, Devyn very quickly became expert in our *Echtran* government, as well."

Yeah, so he could overthrow it! I silently comment to Tristan. Then, out loud, "Aye, it does sound like Devyn would be a valuable ally, but...hasn't he gone into hiding?"

Connor inclines his head. "Yes, well, he's had good reason to avoid the Sovereign's notice, given her prejudice against him. Some of which, I admit, is deserved. He always proved a good friend to me, however."

I look back and forth between the two men. "Then you both really believe I can trust him? I'd hate to accidentally set up Emileia to be hurt...or worse. She *is* my sister, after all."

"Your concern is understandable, Princess." Connor again assumes his fatherly smile. "You may have the impression that Devyn is motivated purely by ambition, but I've known him a long time. He has always cared deeply about what's best for our people—even when occasionally using somewhat...questionable methods in pursuit of that goal."

Biting back a snarky response, I smile uncertainly. "Would he actually be willing to help me, though? He has to know my sister and the *Echtran* Council suspect him of treason, even if they haven't been able to prove it. Won't he assume I feel the same way? I can't believe he'd even talk to me, much less advise me."

"Leave that to me, Excellency." Mayor Alban gives me his own version of a fatherly smile. "I'm confident that when I tell Devyn you're open to displacing Emileia as Sovereign, he'll be only too happy to assist you. Whatever unpleasantness may have occurred between him and your sister, it never involved yourself."

I guess he doesn't know about the assassin Devyn sent after me in November, I think to Tristan, suppressing a snort.

Infusing my voice with relief, I respond aloud, "In that case, I would greatly appreciate you approaching him on my behalf, Mayor Alban."

"Consider it done." His smile is almost triumphant. "You can trust Devyn to have *your* best interests at heart in this matter, Princess. The populace of Fiarway can also be counted on to support you. As you witnessed this morning in the square, they are already heavily predisposed in your favor."

For the remainder of the meal, he and Connor continue enumerating the advantages of me becoming Sovereign—and not just temporarily. Tristan occasionally joins in so enthusiastically I silently ask for his reassurance that he doesn't mean it.

Now that I've started this scary ball rolling, I mostly stay quiet, envisioning possibilities. Not of the things I'd do as Sovereign, as I hope they assume, but of all the ways this scheme could backfire on *us*, instead of Devyn. M's right that he's really smart. Are we smarter?

We'd better be.

Her life might depend on it.

18

FELLBHEIART

(FALL-bahrt): conspiracy; treachery

M

By the time I go to bed that night, doubts about the wisdom of my plan have begun creeping in, though I try to keep them from Rigel. I also realize it's probably just as well my last exchange with Molly wasn't face to face. She may not have my emotion-sensing ability, but she knows *me* well enough she probably would have guessed I'm a lot more nervous about this whole thing than I've let on. But for it to succeed, *she* needs to believe she can do this, so I didn't dare let her suspect I'm not as confident as I pretend.

Of course, Rigel picks up on my worry anyway, as he makes clear once we've both gone to bed. *There's still time to pull the plug on this whole idea,* he sends from his room down the hall, his own worry coming through with the thought. *If Devyn has as much support here as Molly said, trying to arrest him here in Fiarway could get us all killed. You and me, anyway.*

When will we have a better chance, though? I respond. *At worst, he'll totally refuse to leave his lair to meet with Molly. If that happens, you and I can just leave town, maybe blow off that dinner tomorrow night and fly home instead.*

He barely waits two seconds before thinking back, *What if that makes them come after us here, before we can leave? From what Molly said, Mayor Alban's convinced everyone in town is in danger as long as the two of us are*

153

within touching distance of each other. You've seen how Morag acts. It's not just that she doesn't like you, she's obviously scared of the two of us, too. We've seen first hand how dangerous frightened people can be.

We should be safe as long as we stay in the house, I insist. *I definitely won't send you on any errands, where they could have you kidnapped! If I'm wrong and we do feel threatened here, I'll activate the emergency signal in my tracker chip. Then Kyna will send in the troops and we can fly out ahead of schedule. That won't remove Devyn as a threat, though, unless I authorize bloodshed. Which I won't.*

I can tell he still doesn't like this plan, but he doesn't argue any more. Not tonight, anyway.

✦

We're still at breakfast the next morning when the doorbell rings. At my nod, Cormac goes to answer it, his sidearm clearly visible. Rigel told him this morning to be alert for trouble and why, when they were both well out of Morag's hearing.

When he comes back, I'm surprised to see Mayor Alban with him.

"My apologies for interrupting your meal, Excellency," he says, bowing deeply as he enters the breakfast room. "I should have messaged first."

I incline my head, the Sovereign's proper response to a bow. "Not to worry, Mayor Alban, we were nearly finished. Would you care for a cup of coffee or tea?"

He immediately accepts, surprising me again. "That's very kind of you, Excellency. Coffee, please."

Darting a nervous glance at Rigel, sitting to my left, the mayor moves to a chair across from me. "Is there any chance your younger *Costanta* can move a bit further away?" he asks before sitting down. "I realize I'm probably being overly cautious, but it would make me feel much more comfortable."

I almost laugh, but then focus on Alban's emotions and realize he really is scared—way more than when we arrived Friday night. Hm. I did suggest Molly pretend she's afraid of me. Maybe she made us sound really scary? I turn to Rigel.

"Would you mind? We don't wish to frighten our guest."

Rigel responds with a mental chuckle but obligingly gets up to stand a few paces behind me. *I guess the more comfortable he feels, the more likely you can get info out of him,* he thinks to me.

My thoughts exactly, I reply.

Sure enough, Mayor Alban relaxes visibly once Rigel's out of arm's reach, though I still sense plenty of anxiety from him...and guilt. Not surprising, considering what he and Devyn have been plotting. As soon as he's seated, Morag goes to the kitchen to fetch his coffee.

Rather than ask why he's here, I wait for Alban to tell me himself.

After a brief, awkward pause, he does. "I, ah, feel I should apologize for not including you in my invitation to yesterday's luncheon, Excellency. I very much hope you took no offense. Connor Roark and I are old friends, you see, and—"

"Yes, Connor explained the situation when I asked if it was something I'd neglected to put on my schedule. No offense taken. To be honest, I quite appreciated a quiet meal here with only my attendants, after such a busy morning."

"Thank you for being so understanding, Excellency." His smile conveys relief but despite that and his words, I sense an increase in his anxiety.

Perhaps an apology wasn't his real reason for coming here? Again, I wait for him to continue rather than ask questions.

Before the silence once more becomes awkward, Morag returns from the kitchen to set a steaming cup of coffee and a tiny platter with cream and sugar in front of Alban. He smiles his thanks and she returns it—the first smile I've seen on her face. No question where *her* loyalty lies.

With exaggerated care, Alban places a napkin in his lap, then takes his time stirring sugar into his coffee. Only then does he look directly at me, his expression now serious.

"Excellency, I'm afraid there is something else I must tell you, while we're private here. Over the course of my lunch yesterday with Princess Malena and her presumptive Consort, Tristan Roark, it became clear she is not nearly so supportive of you as she has claimed publicly. When I pressed them for details, the two of them confided certain things to me that I found quite...concerning."

I have to hide a smile, thinking of Alban attempting to use "push" on those two when together they're totally immune—and them making him think it worked.

"Concerning?" I repeat with a frown.

He nods. "Because Connor is my good friend, and Tristan is his son, I was reluctant to betray their confidence. Conscience won out, however, and I feel obligated to warn you."

"Warn me? Of what?" I raise an eyebrow ominously while focusing even more closely on his emotions. As expected, his anxiety increases dramatically, but so does his guilt. Interesting.

Alban picks up his cup, then sets it down again without drinking, though he does swallow several times. Gathering his courage?

"You, ah, may have noticed yesterday, in our town square, that your sister received a somewhat more enthusiastic reception from the crowd than you did?"

I grimace slightly. "It was rather hard to miss."

"Yes, well, that outpouring of support was also evident to the young couple in question. So much so, they now feel emboldened to, ah, elevate the Princess's standing at your expense. I'm concerned that she and Tristan Roark may be plotting some sort of coup during your stay in Fiarway, where she can expect more support for such a move than she would in Jewel. In fact, at one point she openly expressed a wish of taking your place as Sovereign, if you could be safely taken out of the way." His words have a rote quality, as if carefully rehearsed.

Why is he telling me this? I think to Rigel, confused. *If he and Devyn are the ones who cooked up the idea of a coup, like Molly said, why would he tip me off?*

Preempting Molly, so you won't believe her if she spills the beans on their plan? That's my guess. They must not know it's too late. Keep playing along for now, Rigel silently advises.

"As you say, this is extremely concerning," I agree after a pause I hope he'll attribute to shock at his revelation. "Surprising as well, given that my sister has always voiced complete support of my leadership. Not that we haven't had occasional differences of opinion in private—particularly since my, ah, lapse in judgment earlier this month," I add on sudden inspiration.

His nod is a little too eager, accompanied by some of the relief he pretended earlier. Because I seem to be buying his story? "Yes, she, ah, mentioned that lapse as one motivation for displacing you. She implied that your judgment can no longer be relied upon, and that your temper—"

"What about my temper?" I snap, frowning.

Alban pales visibly. "Er...that it has become somewhat...unpredictable in recent weeks. Because of that, she asked whether you and your young *Costanta* might somehow be separated, to minimize the risk to her should you learn of her plans. I reminded her that when I made that suggestion Friday night, you rejected it. As you pointed out, he would be unable to protect you if he were elsewhere. Indeed, if she is plotting against you, you need all the protection possible right now, though of course I did not say that."

No wonder he's so scared, Rigel silently comments. *Devyn must have put him up to this, but he's terrified you'll kill the messenger.*

I fight to hide my spurt of amusement, instead schooling my face into an angry mask. "That opportunistic little traitor! I suspected Malena might eventually become dangerous to me, but I didn't think she'd go this far, this soon. Her adoptive mother has insisted for months that my sister and I should have equal standing, but Malena herself always argued against that—even when Mrs. O'Gara hinted that I should step aside in Malena's favor after my little lapse earlier this month." More than just hinted, in fact.

"Your suspicions were obviously well founded, Excellency, though I'm terribly sorry to be the one to confirm it. Such a betrayal by your own sister must be rather...painful." Alban assumes a sympathetic expression, though that's not at all what I sense from him.

"It certainly is," I angrily agree. "But I intend to make sure she feels even more pain."

His pretended sympathy disappears, swamped by renewed fear. "I...I cannot blame you for feeling that way, Excellency. However, I should tell you it's entirely possible she did not come up with this idea on her own. You may not know this, but Connor Roark has always possessed an unusually high degree of persuasiveness, and I suspect his son takes after him in that regard."

"Then you believe *they* put her up to this?" I ask, still frowning fiercely.

He flinches, but manages to nod. "Actually, I...I consider it very probable. You see, during our conversation, she asked whether I thought Devyn Kane—of all people!—might assist her in supplanting you. She can only have learned Devyn and I were once friends from either Tristan or Connor."

"Devyn Kane?" My surprise is genuine this time. I'd assumed Alban would want to keep his name out of this. "What did you tell her?"

"That I have no idea where he is or how to contact him, of course." The mayor acts positively affronted. "If I did, I would have immediately informed the Council, as they've sent word he's wanted for questioning."

Wheels within wheels, Rigel thinks to me. *Now, if Molly hears from Devyn and tells you, you're supposed to assume Tristan or Connor arranged it. They're covering every angle—including Alban's backside.*

I realize he's right—again.

Glowering thoughtfully, I say, "Given my own history with Devyn, it makes a certain degree of sense they might believe he would help with this coup of theirs. I'm glad you were unable to facilitate that. Again, I must thank you, Mayor Alban." I do my best to look and sound grateful. "Considering my sister's apparent popularity in town, it was actually quite brave of you to come here."

"More than you know, Excellency," he eagerly agrees. "As they were leaving my house, Tristan told me to my face that if I breathed a word of this to you, they would tell you the whole idea was mine, and that I've been secretly working with Devyn Kane to remove you from power. I'll admit, that threat gave me pause, for I realized you would be more likely to believe their story than mine." Then, raising his chin proudly like he's posing for a photo, he continues. "I'm happy to say, however, that concern for my personal safety could not overcome my loyalty to you, my Acclaimed Sovereign. I therefore resolved to come here and warn you, as any true patriot would." He reels off those last words quickly, as though wrapping up a prepared speech.

I smile approvingly. "I'm also happy you made the right decision, Mayor Alban. I'll see you're properly rewarded for the loyalty you've shown me." Now that I've figured out exactly what's going on, I have no trouble sounding sincere. "What advice do you have for me?"

He seems taken aback by my question. I guess this wasn't in his script?

"Advice? I...ah...it's not really my place to advise you, Excellency," he stammers. "I simply wished to put you on your guard. As...as my duty to the throne."

Abruptly, he pushes back from the table and stands. "I should take my leave, Excellency, and let you and those responsible for your security —" he nods toward Rigel and Cormac— "discuss any measures you may wish to take. Don't hesitate to let me know if Fiarway's security force can assist in any way. As for tonight's dinner and the procession preceding it, I consider myself personally responsible for your safety. In fact, I will make arrangements for extra safeguards as soon as I leave here."

With another deep bow, he scurries from the room, his coffee still untouched. Cormac follows him out and we hear the front door open and close. Returning a moment later, Cormac confirms he's gone.

"Well, that was...unexpected," I say. "I—"

Don't say anything else! Rigel's thought interrupts me. *Not in front of Morag. She's bugged, remember?*

Oops, good point. I turn to her. "Morag, you may as well clear the table. This news has pretty much killed my appetite." Which it would have, if I believed any of it.

She gathers the empty plates, cups and glasses and carries them to the kitchen. The second she's gone, Rigel whips out his omni and scans the area where Alban was sitting, then peeks under the table.

Yup, I thought so. He planted another bug, this one almost microscopic. Should I—?

No! I think back. *Leave it, even though it seems like overkill. If they're this determined to eavesdrop, I should give them something worth hearing.*

Smart. Diabolical, in fact. Admiration comes through with his thought. *You're pretty good with this security stuff yourself.*

You've taught me well. I wink at him.

When Morag returns to the dining room, Rigel's standing behind me again, his omni back in his pocket.

I try to think of something to say for the benefit of that bug—then realize just sitting around in the breakfast room now we're done eating could make them suspicious. Standing, I turn to Rigel.

"Why don't you and Cormac go into the office and work out what security precautions we can take, in light of what Mayor Alban told me."

Rigel nods and the two of them head to the ground floor office.

Tell Cormac about that new bug, once you're sure it can't pick up what you say, I tell him silently as I follow them out of the breakfast room. *Then find out whether Alban planted anything else while he was here, inside or outside. We need to know exactly what we're up against.*

Will do, he thinks back. *I'll check in soon.*

Morag follows me into my suite, radiating a mixture of confusion and alarm over what she just heard downstairs.

"I'll be in my bedroom," I tell her. Then add, for the benefit of *her* bug, "I need to figure out exactly how I want to deal with my sister ...the traitor."

19

CHABHIL

(KAB-vil): negotiation; debate; (occ.) ultimatum

Molly

Needless to say, after that dinner with Mayor Alban, I don't sleep very well. Tristan does his best to send me soothing thoughts from the bedroom he's sharing with his father, but once he falls asleep I'm on my own. Worst-case scenarios keep running through my head, then make their way into my dreams when I finally do drop off.

It's nearly ten when I drag myself down to breakfast, where I try to act upbeat so Connor won't suspect I'm not fully on board with this terrible scheme to supplant M. But privately, my mind is filled with what-ifs.

Sorcha is clearing the breakfast table half an hour later, when Connor gets a message on his omni. His brows go up as he reads it, then he turns to me with a smile.

"Excellency, as Mayor Alban predicted last night, Devyn Kane has expressed a wish of speaking with you sometime today. Are you still interested in hearing what he might have to say?"

I blink, startled. *Already?*

Sooner is better than later, right? Tristan silently responds.

I guess, but I was kind of hoping M and Rigel would have time to get out of town first.

This was the whole point, right? Tristan thinks to me when I hesitate. *If you can lure him out today, this can all be over!*

161

With that encouragement, I summon a smile for Connor. "Yes, definitely! What time does he want to come over?"

Connor taps out a response to Devyn and a tense few moments—for me, anyway—follow before he gets a reply.

"Ah," Connor says then. "He says he'd prefer to have your initial conversation via holo, as it's not feasible for him to visit Fiarway in person just now."

I was afraid of that. At least he didn't insist I go to him, like M warned me he might. "Um, sure, I guess that'll be okay," I say. "When?"

There's another quick exchange of messages. "He says he can call in ten minutes, if that's convenient for you?"

Again, I'm taken aback by how quickly things are moving. "That... that'll be fine, I suppose. Should I change clothes first?" I glance down at my jeans and turtleneck.

Connor smiles indulgently. "I don't believe that's necessary. But perhaps we should relocate to the living room? I imagine you'll be more comfortable there."

We get up and head that way but before we reach the living room, Connor turns to Sorcha and Gilda, following a discreet distance behind.

"Perhaps you both had better wait upstairs, as you did yesterday."

They both turn questioningly to me and I nod. I'd also like as few witnesses to this conversation as possible.

Like yesterday afternoon, Tristan and I sit side by side on the loveseat, while Connor takes the armchair next to us. I try not to fidget during the few minutes that pass before his omni chimes with the incoming holo-call. As soon as Connor accepts it, Devyn's image appears in the chair opposite the three of us, as though he just teleported in.

"Good morning, Excellency," he says with a sort of seated bow. "Thank you for giving me this audience. Before we speak on more, ah, substantive matters, let me congratulate you on the dramatic elevation of your status since we last met."

That would have been back in Nuath when I was still a Handmaid. I haven't seen him since, unless I count the holo image he projected from that Ossian Sphere in December, when he tried to take over the Council. Remembering the stunned confusion on Devyn's face when we seized control of his Sphere makes me want to smirk, but I don't.

"Thank you, Devyn. As you can imagine, it's been a big adjustment for me."

He nods, his expression understanding. "I'm sure it has. For your sister as well, no doubt."

Way less so, but I pretend to agree. "Definitely. She's not at all sold on the idea of sharing power, no matter how many people tell her how helpful that would be."

"Few leaders are eager to do that," Devyn says sagely. "Even those who've shown themselves...less than adept, shall we say?...at effective leadership."

I have to bite back my instinctive urge to defend M—she's been an *incredibly* effective leader!

"She's definitely been overextending herself," I say instead, which is true. "Her stress was becoming obvious even before Faxon escaped. I'm sure that's why she was so badly affected by experiencing all his memories. She still is, unfortunately."

"I surmised as much from what Alban told me. Apparently she has become extremely unpredictable since that experience?"

I force myself to nod. "I keep offering to help, but she has such a hair-trigger temper now, she doesn't always appreciate it," I say, feeling like a traitor.

"Hm. Perhaps she suffers a touch of paranoia, as well?" Devyn suggests.

"More than a touch," I make myself agree. "I wish she'd go back to the Mind Healers for more treatment, like I've hinted to her once or twice. I'd even be willing to take over for a while, so she can do that, but I'm afraid to suggest it. I...don't think she'd take it very well."

Even in a holo, he positively exudes a sympathetic manner I don't buy for a second. "No, likely not. I must say, Princess, your willingness is really quite selfless, particularly as I understand she has treated you rather poorly of late."

I shrug but don't deny it, even though it's not true at all. "As I guess you heard, I told Mayor Alban last night that I *might* be willing to take over as Sovereign for a while. The trick will be getting Emileia to agree."

"For her sake, I'd suggest you proceed even if she won't. Your sister might not appreciate it at first, but in the long run you'd be doing her an enormous kindness."

Wow, he's good. "That's sort of what I'm thinking. But how? She may not be as fit to lead as she thinks she is these days, but she *is* my sister.

The last thing I want is to see her hurt." There. Now it's out there, my one non-negotiable point.

"Understandable." Devyn's voice is still smooth, though a tiny frown forms between his brows. "I agree that should be avoided if at all possible."

Nope, not good enough.

"I did tell the mayor I'd appreciate your help in this, Devyn, but not if it means harming Emileia in any way. Or Rigel Stuart, either, for that matter. Just so we're both clear on that."

The frown is more pronounced now. "That...may be somewhat diffi-cult to guarantee, Excellency. But let's set it aside for now, shall we? The important thing is that we both agree you are better equipped for the Sovereignty than your sister, particularly given the unfortunate after-math of her heroic effort to locate Faxon. Not only are you better suited temperamentally, but in terms of your life choices since learning of your heritage. I'm right, am I not, that you eventually mean to pair with Tristan Roark?"

Tristan's hand, firmly clasping mine this whole time, gives a convul-sive twitch. So does mine. It's not something we've ever discussed *directly*.

"I...ah..." I stammer.

"That is our hope, sir, yes," Tristan says firmly, now giving my hand a squeeze. *Sorry,* he thinks to me at the same time. *We can talk about it later, but right now—*

Got it, I think back, trying to force my heart to beat normally again as I nod to Devyn, probably looking every bit as flustered as I feel.

He continues smiling benignly upon us both. "Alban tells me everyone in Fiarway has been commenting on what a handsome—and appropriate—couple you make. I realize you are both still young, but presenting a high-ranking Royal as your intended Royal Consort will absolutely further our people's acceptance of you in lieu of your sister. You must be aware there is still substantial resistance among them to Emileia's choice."

I again feel like a traitor nodding, even though I'm well aware it's true. People can be so stupid! "She knows that. How can she not? It's yet another thing adding to all the stress she's under."

"Yes, I recall she herself blamed stress as a factor in her deplorable actions earlier this month. You're perfectly right that she needs time away from her duties for the sake of her health, both mental and physical. And, Princess, the only person who can possibly give her that necessary respite is you."

Again, I'm impressed in spite of myself by how reasonable he can make treason sound. If I didn't know better, I'd almost believe becoming Sovereign *is* the kindest thing I can do for M.

"I...I never thought of it that way before," I admit, as though I'm nearly convinced.

"Perhaps you should." Though he can't possibly be using any kind of "push" via hologram, I can see how the certainty in his voice would have a similar effect. No wonder he nearly got himself Acclaimed Sovereign last spring!

Before I can respond, Tristan speaks up again. "Hasn't Emileia told you she never actually wanted to be Sovereign?"

"Lots of times," I confirm, giving his hand a grateful squeeze. "In fact, the *only* reason she agreed to go to Nuath and be Acclaimed was to save it from the Grentl. Well, and to keep Rigel from being hurt or killed when he was being held in Dun Cloch. From the very start, she's had zero desire to be a leader or have all this power. Or pressure. I'm not sure she does even now, but she hasn't had a choice."

"Then it will be an act of mercy for you to give her one, Princess."

Because I can't give in before he comes here in person, I act uncertain. "Even if you're right, I don't think I'm ready for that. After all, Emileia had advice from the *Echtran* Council, then Regent Shim, while she was getting up to speed. The only person I've had to advise me so far is her. How can I lead with so little experience?"

A satisfied smile spreads across Devyn's face. "By relying on those of us who do have that experience, of course, just as your sister did. I myself would be honored to be numbered among your advisors. Not to appear self-serving, but you would be hard pressed to find anyone more qualified. Isn't it true that at one point my name was put forward as a potential Earth Regent for Emileia?"

"That's right, I'd nearly forgotten! Of course, she rejected the idea, because of your role in erasing Rigel Stuart's memory last spring."

He sighs. "Yes, I rather doubt she'll ever forgive me or the others involved in that, though to this day I believe we acted for the best. The boy was a definite security risk, totally apart from the problems presented by their potential pairing. No one can deny that once the distraction of a teen romance was removed, Emileia did a superb job of convincing Nuathans to relocate to Earth, thereby extending Nuath's power supply by several years."

Only because of that antidote she was given to counteract her graell *sickness,* I think indignantly to Tristan. *She was still totally miserable, though. It was heartbreaking to watch.*

Aloud, I say, "She really did do an amazing job. We were all proud of her."

"But now....?" He lets the words hang in the air.

"I guess she *is* more distracted with him around. I also suspect if she ever had to choose between being Sovereign and keeping Rigel around, she'd choose him."

"That alone makes her a risk to our people, wouldn't you agree?" Devyn asks, his expression revealing nothing but concern.

Though I *don't* agree, I pretend to. "Yes, I suppose it does." *Of course, I'd do the exact same thing if it was you,* I silently assure Tristan.

He sends a rush of love and support my way. *You're doing great—you've about got him reeled in. Now to convince him to come here to talk in person. That's the whole point of this, right?*

"I really would appreciate your help if I'm going to do this, Devyn," I finally say. "Can you come to Fiarway sometime this week, so we can talk in person about how I should proceed?"

As I feared, he shakes his head. "Much as I'd like to, Excellency, I feel it would be far too risky with your sister and Rigel Stuart staying in town. Emileia's animosity toward me is well known—you referenced it yourself—and we all know how lethal that pair can be. I'm more than willing to send a car to bring you to me, however, well outside Fiarway."

Exactly what M warned me against! "I'm sorry, I'm not at all comfortable with that," I tell him. "Though we kept it out of the news, there was an attempt on my life the day after my sister disclosed my identity to the Council, and some believe it may have been at your urging."

Off to the side, I see Connor shift uncomfortably in his chair. Devyn, meanwhile, assumes a pained expression.

"Ah, yes. Connor told me about the speculation surrounding that assassination attempt, but I assure you, Princess, I had absolutely nothing to do with it. The man involved was found to be mentally unstable, was he not? If he claimed to be acting on my orders, he was terribly deluded."

Father told me the same thing, Tristan thinks to me. *I didn't buy it then, either.*

Neither do I, but I force a relieved-looking smile. "I'm very glad to hear that. But I also remember how you tried to force my sister and the Council to name you Regent just a month after that, with an Ossian Sphere full of antimatter."

Now he manages to look chagrined. "I freely admit that was an unforgivable overreach on my part, Princess, though I had no intention of weaponizing that antimatter. Its sole function was to enhance the Sphere's persuasive properties. However, your sister proved more resistant than I expected."

I have to suppress a secret grin at that.

"Or perhaps the Sphere itself was defective," he continues, "as I was unable to maintain control of it. It no longer poses a threat, of course, as it subsequently self-destructed, likely due to incompetence by my engineers. The experience taught me a valuable lesson about trusting the wrong people and, more importantly, that I should never ignore my true strength—diplomacy. *That* is what I propose to exert on your behalf."

I summon a grateful smile. "I appreciate that, Devyn. Still, the only place I'm willing to meet in person is here. Surely we can arrange that without my sister finding out?"

"I'm sorry, Excellency," he says with seeming regret. "Even for so worthy a cause, I'm not willing to take that risk. Perhaps if she and young Stuart can be detained somewhere—safely but separately—while you and I meet and finalize our plans?"

"Detaining them against their will could easily get one or both of them hurt," I object. "That's a risk *I* won't take."

Time to go to plan B? Tristan silently asks.

M won't like it, but I was just thinking the same thing.

"I have a better idea," I continue aloud. "My sister is scheduled to fly to Dun Cloch tomorrow evening. Why don't we simply wait until she leaves Fiarway to meet in person? You'll be able to come here without any risk at all once she and Rigel are gone." It'll mean calling in Kyna's troops myself, but I'm more than willing to do that to keep M and Rigel safe.

Devyn frowns thoughtfully, then slowly nods. "I suppose that's reasonable. Particularly if we can have your sister placed under the care of Dun Cloch's Mind Healers when she arrives there. Your primary goal is to ensure Emileia receives the treatment she so clearly needs, is it not?"

"Yes," I confirm, even though M is as mentally sound—now—as anyone. More than most people, in fact!

"Even if it requires she be involuntarily committed to a Mind Healing facility?" he asks. "Are you willing to authorize that?"

I only hesitate for a moment, since if all goes according to plan, Devyn will be under lock and key before it matters.

"Absolutely," I tell him. "I'm willing to do anything necessary to restore my sister to full mental health...to include acting as Sovereign while she receives more treatment."

He smiles. "In that case, I should be able to offer you substantial assistance toward that goal." Devyn then continues, "I understand you and your sister are both to attend a formal dinner this evening?"

I nod, wondering where this is going.

"I believe I'll speak with Alban about using the occasion to set the stage for a smooth transfer of power once Sovereign Emileia is safe in Dun Cloch. Meanwhile, I must caution you not to breathe a hint of this to your sister, should the opportunity arise. If she were to learn I'm residing nearby, she would likely take action against me."

"No, I won't say anything to her." Not out loud, anyway.

Devyn's smile now borders on smug. "Thank you. For now, I will bid you good day and eagerly anticipate our next chat—in person—as soon as I can safely visit you. To your very good health, Excellency." Standing, he bows deeply to me, right fist over heart, before his hologram vanishes.

Swallowing, I exchange a glance with Tristan, who also looks a bit startled by Devyn's abrupt disappearance. Then we both look at Connor.

"I must say, Excellency, you handled that interview extremely well, displaying a maturity beyond your years." Though he speaks approvingly, Connor's air of surprise is less than flattering. "All things considered, it was probably wise of you to refuse Devyn's offer to have you brought to him. While I hope he has now truly abandoned his earlier ambitions, I suppose we shouldn't entirely disregard his past actions."

"My thoughts exactly," I agree. "There's no denying he could be a huge help to me, but first I need to be positive I can trust him. For now, I thought it better to be...cautious."

Somehow I need to tell M she really does have to fly to Dun Cloch tomorrow after all, I add silently to Tristan.

Maybe at that dinner tonight? he suggests.

"Yes, caution is always advisable when dealing with someone like Devyn," Connor agrees, oblivious to our mental exchange. "Though as I said—"

The living room vidscreen suddenly chimes and he breaks off. Turning, we all see the screen flashing a priority notification—to Princess Malena, from Sovereign Emileia.

"You'd...you'd better open it, Princess." Connor's voice shakes slightly.

Going to the vidscreen, I identify myself with my thumbprint. An instant later a message window opens, to display a chillingly formal summons.

"Uh-oh," Tristan and I say together.

20

ULMUCHAN

(UHL-muh-khan): preparation

M

Morag follows me upstairs, but I tell her I need privacy to think and shut her out of the bedroom. There, I sit in the armchair near the foot of the bed and stare at the wall, mentally replaying everything Alban told me at breakfast. Rigel's guess is probably correct that he came here to preempt anything Molly might tell me, though I suspect his main motivation was to cover his own sorry butt. I also suspect Devyn coached him on what to say, which would explain why his words sounded so rehearsed.

The question is, what's next? Have he and Devyn abandoned their plan to separate us and help Molly take over as Sovereign, now that Alban's spilled the beans? More likely, they're hoping all his assurances of loyalty will lull me into a false sense of security before they make their move.

In that case, Rigel and I need to be extra alert for whatever they may be planning...unless it'll make Molly's story more convincing to let them carry it out? From what Alban said, she's apparently claiming I really am dangerous as a reason to supplant me—something I suggested myself.

Will they use that excuse to mobilize the whole town against me? If that story spreads beyond Fiarway, it'll undo most of my efforts to reassure people I'm fine—and safe—after Gwendolyn Gannett's exposé. But

170

trying to refute it now could potentially put Molly in danger—the last thing I want to do!

Ugh.

Have you told Cormac what's going on? I think to Rigel at that point in my ruminations. *What did he say?*

That he already doubted Alban's story. Still, he's relieved to know Molly's not actually planning to betray you. He and I are doing another thorough sweep of the whole downstairs right now, then we'll search the outdoor perimeter.

I bite my lip. *Maybe you should stay in the house and let Cormac do the outside stuff. They might already have someone lurking, waiting for an opportunity to nab you. After Alban made such a big deal about guaranteeing our safety for that dinner this evening, I doubt they'll wait that long.*

You may be right. I'll finish the inside sweep myself, while Cormac does the perimeter. I'll let you know what we find, if anything.

While they're doing that, I work on coming up with something I can do at my end to bolster whatever Molly's telling Alban—and maybe Devyn, too, by now? I'm positive he won't leave his fortress unless he believes she's totally on board with whatever he suggests.

Hm. Maybe if I say or do something that makes it seem like I'm threatening Molly, she can pretend she's so scared of me she's desperate for his help?

Pulling out my omni, I start outlining exactly what I should say to her—and how. And when.

Twenty minutes later, Rigel reaches out with his update. *Good thing it was Cormac who did that outside sweep. Two brutish-looking guys were loitering within sight of the house, watching the front door. He would have questioned them, but they ran off as soon as he approached them. Then he spotted some kind of device stuck to the side of the house, up near the roof line. It must have been put there last night or while Alban was here, because it wasn't there yesterday. We think it's something to either intercept or block communications, but testing that theory could tip them off we've noticed it. Ditto disabling it with an energy weapon.*

I think for a moment. *I'll send an innocuous message to Nara asking when the next Council meeting will be. She's usually quick to answer. If she doesn't, maybe you can try messaging your dad.*

Good idea.

We break off our mental communication and I send my question to Nara. It *seems* to go through, but until she replies...

Ping! *Kyna told us to plan on our usual Saturday evening time slot once you and Princess Malena return, Excellency,* comes her prompt response. *Of course, that can be postponed if either of you would prefer to rest an extra day or two.*

I fire off a quick thanks, then confirm to Rigel that my omni still works.

Then we can assume everything's definitely being monitored now, if it wasn't before. You absolutely shouldn't risk contacting Molly again.

Unless it's something I want *them to intercept?* I think back.

What—? Oh! Clever.

Grinning, I pull up the notes I just made on my omni and start composing a message.

21

COMBLACHT

(KOHM-vlakt): fight; conflict

Molly

Even though Tristan and Connor can see the vidscreen as well as I can, I read M's priority message out loud.

"I, Sovereign Emileia, hereby request Princess Malena's attendance at half past noon today for a luncheon at my lodgings. Tristan and Connor Roark are welcome to accompany you if they wish, as are your personal attendants. Please be punctual."

I turn back to the others, pretending—well, mostly pretending—to be nervous. "I...I guess we'd better go, huh? That last bit makes her sound kind of pissed."

Tristan acts concerned, too, though we both assume this must be part of M's plan. Exactly *which* part, we can't know for sure—yet. Hopefully she'll explain once we get there?

Connor, who's totally unaware of the plan, looks genuinely worried. "Do you suppose she could have learned of your conversations with Devyn and Mayor Alban?" He darts a glance at me, then Tristan, then me again.

I suck in an alarmed-sounding breath. "Oh, wow, I hope not! But... how could she?"

Other than this whole deception being her idea? comes Tristan's amused thought.

Then she ought to pretend to be clueless, shouldn't she? I think back.

Maybe she will? Guess we'll find out soon enough.

"We don't dare refuse her summons, of course," Connor says after a moment. "I wonder if she'll expect formal attire?"

"Knowing M, I normally wouldn't think so." I frown. "But considering her wording...maybe?" I reread her message. "We're supposed to be there in less than an hour, so we should probably start getting ready."

⁎

"Sure, okay," I tell Sorcha half an hour later, when she again holds up a tiara to go with one of my formal Princess dresses. If I'm going to pretend I want to become Sovereign, I may as well do the thing right. "Maybe my sister will see it as a sign of respect."

When I join Tristan and Connor downstairs, they're also dressed more formally than any of us were for dinner last night. Tristan's in another traditional Consort ensemble instead of his smoking-hot Bodyguard uniform, though of course he's still gorgeous.

His eyebrows go up appreciatively when I enter the living room. "Wow, you look amazing!" he tells me. "Every inch a Princess."

I self-consciously reach up and touch the tiara nestled in my hair. "Too much? Will this give M the wrong impression, do you think?"

"Not at all, Excellency," Connor assures me. "Your attire is perfectly fitting for your station. Did your sister not wear a tiara for formal occasions before she was Acclaimed?"

Only because I insisted she wear one, over her protests. "Well, yes. Not that she actually *said* this lunch would be formal."

"Treating it as such is a way to denote respect." Connor echoes my words to Sorcha upstairs. He speaks soothingly, but the tightness around his eyes betrays his worry.

"Let's hope M sees it that way, and not as a challenge," Tristan comments. Then, just to me, *A challenge would fit right into her plan, though, right?* I can sense he's more than a little nervous, too.

His father frowns at that. "Surely not? Arousing her suspicions would be, ah, premature at this point, based on what Devyn said earlier."

"Assuming she's not already suspicious." I again pretend more nervousness than I'm feeling—a little more, anyway. "Either way, we'd better get going. She told us not to be late."

Nodding, Connor hurries out to the garage, the rest of us on his heels.

We arrive at the VIP residence at two minutes to twelve. Before Connor can even ring the bell, the door is opened by an impassive Cormac.

"The Sovereign requests that you join her in the breakfast room," he informs us, his tone as chilly and formal as M's message was. "Follow me, please."

The only other time I've been inside this house was as M's Handmaid last August, when we spent a day and a half in Fiarway after we got back from Mars. At the time, I was so focused on acting the perfect *Chomseireach* that I barely noticed the opulence—though of course it's nothing compared to the Royal Palace in Nuath. Now, I can't help comparing it to Connor's comparatively modest home.

Silently, we follow Cormac to the smaller dining room, where M is already seated at the head of the table with Rigel on her left. Like Tristan, he's dressed as a Royal Consort instead of a Bodyguard. As we enter, Cormac goes to stand behind M, next to Morag.

"Welcome." M's expression gives nothing away. "Thank you for coming so promptly on short notice." Her voice doesn't give anything away, either—chilly, but not angry.

I hesitate for a second, then move to the chair at the foot of the table, opposite her. Only then do I notice the finger bowls, one at each of five place settings. M's has the traditional green orchid denoting the Sovereign's place. Mine doesn't.

"Thank you for inviting us," I cautiously reply, watching her carefully for the slightest sign of...anything.

Meeting my gaze, she gives me the barest ghost of a wink. Reassured, I sit down.

Connor and Tristan both bow to her, then take their own seats—Tristan to my left, Connor on my right. There's no place setting or finger bowl to M's right—that chair stays empty.

Looking at M again, I rest my arm against Tristan's and attempt a silent question, hoping she can hear me, since we're a little farther apart than we were on the plane. *What's going on?*

Almost to my surprise, she immediately replies. *I'll explain in a minute. They can hear everything we say, so for now just play along. Maybe comment on the finger bowls?*

"What's with the finger bowls?" I obediently ask, glancing pointedly around the table. "I thought you hated these things."

Her smile doesn't reach her eyes, though I suspect—hope—that's for the benefit of Connor and the two Handmaids. "Normally that's true, but today I felt you needed a reminder of my station...and yours. Some rather disturbing rumors have reached me, Malena. I brought you here to confirm or deny them."

"Rumors?" I glance at Connor, but he looks alarmed rather than guilty.

"That's right. We can discuss them over the meal." M nods to Rigel and they go through the whole finger-dipping ritual with her bowl, then Rigel's, then the rest of us with our own stupid little bowls.

Once that's over, M turns to her Handmaid. "Morag?"

Her temporary Handmaid motions to Sorcha and the two of them go into the kitchen, then return a moment later with trays of food. As they serve everyone with soup and a variety of small sandwiches, I notice M's arm is still touching Rigel's, so I try reaching out to her again.

Can you at least give me a hint?

I will while we eat, she responds without looking at me. *I picked soup and sandwiches to make it easier to keep contact with our guys.*

I pick up my spoon, desperate to hear what M's up to, but Gilda clears her throat.

"Excellency, if I may?" She hands a tiny dish I hadn't noticed to Sorcha.

Considering the act M's putting on, and that Gilda doesn't know it's an act, her concern is understandable.

M reinforces that thought. "Probably wise, all things considered," she tells Gilda—and me. "Cormac, will you do similar honors?"

Her older Bodyguard has Morag serve him a sample of M's soup and sandwich as Sorcha does the same with Gilda. Then our adult Bodyguards carefully taste each dish.

I'm always struck by how stupid this formality is, since if either of us were going to poison the other, we'd be smart enough to use something that wouldn't work instantly. But it's traditional, so we all go through the motions.

Finally M picks up her spoon, signalling everyone else can eat, too.

I swallow two mouthfuls of tomato soup without really tasting it before asking, "Now, what are those rumors you want me to confirm or deny?" *Has something changed since we texted yesterday?* I think to her, my arm still lightly touching Tristan's.

Yes—I'll explain this way while we eat. Everything we say out loud is being monitored so we need to stick to the plan for now. Before I can react, she says aloud, "Don't pretend ignorance, Malena. I couldn't help noticing yesterday morning how much more popular you are in Fiarway than I am, despite this being your first visit since the truth about you came out. Clearly *someone*—" She looks pointedly at Connor— "has been working to influence public opinion here."

Connor, who just took a sip of his iced tea, sputters. "Surely, Excellency, you don't think that I—!"

"Actually, I do," she interrupts. "You and your son have everything to gain by convincing my sister to replace me as Sovereign. As does she." M turns a way-too-believable glare on me. "No wonder you invited me to accompany you here. Where better to attempt a coup, than in an *Echtran* enclave where the majority already favor you over me."

Admit it! Play along! she thinks to me across the table.

I force myself to return her glare as I improvise. "A coup? You're even more paranoid than I thought," I say, then silently add, *I told Connor and Alban you've been acting kind of crazy since the whole Faxon thing— enough I should maybe take over for a while. That seemed more believable than pretending I've secretly wanted to replace you all along. Don't be mad, okay?*

Mad? I think it's brilliant!

Relieved, I continue aloud. "Admit it, Emileia, you haven't been fit to lead since you spent all that time in Faxon's memories. I tried to pretend otherwise, but Connor and Tristan helped me see the truth—that *I'm* what our people need right now. You need help. You may *think* that Mind Healer cured you, but it's obvious you didn't get nearly enough treatment."

"So you'll justify deposing me by claiming it's for my own good?" she flares. "Are you telling people I'm too crazy to be Sovereign now? I saved Nuath from Faxon! Is this the thanks I get?"

"The Faxon thing just pushed you over the edge," I retort, remembering what Devyn said this morning. "But from the very start, you've been too blinded by love—or ego—to see what a distraction your non-Royal boyfriend is. He's held you back all along from being the leader our people deserve."

She flinches slightly. Going after boyfriends *is* below the belt, but I'm making this up as I go, trying to make it sound good for our unseen listeners.

Sorry, sorry! I quickly think to M, but she still retaliates in kind.

"Blinded? Me? When you ignored how your boyfriend only became interested in you after he found out you're my sister? The whole reason he moved to Jewel was to replace Rigel as *my* Consort, remember? When that didn't work, you became his consolation prize."

Now I'm the one who flinches. Ouch!

Tristan sends me a reassuring dose of love. *We know the truth. So does M,* he reminds me. *This is just an act.*

"I should have paid attention to the warning signs sooner," she continues when I don't reply. "Especially when Connor started visiting Jewel again. For all we know, he's still in league with Devyn Kane, who nearly had you killed last year. I'm sure he'd *love* to see you replace me as Sovereign. With Connor in his pocket and Tristan as your Consort, Devyn could call the shots. But if you think I'll just let you push me out of the way, you're *dead* wrong."

"That wasn't my plan when I came to Fiarway," I admit, since Devyn, Alban and Connor already know that. "But since getting here, I've realized it would be the best thing for both of us. Especially since you never wanted to be Sovereign in the first place!"

M blinks. Because it's true? She obviously didn't expect me to say it. But she only hesitates for a second before wading back in. "And you do? That's quite the dramatic reversal from what you were telling me and everyone else less than a week ago! You know how persuasive Connor and Tristan are. Can't you see they've brainwashed you? Did *they* convince you to wear that tiara, or was that your idea?"

"*You're* the one who insisted I learn all this Sovereign stuff," I angrily remind her. "You told me you needed help, and you obviously do. Or maybe you just wanted to spend more time with your boyfriend and less time doing your job? Well, if you won't do it, I will!"

"You...you backstabbing little traitor!" she practically shrieks at me. "I trusted you! Even when you were only my Ag Handmaid, I treated you better than you had any right to expect! But wow, give you just a taste of Royal privilege and you're suddenly as power-hungry as your boyfriend and his father. I feel like I barely know you anymore!"

M looks like she's on the verge of tears. I am, too. It's horrible hearing her say such hurtful things and even more horrible saying such awful stuff myself.

"Me? *You're* the one who's totally changed from the sister I knew!" I'm about to elaborate, but realize I'm shaking. We both need a break—and I need to find out the real reason she's making us do this. "Fine. Whatever. You're obviously determined to believe the worst about me, but I came here to eat lunch, so that's what I'm going to do."

Still glaring at her, I swallow another spoonful of now-cold soup, then stuff half a little sandwich in my mouth and start chewing. M looks like she's about to lash out again, but then huffs out a disgusted breath and takes a bite of sandwich, too.

Rigel and Tristan trade fake—I hope?—dirty looks, and also start eating. Connor just sits there, looking stunned. Though I can't see Gilda's or Sorcha's expressions behind me, they're probably just as shocked—and Morag's mouth has actually fallen open. Cormac looks as stoic as ever, but M may have clued him in on this part of her plan. Like I need to be!

Okay, what's the deal? I ask M silently while I chew. *Why are we doing this?*

Mayor Alban dropped by this morning to warn me you might be plotting against me.

I nearly choke on my sandwich. *What? That doesn't make any sense! Does it?*

We think he wanted to cover his butt in case you spill the beans on their plotting. He also planted another bug while he was here, right in this room, which gave me the idea for this lunch. My guess is he and Devyn want to turn us against each other, to make their work easier while they sit safe on the sidelines. The last thing they'll want is for us to team up against them when they make their move.

That *does* sound like Devyn's deviousness.

Speaking of Devyn, I think to her, *he holo-ed in this morning and we talked for nearly an hour.*

And?

I swallow, take a sip of my tea, then another bite of sandwich. *He's totally onboard with helping me replace you, but when I asked to meet in person he suggested I come to him. I said no but he insisted he'll only come to me if you and Rigel are out of the way, somewhere you can't threaten him. Except I'm afraid he wants you ALL the way out of the way.*

M starts eating her soup, though it's got to be as cold as mine is. *What did you tell him?*

That I'm only willing to take over so you can spend more time with the Mind Healers, and I absolutely won't risk either one of you being hurt. I tried to convince him we could meet at Connor's without you finding out, but he wouldn't go for that. So I told him you're leaving for Dun Cloch tomorrow and we can meet once you're gone. He agreed to that, on condition I have you committed to a Mind Healing facility there.

Her eyes widen with alarm, though she quickly tries to hide it. *I can't leave you to deal with Devyn on your own! What if he figures out this was all an act and turns against you?*

You promised, I sternly remind her.

I only promised we'd leave if Devyn wouldn't talk to you at all. I'm the one who came up with this plan, so it's not fair to make you handle the riskiest part of it by yourself.

I knew she'd be stubborn about this—delegating has never been M's strong suit.

You're not making me. What's not fair is expecting me to put you at risk! I'd tell you to skip that dinner tonight, but that might tip Devyn off that I tipped you off. He was obviously worried I might. He said something about using tonight to lay the groundwork for me taking over—probably Alban singing my praises or calling your sanity into question or something. So he wants us both there.

It might also make Alban suspicious if I bail on the dinner after he promised to be personally responsible for our safety tonight, M responds. *If either of them guess you warned me, it could put you in danger.*

"How's the food?" she asks aloud before I can respond, breaking what must seem to anyone listening like a really long silence.

"The *food* is fine." I match her snarky tone. "But you're not. I wish you could see that."

Her eyes narrow dangerously. "Don't start again, Malena."

I shrug and pick up another little sandwich. *Either you agree to take that flight tomorrow night or I ditch the whole plan and call in Kyna's troops myself as soon as I leave here.*

And risk getting all those people killed? Her mental "voice" is appalled.

Better them than you. Our people need their Sovereign!

M frowns down at her plate, obviously thinking hard. *You win,* she finally thinks to me. *But once I leave, you have to be super, super careful! Promise?*

I promise. And you be super careful during Alban's dinner tonight.

I will.

Her assurance lets me relax enough to suddenly notice I'm eating tuna, which I've never liked.

Tristan sends me a silent apology. *I should have let you know when you picked it up but I didn't want to distract you.* He's been listening in to our whole silent exchange, of course. I assume Rigel has, too.

Then, apparently deciding we've stayed quiet long enough, M speaks up again, "You'll never get away with this, you know." *Sorry about the tuna, I forgot,* she adds silently, almost making me laugh.

"I plan to let the Council know what you're up to," she continues aloud. "Trust me, if you continue on this path, you won't like the reception you'll get when you return to Jewel—if you even have the nerve to go back. I'll also tip off the governor of Dun Cloch, in case you were planning to undermine me there, too."

I'm so relieved we're on the same page again, it takes extra effort to maintain my fake hostility. "Wow, you're even more unhinged than I realized. It would probably be safer for everyone if you just skipped that dinner tonight." If I can get her to concede that point, too, I'll worry even less.

No such luck.

"You'd like that, wouldn't you, Malena?" she demands, half-rising like she wants to launch herself across the table at me. "No way I'll let you undo all the good I accomplished with my speech yesterday! Not only am I going to that dinner, I'm going to be on high alert for whatever duplicity you have planned. Maybe *you* should stay home, if you don't want to be publicly humiliated!"

Sitting back down, she again rests her arm against Rigel's. *There. That should discourage them from attempting anything too obvious tonight.*

I grudgingly admit—silently—that she's right, but for the sake of those hidden bugs and Connor, I huff out a disgusted breath.

"What, let you attend alone so you can go on some demented rant to everyone about me being a traitor? Not a chance! I'll be there. Maybe by then you'll have calmed down enough I can talk some sense into you before you do anything *too* crazy."

22

PHAERAID

(parr-OYD): procession; parade; display

M

"Don't call me crazy!" I yell at Molly—like crazy Mr. Farmer once yelled at me. *Anything else you need to tell me?* I then ask silently as we keep glaring at each other.

Not that I can think of, except how much I hate doing this, she thinks back. *Sorry about some of the stuff I said.*

I suppress a smile. *Ditto.*

So we're on the same page now? Privately, I mean, she adds, since we've been doing our best to give the impression we're anything but.

I guess so. Though I really don't like leaving you here to deal with Devyn on your own.

She gives me a patient look and reminds me, *I have Tristan. Once Devyn's in the same room with us, it should be a piece of cake to lull him into a false sense of security long enough for me to activate my tracker. I'll let Kyna know ahead of time to expect it.*

Reassured, I again realize we've been quiet a little too long. Clearing my throat, I glance around the table. "Would anyone like dessert?"

Connor flinches visibly. He's barely eaten a thing, his emotions an intense mix of fear and guilt after the accusations I made earlier.

For a moment Molly and Tristan look like they're struggling not to laugh at such an anticlimactic question.

"All your unfounded suspicions have killed my appetite," Molly replies. "Who told you I was plotting against you, anyway?"

"Like I'd tell you? I owe them better than that for cluing me in, especially since I was warned you might retaliate against them if you knew."

Molly jumps to her feet. "That's it. You're being completely ridiculous, but I don't have to sit here and listen to how awful you think I am."

Tristan gets up to accompany her. After a startled moment, Connor also scrambles to his feet.

I whirl on him. "You're not to say a word about any of this once you leave here. Do you understand?"

Connor blinks at me, clearly taken aback. "I...ah..."

"My sister and I have worked hard to present a united front, despite our private disagreements. I won't have that undermined, even now. Especially now."

I direct another glare Molly's way, then follow them to the door. Cormac opens it for them, but before Molly can step through, I seize her by the arm, determined to further cement the impression we've tried to give.

"You should know better than to try to cross me, Malena." I try to make my tone as threatening as my words. "You've seen what can happen to people who do."

Since touching makes telepathy so much easier, I quickly add, *I know you can do this, Molly. Just stay the course until Devyn's out in the open—but please, please be careful!*

"Is that a threat?" she demands. Though her expression appears outraged, her mental reply is reassuring. *I already promised I would. And tonight, all four of us need to be alert, just in case. I never liked this plan, but I'll do everything I can to make it work. Meanwhile, please stay safe, M!*

You, too, I think back.

For a long moment, we lock gazes.

Then, aware of all the interested eyes on us, she roughly shakes me off. "I'm not afraid of you, Emileia, not anymore. I'm done being your lapdog. Find someone else to kick around!"

With a swirl of her royal blue skirts, she sweeps through the door and down the front walk, flanked by the rest of her party.

I watch with mixed feelings as she gets into Connor's car, parked at the curb. Near the end of our faux fight, I sensed actual anger from her.

Did she intentionally project that, or is she truly pissed I'm forcing her to go along with this plan? Now I wish I'd asked. Either way, I'll simply have to trust her, like I said I would.

Closing the door, I turn to face Rigel, Cormac and Morag, hovering near the back of the foyer. Mindful of Morag's bug, as well her likely allegiance, I haughtily lift my chin.

"I clearly overestimated my sister's loyalty to me—and underestimated her gratitude for everything I've done for her. So be it. My path is now clear. Tomorrow I fly to Dun Cloch, then on to Jewel, where the people are truly loyal to their Sovereign. Once safe from Malena's treachery, I'll be able to gather the necessary support to ensure she can't possibly supplant me."

I march to the staircase, then pause, my foot on the bottom step, to look back at the others, still standing frozen in the entryway. "Rigel, come with me. Morag, I release you from your duties. You're free to go."

To my surprise, she shakes her head. "No, Excellency, I was given this post by Mayor Alban and will continue to serve as your *Chomseireach* until he tells me otherwise. I cannot allow you and your young *Costanta* to go upstairs unchaperoned."

I glare at her, irritated but also a little impressed. I expected my displays of temper to scare her off, but she must be made of tougher fiber than I thought. All I can do is continue making use of her as Alban's spy.

"As you will. Come, Rigel." I make it an order, though I accompany it with a silent apology.

He obediently falls into step just behind me. *No need to be sorry, you're doing great. By now, Devyn and Alban should totally believe Molly's willing to go along with their coup. You just made her job easier.*

I hope so. But only time will tell whether my performance pays off or backfires—maybe on both of us.

⁘

Upstairs, I have Morag help me change into something more comfortable than the Sovereign gown I chose for the lunch confrontation. When we return to the sitting area, I imperiously inform her that Rigel and I again need a period of direct contact to keep us at optimum health.

Just like yesterday, we sit together on the couch and clasp hands, while Cormac stands at attention and Morag glowers her disapproval.

Should we double check whether Devyn's still in his lair? Rigel asks silently when I don't send him any thoughts right away. *Or did you have something else in mind?*

Oh, I guess we can check on Devyn real quick. Mostly, I just need some serious recharging after that lunch.

He gives my hand a sympathetic squeeze. *I know that was hard on you. Hard on Molly, too—I think.* I can tell Rigel's still bothered by a few things she said to me. So am I.

I also thought it would be good for us both to be at our best ahead of tonight, just in case, I add. *If things go south, we might need to react quickly.*

Good thinking, he agrees. *Odds are everything will be fine—safe, anyway. After all Alban's assurances, he'd be outing himself as a traitor if he threatens us in any way, but it's always good to be prepared. I just wish we could manage some real alone time. I love you, M.*

Ditto, on both counts. I send all the love I can through our touch, wishing I could kiss him instead. *All right, let's see what Devyn's up to.*

Now that we know where to "look," it takes less than five minutes to confirm he's still in his mountain fortress. Once we do, I focus on his emotions—something I didn't attempt yesterday, I was so eager to send Cormac after him.

What I sense is encouraging—for our plan, anyway. Devyn's in a great mood. Elated, even.

Can you pick up anything he's saying? Rigel asks. I've occasionally been able to do that in the past, though never from this far away.

I focus harder and dimly hear, "—proceed as planned?" Then, in what's unquestionably Devyn's voice, "Yes. Afterward, we can implement the next phase."

I sense whoever he's talking to moving away, but keep my focus on Devyn himself. He's no longer talking, instead seeming intent on something he's looking at or reading. Unfortunately, I can't actually read minds this way, useful as that would be right now. Frustrated, I keep trying until Rigel stops me.

You're wearing yourself out, M. That's the exact opposite of what you said we should do right now.

He's right, as always. I pull back my focus until I'm only sensing Rigel—the one person I most want to be connected to. At once, strength and clarity flow through me, alleviating the strain I was just causing myself.

Thanks. You always know what's best for me.

Part of my job. The blast of love he sends my way is laced with amusement.

We keep holding hands for another half hour, sending loving thoughts back and forth while trying to keep worry at bay. Every now and then I recall one of the hurtful things Molly said today, but each time Rigel reminds me it was all an act that I insisted on.

It's thirst that finally compels me to let go of Rigel's hand, after a final, fortifying exchange of love. A glance at my omni shows we've been sitting here together for nearly an hour.

About the same amount of time we spent yesterday, so if Morag reports back we'll at least seem consistent, Rigel silently remarks.

Good point. That'll make it even less likely anyone will guess the main point of this trip was to track down Devyn.

Not that anyone outside the Council and the Bond Squad knows about this particular ability of ours. I hope.

Since my suite doesn't have its own recombinator, I ask Morag to bring up a pitcher of water and glasses for everyone. She starts to protest, but I point out that Cormac will remain in the room with Rigel and me, so she grudgingly complies. The second she's gone, I grab Rigel for a kiss long enough to give us both an extra boost of vitality, if nowhere near as long as we'd both like.

I'll take it, though, he sends when we reluctantly part at the sound of Morag's approaching footsteps. As always, Cormac gives no indication he noticed anything.

Morag comes in bearing a large pitcher of water and three glasses—not four. I hope she got something for herself while she was downstairs, but I doubt it. I gratefully gulp down a glass of water, then refill it. Intense mental exertion always seems to make me thirsty for some reason.

After that, I go into my bedroom to make another brief, super-secure call to Kyna. I let her know about Molly's initial holo-talk with Devyn, and his refusal to meet with her in person until Rigel and I leave Fiarway.

"So I will be taking that flight to Dun Cloch tomorrow evening.

Once I get there, I'll wait till I get word Devyn's been captured before publicly denouncing Alban, just to be safe."

"Probably wise, Excellency. It would be a shame to lose our chance to arrest Devyn at this point. Do please be careful until you're safely out of Fiarway, however."

I promise her I will.

By now it's late afternoon. I wonder if Molly's spoken with Devyn again since our faux-acrimonious lunch? I also wonder whether Devyn had already heard our conversation from that faux-acrimonious lunch when he said, "Proceed as planned." Probably? Good news, if so.

I'm still thinking about that when the sitting room vidscreen lights up with a call from Mayor Alban.

"Good afternoon, Excellency." His image bows deeply to me. "I hope you've enjoyed a relaxing day, despite the somewhat worrisome news I brought this morning?"

I incline my head in response to his bow. "Not particularly, though I'm trying to rest a bit now. I invited my sister to lunch and, while we had a bit of an argument, I feel we've now reached a greater degree of understanding."

"That...is good to hear, Excellency." Only a slight raising of his brows betrays his surprise at my assertion, at odds with what he must have heard. "I, ah, did hope I was mistaken about her intent. That should make this evening's festivities much more pleasant for you both. I'm calling to acquaint you with the details of the procession in advance of tonight's dinner, which will allow all of Fiarway's residents to pay their respects to you both."

"Oh, yes, you did mention a procession. What do I need to know?"

"A car will arrive for you and your attendants at six. You'll be driven along a route passing through much of Fiarway before terminating at our Town Hall shortly before seven. Another car will transport your sister and her attendants." Like this morning, his words have a rehearsed quality.

Rigel speaks up from behind me. "No offense, sir, but are you certain this will be safe? Given previous attempts on the Sovereign's life—"

"Absolutely! Did I not say this morning I would personally ensure the Sovereign's safety?" The mayor's smile is just short of condescending. "Both the Sovereign and the Princess will be protected by force shields, though their cars will appear to be open. We're taking no risks whatsoever."

"I appreciate your caution, Mayor Alban." I smile my thanks, wishing I could read his emotions. "I'm sure my sister will, too."

He bows again. "I'll see you this evening, then, Excellency. I quite look forward to it."

The call ends and I look over at Rigel and Cormac. "Are you both still okay with me being in this motorcade?"

"With the precaution he mentioned, it should be safe enough, Excellency," Cormac says. He glances at Rigel, who nods.

Let's be alert for anything, though, he thinks to me. *It's possible they'll use it as an excuse to separate us.*

I silently assure him I won't let that happen, then turn to Morag. "Let's decide what I should wear for this parade-thing and the dinner tonight, shall we?"

Molly was always eager for any chance to dress me up. She still is, in fact. Morag, not so much.

"Of course, Excellency. I'll begin setting out ensembles for your approval now."

Two hours later, resplendent in the same sumptuous lavender gown I wore in last fall's Homecoming parade as Junior Princess, I wait in the foyer with my attendants. Rigel is again dressed in Consort attire instead of his Bodyguard uniform, which should justify him sitting next to me rather than separately. We both agreed that would be safer.

At one minute to six, the doorbell rings and Cormac opens the door. It's our same driver as before, now dressed in formal livery. Behind him, a bright red convertible limo is parked at the curb. Bowing, the driver conducts me to the flashy car, Rigel on my left and Cormac and Morag following behind.

"Excellency, you and your, ah, Consort are to sit here, with your attendants in the seat behind." The driver gestures to two generous seats in the middle of the vehicle. "All of us will be protected by a force shield I'll engage as soon as we leave. We'll join the rest of the motorcade, waiting two blocks from here, after which we'll make our way through all of Fiarway's major streets as we progress to the Town Hall."

Like Alban's, his speech is clearly rehearsed, which reminds me to focus on his emotions. I pick up a trace of nervousness, but nothing worse. Nothing that feels the least bit sinister, anyway.

Good to know, Rigel thinks to me, but still insists on doing a security sweep of the vehicle before I get in. The man stands back while Rigel and Cormac both scan the whole car with their omnis, after which they report it safe.

Rigel helps me into the middle seat, then takes his place next to me while Cormac and Morag get in behind us. Once we're all seated, the driver pushes a button on the dash and a barely-perceptible transparent dome forms around the entire top half of the car, emitting a faint hum. The force screen's energy makes all the hairs on my arms stand on end, reminding me of the very first time I was near Rigel, a year and a half ago.

The red limo pulls away from the curb and passes several houses before turning left. A long line of black cars is waiting at the next cross street. When we reach them, I see a stretch convertible identical to this one, only white, at the rear of the line with Connor driving. Molly's in the middle seat with Tristan next to her, Gilda and Sorcha behind them, presumably also protected by a force shield. Turning right, our car takes its place at the head of the line.

Looks like I still get precedence over Molly. For now, I think to Rigel as we begin driving slowly forward, leading the procession. *I wonder how long that'll last?*

Probably until we leave Fiarway, he sends back. *As of this morning, Alban was still pretending to be on your side.*

I wish Molly were close enough to contact telepathically, but there are nearly a dozen cars between us. Hopefully we'll get a chance to talk when we reach the Town Hall.

The procession creeps down one street after another, zigzagging through Fiarway. People line our route, waving and cheering as we pass. A lot of houses are decorated with brightly-colored flags and banners—many displaying Princess Malena's name, though a few also honor Sovereign Emileia. Though I know full well why that is, it still stings a little. I make a point of smiling and waving at everyone, doing what little I can to counter Devyn's influence.

We're moving so slowly and taking such a roundabout route, it takes more than forty-five minutes to traverse little Fiarway. Eventually we reach the Town Hall, an imposing building right on the main square.

Instead of stopping out front, like I expect, we continue around to the side, where a large door retracts into the ground. A ramp leads down to an underground parking garage, much like the ritzy guesthouse in Tully-mayne, Nuath, where I stayed until I could be Acclaimed.

Our car has barely started down the ramp when I suddenly feel disoriented. Blinking rapidly, I shake my head and look around. To my surprise, we're already parked near an ornate underground entrance with gilded double doors. Did I black out for a second?

I turn to Rigel and, to my shock, discover he's gone. Confused, I glance behind me and see Morag and Cormac still sitting there, both also blinking as though just waking up. Rigel is nowhere to be seen.

"Rigel?" I call aloud, now looking around me more wildly. *Rigel?* I repeat silently, but at top telepathic volume. He doesn't answer, audibly or silently.

Scared now, I turn to the driver. Though he also looks dazed, he's already out of the car and coming to open my door. "What just happened?" I demand. "Where's Rigel?"

He doesn't answer, but I sense a distinct trace of guilt from him that wasn't there earlier. If he doesn't know, he must suspect, at least. Turning all the way around, I see the other cars from the procession still entering the parking garage. Whatever happened, it can't have lasted more than a few seconds.

"Cormac? Did you see where Rigel went?"

My Bodyguard shakes his head, alarm now mingling with his confusion. "No, Excellency. It's as though...as though he simply vanished out of the car."

"Morag?" I ask my churlish Handmaid.

She seems as genuinely confused as Cormac, and only slightly less alarmed. "I saw nothing either, Excellency. He was sitting beside you, and then he wasn't."

Mayor Alban hurries up just then. "Excellency? Are you all right?"

"No, I'm not! What have you done with Rigel?"

"I?" He looks convincingly startled but I sense nothing from him but intense guilt, tinged with fear. "Nothing, I assure you."

Angry now, I glare at him. "You were in the car right behind us. You *must* have seen what happened?"

My Royal "push" isn't as strong as Molly's, but it's enough to force an answer.

"He...ah...I was told he'd be taken somewhere safe, Excellency," the mayor stammers. "I'm to escort you inside."

"Forget it. I'm not going anywhere until—"

Breaking off, I again reach out mentally for Rigel. *Can you hear me? Where are you?* I "listen" as hard as I can for several seconds. He doesn't reply—which must mean he's not conscious. I *won't* consider the alternative.

Trying hard not to panic, I reach into the hidden pocket of my formal gown for my omni, so I can ask Molly if the plan was changed. At this point I'm less concerned about secrecy than making sure Rigel's okay.

Instead of my omni, though, my hand encounters a stiff piece of paper that turns out to be a small envelope. Nothing's written on the outside, so I rip it open. Inside is a single sheet of paper containing a brief, typed note with no signature:

If you wish to see Rigel Stuart again, you will behave this evening as if all is well. We'll talk soon.

23

EGINNTACHT

(egg-EEN-tok): confusion; uncertainty

Molly

My face is stiff from smiling by the time we finally reach the Fiarway Town Hall at the end of that endless procession-thing. It's a relief to see the line of cars ahead of us disappearing through the entrance to what I assume is an underground parking garage, like some of the more important buildings in Nuath had. When we're finally out of sight from the crowds, I let my cheeks relax.

Ugh, I think to Tristan, sitting next to me in the convertible white limo. *This is just one of the many, many, MANY reasons I never want to be a Sovereign myself!*

You're doing great, he thinks back. *Like somebody who was born to this.*

That does *not* improve my mood. I've been on edge all afternoon, ever since that weird, upsetting lunch with M. I know our "fight" was fake, staged for whoever was listening, but it felt a little too real—especially as I was leaving. No matter how many times I tell myself M only said those things to make her sound irrational, and like the two of us don't get along, I'm finding some of her words hard to forget.

I half expected another call from Devyn afterward, since according to M he was bound to hear, or hear about, everything we said. Should I be worried that I didn't get one? Or is that a good sign?

He did say your next meeting would be in person, after M and Rigel leave

192

Fiarway, Tristan silently reminds me. *I'm sure he'd have let you know if he changed his mind.*

Would he, though? What if—

I break off my thought at the sight of people gathered around M's car, the red one, way up ahead.

"What's going on?" I ask aloud. Not that anyone in this car would know.

Fighting a sudden sense of dread, I reach for the car door, only to discover there's no handle on the inside. Connor, behind the wheel in front of me, merely shrugs and continues driving forward at a snail's pace behind the long line of other cars. It seems like forever before we finally reach the ornate underground entrance, the commotion I saw now over.

M's red limo has already pulled away from the curb, empty except for the driver. M is nowhere in sight as we park in the spot it just left. I'm anxious to get inside and make sure she's okay, but Connor takes a maddeningly long time to disengage the force shield and get out of the car. By the time he opens my door, I'm practically bouncing with impatience.

"There were a bunch of people crowding around M's car a few minutes ago. If something's wrong, we need to find out what."

Connor glances toward the entrance, showing only mild concern. "Likely just excitement by the staff at receiving the Sovereign. We'll ask once we reach the banquet hall."

Tristan and I precede the others through the double doors and up an elegant staircase. I try to hurry, but my formal royal-blue gown slows me down. I have to lift the front carefully if I don't want to trip over the hem. At the top of the stairs, we're greeted by a smiling Mayor Alban.

"Welcome, Excellency." He bows deeply. "Please allow me to escort you to the banquet hall. The rest of the guests are already assembled there."

Great. So I have to make a grand entrance on top of everything else. I almost ask the mayor why M and I aren't making our entrance together, but remembering the role I'm supposed to be playing, I hold off.

Our small group proceeds down a plushly carpeted hallway to another set of double doors that open into a lavish dining hall that reminds me of the one in the Royal Palace in Nuath. Approximately two dozen guests are seated at a long table set with glittering crystal and flatware. At my entrance, they all rise and bow in unison, chanting, "*Faoda byo Banfriansa Malena!*"

Taken aback, I stop cold, scanning the big room for M. When I spot her, seated at the far end of the table, I relax. She looks fine. Then I tense again. Where's Rigel?

Silently, I repeat that question to Tristan.

Dunno, he replies, sounding worried himself now. *But he can't have been taken away by force, or M would look a lot more upset.*

He's right—though when I look more closely at M, I see definite signs of strain around her eyes and mouth. Cormac and Morag stand behind her in their traditional positions, but the chairs on either side of her are empty. I start toward her, but Alban clears his throat.

"Excellency, you're to sit here." He indicates the head—or foot?—of the table, the end nearest to me and farthest from M.

I reluctantly move to that chair, then notice the fingerbowl at that place contains a green orchid. Frowning, I look down the length of the table again and see M's fingerbowl has one, too. It still feels inappropriate for me to have an orchid, but not as bad as if I were the only one so honored. Still on edge, I allow Tristan to pull out my chair for me.

When I sit, the rest of the guests do, too, making me wonder—hope—they greeted M the same way they greeted me, except with *Thiarna* (Sovereign) *Emileia*. Not that I can ask anyone.

As Tristan takes the seat on my left, in the Consort spot, Connor and Mayor Alban confer quietly together a few paces away—too quietly for me to eavesdrop. Returning to the table, Connor takes the chair on my right and Alban steps close to my shoulder.

"Would you perhaps like to say a few words, Princess?" he asks.

"Me?" My voice almost squeaks, but not quite.

Stick to the plan, Tristan silently reminds me.

"Er, okay." Smiling down the table at all the guests, I say, "Thank you all for the hospitality you've shown me and my sister." I nod toward M. "We're both grateful for our warm welcome here and look forward to future pleasant visits to Fiarway."

I know M usually says more than that, but I'm feeling too unsettled right now to come up with anything longer.

"Thank you, Excellency," Alban says loudly enough for everyone to hear. Then, more quietly, "Feel free to begin the pre-dinner ritual as soon as I'm seated."

With another little bow to me, he walks to the other end of the room and takes the place to M's right, leaving the traditional Consort spot still empty. Where *is* Rigel? Did Devyn and Alban kidnap him after all? More alarmed than ever, I try to catch M's eye. Looking up, she meets my gaze with an intensity that makes me suspect she's trying to send a mental message. I touch Tristan's hand and listen as hard as I can, but don't hear anything.

Are you okay? I try sending to her, but it's obvious she can't hear me, either. Not surprising, since we're more than thirty feet apart and Rigel's not here, but still frustrating.

As we both hesitate, Alban nods to M, then down the table to me. "Excellencies?"

Tristan picks up my fingerbowl, but I keep watching M instead of dipping my fingers. Without Rigel here, who—? Then Morag steps forward to hold M's bowl out to her.

Oh. Right. I did read that's the proper procedure when a Sovereign's Consort isn't present, or if he or she doesn't have one at all, like Sovereign Vevilana, Nuath's "virgin queen." Gazes still locked, M and I dip our fingers and dry them simultaneously, after which our attendants go through their own finger-dipping rituals. In Rigel's absence, Tristan's finger dip is what signals the rest of the guests to do the same, so the meal can finally begin.

The food's probably great but I barely taste it, I'm so focused on M, trying decipher from her expression what's going on, since we can't use telepathy. Questions swirl through my mind. *Did* Devyn have Rigel kidnapped after all? Why, when he agreed to wait? Because of something he overheard from our lunch?

Finally, unable to stand it any longer, I turn to Connor. "Rigel Stuart was in my sister's car during the procession, but he's not here now. Did Mayor Alban tell you where he went?"

Connor's smile looks forced. "He, ah, informed me young Stuart agreed to take his meal separately, rather than cause the guests undue anxiety. Apparently, some are still alarmed by seeing the two of them together after recent revelations about their combined power. Alban seemed quite relieved that the boy proved so understanding."

Even without M's emotion-sensing ability, I can tell he's uncomfortable. Maybe because he doesn't really believe Alban's explanation?

"So...is he in the kitchen or something?"

"I imagine so, though the mayor didn't specifically say." Connor doesn't quite meet my eye as he answers.

Should we try to get more out of him? I silently ask Tristan. *Because I'm almost sure he either knows or suspects more than he's saying.*

Not here, he thinks back. *We're pretending we're on Alban and Devyn's side, remember? Probably safer for now to act like we believe everything's okay.*

I don't respond, even mentally, wondering again whether Tristan's a little *too* invested in this plan of M's—way more than I am. I'm careful to keep that thought strictly to myself, though.

✦

The dinner seems interminable as course after course is served, none of which I enjoy. I'm too worried about M.

As the meal progresses, she looks more and more unhappy. Even a little scared. I've hardly ever seen M scared before, which scares *me*. She barely touches her food, but twice more as we're eating she looks like she's trying to send me a mental message that never comes through. I try, too, three different times, with no more success.

Finally, *finally*, the dessert course is served. I dismiss Sorcha and Gilda to get their own dinners in the kitchen and apply my spoon to the frozen concoction in front of me. The sooner I finish, the sooner I can leave the table without giving offense and talk to M. Except as I take my last bite, I remember M's the one who's supposed to signal the end of the meal.

I try to catch her eye again, but now she's making little circles with her spoon in her dessert dish, like she's retreated to another world.

Long minutes pass as I stare at her, but she never looks up. By now, pretty much everyone's done eating. The guests start quietly chatting among themselves, some sending curious glances M's way. Desperate to hear her explanation for what's going on, I finally take matters into my own hands. Forcing a smile, I again address the room.

"Thank you again, Mayor Alban, for this delicious dinner, and thank all of you for joining us tonight. My sister and I wish you all a very pleasant evening." On the last word, I shove to my feet, catching Tristan by surprise—though he belatedly puts a hand on my elbow like he helped me up.

Connor blinks at us, equally startled by my abruptness. "Ah, perhaps we should linger for a bit, Princess?" he quietly suggests. "Allow more people to make your acquaintance? Alban mentioned something about after-dinner cocktails—"

"Maybe later. First I want to talk with my sister." Stepping away from the table, I head in her direction.

The guests also start getting to their feet, many looking confused by how suddenly I ended the meal. Now that I think of it, M did usually hang around for an hour or so after those formal dinners in Nuath. Oh, well.

As I move toward her, M finally looks up, a question in her eyes. I've got questions, too, but I'd rather ask them silently. For that, I need to get close enough to touch her.

C'mon, I think to Tristan, grabbing his hand. I start making my way around the table, but I've only taken a few steps when a woman smilingly blocks my path.

"Excellency, I'm so pleased to finally meet you. I'm Helva O'Connell, president of Fiarway's merchant guild."

"Oh, um, nice to meet you." I summon a quick smile before stepping past her, trying not to be *obviously* rude.

Unfortunately, she's not the only person determined to introduce themselves as I try to get to my sister. I do my best to be polite to each one, though nearly all my attention is on M. Still seated, she looks like she's arguing with Mayor Alban. About Rigel?

"Yes, I hope we can talk more later, too," I absently reply to the head of something-or-other, gushing about how great it is to have a second Royal heir. I step around him, determined to do no more than smile at anyone else before I reach M. But even as I think that, I hear her voice.

"No, please!" She's on her feet now, backing away from Alban and shaking her head. "Really, that won't be necessary."

As I watch, M stumbles against her chair and nearly goes down, but Cormac lunges forward to catch her in time. Exclamations break out, punctuated by a few screams.

"The Sovereign!"

"What happened?"

"Is she all right?"

Mayor Alban takes control, telling everyone to stay back as he moves to help Cormac support M—who's still conscious, much to my relief. Then two burly men who were standing unobtrusively against the wall come forward to flank Cormac and the mayor as they lead M away.

I start shoving my way past people, no longer caring about being rude. "Excuse me! Excuse me! Let me through!"

Tristan helps to clear a path for me, but just before we reach the other end of the table, M is hustled out of the room through a door behind her.

M? Can you hear me? I think to her as hard as I can while clinging to Tristan's hand.

For a second I almost think I hear a faint echo of her voice in my head, but then it's gone.

Pushing past the last few people, we finally reach the door M just disappeared through. Tristan's reaching out to open it when Mayor Alban comes back through it from the other side.

"Everyone, please! Calm down!" He holds up both hands, palms out. "The Sovereign became briefly confused and agitated, but appears to have suffered no physical harm. She is now being attended by our best Healers, who will more fully evaluate her condition and provide whatever care is needed. I hope to have more information tomorrow, which I'll share with you via Fiarway's local network."

His little speech sounds suspiciously prepared. At its conclusion, he sends me a quick half-wink that confirms my guess. Whatever's really going on with M and Rigel is clearly part of Devyn's plan—but definitely *not* what we agreed to! Though I pretend to be reassured for Alban's benefit, I'm anything but.

He turns away then to offer individual reassurances to various people coming up to him. I move toward him, planning to ask where M is being taken, but Tristan tightens his grip on my hand. *Going along with their plan is what M wanted you to do, remember?*

But what is *their plan?* I think back, trying hard not to panic—and especially not to *look* like I'm panicking. *Devyn said he'd wait until they left Fiarway!*

I know. But playing along is still following M's plan, Tristan insists.

This wasn't part of her plan! I protest. *She never would have agreed to be separated from Rigel.*

Probably not, he admits, *but you were super clear you won't tolerate either of them being hurt. When Devyn comes to meet with us in person, you can let him know that if they are, you'll see he pays the ultimate price. He won't dare harm them after that.*

I stare at him disbelievingly. *We can't know that! Whose side are you on, anyway? I'm not willing to risk M to catch Devyn, but it sounds like you are.*

Tristan blinks, then looks stubborn. *I don't want M or Rigel hurt. Of course I don't! But yeah, I really, really want Devyn removed as a threat. He tried to have you killed, remember? If we don't go through with this, he might succeed next time. That's what I'm not willing to risk!*

Though I appreciate his concern, I refuse to trade M's safety for mine. I'm about to tell him so again when I notice the crowd around us has thinned and Alban is looking at me. Determined to find out *something* about what's going on, I give him what I hope looks like a conspiratorial smile as I move to his side.

Alban's return smile is definitely conspiratorial. "You should know, Excellency, that your sister proved herself even more unbalanced than we suspected," he confides before I can ask any questions. "Before I had her helped out of the room, she was on the point of publicly accusing you of treason. Clearly, I couldn't allow that."

"What did you do to her?" Now I'm even more scared for M.

"Merely gave her a little something to calm her nerves, as she was becoming extremely overwrought," he smilingly assures me. Even without my mum's ability, I'm positive he's lying. "Healers are attending her now, so why don't you have Connor take you and Tristan home?" the mayor continues. "I'll contact you in the morning about your sister's condition before making any general announcement. Meanwhile, do try not to worry. I assure you, she's getting the best possible care."

I don't believe that, either—those big dudes who hustled her out of the room were *definitely* not Healers! The only thing that keeps me from accusing Alban of treason on the spot is the fear it could make things even worse for M.

Again forcing myself to smile, I thank him with fake effusiveness and turn toward Connor, Gilda and Sorcha, all hovering a short way behind Tristan and me. Connor must have heard everything the mayor just said, because he immediately motions me back toward the main doors of the banquet hall.

"We should go home, Excellency, where we can await further word from Mayor Alban. I'm sure everything will be fine."

There's an uneasiness beneath his apparent concern I can't help noticing, but I just nod.

"All right. Let's go." *The second we get back, I'm calling Kyna,* I silently warn Tristan as he escorts me out of the big room. *This has gotten way out of hand. Maybe she'll have an idea what to do now.*

Though I can tell he doesn't like that idea, he doesn't argue as the three of us go down the ornate staircase to the underground garage, where Connor's car is waiting. He drove it to the Town Hall before the procession, so we go back in that instead of the white limo I rode in earlier. I'm glad to be less visible, but don't dare let down my guard while sitting up front with Connor.

Are you sure—? Tristan finally starts thinking to me when my omni vibrates in the hidden pocket of my fancy gown. Frowning, I fish it out and look at the screen. It's a message from Devyn.

The first phase of our plan has been successfully completed ahead of schedule, Excellency. Tomorrow I can safely call on you at Connor's house, as you requested, to discuss our next steps. I'll reach out to him in the morning to arrange a time. Meanwhile, I wish you a very good night's sleep.

24

SOHNNIHE

(SON-ye): trapped; held captive

M

I'm still groggy as two strange men and a woman bundle me into a van in the underground parking lot of Fiarway's Town Hall. I look around for Cormac and see him a few feet away, looking anxious and confused. Next to him, Morag also appears confused, though less worried.

"Where are you taking me?" I ask, sandwiched in the middle seat between the woman and one of the men. The other man motions Cormac and Morag into the seat behind me, then gets behind the steering wheel.

"Back to your temporary residence, Excellency," the woman replies. "Healers will attend to you there. The mayor thought asking you to mingle with other patients at the Healing facility would be unseemly."

I frown at her. "Healers? What's wrong with me?"

Her smile is stiff and forced. "That is for the Healers to determine, Excellency."

Though I already tried more than a dozen times during that endless formal dinner, I again reach out mentally for Rigel. *Can you hear me yet? Please let me know you're okay!*

There's still no answer.

Dinner was pure torture, forcing myself to behave as normally as possible in case Rigel's life was on the line. Why, *why* did I insist on this

201

stupid plan to catch Devyn? I managed to convince myself, along with Molly and even Kyna, that it was practically foolproof, but I was obviously very wrong. Now I'm terrified Rigel will pay the ultimate price for my stubbornness. That's the only reason I didn't activate my tracker chip after he disappeared.

All through the meal I also kept trying to reach Molly telepathically, to tell her to abort the plan, but without Rigel to boost me, it was hopeless. Even if he'd been there, I doubt it would have worked at that distance, especially considering how hard it was to focus through my mental turmoil and the after-effects of whatever gas they used in the car. I'm pretty sure Molly tried from her end, too, with no more success. Maybe she wanted to tell me Devyn changed the plan? Did he somehow force her to go along with this?

I'm not sure exactly what happened at the very end of the dinner. Molly was starting to come toward me when I felt a tiny prick in my right arm—the one closest to Alban. A second later, my heart started racing like I'd been given a shot of adrenaline. Alban pretended to be concerned, but I could tell he was faking. He then offered to give me something to calm my nerves and I reacted...badly. What did I say, exactly? I don't remember.

I do remember trying again to reach Rigel, and then Molly. For a second I almost thought Molly heard me, but things were going fuzzy by then, so I might have imagined it. I vaguely recall Cormac catching me before I hit the floor, but not much else. Did I pass out again?

"Here we are, Excellency," the man driving the van announces, and I'm startled to see we're already back at the guest house.

"I'll help you out, Excellency," the woman beside me says. "Then your *Costanta* and *Chomseireach* can take you inside. A team of Healers should arrive shortly."

Too confused to protest, I allow her to hand me out of the van, then take Cormac's arm to go up the walk. The van drives away before we reach the front door. Shakily, I palm it open and the three of us go inside.

"Come, Excellency, let's get you upstairs." Cormac's voice reflects his concern. I lean heavily on his supporting arm as we ascend the staircase, with Morag bringing up the rear.

The first thing I do once we're in my suite is reach for my omni before remembering it's gone. I reread note that was left it its place—is it from Devyn or Molly? Until I hear from *someone*, I have no way to know.

"Cormac, do you still have your omni?"

He nods. "They took my weapon, but I keep my omni in an inside pocket, which would have made it more difficult to find quickly."

"Good. If you can get a signal out, we should—"

Cormac stops me with a warning look, followed by a quick glance at Morag, reminding me she's still bugged. It was my idea to pretend we didn't know, but with my stupid plan in shambles that seems pointless.

"Will you please ensure our privacy, Cormac?"

With a nod, he takes out his omni, points it at Morag, and does whatever it is he and Rigel do to render listening devices inert.

In response to her startled expression, I smile grimly. "I'd rather not be spied on anymore, Morag. The device you've been wearing is disabled now, so you may as well take it off."

"Device?" Her apparent confusion is totally feigned.

"In your armband," Cormac clarifies. "I presume it was given to you by the mayor?"

She goes pale and gasps, the biggest display of emotion I've seen from her. "You...you knew? Then why—?"

"Of course we knew," I tell her. "But I chose to pretend not to, since it was already obvious we shouldn't say anything in front of you that we didn't want reported back. From the start, that bug only picked up things I wanted your, ah, handlers to hear. But I'm done playing their games now that they've kidnapped Rigel. Do you know what they plan to do to him?"

Still looking aghast—and scared—she shakes her head. "N-no, Excellency! I was merely ordered to stay as close to you as possible, and to prevent you from being alone with him. M-Mayor Alban did tell me the armband would monitor my surroundings, but he claimed its primary function was to protect me from those electrical charges you and young Stuart generate."

A mirthless laugh escapes me. "Trust me, no device would have protected you if we'd zapped you full strength—not that there was even the slightest risk we'd do that. The night we arrived, I told you—and Alban—we posed no danger to anyone. Though right now I'm so pissed at Alban I'd be tempted... Are you *sure* you don't know anything about their plan?" I add some "push" to my question.

"I'm sorry, Excellency, no." Unfortunately, I sense only regret, not duplicity. "If...if I was somehow instrumental in helping them capture or harm your young *Costanta*, I'm genuinely sorry for that, too," she adds. "Mayor Alban insisted that by acting as your temporary *Chomseireach*, I was serving a necessary function. He...he said I would be regarded as a hero for voluntarily putting myself at risk for the greater good. I... believed him."

The main emotions I sense from her now are embarrassment and contrition, her earlier hostility barely noticeable at all.

"I'm sure he can be very convincing," I tell her gently. "Most Royals are. That doesn't mean they're always right—or honest. I personally learned that the hard way, well before I was Acclaimed Sovereign. Perhaps I'll tell you that story sometime. Cormac, are you able to call or message out?"

He pulls up his omni's control panel, touches a few holographic buttons, then shakes his head. "The comm block we suspected earlier is now thoroughly in place, Excellency. No signal can get through this dampening field. Shall I try from outside?"

I nod and he goes downstairs—then returns a moment later to report that the front door is now sealed shut. "I was unable to force it, though I did try."

"Seriously? They actually locked us in?" I was pissed before, but now I'm furious. "I'm the Sovereign! How dare they?"

Morag looks—and feels—scared now. But before I can reassure her, she says, "There is a back entrance, Excellency. Shall I—?"

"Yes, please." I smile my gratitude. "Thank you, Morag."

To my surprise, she actually smiles back before leaving.

The second she's gone Cormac turns to me, positively radiating guilt. "Excellency, I must apologize. I truly believed you were suddenly taken ill, but clearly that was not the case. Had I realized in time and acted, I might have prevented—"

"No, Cormac, this isn't your fault. I was intentionally pretending everything was okay. Because of this." I hand him the note that was left in my pocket.

His eyes widen as he reads it. "Then the mayor—?"

"I don't know for sure who wrote it. But just after the dinner ended, Alban gave me something that nearly made me pass out. I'm sure he waited till you weren't looking to stick me with whatever it was. Besides, if you *had* intervened, they might have taken it out on Rigel, so it's just as well you didn't."

Frowning, he nods, though his guilt doesn't fade completely. I suspect it'll take him a while to get past what he clearly considers a dereliction of duty.

A moment later, Morag returns to confirm what I assumed was the case. "We do appear to be completely locked in, Excellency. I'm sorry. I never expected—"

"No, I know. There's no reason you would have. I didn't think they'd go this far either, even if my sister does enjoy greater support here than I do."

Though I'm still having trouble focusing properly, I try to think through my situation and what to do about it. Locked in, unable to contact anyone, even Rigel…my options are pretty limited.

Is Molly still sticking to my original plan? Did she agree to this? I do remember saying she could go along with anything short of getting me or Rigel killed—which, in retrospect, was pretty stupid. I think about some of the stuff I said to her at lunch, especially toward the end, and wonder if I brought this on myself. My goal was to convince our eavesdroppers Molly had told them the truth about me, but maybe I came on *too* strong? Maybe if—

"Would you like a cup of tea, Excellency?" Morag asks, interrupting my spiraling thoughts.

I blink at her until her question penetrates, then nod. "Tea would be nice. Thank you, Morag. Peppermint, please." That should help clear my head better than chamomile. I need to restore my wits if I'm going to have any chance of outsmarting Devyn. Unless it's already too late?

Morag comes back a few moments later with a steaming cup of peppermint tea and a small plate of ginger cookies.

"I…noticed you didn't eat much at dinner, Excellency," she explains, setting them both on the little table next to me.

Thanking her, I lean back in the cushy chair and sip my tea, trying to force my brain to function. I also try again to contact Rigel, but with no more success than before. Could whatever drug Alban gave me be interfering with my telepathy? I devoutly hope that's all it is.

Cormac and Morag both hover worriedly as I finish my tea and a couple of cookies. Then Morag tentatively asks if I'd like her to help me get ready for bed.

"I'm sure you'll feel better in the morning, Excellency. No doubt the Healers you were promised will arrive then, as it's now rather late. The people who brought us back did say they'd be attending you."

"Yes, I remember."

Now that my mind's clear enough to recall nearly everything from earlier, I seriously doubt any Healers will show up tomorrow, or at all. Devyn and Alban won't want me interacting with anyone who could possibly interfere with their plans.

"Perhaps by then Mayor Alban will also have persuaded your sister to release you," Morag adds encouragingly.

I open my mouth to deny that Molly would have done this to me but realize I can't know that for sure.

"Bed sounds good," I say instead, "but I can get ready on my own. I'm feeling much more myself now. I'll see you both in the morning. If nothing has changed, we can discuss our options over breakfast."

Cormac nods, and after a second, Morag does, too.

With a parting smile, I go into my bedroom and shut the door, hoping *that* won't seal behind me. For all I know, they plan to starve me to death.

On that thought, I try again, harder than ever, to reach Rigel's mind. When there's still no sign of it, I stifle a sob. What if Devyn already had him killed? Wouldn't that be the surest way to guarantee we can't ever threaten him again? Though I've been trying to hold it at bay, I'm now gripped by the same terror I felt a year and a half ago, when Rigel was nearly executed in Dun Cloch. What if this time—?

No! I won't give in to despair. Not yet. We've faced challenges before and we'll get through this one, too. I keep telling myself that the whole time I'm washing my face, brushing my teeth and changing into my nightgown.

I climb into bed, hoping a good night's sleep will purge the last of the fog from my brain so I can figure out a solution tomorrow. That is, if I can sleep at all, worried as I am about Rigel.

I'm glad I thought to load my old favorite, *Jane Eyre*, onto my Martian book-scroll before leaving Jewel. I've read it so many times, it can usually be counted on to lull me to sleep. Sure enough, by the end of the first chapter my eyelids are getting heavy. Snapping the screen back to pencil size, I set it on my nightstand and roll over.

M? Are you there?

Rigel's voice in my head makes me sit bolt upright in bed.

Rigel? I think back, hardly daring to hope. Did I really hear him, or was I already dreaming?

Yes! Where are you? His mental reply is accompanied by relief tinged with worry. *Are you okay?*

I nearly laugh with relief of my own. *Me? I'm fine. I'm back in the VIP guesthouse, totally safe. What about you? Did they hurt you? Where are you?*

Not sure yet, I just woke up. Someplace with a bed, is all I know. The last thing I remember is going into that underground garage at the Town Hall at the end of our parade through town.

Even though he can't see me, I nod. *That's where they gassed us—all of us inside that force dome, including the driver. I was out for less than a minute, I think, but when I came to you were gone. Neither Cormac or Morag saw what happened and nobody else would admit to anything. Whoever it was took my omni and replaced it with a note threatening you if I didn't act normal during dinner. But I did such a lousy job of that, I was afraid they might— But you're alive! I was so, so worried about you, Rigel!*

I'm fine. Right now, anyway. I'm really sorry for what they put you through, M. I love you!

I love you, too, Rigel, so much! I take a moment to bask in my immense relief before making myself think again. *Now that we can communicate, maybe together we can figure out what's going on. I'm safe, like I told you, but I'm locked in and Cormac confirmed they've put a total comm block on us. No messages can get in or out—except between us!*

I get the impression of a mental chuckle from him. *Yeah, Devyn must not know about our range—unless Molly or Tristan told him?*

No! They wouldn't do that.

Are you sure? Sounds like they didn't warn you about me being hauled off before that dinner. What did Molly say when you asked about it afterward?

I frown into the darkness. *I never got a chance. They seated us at opposite ends of a really long table, and without you there we couldn't use telepathy to talk. We never got close enough to touch before Alban drugged me again and I was taken away.*

Sounds like they made sure Molly would have plausible deniability about whatever happened.

Or they changed the plan themselves and wanted us both to think it was the other one's idea, I suggest. *I can't believe Molly would betray me like that. I trust her.*

There's a pause before he replies. *Until there's proof you can't?*

That stops me for a second, but then I shake my head. *Even if it looks that way, I'm sure it'll be something Devyn's done. Maybe with Connor's help.*

Sorry. Guess I'm feeling a little paranoid right now. Tell you what, give me five or ten minutes to try to figure out where I am and I'll reach out again. Think you can stay awake that long?

I was sleepy before, but talking with Rigel has me wide awake. *Definitely! I'll be here. Tell me what you find out.*

I try to read to pass the time, but I'm too keyed up now. Finally, after what feels more like half an hour, Rigel contacts me again.

You still there? Good. I can't be positive, but I think I'm in Devyn's actual fortress. This room probably belongs to one of his security guys. Definitely not a cell, like that thing in Dun Cloch. There's even a real bathroom. And a vidscreen, though it doesn't seem to work. They must have disconnected it.

His mention of Dun Cloch rattles me, but I shove my foreboding aside. *Do you think you can fix it, the way you did at your grandmother's place back in Nuath?*

I'll try, but no promises. I spent a couple minutes listening at the door—locked, obviously—and heard people talking. Couldn't hear much, but it sounds like big plans are afoot. Everything's quiet now but I'll try to find out more later. Guess there's not much either of us can do tonight, though, except sleep. You said they drugged you, too?

Twice, actually, I admit, fighting off a sudden wave of exhaustion. *First when they gassed us all at the start, then after dinner, when Alban stuck me with something. It's mostly worn off now, but I'm still a little out of it.*

From more than three miles away, Rigel sends me a warm wash of love. *Sleep then, sweetheart. Tomorrow we'll both be fresher, better able to plan. I love you!*

I love you, too! And you're right—we'll get through this, like we have everything else.

We will. Nothing but confidence comes through with his thought. *Together. Like always.*

Together, I reply, sending back all the love I can.

Then, overcome by the events of the day but secure in Rigel's love, I drift off to sleep.

25

BREAG FIONN

(brag fin): discovery of a lie; detection of falsehood

Molly

I reread Devyn's message, trying hard not to freak out right here in Connor's car.

What's wrong? Tristan sends in response to my emotional turmoil.

I silently recite Devyn's text to him before tucking my omni away. I'd rather not say anything to Connor just yet, though if he's a party to getting M or Rigel hurt...

You told Devyn flat out you wouldn't allow that, Tristan reminds me after a startled second. *It sounds like they've gone back to the original plan Alban told us about yesterday, to keep them apart—but safe.*

We can't know that! What if he has them both killed? That would force *me to be Sovereign, which is exactly what he wants!*

From behind me, I feel the calm Tristan's trying to project my way, but it does more to piss me off than calm me. Sensing that, he instead tries talking me down again.

Devyn only wants you to be Sovereign so he can call the shots, right? He has to know if he hurts M or Rigel, you'd never trust him again and would even retaliate for that kind of double-cross. It's in Devyn's best interest to keep them both safe for now—and he always puts his own interests first.

As his reasoning penetrates, my panicked heart rate and breathing start to slow. He's right. Devyn would be stupid to kill them now, knowing it would alienate me forever, and Devyn's anything but stupid.

Thanks, I send back as Connor pulls into his driveway. *But I'm still calling Kyna as soon as I get upstairs, because M's plan has spun way out of control.*

Ten minutes later, that's exactly what I do.

Kyna answers surprisingly quickly, considering it's two hours later in Washington, DC. "Princess? Is there a problem?"

"Yes. It, um, seems M and I have miscalculated a bit," I admit. "Everything seemed to be working as of this morning. I'd convinced Devyn to talk to me in person once M left for Dun Cloch tomorrow. As soon as he showed up here, I was going to have you send in your security guys to arrest him, just like M wanted. But tonight Devyn changed the plan without telling me. He had Rigel hauled off right before our formal dinner, and then M was taken away practically the second it ended. Mayor Alban said she had a health emergency, but I think he caused it."

Kyna sighs. "I was afraid of this, or something like it. Do you know where the two of them were taken?"

"Not yet, but Devyn messaged he'll be coming here in person tomorrow morning, so I'll make him tell me. M *might* be at Fiarway's Healing facility, since Alban mentioned her being attended by Healers, but Rigel's probably locked up somewhere."

I go on to relate the holographic conversation I had with Devyn this morning, including my insistence neither of them be hurt no matter what. "He agreed to that, but he also said he'd wait till they left. I never should have trusted him."

Kyna makes a sound suspiciously like a snort. "No. He's proven his untrustworthiness several times over. The troops I sent are standing by, so if he follows through on his plan to visit you in person tomorrow, we can have him apprehended."

"Not if he's holding M and Rigel prisoner!" I protest. "For all we know, he's left orders to have them both killed if anything happens to him!"

A long silence greets my words. "A valid concern," she finally concedes. "I don't suppose you or the Sovereign had a plan for how to proceed under this scenario?"

"No, we haven't had a chance to talk privately since lunchtime today, when we both still thought she'd be flying out of Denver tomorrow night. Oh, I guess you should cancel those plane tickets."

"Not an issue. The same chartered aircraft that brought the security force to Fiarway is waiting to take the Sovereign and her attendants to Dun Cloch. I'll simply tell the pilot to stand by. You're certain Devyn means to call on you in person tomorrow?"

I pull up his last message and read it aloud to her. "He's pretty gung-ho to help me take over as leader," I add. "I'll get everything I can out of him when he gets here."

"Please do, and report back when you can. I'll keep the security force on hold until you give me word they can safely move in."

As I disconnect the call, I wish more than ever I'd never let M talk me into this crazy plan. We both should have known Devyn would outsmart us. But as long as he continues to believe I'm on his side, maybe I can still salvage things. It's all I have to work with now.

+
+ +

Devyn's text may have wished me a good night's sleep, but I definitely don't get one. For the second night in a row I toss and turn, my mind a morass of worry. It's past nine when I drag myself down to breakfast.

I try to conceal my lack of sleep with extra makeup, but apparently it doesn't work.

"Excellency, are you feeling quite well?" Connor asks when I join him and Tristan in the dining room. "You look a bit...peaked. I do hope a cup or two of tea will perk you up, as today promises to be rather an important one."

I give him a sharp look. "What do you mean? Did you hear something about my sister? How is she?"

Connor holds up a hand to stop my flow of questions, his expression now apologetic. "I'm sorry, Princess, I didn't mean to worry you. I've heard nothing further about the Sovereign's condition as of yet. I simply meant that you may be called upon to take her place as early as today, should the Healers determine she is currently unable to serve."

Does he know more than he's saying? I think to Tristan.

Maybe? he silently replies. *He got a message from someone just before we went to bed last night, probably either Devyn or Alban.*

Even so, I pretend to take Connor's assurance at face value—for now. "I hope Emileia will be okay," I say, holding my plate out to Sorcha, so she can spoon eggs and hash browns onto it. "But I guess you're right that I need to be prepared in case she's not."

If Devyn's gone back on his word and hurt either her or Rigel, I'll have him executed, or at least memory-wiped! I mentally fume to Tristan as I take my first bite.

Tristan puts a calming hand on my arm. "I'm sure everything will turn out fine." *We just need to stick to the plan,* he silently adds. *Devyn's message said he's going to leave his fortress and come here today. That was always going to be step one, right?*

It was. Now it's to make sure M and Rigel are safe!

He has no answer to that.

Though I'm too anxious to be very hungry, I make myself eat most of what's on my plate and drink two cups of strong tea. I need to be fully alert when Devyn gets here, if we're going to outsmart him. Clever as he is, it won't be easy.

I'm just finishing my second cup when I get a call from Mayor Alban.

"Excellency, I promised last night to give you first word on your sister's condition when I received it, which I did a few minutes ago."

"Yes? And?" I ask eagerly. "Will she be all right?"

There's a pause long enough to worry me before he replies, "It's too soon to say, I'm afraid. Our Mind Healer believes the Sovereign suffered a mental break of some sort. Clearly you were correct that she is not nearly so recovered from her recent traumatic experiences as she wished us to believe."

Like last night, his words sound almost scripted. By Devyn?

"They assure me she is being kept quite comfortable." Alban's voice is irritatingly soothing. "She's being attended at the same guest house where she's been staying, as the Healers felt familiar surroundings might be more calming."

So they can continue spying on her, I assume. "Who, exactly, is with her?" I ask when he pauses again.

"Two Healers, along with her primary *Costanta* and the *Chomseireach* I assigned to her on her arrival here."

At least Cormac's with her. But— "Not Rigel Stuart?"

"No, it was considered safest they be kept apart, given her unstable state. No one wants a repetition of the regrettable incident that occurred earlier this month. Given the hostility she displayed toward you yesterday, I'm sure you agree."

Does he realize he just admitted to eavesdropping? Rather than comment on that, I ask, "Where is Rigel right now?" Without him, M really will be sick soon. So will Rigel, making it even harder for them to resist whatever Devyn has planned. "I hope he's also safe and in comfortable surroundings? I know my sister would insist on that, at a minimum."

"Of course her young *Costanta* is safe, Princess!" Alban sounds surprised I would even ask. "Perfectly safe. Comfortable as well, according to the report I was given this morning. Your sister need not worry about him, as I'm sure she's been informed. But...I should let you go, as I believe you have an important meeting to prepare for. I will attempt to assess your sister's condition in person later today, and speak with you again afterward. Your very good health, Excellency."

He disconnects the call before I can thank him—or demand to know exactly where Rigel is.

"Devyn messaged me while you were talking with the mayor, Princess," Connor tells me as soon as I put my omni-phone away. "He suggested calling on you here in half an hour, if that meets with your approval?"

Despite feeling overwhelmed by how quickly things are moving, I nod. The sooner I can get answers out of Devyn, the better. "Yes, that'll be fine."

"Perhaps you'd like to change your attire first?" Connor runs a not-quite-critical eye over the jeans and casual sweater I threw on after sleeping so late.

"Oh. Right. Good idea." Devyn deserves no such consideration after going back on his word, but it might help me feel more confident. "I won't be long."

Sorcha follows me upstairs and helps me swap out my jeans for the pale blue skirt and embroidered darker blue tunic she set out before I went to bed last night. A glance in the mirror confirms I look a lot more regal in this outfit. I *have* to stay in control of this interview, even while pretending to believe whatever Devyn says.

Connor and Tristan are already in the living room when I go back downstairs. I join Tristan on the loveseat just as the doorbell rings. Smoothing out my skirt, I lift my chin and assume the persona of a Princess about to hold an audience.

Fake it till you make it, I tell myself firmly. Until M and Rigel are both safe and Devyn's under lock and key, I need to act like I was brought up

Royal instead of an Ag orphan. M's and Rigel's lives might depend on how well I can carry this off.

Trust me, you look every inch a Princess, Tristan assures me, giving my hand a squeeze. *Ready to activate your tracking chip so Kyna's troops can nab him?*

Not till we know what he's done with M and Rigel! Acting too soon could get them both hurt—or worse. I told Kyna the same thing last night.

Reining in his impatience to eliminate Devyn as a threat to me, Tristan grudgingly agrees. *Soon, though...*

"Welcome, Devyn, welcome." Connor steps forward to greet his friend when Gilda shows him into the room. "It's been too long."

"It has," Devyn agrees, smiling benignly on all of us. "I intended to call on you last week, but the time got away from me."

In other words, he was too busy plotting with Alban how to take advantage of our visit, I think sourly to Tristan while politely returning the traitor's smile.

"Thank you for receiving me on rather shorter notice than we originally discussed, Excellency." Devyn bows deeply, right fist over chest.

I acknowledge his bow with the traditional head inclination everyone's made me practice. "I appreciate your willingness to meet with me here, where I'm more comfortable."

His smile broadens. "As you rightly pointed out, face-to-face is the best way to discuss the rather delicate matters we must now decide."

"Matters I was led to believe would wait until after my sister left Fiarway." I only let mild annoyance color my tone, though I feel more like shouting accusations. "Why was I not informed about this change of plans?"

Devyn moves to the chair facing me and sits down before answering, a delay that's not *quite* disrespectful, though it comes close. Giving himself time to think?

"After we spoke yesterday, I was made aware of an incident that convinced me waiting would be unwise," he cautiously replies. "Is it true, Excellency, that your sister summoned you to her lodgings yesterday, where she directly threatened you?"

I turn a questioning frown on Connor, who immediately looks guilty.

"I, ah, may have related what she said to you as we were leaving," he admits. "I felt Devyn should know the potential danger she poses to you."

Everything M said yesterday was to convince Devyn and Alban they'd succeeded in turning us against each other, but it apparently worked *too* well—and backfired. All I can do now is continue playing my part, at least until I get more details.

"My sister was understandably angry after Mayor Alban told her I was conspiring against her—something else I didn't expect and never agreed to. Did you authorize him to do that?"

Rather to my surprise, Devyn nods. "I thought it prudent to discover how violently Emileia would react to such news—which she should have had no reason to suspect before Alban's visit, if what you've told me is true. As I feared, she was only too eager to believe him. You've claimed your sister has no love for power, but you saw how quick she was to assert it, to put you in your place. Given her stated intention of discrediting you, I thought it unwise to let her leave Fiarway. Her authority still exceeds yours, making your ability to have her involuntarily committed in Dun Cloch uncertain. Should she return to Jewel, she would likely have more than enough support to move against you. Surely you don't wish that any more than I do?"

"No," I admit, thinking furiously, "but you should have informed me first. I was very worried last night, not knowing why Rigel Stuart disappeared early on, or where Emileia was being taken after the dinner."

"For that I do apologize, Excellency. In retrospect, I suppose my message to you last night could have been clearer."

I nearly roll my eyes at that understatement. "Yes, it certainly could have. You might at least have confirmed that both she and Rigel Stuart are still safe. Unless they're not?" I add some "push" to that question, needing a completely truthful answer.

"Of course they are, Princess, perfectly safe. You were quite clear they mustn't be harmed."

Devyn *seems* sincere, but I know better than to take anything he says at face value. Tristan silently agrees.

"If I discover they were—" I begin warningly.

"You would be well within your rights to not only end our association, but to take action against me. I'm fully aware of that, Excellency," he assures me. "It is no more to my advantage to betray your trust than it would be to yours to betray mine."

Ah, he's getting tricky now, Tristan thinks to me. *Try to pin him down, get more specifics. Then maybe we can still have him arrested before he leaves here.*

"So what exactly did happen last night?" I ask, earning Tristan's silent approval. "Mayor Alban told me this morning my sister had a mental break, but it looked to me like he said or did something after dinner that upset her—enough to justify having her taken away. He also told us Rigel Stuart left her side willingly, which I find hard to believe. If you and I are going to trust each other, let's start with some honesty right now."

If Devyn is startled by my directness, he covers it quickly. "Very well," he replies after only the slightest hesitation. "Once it became clear our original plan of letting your sister leave Fiarway was untenable, we had to put another in place quickly, which is why you weren't informed ahead of time. I feared you might become concerned enough about her safety to warn her, which would have risked endangering us all. Alban and I arranged to have Rigel Stuart removed before he and the Sovereign entered the Town Hall. A harmless gas rendered them both unconscious while he was taken away, to avoid any sort of scuffle that could have resulted in injury."

"Taken where? Mayor Alban said my sister is back at the guest residence?"

"Yes," he confirms. "We thought that a safer choice than the local Healing facility, where it would be difficult to prevent her interacting with others. According to Alban, your sister was about to accuse you of treason at the dinner's conclusion. To prevent that, he gave her a mild sedative so she could safely be led away before alarming the other guests."

So much for honesty. I'm *positive* that's not all Alban did!

"While it's true most of Fiarway's residents would prefer to have you as their Sovereign," Devyn continues, "that sentiment is not—yet— universal. Taking your sister to the Healing facility would have risked her enlisting the aid of someone who still supports her. Now, Alban can plausibly claim the Healers feel they can keep her more comfortable at the guest residence."

I frown. "But is she actually a prisoner there?"

"Not the term I would choose, though technically accurate, I suppose, as neither she nor her Bodyguard can leave the building or contact anyone outside it. Again, this is to prevent her from acting against you while we arrange to have you installed as temporary Sovereign."

If he's telling the truth—and it makes enough sense he probably is—it *should* mean M is safe for now. Except for being locked up and completely incommunicado.

"What about Rigel Stuart?" I prompt when he pauses.

Devyn allows himself a slight smile. "He is also safe, comfortable and secure, similarly unable to communicate with anyone."

Except maybe M?

"Here in Fiarway?"

"No, I felt it wiser to have him taken to a location I can more directly monitor and control, outside of town. He was kept unconscious long enough to transfer him to his current lodgings—again, to avoid any sort of struggle that might have risked him being hurt."

He's probably in Devyn's own fortress, then, Tristan silently surmises.

Probably, I agree. *Though I don't see how knowing that helps.*

"Is he awake now?"

Devyn nods. "I'm told he regained consciousness late last night and ate the meal provided him this morning. I really have taken great care to respect your wishes, Princess. You have no reason at all to worry about young Stuart's health or safety...so long as we continue in accord."

Ah. Exactly what I was afraid of! "Surely, Devyn, you didn't mean that to sound like a threat?" I ask with forced mildness.

"A threat?" His brows go up in clearly-feigned surprise. "I prefer to think of it as insurance. Having trusted the wrong people at least once in the past—" he flicks a glance at Connor, who flinches— "I simply wish to minimize the chance of it happening again. In this case, I don't foresee it becoming an issue, as your goals and mine appear to be aligned. You want to ensure your sister gets the help she needs, and I want to ease your transition to Acting Sovereign while she receives treatment."

Drawing on Tristan's persuasive ability as well as my own, I smilingly project the trust and complacency I want Devyn to feel. "When you put it that way, it makes perfect sense. I'm sorry if I sounded suspicious just now."

"No apology necessary, Excellency. Caution is never out of place. Now, if I've set your mind at ease about your earlier concerns, I recommend we discuss our next steps."

Now? Tristan thinks to me then. *If they're both safe where they are, you should call in Kyna's troops! They can arrest Devyn, then rescue M and Rigel.*

It's too risky! I think back. *Even if they're safe right this moment, if those troops show up, Devyn could order Rigel killed before anyone can get to him. M would never, ever forgive me if that happened. And if he has M killed, too, I'd never forgive myself! I need to play along until we're* positive *he can't do that.*

"What do you think I should do first?" I ask, with just enough "push" to convey my complete willingness to be advised.

Devyn smiles, visibly relaxing. "You can begin by taking over your sister's obligations for the rest of today. I had Alban forward her schedule to me."

He pulls out an omni—not a spiffy cellphone-looking one like mine, I'm secretly pleased to see—and brings up a holo-screen, which he angles so I can read it, too.

"This shows her speaking at the school during their lunch hour," I observe. "I don't know what she planned to talk about, though."

"They're children." Devyn shrugs. "I'm sure they'll be happy with anything you say, they'll be so thrilled to have you in their midst."

Thrilled? By me? I can see how a visit by the actual Sovereign might have impressed them, but—

They'll be just as excited to have you there, Tristan silently assures me. *If you're determined to keep playing along, you might as well do it right. Hopefully it'll only be for a day or two.*

"Should I also attend that meeting with the planning commission this afternoon?"

"Of course." Devyn goes on to suggest several other meetings and appearances I can schedule during the rest of my week in Fiarway, to cement the idea that I'm stepping fully into M's shoes. I ask a few questions, always deferring to his judgment on any particulars.

Fifteen minutes later, satisfied that I'm prepared to follow his advice going forward, he gets up to leave.

"You're expected at the school in less than an hour, Excellency, so I'll let you prepare for your first speech as Acting Sovereign. Alban should shortly be releasing a statement on your sister's condition, which will explain why you're taking over her duties. If you'd like, we can speak again this evening. We still have several issues to resolve before you return to Jewel."

"Um, about that. My sister will be expected back at school after spring break—by the *Duchas,* anyway. What excuse will we give if she doesn't show up?" I don't have to fake looking worried—I *really* hope I can drop this charade sooner than that!

His smile is supremely confident. "Leave that to me, Princess. I already have a strategy in mind, which I'll explain when we talk next." He bows to me, takes a step toward the door, then turns back.

"One other thing. It's possible that when word of Alban's statement spreads beyond Fiarway, you'll receive conflicting, if well-meaning, advice from various quarters, to include the *Echtran* Council. I recommend you agree to nothing without first consulting me. That is, if you want to ensure the continued well-being of young Stuart...and your sister."

26

HIARMARTI

(hee-ehr-MAHR-tee): consequences; results; price to be paid

M

Other than a slight headache, I feel fine—physically—when I wake up the next morning. Of course, the very first thing I do, even before getting out of bed, is reach out mentally to Rigel.

Are you awake yet? How did you sleep?

To my great relief, his reply comes immediately. I didn't dream last night's conversation after all!

I've been awake for nearly two hours, sleepyhead, but I slept pretty well. Guess you did, too?

Obviously. Without my omni, I have no idea what time it is. *What have you been doing since you woke up? Did they give you breakfast, I hope?*

He assures me they fed him, even if oatmeal and coffee weren't what he'd have ordered if given a choice. *My first time drinking coffee, believe it or not. I'm not a fan, but I think the caffeine gave me a brain boost. I've been pretty busy.*

Doing what?

Rigel describes the room he's in, which he's now thoroughly explored. *It's worlds better than that death-row cinderblock cell in Dun Cloch that Lennox stuck me in,* he adds.

I shudder at the reminder. Until he finally answered me last night, all I could think about was that horrible time I came terrifyingly close to losing him forever.

220

Did I mention this place has an actual bathroom, complete with Martian shower and toilet? I expected to find a security camera on me, but there's no sign of one, just a speaker over the door. Seems to be for broadcasting orders and general announcements, though, not monitoring this room. I've poked around inside it and think I can rig it to listen in to all the other speakers in the complex. That would let me learn a whole lot I can pass along to you.

Wow, you have been busy! I think back, impressed. *Maybe you should drink coffee more often.*

While I'm here, anyway. The amusement accompanying his thought reassures me he's not becoming despondent—yet. *Otherwise, yuck. What's happening at your end? Though I guess you don't know yet, since you just woke up?*

He's right, I don't—but I need to find out. I suggest he go back to tinkering while I get dressed, eat breakfast and try to discover what explanation people are being given for whatever happened at the end of last night's dinner. Molly's probably worried sick about me, but even if I could contact her, I wouldn't know what to say until I learn more—if I can.

Stretching, I get out of bed and head to the bathroom, then throw on a pair of jeans and a turtleneck. As far as I know, nobody's here I need to impress, so I might as well be comfortable.

Cormac and Morag are waiting in the sitting room. At my appearance, Cormac bows and Morag jumps up from a chair and hurries toward me.

"Excellency! We were becoming concerned, but didn't wish to wake you if you were still asleep. How are you feeling this morning?" She seems as genuinely solicitous as she was last night.

"I'm fine," I tell them both. "What time is it?"

Morag points to the vidscreen, where the time is displayed in one corner, something I didn't notice when I still had my omni.

"Oh, wow, it's already ten-thirty? I'm sorry! I hope you didn't wait on me for breakfast?"

Their expressions answer me even before Cormac says, "We did, Excellency, but I took the liberty of making a full security sweep, and a more determined effort to force an exit from the building, though again without success."

"Thanks for trying, at least. As for breakfast, let's take care of that right now. The recombinator's still fully stocked, right?" Morag nods. "Good. At least this prison is well-provisioned. Come on."

They both seem rather taken aback by my perkiness—no wonder, since they have no idea I began the day "chatting" with Rigel. Just knowing he's alive and unharmed is enough to boost my mood.

When we reach the breakfast room, I ask Cormac to please deactivate the new bug Alban planted yesterday. "If he wants to know what I'm up to today, he'll have to come here in person," I add, in case the things are still working with this comm block in place. I hope he does show up. Not only am I eager for any news, I have a few choice things I'd like to say to his face.

While Cormac complies, Morag disappears into the kitchen. She returns a few minutes later, not with one of those little menu tablets, but a steaming platter of eggs, bacon, hash browns, scones and jam. Cormac helps her set it all out, then she hurries back to the kitchen for a big pot of tea...and three cups.

"I, ah, thought perhaps we could all use a proper breakfast, Excellency, if that is all right?"

I grin at her. "An excellent idea. I'm glad to see you loosening up a little, Morag. Please, have a seat."

Smiling shyly in return, she cautiously sits down.

As the three of us polish off our hearty breakfasts in near silence, I mentally reach out for Rigel again. Now that my initial surge of relief has faded, my anxiety for him is creeping back.

Everything still okay there? I send while shoveling more eggs into my mouth.

A full minute passes, long enough to worry me, before his reply comes through.

Yes, sorry. I was in the middle of something kind of fiddly. Without tools I've had to get a little creative, but I just finished rigging my speaker to monitor sound complex-wide. Next I'll tinker with the vidscreen. I'd love to hack into the master controls for this place, but I'm sure it's got all kinds of firewalls in place to prevent access.

Beyond impressed, I suppress a smile. *All I've accomplished is breakfast. Oh, and prying Morag out of her prickly shell. She's acting almost friendly now that we're all locked in here together. I guess nobody warned her this could happen.*

We chat for another couple of minutes, then I encourage Rigel to get back to work. If he can figure a way to hack into Devyn's computer system, we'd have tons of info to share with the Council and *Echtran* security. Assuming, of course, we both escape from Fiarway alive.

Unfortunately, our odds of that start looking worse a few minutes after I return to my suite. I'm suggesting to Cormac that we should try forcing one of the downstairs windows, when the parlor vidscreen lights up with a priority announcement from Mayor Alban.

"Huh," I comment. "So signals can get *into* this house, just not out?"

Cormac reminds me that's how the comm block worked when I put Devyn, Mr. O and Nels Murdoch under house arrest in the Royal Palace in Nuath. The same was true for Allister and Lennox in Dun Cloch, now that I think of it.

"Shall I—?" Cormac asks, gesturing toward the screen.

I nod and he clicks to activate it. A second later, Alban's face appears, looking grave.

"By now, most of you have probably heard about Sovereign Emileia's near-collapse during last night's official dinner in our Town Hall. I have now spoken at length with the Healers attending her. It appears she suffered some sort of mental break, but I am assured that she is receiving the care necessary to stabilize her condition until she can be transferred to our top Mind Healing facility in Dun Cloch. At this time, it is unknown whether, with sufficient treatment, she will one day recover to the point she can resume her position and duties as Sovereign. Fortunately, Princess Malena has agreed to fulfill the Sovereign's ongoing obligations while her sister is incapacitated. Be sure to thank her, should you see her about town during the remainder of her visit here. Meanwhile, all of our thoughts and prayers are with Sovereign Emileia, as she begins her long journey back to full health."

The screen goes blank and I look over at the others. "Well. Isn't that interesting? Do you suppose those Healers somehow snuck in during the night, examined me, and snuck back out?"

Morag looks shocked, but Cormac chuckles. "That's clearly not possible, Excellency. However, it does make me wonder whether the mayor intended for you to see this broadcast, which I assume was sent to everyone in Fiarway."

"He may not care," I reply. "Why would it matter, if we're never allowed to talk to anyone again?"

My words produce a sharp spike of fear from Morag. "N-never, Excellency?" she stammers.

"I'm sorry, Morag, I don't know what he intends to do with us. Maybe he just wants me kept out of the way while they set my sister up to take my place—here in town, anyway. How they'll convince everyone, everywhere, to accept that, I have no clue. I'm sure they have a plan, though."

I wonder how much of that plan Molly's aware of at this point? Whatever it is, I expect she'll pretend to go along with it if she thinks it'll keep me—and Rigel—safe. Since we both thought Devyn would wait till I left Fiarway to make his move, she's probably playing things by ear now. Stupid of us to have trusted him even that much, I realize in retrospect.

Going to the vidscreen myself, I bring up the interactive panel to see if I can send anything out this way, like I did with the message I sent Molly yesterday. I can't. All I get are error messages. Ah, well.

"Let's see if any of the windows will open," I suggest to Cormac. "Shouting for help might not be very regal, but if it works..."

We go from window to window through the whole house, but none of them will budge. Morag helps, too. In fact, she suggests trying to break one, apparently still spooked by the idea of being trapped here long term...or worse.

Unfortunately, that doesn't work, either. Whatever the windows are made of, nothing we hit them with seems to have the least effect.

"I guess there's nothing for us to do but wait," I finally tell the others. "Feel free to read or something, to pass the time."

Without my omni, I can't access my backlog of waiting petitions to work on, so I take my own advice and open my book scroll. Instead of fiction, though, I start researching the definitions and penalties for treason. Might as well be prepared if I ever get out of this.

A slow hour passes, during which I keep wondering what Molly's doing. I was supposed to give a talk at the school today. Is she doing that in my place? What about my visit to the planning commission, to discuss future influxes of immigrants during the next few launch windows? I'd planned to go straight from that meeting to Denver to catch my flight out tonight...which I'm obviously going to miss. Has Molly told Kyna what happened? I wish I knew!

Twice, I get brief updates from Rigel. He hasn't yet figured out how to hack into the fortress's computers but has managed to disable the lock on his door. He doesn't dare venture out, though, in case Devyn's guards have been told to shoot him on sight. By eavesdropping through the sound system, he learned Devyn himself left the place for a little over an hour. To meet with Molly? If so, I doubt she'd dare call in Kyna's troops with Rigel and me both being held hostage.

"It's past lunchtime. Let's go downstairs and get something to eat," I finally suggest. I'm not very hungry after that big breakfast, but it's something to do.

We're halfway down the grand staircase when the doorbell chimes.

Cormac's eyebrows go up and he hurries down to the door—which still won't open.

"Some concerned Fiarway citizen might be bringing a casserole or something," I theorize. "Maybe whoever it is will call for help when we don't answer."

But then the door opens from the other side and Mayor Alban steps through, flanked by two burly men—obviously bodyguards. I immediately give Rigel a mental heads-up, so he can listen in.

"Ah, Excellency!" Clearly startled to find me almost in his face, Alban sketches a quick bow. "I'm, ah, delighted to find you looking so recovered."

"From whatever drug you gave me last night? Yes, I'm fine today. As I'm sure you knew I would be," I reply acidly. "I found your explanation for what happened...interesting."

He blinks. "Oh, then you—?"

"Yes, I saw your broadcast. Wasn't I supposed to?" As he flounders for an answer, I give him a mocking smile. "But where are my manners? We were just about to have our midday meal. Won't you join us?"

Alban darts a furtive look at each of his hovering goons, then at Cormac. Apparently reassured by the odds, he forces an answering smile.

"That's, er, very kind of you, Excellency, under the circumstances."

"Circumstances I'd like you to explain to me while we eat."

Again he hesitates, then nods. "Of...of course, Excellency. Please don't think... That is..."

I motion him toward the breakfast room and he stops his stammering long enough to scurry past me with another respectful nod. He seats himself in the same chair he sat in at breakfast yesterday, his two security guys standing at attention behind him. I take my time sitting opposite him. I'm enjoying his discomfort more than I probably should, but I'm not feeling especially charitable toward him just now.

In response to Morag's questioning look, I ask her to bring out two orders of salad and mac and cheese, then turn to look squarely at Alban.

"Now. Suppose you tell me what's going on? Why am I being held prisoner, under what appears to be a complete communications embargo? Most would consider what you've done to your Sovereign treason. Is there any reason I shouldn't?"

Alban swallows convulsively a few times before answering. "Please believe me, Excellency, everything that has occurred since yesterday afternoon was decreed by Princess Malena. I argued most strenuously against it!"

I regard him narrowly. "You're claiming my *sister* ordered me imprisoned here and cut off from anyone I could have contacted for help?"

"I, er, yes. I did warn you yesterday, Excellency, that she's being heavily influenced by Connor Roark and his son, both of whom have always been extremely ambitious. I assumed you would take precautions, but instead I understand you deliberately antagonized, even threatened her? After witnessing that, Connor and his son no doubt found it easy to persuade her such extreme measures were justified."

"You still maintain Devyn Kane has no hand in this?"

"I...ah...he and Connor are still rather close, so it's *possible* he has contacted your sister to offer advice, though of course I have no personal knowledge of that."

Though I'm fully aware Alban is in this thing up to his neck, the less he suspects I know, the better. "What about Rigel? You promised me at dinner last night he was safe. Can you confirm that? Do you know where he was taken?"

Again, the mayor hesitates. "Not...precisely. I did ask your sister, knowing you were likely to inquire about him, but she would only say he's being securely detained outside of Fiarway."

"So you haven't even made sure he's still alive?" I add a little sob at the end of my question.

The more frantic I seem about Rigel, the less likely Alban—or

Devyn—will suspect he and I are already in contact, which alone could be enough to get him killed.

The mayor's expression becomes convincingly sympathetic, though that's *not* what I sense from him. "I...I'm certain he is, Excellency. You sister assured me—"

"But you don't *know!*" I cry. "Since you've made sure I can't call Malena myself, you can be the one to tell her I *demand* to talk to Rigel. Today!"

"I...I don't—"

Again, I cut him off. "You claim you're not complicit in this plot against me, but *you're* the one who drugged me last night so I could be locked up here."

"No, no, that was also your sister!" he insists, his alarm spiking again. "She told me that ampule contained something to negate the physical symptoms you and young Stuart apparently suffer when you're apart for any length of time. I believed her."

Wow, they've come up with plausible explanations for everything, Rigel comments from six miles away. *If Molly really did authorize this, she probably* would *have told them to give you that antidote—not that they'd have any in Fiarway.*

They could have lied to her about that, I think back, though I can't believe Molly actually okayed this.

"Aren't you still the mayor here?" I demand of Alban before my silence can become noticeable. "You know full well my sister is committing treason, so why haven't you had her arrested? Yesterday you said I could count on your security force, if needed."

"Yes...well...I, ah, may have been mistaken about that," he admits, shrugging apologetically. "While I was aware of your sister's popularity in Fiarway, largely thanks to Connor Roark, I had no idea her influence had extended into my own inner circle. More than half the town is now convinced you really are dangerous, a belief your sister has encouraged since arriving here. Much as it pains me to say so, Excellency, beyond your little speech in the square Saturday, your own actions have done little to dispel that notion."

He's right, I realize. All the stuff I said to Molly at lunch yesterday— for Alban's and Devyn's benefit—did just the opposite. My goal was to convince them they'd succeeded in turning us against each other, so they'd completely buy into Molly's pretense. But by hurling accusations and threats at her, I foolishly played right into their hands.

Assuming everything I said to Molly yesterday was recorded, they can totally use my words against me. Not just to demonstrate I'm unfit to be Sovereign, but to keep Rigel and me apart...permanently.

27

DHUALGIS CUMANN

(doo-AHL-gus koo-MAHN): benevolent duty; royal obligation

Molly

The second Devyn is out of the house, Connor again congratulates me on how well I handled the interview.

"I must say, Princess, I was quite impressed by the insightful nature of your questions. I hope the answers you received were sufficient for now, and that you are reassured you may trust Devyn—and myself—to advise you going forward?"

"Yes," I lie. "I'm much more convinced now we're doing the right thing. I just hope the Mind Healers really can help my sister get better. I…I miss the person she used to be."

Again with the fatherly smile. "I'm sure they will—eventually. Please try not to worry about her, Princess. Both Alban and Devyn assured us—"

Just then, the living room vidscreen lights up, announcing an emergency broadcast from Mayor Alban. Connor hastily activates the screen.

I listen, appalled, as the mayor solemnly informs Fiarway's residents that M is so mentally unstable she'll be shipped off to the Mind Healing facility in Dun Cloch. Then he not only implies she might never recover, he tells everyone how grateful they should be that I've agreed to take over all her duties, effective immediately.

Yikes! I think to Tristan in a panic. *It sounds like their coup is already a done deal!*

229

Connor, meanwhile, is smiling. "There now, Princess. I'm sure it's a relief to know your sister will receive the very best care. I must agree with the mayor that our people are exceedingly lucky to have you. Particularly in a situation such as this, which no one could have foreseen."

Because this whole situation was created by Devyn and Alban! I silently fume to Tristan. *I'm going to make sure they're both charged with treason if we can get M and Rigel safely out of this mess!*

Agreed, he sends back. *But meanwhile...*

I have to keep playing along. I know. Ugh.

My only response to Connor is a tight smile, though I feel more like yelling at him for being okay with all this. Turning away before I give into the temptation to say what I think, I head for the stairs.

"I'm going to get ready for that school thing," I say over my shoulder. "Let's plan to leave in twenty minutes."

Upstairs, I shut myself into Connor's master bedroom, telling Sorcha and Gilda I need a few minutes alone. Activating my noise-canceling app, I call Kyna. To my dismay, it goes to voice mail. Rather than leave a message, I disconnect, wondering how long I should wait before trying again. Before I can decide, she calls me back.

"I apologize for not answering immediately, Princess. I was forwarded the broadcast Fiarway's mayor made a few minutes ago and thought I should watch it before speaking with you. Have you seen it?"

"Yes, that's why I was calling. You're someplace private, right?"

She assures me she is, then says, "Based on what you told me last night, I assume you place no more faith in Mayor Alban's assessment of your sister's condition than I do?"

"No. In fact, I seriously doubt a Healer has even seen her. Devyn came here in person less than an hour ago, claiming he only broke his promise to wait until M and Rigel left town because M threatened me yesterday. She did, but only because we knew they were listening to our whole conversation."

I explain how I'd told them both that M was still suffering after-effects from spending time in Faxon's memories and needed more Mind Healing treatment to recover. "That seemed like my most believable excuse for wanting to take her place, but now they're using it against her."

"So it appears," Kyna agrees. "Where is the Sovereign now, if not at a Healing facility?"

"According to both Alban and Devyn, back at the VIP guesthouse. But now she's locked in, and blocked from making or receiving calls."

Kyna's silent for a second, then asks, "Why did you not have had Devyn apprehended while he was at Connor's home?"

Seriously? "Because I didn't want to risk him ordering M or Rigel killed!" I refrain from adding, *duh.* "He swore they're both still safe, but made it clear they'll only stay that way if I follow his advice and take over as Sovereign."

Again there's a pause before she responds. "Hm. Did he say where Rigel Stuart is being held? Not with the Sovereign, I assume."

"We think he's in Devyn's fortress outside Fiarway, though he didn't directly tell us that. Devyn did imply that if he himself felt at all threatened, Rigel would pay the price. Maybe M, too. As long as he controls if they live or die, I can't think of anything to do but keep playing along, pretending I want to be Sovereign. Unless you have another idea?"

I hold my breath, waiting for her answer. Kyna's really smart, smarter than me or even M...though I'm half-tempted to ask why she ever gave M the okay for this awful plan.

"I'm afraid I don't," she replies after a moment, much to my disappointment. "However, if Mayor Alban does send the Sovereign to Dun Cloch, as he indicated, we can intervene there to free her."

"Unless Devyn's still holding Rigel hostage, which he probably will be," I remind her. "Anyway, I'd better go. Devyn has me taking over M's appointments as part of his plan, and I need to get ready for the first one. Oh, um, do you think you could hold off telling the rest of the Council what's actually going on? Especially my mum?"

Kyna's voice holds a faint trace of amusement when she responds. "I understand your concern, but everyone's sure to hear about Alban's broadcast by the end of the day. The Council will need to be told something. I'll consider how best to explain. Keep me apprised of any further developments, and I'll attempt to come up with an alternative strategy for you. Whatever happens, do please take care, Princess. Our people absolutely cannot afford to lose both you and the Sovereign."

"I will," I promise, trying not to even think about that. "Thanks, Kyna."

Deactivating my silencing app, I open the bedroom door so Sorcha can put the finishing touches on my appearance before we leave.

A few minutes later, Connor drives me to the school to give my talk, which I haven't even had time to think about, much less plan and rehearse. I hope I don't crash and burn.

You won't, Tristan thinks to me. *You've always been great at coming up with stuff on the fly.*

Never with this much on the line.

Connor parks in front of the school and we follow him into the building, where we're greeted by the principal.

"Thank you for coming, Princess. I've informed the students you will be speaking to them in place of your sister." She gives me the requisite bow, her smile tinged with worry. "Please accept my sympathy. I'm sure you must be very upset over the Sovereign's apparent relapse."

"Yes, I am." I don't have to fake my distress. "I very much hope this will turn out to be just a temporary setback for her, but it's too soon to know."

With an understanding nod, she escorts me to the lunchroom, where over fifty elementary and middle school students are assembled. The principal hands me a tiny mic-button, which I stick to my neckline as I walk to the front of the room.

"Hello, everyone." I'm startled by the magnified volume of my voice and remember M saying she also had to get used to that. "I won't keep you from your meal for long, but I'm glad to have this chance to see all your bright, young faces. You give me hope for the future of our people, no matter what challenges we may face as we work to make this world a better one, for both *Echtrans* and *Duchas.*

"You may not have had many chances to interact with the *Duchas* yet, but I've found most of them are well worth befriending. I'd never spent time around them, either, so I was pretty nervous when I first moved to Jewel a year and a half ago. Soon, though, I realized they're not that different from us, even if we enjoy a few natural abilities they lack. On school days, I actually spend more time around them than I do with *Echtrans,* and they're not scary at all.

"As I expect you all know, more and more of our people will be coming to Earth from Mars over the next few decades, to lessen the strain on Nuath's power. Our few all-*Echtran* communities aren't big enough to house everyone, so a substantial number of us will need to live in *Duchas* towns and cities. Among your other studies—" I glance over at the half-dozen teachers standing along one wall— "I hope you'll receive lessons on both what to expect and what will be expected of you if your family is asked to relocate to, say, the Denver suburbs or somewhere similar.

"I'm sure your teachers would like me to tell you to apply yourselves to your schoolwork, and you should, but I also encourage you to enjoy this time of your lives. These school years pass all too quickly, but the friendships you make now can last your whole lives. And friendships, I've learned, can carry you through just about anything. Treasure them.

"You've been a lovely audience—thank you for listening so attentively! Now, I'll let you get on with your lunch period and wish you a wonderful day."

At a signal from the principal, the whole student body rises to its feet and bows to me.

"*Faoda byo Banfriansa Malena!*" they exclaim in near-unison, something they must have been made to rehearse ahead of time.

I'm relieved they kept the *Banfriansa* (Princess) at least, unlike those few in the crowd Saturday morning who substituted *Thiarna* (Sovereign). I probably wouldn't have been able to stop myself from correcting them, even knowing Devyn might have spies here.

Smiling, I do the head-incline thing and move toward the exit, where Tristan and Connor are waiting. Along the way, I give the mic-button back to the principal, who follows us out into the hall.

"Thank you so much, Princess! You set the perfect tone. These children will now have a story they can tell for the rest of their lives. Please extend my well wishes to your sister when you're able to speak with her."

I promise I will, determined to convince Devyn to let me do that. Soon!

On the way back to Connor's for lunch before my—M's—two o'clock meeting with Fiarway's Planning Commission, I check my omni and see a missed call from my mum. Ugh. I'd rather not talk to her right now, but might as well get it over.

When we get to the house, I excuse myself upstairs so I can return her call without anyone—except Tristan—listening in. She answers immediately.

"Hi, Mum. I'm guessing you heard—?"

"Yes, I did!" she breaks in excitedly. "I do hope Emileia is all right? Needless to say, the entire Council is concerned about her." At least she's not gloating, though I suspect that's coming.

I'm reluctant to tell her what really happened, remembering how chummy Mum and Dad were with Connor last weekend. She'd either be scared to death or put even more pressure on me. Maybe both.

"So am I," I reply. "The Healers haven't let me talk to her yet, but I hope to soon. Tomorrow, at the latest."

"Meanwhile, I suppose you'll need to assume a bit more responsibility?" she asks then, just like I knew she would. "It sounds as though Emileia may not be able to resume her duties for some time. Do you happen to know whether she and Rigel were able to locate Devyn Kane before her collapse?"

I decide it's safest to be cagey about that, too. "I was going to ask her during last night's dinner, but we were seated at opposite ends of a really long table and I never got a chance before—"

"Before she collapsed? The mayor did say that's when it happened. Such a pity. I'm sure you're upset Molly, but you mustn't let this opportunity go to waste. While I of course hope for Emileia's full recovery, this is a chance for you to demonstrate your own leadership abilities. I'm sure Connor and Tristan agree."

"We, um, haven't talked about it yet, but I want to hold off making any big decisions until I see M for myself."

I may have to pretend to Devyn I'm on board with playing Sovereign, but I do *not* want my mum to believe that!

"Yes, well, I suppose it's early days yet. And as I said, we all hope Emileia will soon be herself again. But should it happen she's not—"

"Thanks, Mum. I'll call you tomorrow, okay?" I disconnect before she can press her point any further.

She really does care about you, Tristan assures me from downstairs. *Come have some lunch. That'll make you feel better.*

I'll be down in a minute, I tell him, ignoring the rest of his comment. I'm starting to feel like absolutely everyone, maybe even Tristan, is herding me toward a role I never wanted.

⁺₊

After lunch, Connor drives me back to the Town Hall for my meeting with the Planning Commission. I expect it to be the kind of boring stuff M wants to delegate to Kyna, but it's more interesting than I expect, all about creative ways to accommodate the next influx of immigrants from Mars.

"Assuming they'll again ask families with young children to settle in *Echtran* communities after their Orientations, we wish to be better prepared than we were last summer," Lars, the head of the Commission tells me. "We received numerous—justified—complaints about the temporary lodgings we slapped together for first wave. Those have all been vacated and dismantled now, to be replaced by sturdier, potentially permanent residences in advance of the next launch window."

He points out the areas already set aside for the buildings they intend to erect over the next year—apartments and single-family homes. Uncomfortable as I am being here in M's place, I can't help visualizing the end result. I even make a couple of suggestions, which are gratefully received.

"Thank you so much for your time, Princess," Lars says as we're leaving an hour later. "And for your input on easing the newcomers' acclimation to Colorado's weather, as well. I look forward to sending you photos of the finished project early next year."

I open my mouth to tell him M will be receiving those pictures, not me, then shut it again. Much as I want to insist she'll be resuming her position soon, I don't dare until Devyn's been dealt with.

We've only been back at Connor's for a few minutes when he gets a call from Mayor Alban, asking if he can drop by. Since I have some pointed questions I'd like to ask the mayor myself, I readily agree.

Twenty minutes later, Alban is shown into the living room, where Connor, Tristan and I are having our afternoon tea and biscuits. Bowing elaborately to me, the mayor moves to the chair next to Connor. As before, Gilda and Sorcha are sent upstairs so we can talk privately.

"Thank you again, Excellency, for seeing me," Alban begins, pouring himself a cup of tea. "As promised, I called upon your sister earlier to verify her status with my own eyes."

"Yes? And?" I lean forward eagerly. "How is she?"

Sadness etches his features. Though I'm sure he's faking it, I brace myself.

"I'm sorry to tell you the interview did not...go well. The Sovereign acted even more deranged than I expected, hurling accusations and even threats. She, ah, asked me to relay them to you. I'd prefer not to repeat most of what she said, however, as I'm sure she'll regret those words once she completes the treatment she so obviously needs."

"Can you at least give me the gist of what she said?" I press. He'll probably lie through his teeth, but I need to know what he intends to tell others.

He shifts uncomfortably in his chair. "Er, among other things, she accused you of having young Stuart murdered, then rather graphically described the retribution she intends to inflict upon you. It was...quite horrific to hear."

"Murdered?" My hand, firmly clasped in Tristan's, twitches convulsively. "Does she—? That is, why does she believe he's dead?" *If they really did kill him, I'll help M do every one of those awful things to them!* I fume silently.

I'm sure they didn't. Tristan gives my hand a reassuring squeeze. *I hope.*

"Honestly, Princess, I have no idea." Alban shrugs, hands innocently spread wide. "I repeatedly assured her that he's fine, but she refused to believe me and kept demanding she be allowed to speak with him."

"Can't you let her do that? Surely that would be the quickest way to calm her down?" *Unless...?*

He shakes his head, spiking my worry for Rigel higher. "It simply isn't feasible at this time. I attempted to tell her something might be arranged later, but she was beyond reason. The Healers feel the sooner she can be consigned to a dedicated Mind Healing facility, the better— for her own safety, as well as that of others. I'm terribly sorry, Excellency. I did hope to have better news for you."

Faking a sob, I manage to squeeze out a tear. "I'm sorry, too. Poor Emileia! Is there any chance I can speak with her myself, even remotely?"

The mayor shakes his head with pretended regret. "I strongly advise against it, Princess. Indeed, the Healers have insisted she receive no calls or visitors at this time, as she is so easily provoked to violence. Nor would you wish to hear the things she is saying about you. Indeed, given her current state, she would almost certainly try to do you an injury were you to visit her in person."

"You're *sure* Rigel Stuart is still alive?" I add some "push" to my question this time.

Alban nods, but my relief is short-lived. "I've been given no reason whatsoever to believe otherwise, Excellency. In fact, I've been told he's quite safe."

In other words, he doesn't actually *know*. But M should! At least if Rigel's within a few miles of Fiarway—and conscious.

Keeping my "push" in place, I frown at Alban. "For your sake, I hope what you've been told is true. If either he or my sister are harmed—at all —I will hold both you and Devyn *personally* responsible."

Alban's eyes widen. "I...ah...of course, Excellency. I'll, um, reconfirm with Devyn, but I'm sure—"

"Yes. Do that. And figure out a way for me to see my sister—if not today, then tomorrow. If a personal interview can't be safely arranged, I'll settle for a holographic one. I also want to speak with her Healers. You're free to relay what I've said to Devyn, though I intend to speak with him again myself very soon. He promised to advise me in my role as Acting Sovereign, and if what you tell me is true, I'll need that advice right away."

Thoroughly intimidated now, Alban swallows convulsively and bobs his head. "Of...of course, Excellency," he repeats. "I'll contact him as soon as I leave here."

"Please do," I reply in a more pleasant tone, easing up on my "push." "Thank you for coming, Mayor Alban."

At what's clearly a dismissal, he hastily gets to his feet, regarding me with a lot more respect than he did on arriving. Good. I may have to let Devyn believe he's controlling me, but I'd rather Alban take *my* orders, if push comes to shove.

"I...I give you good day, Excellency," he says, bowing more deeply than when he came in. "Connor, Tristan." With a last, nervous smile, he scurries out of the room.

"Again, I'm impressed, Princess," Connor exclaims when the front door closes. "If I ever doubted whether you have the strength of will necessary to be Sovereign, I do so no longer. Based on everything I've seen today, you'll be at least as strong a leader as your sister was, even at her best."

![28]

CHOMHAERLE

(KOM-ahr-lee): advice; counsel

Molly

"Er, thanks," I respond to Connor.

Alban's visit was upsetting enough, listening to all the awful stuff he said about M and not daring to refute it. Connor's praise comparing me to M—referring to her in the past tense—makes me feel positively sick.

"I think I'll go up to my room until dinner," I tell Tristan with a mute apology. "I...need to do some thinking."

Aware of my turbulent emotions, Tristan nods, his eyes holding nothing but sympathy. "You want things informal again tonight?"

"Please." I attempt a smile for both Tristan and Connor—one I'm sure fails miserably—then make my escape.

Sorcha appears as I reach the upstairs hallway. "Is there anything I can get you, Excellency?" Judging by her worried expression, my distress must still show.

"Another cup of tea, please, but give me a few minutes." With another lame attempt at a smile, I shut myself into Connor's master bedroom and sink onto the bed. *What have I done?*

Though my thought wasn't specifically directed to Tristan, he answers. *You're doing what M asked you to do. I know you don't like hearing it, but Father's right—you were great just now with Alban. He and Devyn need to understand they'll face terrible consequences if they hurt M or Rigel.*

Unless they already have! Why would M assume Rigel's been killed? I ask, desperately needing reassurance.

Either Alban was lying about that, like everything else, or she was putting on an act for him. But you struck just the right tone a few minutes ago, making your wishes clear without directly calling him a liar. He won't dare let Devyn harm them now.

The knot between my shoulders starts to relax. *I hope you're right, but we're nowhere near out of the woods yet.*

You'll get us there, he thinks back. *All of us—you, me, M and Rigel. And get Devyn hauled off for good. You'll see.*

I appreciate his complete confidence in me, but I'm still uneasy. I wish I could verify for myself—*now*—that M and Rigel are still okay.

When a call from Kyna lights up my omni a moment later, I wish it even more fervently. Hastily engaging my silencing app, I answer.

"Princess, I know you asked me to hold off on informing the Council about your sister's plan, but—"

"They're freaking out about Alban's broadcast this morning?" I guess. "I already got a call from my mum."

I decide not to elaborate about how excited she was at the idea of me taking over as Sovereign.

"You could say that," Kyna confirms. "Not surprisingly, they're demanding answers—as will many others, as word spreads. Some explanation will have to be given. Devyn will likely have anticipated this, clever as he is."

Though I hadn't thought about it till now, she's probably right. "What did you tell them?"

"That I have reason to believe Alban exaggerated the matter. I promised to speak with you and also with the Sovereign, if possible, and report back.

I frown, pondering. "I guess you should tell the Council about M's plan," I finally say, "but make it super classified. I definitely don't want to risk anyone leaking it to Devyn."

Kyna agrees sharing the plan is the easiest way to allay their concerns about M's sanity, if not her safety. "As for a more public, official explanation—"

"I'm willing to bet Devyn's already decided what it should be," I realize as I say it. "If he makes me record something, I'll insist it not be broadcast until M's been evaluated by the Mind Healers in Dun Cloch, by which time she should be safe from him."

"A clever strategy, Princess, and one I hope he agrees to. I'll leave it to you to determine when it is safe to have him apprehended."

Feeling slightly more confident we might all get out of this mess alive, I end the call just as Sorcha taps on the door to bring me my tea.

Half an hour later I go back downstairs, only to have Connor inform me Devyn's coming for dinner.

"I assumed that would meet with your approval? You did tell Alban you wished to see Devyn as soon as possible."

I suck in a breath, then nod, girding my loins for the next round in our battle of wits. "Yes, I do. What time will he be here?"

Connor glances at his omni. "Soon, I believe. He indicated he'd like to talk with you before we eat—and possibly afterward, as well. Are you...are you quite sure this is the course you wish to pursue, Excellency?" he adds in sudden concern. "I would hate to think Devyn and Alban are persuading you to do things you'll later regret, much as Devyn did with me last year."

I regard him with surprise. *Did you put him up to this?* I quickly think to Tristan.

Nope, he replies. *This is all him. Kind of glad to hear it, too.*

So am I, inconvenient as it might be right this moment. "I'll try hard not to let them do that," I carefully assure Connor. "But for now this seems like the best way to get my sister the help she needs without letting our people down. Her well-being is still my first concern. I won't let Devyn or Alban make me forget that."

His expression relaxes into a smile. "I'm sure you won't, Princess. You've demonstrated surprising strength of will so far, but given my own experience with Devyn, I felt obliged to put you on your guard."

"I appreciate the reminder," I tell him—and mean it. If Connor is forced to make a choice between Devyn versus M and me, I'm far more confident now he'll come down on our side. I hope.

The doorbell rings a few minutes later, and Devyn is again ushered into the living room. Despite Connor's caution to me just now, he solicitously offers his old friend a drink.

"If you have a red wine open, that would be nice," Devyn replies. Then, bowing to me, he takes the same chair Alban sat in earlier. "I understand you received some less than pleasant news from the mayor, Excellency?"

"Yes," I confirm. "I had no idea my sister's condition had deteriorated so rapidly...if it really has?" I carefully apply just a bit of "push," hoping to force an honest answer without him noticing.

Devyn acknowledges my skepticism with a half smile. "Alban may have exaggerated slightly, but that works to your advantage. The more compromised she's believed to be, the more easily people will accept you as her replacement."

Realizing he's exerting a substantial amount of "push" himself, I pretend to be affected. "Oh. Good point. Then I guess I came down a little harder on Mayor Alban than necessary."

"Yes, he told me you were quite adamant that you would hold both of us accountable should any harm come to your sister or young Stuart. Fortunately, I can readily assure you they are both perfectly fine at the moment."

At the moment? I think to Tristan, tamping down my sudden alarm. In response, he tightens his grip on my hand, sending reassuring vibes my way.

"I very much hope that will remain the case." I allow myself a slight frown. "Surely I've made my feelings on that clear by now?"

"You have," Devyn agrees. "And as we remain in accord, you have no need to worry about them."

Because he's still using "push," I force my expression to relax into complacency. "I'll try not to. You said this morning that my path is clear, but you didn't say much about what that path should be, other than honoring my sister's obligations in Fiarway."

"I hear you carried off both appearances flawlessly," he says approvingly. "Those in attendance were impressed. Well done."

"Thank you," I reply, exuding a gratitude I don't come close to feeling. "But what's next?"

Smiling, he pulls out his omni. "As it happens, I've thought of two steps you can take this evening, the first being a call to *Echtran* Council leader Kyna Nuallan. Unless she's already contacted you?"

Though he's using "push" again to force an honest answer, I have no trouble lying to his face. "She did leave me a message a couple hours ago. I wasn't sure what to tell her, so I haven't returned it yet."

"A wise choice," he says, showing no trace of suspicion. "I suggest you do so now. You can confirm everything Alban said about your sister's condition, and request her assistance in having Emileia transferred to Dun Cloch's Mind Healing facility tomorrow."

Perfect! I think to Tristan, though I pretend to be startled. "So soon? Can't I at least speak with my sister in person before she leaves Fiarway? I'd very much like to form my own opinion of her condition. Not that I don't trust Mayor Alban..."

"A reasonable request," Devyn agrees, surprising me. "I'll arrange for you to visit her tomorrow morning. I'm sure you'll find her removal justified after speaking with her."

I try to decipher his expression, wondering what the catch is, then remember I'm supposedly still under his sway. "Thank you." I smile, again projecting gratitude. "I appreciate that."

He returns my smile, then says, "I recommend you place that call, now, before dinner, as it's two hours later in Washington, DC. Tell her that for everyone's safety, your sister will be sedated for the transfer, as she's shown a tendency to become violent."

"Violent? Really?" I was sure Alban was lying about that.

Devyn lifts a shoulder. "Suggesting the possibility will justify sedating her. We are agreed *you* are the Sovereign our people need right now, are we not? To ensure a smooth transition, it will be best if your sister has no opportunity to oppose it before she can be safely sequestered in Dun Cloch. I have a few trusted allies there who can take over her care—and security—once she arrives."

"Oh." I swallow the bile rising in my throat. "I...I guess that's a good point. As long as she isn't hurt. At all."

"If anything, sedating her will make that much less likely. Now, if you're ready to make that call?" I feel an increase in the "push" he's trying to use on me. "If you allow me to hear her end of the conversation, I'll be better able to advise you going forward."

Under Devyn's watchful eye, I take out my omni, trusting Kyna will realize what's going on after our conversation earlier.

She picks up almost immediately. "Princess?"

"Hello, Kyna," I respond before she can say anything else. "I'm really sorry I didn't return your call sooner. I guess you heard about Mayor Alban's broadcast?"

There's a slight pause at her end before she says, "Yes, I'm afraid I did. I would have called you immediately, but thought you might need time to adjust to such upsetting information before being asked to assume the role of Acting Sovereign. Though if you recall, Emileia herself recommended you for that position earlier this month."

"I know. At the time, I didn't feel prepared for so much responsibility, but now it sounds like I don't have a choice. I guess we may as well make it official, if you think that's best."

"As you say, we haven't much choice if your sister is as irrational as Mayor Alban claimed. Have you been able to speak with her yourself?"

Watching Devyn, I carefully reply, "Not yet. The Healers and Mayor Alban recommended against it, though I hope to visit her tomorrow. I'm told Fiarway only has one Mind Healer and lacks the resources Emileia needs, so the plan is to send her to the big Mind Healing facility in Dun Cloch. Can you arrange that?"

"If that's what you believe is necessary, Princess. When?"

"Sometime tomorrow? Is that possible?"

When Kyna pauses again, I suspect she's moderating her tone so Devyn won't guess this is exactly what we wanted. "Yes, I can have a chartered plane waiting at Denver's private runway by morning."

I happen to know there's already one there—the same plane that brought her strike force here yesterday.

"Thanks, Kyna. I knew I could count on you." Devyn raises his eyebrows then, as a reminder. I give him a tiny nod and add, "The Healers strongly suggest she be sedated for travel. Apparently her behavior has become unpredictable, so they think that will be safer."

Devyn nods approvingly to me, then signals that I should end the call.

Nodding back, I hastily say, "Um, I should probably go. We were just about to have dinner. Let me know once her flight's arranged, okay? Maybe by morning I'll have better news."

"That will be my sincere hope, Princess. Good night."

I disconnect the call and look at Devyn questioningly.

"Very well done, Excellency," he congratulates me with a smile. "I'm sure she perceived nothing beyond sincere concern for your sister."

I force an answering smile. "I *am* concerned about her. Can I really visit her tomorrow?"

"Of course. I'll even come with you as an extra precaution should she threaten you again. By the time we leave her, I'm confident you'll have no more qualms about assuming the role of Sovereign."

Something in his phrasing strikes me as ominous. He clearly has more in mind than just letting me talk to M...but what?

Though dinner is informal—not counting the food tasting Gilda still insists on—it's awkward, at least for me.

Devyn and Connor, by contrast, seem totally at ease, chatting about the "old days"—first on Mars, then after relocating to Earth when Faxon began his reprisals against our *fine*. I remember my dad's rants about all the Royals who left back then, calling them cowards. Good thing he's not here tonight.

While they talk, I carry on a silent conversation with Tristan.

If Kyna outs Devyn once M is safe in Dun Cloch, I'm scared he'll take it out on Rigel. How do we keep him from doing that?

We still have no actual proof Rigel's even alive, he reminds me. *Maybe after dinner you should ask to talk to him? You can say you want to reassure M he's okay when you see her tomorrow.*

Good idea, though I'll bet he comes up with some reason I can't.

Tristan touches my hand reassuringly. *Then we'll both lean on him, hard, until he agrees.*

When dessert is served, there's a lull in Connor and Devyn's conversation. I take that opportunity to speak up.

"Devyn, you and Mayor Alban have both said Rigel Stuart is okay, but is there a chance I can talk to him after dinner? I'd love to be able to reassure my sister he's fine when I see her tomorrow. It sounds like she's super worried about him, which makes sense considering they're *graell-*bonded."

As I expect, Devyn frowns. "That may not be feasible, Excellency. The logistics—"

Grabbing Tristan's hand under the table, I summon a charming smile...and plenty of "push."

"I'm sure *you* can figure out a safe way for me to speak with him. I've always admired your ability to assume control in every situation, including this one. Early on, I wasn't sure becoming Sovereign was a good idea, but you've helped me see it will eventually make everyone happier, including my sister. But this would be a way to make her happy right away."

Though the crease between his brows doesn't completely disappear, Devyn slowly nods. "I appreciate your confidence in me, Princess. I suppose, if it means so much to you, I can reach out to those guarding him to see if young Stuart can speak with you for a moment…though I must again insist on listening to your conversation."

"That'll be fine," I assure him. "I just want to hear his voice, hear him say he's okay, so I can tell my sister tomorrow."

Tristan and I keep our "push" in place as we all return to the living room a few minutes later. "Can we call him now?" I ask as we sit down.

Though Devyn still looks a little conflicted, he pulls out his omni. "Yes, it's me," he says to whoever answers. "Go to the Stuart boy's room and put him on briefly. Princess Malena wishes to be assured of his well-being."

I hear an incredulous-sounding male voice at the other end exclaim, "But you said—"

"Never mind what I said. I'd like to do her this favor. Yes, we can wait."

Devyn smiles over at me and I smile back, emanating trust and gratitude.

Two minutes pass, then three. It's getting harder and harder not to let my anxiety show, when—

"Mol— Er, Princess Malena?" It definitely *sounds* like Rigel's voice.

"Yes, Rigel, it's me. Are you all right? They haven't hurt you?" I dart a glance at Devyn, who appears the very picture of innocence with an I-told-you-so expression.

When Rigel responds, I'm even more sure it's really him. "No. At least not yet. They're even feeding me. Are you and—?"

"Tristan and I are still at Connor's," I interrupt before he can say too much. "Have you—?"

Devyn disconnects the call before I can finish my question. "I'm sorry, Excellency, but I'd prefer not too much information be exchanged just yet. There will be time for that later, once your position is secure."

Too late, I realize I was so relieved to hear Rigel's voice I let up on my "push." Oops.

Same here, Tristan silently admits. *He sounded good, though! Hope you get a chance to tell M tomorrow.*

"Are you satisfied the boy is indeed unharmed?" Devyn asks when I don't respond.

"Yes. Thank you!" I enthuse with "push"-enhanced gratitude. "I am worried he and my sister will both get sick, though, if they're kept apart too long. It's the down side of their *graell* bond. Will Rigel be allowed to join her in Dun Cloch?"

Then it would be totally safe to have Devyn arrested.

"At some point, certainly," he agrees, though with a smile I don't completely trust. "Until then, we can arrange for them to receive the antidote developed for them in Nuath last year."

"How—?" I glance at Connor, assuming that's who told him about that.

But Devyn, apparently guessing my thought, says, "Actually, Princess, it was your father who mentioned the antidote Morag Teague developed for her grandson and Emileia, back in Nuath. Clearly, it works quite well."

That must have been when they all secretly agreed to erase Rigel's memory...and lie to M about it. I felt terribly betrayed to learn my Dad would do such a thing to M.

Yeah, that was pretty bad, Tristan silently agrees, picking up on my emotion. *But he's mostly redeemed himself since, right? So it's possible.*

Tristan's clearly thinking about his own father.

True, I agree. *But him knowing about that antidote takes away my argument for letting Rigel go—or even keeping him alive,* I think worriedly to Tristan.

You'll convince him anyway, Tristan confidently responds. *I'll help.*

"Now, with that matter settled," Devyn continues when I don't reply, "there is one more thing I'd like to accomplish this evening."

With an effort, I refocus my attention. "Oh? What's that?"

"I'd like you to record a brief statement, to be broadcast via MARSTAR once your sister is securely situated in Dun Cloch. To save you the trouble, I've taken the liberty of composing a script you can read." He taps a button on his omni and a holographic teleprompter appears. "Let me know when you're ready and I'll begin recording."

I look over the displayed text, increasingly appalled as I read through to the end. No way I'm recording something like this!

"'Dangerously insane?'" I repeat, pointing. "That's...pretty extreme. Anyway, shouldn't this wait until after Dun Cloch's Healers really have had a chance to evaluate my sister?" Before that can happen, M, at least, should be totally safe.

"Their evaluation hardly matters," Devyn replies with an unpleasant smile, "though I've been assured it will reflect whatever I suggest. The point is to make your claim to leadership unassailable, which this will."

As he speaks, he intensifies his push to the point I feel an instant's temptation to capitulate before shaking it off. If I argue any more now, he might suspect I've been resistant to it all along. Swallowing, I force myself to nod.

"Okay. I'm ready."

Touching the record command, Devyn signals me to start. Reminding myself these awful words will never be broadcast anyway, I face the camera and start reading.

"Hello, everyone. I'm sorry to say I have some very distressing information to share with you. Many of you are likely aware by now of the broadcast Mayor Alban of Fiarway made on Monday, about my sister Emileia's unexpected health incident. As promised, she was sent to Dun Cloch to be thoroughly evaluated by our top Mind Healers, who have now determined she has suffered a near-complete mental breakdown. I was allowed to visit her briefly before she left Fiarway and can confirm her condition was far worse than I'd hoped. Mayor Alban admits he was intentionally vague in his original broadcast, to avoid causing undue worry before tests could be run. Now, unfortunately, it is my unhappy duty to report that the Mind Healers consider Emileia dangerously insane, posing a risk to herself and others. As you may imagine, this news is personally devastating to me. I refuse to give up hope that, with sufficient treatment, my sister will one day be restored to the person I once knew and loved. Until that happy outcome, however, the *Echtran* Council has asked me to take her place as your Sovereign, immediately and for the foreseeable future. I've been assured that, with sufficient guidance, I am well equipped for the role. I must trust they are right. Thank you all for your support, and for your continuing prayers for my sister. Long live Former Sovereign Emileia."

By the time I finish reciting, I'm starting to cry—for real.

"Well done, Excellency," Devyn declares, putting his omni away. "The tears at the end were a nice touch."

His words fill me with such fury I can barely conceal it. *We have* got *to take this monster down!* I silently fume to Tristan.

We will, he promises, his own anger mingling with his sympathy for me. *One step at a time. By tomorrow night, M should be safe. Then we'll get to work on rescuing Rigel. Maybe we'll find out tomorrow M already has a plan.*

Maybe. Even if she does, I have an awful suspicion Devyn still has at least one more trick up his sleeve.

29

EALU

(AY-loo): to break free; escape

M

I'm even less hungry by dinnertime than I was at lunch—one of the early symptoms of Rigel-deprivation—but I go through the motions of eating. Both to reassure Cormac and Morag I'm okay, and to keep up my strength as much as possible. I suspect I'll need it.

Though it's barely seven when we finish dinner, I'm tempted to go straight to bed and put an end to one of the longest, most boring days I've endured since becoming Sovereign. Even those mind-numbing, back-to-back meetings in Nuath were better than this.

Or maybe not. Then, I believed I'd never see Rigel again—or if I did, he wouldn't remember me. At least now we can talk to each other long-distance, secure in our love, if not our future.

Much as I want to believe Molly will make sure we both get out of this alive, we currently have no guarantee. All day, as hour after dreary hour passed with no word from anyone or any idea of what's going on at her end, my faith in her has become harder and harder to cling to.

Everything still okay there? I send to Rigel when I get back upstairs. I shouldn't distract him while he's trying to hack into Devyn's systems, but our sporadic mental conversations have been my only bright spots during this endless afternoon and evening.

Sorry, he replies after a few seconds. *I've been digging deeper and deeper into the vidscreen menus and wanted to back all the way out before answering.*

I'm still making progress, but it's been slow. One of Devyn's goons checks on me every hour or two, so I have to be ready to hide what I'm doing at a moment's notice. Makes what's already tricky even trickier.

I'll let you carry on, then. What you're doing is way more important than anything I can accomplish here—which is basically nothing.

The sympathy I sense from him is tinged with amusement. *I'm sorry you've been bored. When we get out of this, I promise to make it up to you.*

I appreciate he said "when" instead of "if," like it's a sure thing—even if it was only to boost my spirits.

To distract myself from the temptation to keep talking with him, I open my scroll-book to a novel I've been looking forward to reading. That works for maybe half an hour, but then I start losing track of what's on the page, my mind circling back—and back—to everything I should have done differently, starting before we ever left Jewel.

Finally, I give it up and start getting ready for bed. I've just started brushing my teeth when Rigel reaches out to me—the first time today he's initiated contact. *You still awake?*

Yes! I hastily rinse off my toothbrush. *Can you talk more now?*

Yeah. I'm taking a break, since someone's scheduled to check on me soon. Anyway, I think I've done almost all I can from here. Way more than I expected, actually. You want all the details?

I almost laugh out loud at such a silly question. *Of course! Tell me everything.*

He starts listing everything he's accomplished today. As I change into my nightgown and snuggle into bed, I listen attentively.

After rigging his speaker to pick up sounds from all the others, he started listening in on conversations throughout the fortress. From just that, he learned how many total guards Devyn has—eleven—and that they're all armed with Martian energy weapons.

I think a few also have Earth-style rifles— I heard one mention what a pain they are to clean. They work in shifts. Six guys standing guard or patrolling outside during the day and four at night, with someone always monitoring the exterior cameras from inside. I can tap into those now from my vidscreen.

I'm impressed all over again by his hacking skills. *Anything else?*

Kind of a lot, yeah. He goes on to describe how, by degrees, he gained access to nearly all of the complex's internal and external systems.

I was surprised at first there's no camera to keep an eye on me in here, but then

I found out that up until recently, this room belonged to one of Devyn's top guys—Murgh Gall, the mob leader we took out at NuAgra.

Nice of him to say "we," when it was totally me who killed that guy. Rigel tried to stop me.

Apparently he was high enough in the pecking order to rate some special perks—like no cameras and an interactive vidscreen. Most of the other rooms are monitored, but this was apparently the only one empty when they brought me here. Guess they didn't want to take the time to shuffle people around.

Devyn probably didn't warn any of them about it ahead of time in case it didn't work out. He likes to hedge his bets, I comment. *So did you figure out how to control anything from there?*

Yep! So far, I can— Oops, somebody's coming ahead of schedule. Feel free to listen in.

We agreed months ago not to do that without permission, to avoid the embarrassment—and ethical issue—of eavesdropping on other people by accident. Both of us also need a *little* privacy sometimes. Now, though, I maintain my connection with Rigel's mind so I can hear everything he does.

After a series of beeps, there's a click and what sounds like a door opening. "You. Stuart. Princess Malena wants to talk to you."

My heart leaps into my throat, thinking Devyn's trapped Molly in his fortress, too, but then I realize Rigel's been handed a phone or omni. "Mol— Er, Princess Malena?" he says.

"Yes, Rigel, it's me," Molly's voice answers. "Are you all right? They haven't hurt you?"

"No. At least not yet. They're even feeding me. Are you and—?"

Molly interrupts with, "Tristan and I are still at Connor's. Have you —?" Her voice abruptly stops.

"Hello?" Rigel says. "Princess? Molly?" No answer. "I, um, guess she hung up," he tells the man who brought the phone.

The guy just grunts and a second later I hear a door closing and more beeps—locking Rigel back in, I assume.

Okay, that was weird, he thinks to me. *Do you think she managed to swipe Devyn's phone, then got caught?*

I hope not, I respond worriedly. *Maybe she convinced him to let her talk to you, to prove you're still alive? If he was right there, she wouldn't've wanted you to say anything that could tip him off about our plan. He might have grabbed the phone back when she started asking too many questions.*

Rigel admits my theory sounds more likely. *Then she must still be going along with Devyn's plot for her to take your place.*

Pretending to go along, you mean.

He hesitates for a second or two, then replies, *Right. That. Here's hoping, anyway.*

Rather than argue against his doubts, which I've been trying really hard not to share, I return to the previous topic. *You were about to tell me how much you can control from your room now.*

Oh, right. I haven't been able to test most of it yet without risking somebody noticing, but I'm fairly sure I can lock or unlock all the doors in this place remotely, including mine. I also got far enough in to see and edit the work schedules, alert sequences, even the menus. Maybe I should dial myself up a better breakfast for tomorrow, he jokes.

Glad you still have your sense of humor, I reply, smiling, but his next words wipe the smile off my face.

Better to laugh than freak out. Scrolling through their schedules, I found out they expect to reassign this room in a couple days. Trying not to speculate why. Or to give into this headache.

You, too?

Along with mostly losing my appetite, I've also felt the first twinges of that symptom of separation sickness.

Yeah. One reason I wanted to work fast, before my mind starts going fuzzy. I'll drink their nasty coffee again tomorrow, in case it helps me think. Guess we really should have brought along some of that antidote, huh? Just in case?

Not that we had enough warning we'd have known to use it, I remind him. *At least we can talk like this. Together, maybe come up with a plan,* I add, doing my part to look for silver linings.

He sends an extra surge of love my way. *Good point. Anyway, I plan to run a few tests once it's just the night shift on duty. Less likely anyone will notice if I screw something up. I'll let you know in the morning if I've thought of a way to spring myself from this place—though how far I'd get on foot in the middle of the mountains, I'm not sure.*

If you can escape, do it! I tell him. *We can figure out the rest once you're out of danger.*

Rigel free of Devyn's control would be a *huge* weight off my mind. I —mostly—doubt Devyn intends to kill me anytime soon, but if he and Alban actually ship me off to some Mind Healing ward in Dun Cloch, they may see Rigel as nothing but an extraneous detail to be eliminated.

I shudder, but try to keep that fear to myself. The longer Rigel can stay upbeat, the more likely he is to engineer his own escape.

I don't sleep nearly as well as I did the night before. Then, between my massive relief at finally hearing from Rigel and still having traces of that drug in my system, I passed out with a smile, sure everything would be okay. Now, after way too much time to think things through, our prospects don't seem nearly as rosy.

I want desperately to believe Molly's still trying to make our original plan work, but doubts keep creeping in. She must have been awfully persuasive for Devyn to let her talk to Rigel, if that's what happened. A good sign, surely? Unless she overplayed her hand at the end of the call and made Devyn suspicious...

More than once during the night, I remind myself that Molly and Tristan together are scary good at disarming suspicion. They've even used that joint power successfully on cops more than once. It also works on *Echtrans*—Alan at school, as well as on Connor and Alban. Still, I can't help feeling Devyn might present an extra challenge.

After waking up for probably the dozenth time, my mind again teeming with worries, I give up trying to go back to sleep. It's light outside, so I might as well get up. First, though, I reach out for Rigel, touching his mind ever-so-lightly to see if he's still asleep.

He is.

For all I know, he was also up most of the night—though probably more profitably employed than I was. Reining in my impatience for an update, I roll out of bed and head to the bathroom for a pre-breakfast shower.

Pulling on a robe afterward, I open my bedroom door and find Morag and Cormac already in the sitting room.

"You're both up early," I greet them.

"As are you, Excellency," Cormac responds, rising to bow. "I took the liberty of attempting to connect to a newsfeed with the vidscreen, but was unsuccessful."

Morag also bows, then comes forward. "Shall I help you dress before breakfast, Excellency?"

"Sure. Thanks." I motion her into the bedroom.

In hopes it'll give me extra confidence to face another uncertain day, I let her array me in an outfit more appropriate to my station than yesterday's jeans. I forego the tiara, though, which seems a little silly when it's just us here.

I have even less appetite for breakfast than I did for dinner last night, but I ask Morag to make my tea extra-strong. If caffeine helped Rigel to think, maybe it'll do the same for me.

Morag presses me to eat more than tea and a slice of buttered toast, but I shake my head. "Thanks, but I wasn't kidding about needing regular physical contact with Rigel to stay healthy. He's probably not feeling great now, either—wherever he is."

She looks stricken. "I'm sorry if I didn't seem to believe you earlier, Excellency, and for making things more difficult for you. Mayor Alban said—"

"I know. You had no reason to doubt what he told you, when you hadn't even met me. I appreciate you trying to make up for it now."

Her renewed feelings of guilt subside as I smile at her.

Cormac is also watching me with concern, though he doesn't say anything. I wish I could reassure him that Rigel's safe and might even manage to escape today, but I don't dare. Nobody in Fiarway knows about our telepathic range except Molly and Tristan, and it's safest to keep it that way. That is, unless....

No! I refuse to believe they'd betray us like that.

Finishing my tea, I mentally check in on Rigel again. Earlier I could tell he was still deeply asleep, but now he feels much less so.

Are you awake yet? I send, keeping my mental "volume" low in case he's not.

This time he responds right away. *Yes! Sorry if you tried earlier. I didn't fall asleep until sometime after four, but I put the time to good use. I only stopped when I started having trouble focusing.*

I'm glad I let you sleep, then. Give me an update when you get a chance—though maybe have some breakfast and coffee first?

His mental chuckle isn't as strong as last night, but reassures me all the same. *Doubt I can eat much, but okay.*

Neither could I, but I took my tea extra strong. Here's hoping between us we can make something positive happen today, before we get too— You know.

Yeah. I know. Love you, M.

I return the sentiment wholeheartedly, then stand up from the table. "Sorry, I zoned out for a minute. I'm afraid I didn't sleep great."

"Understandable, Excellency." Cormac exudes sympathy. "If there's anything I can do, you need only let me know."

"Thanks, Cormac." I smile my appreciation for his unwavering support. "I will."

Morag also expresses her willingness to help, her sympathy still mingled with guilt. She quickly clears the table and we all go back upstairs—where there's still nothing to do. Fortunately, before I go too stir-crazy, Rigel contacts me again.

I can give you that update now, if you're somewhere it won't be too obvious we're talking.

Since I'm just sitting with my book-scroll trying to read, I eagerly tell him to go ahead. *You said you made progress overnight?*

Even more than I expected. Devyn's internal security isn't nearly as tight as you'd think for a guy that paranoid. Maybe he figures there's not much to worry about here in his own lair, surrounded by obedient minions. He must have a really low opinion of their initiative or intelligence. I hacked so far in, I'm pretty sure I can take control of the whole place with just a few more keystrokes. The timing will be super tricky, though.

Will he ever stop impressing me? Probably not. *Wow, you really were busy! What do you mean about the timing?*

Since Devyn's obviously the smartest guy in the place, it'll be safest to wait till he's not here. Digging into the logs, it looks like whenever he leaves, he transfers the master controls to his first-in-command. If he goes out today, and I have enough warning, I should be able to reroute the controls to my vidscreen without triggering an alert. Any other time it would. Devyn's at least taken that simple precaution.

Though I don't understand the technical aspects of what Rigel's talking about, I totally trust that he does. *Will you know when he leaves? If he does?*

I think so, unless one of his guards happens to check on me right at that moment. Since breakfast, I've been monitoring everyone's whereabouts, but the one person without a tracker is Devyn. Still, assuming they use the same protocol as when he left twice yesterday, I'll be able to tell by what everyone else does. Once I seize control of the system, I'll have to disable a string of automatic safeguards in order, like knocking down a bunch of electronic dominoes—that part could take at least an hour. But then I should be able to escape no problem. The main risk would be Devyn coming back before I finish.

I don't even want to think about that. *I wish I could tell you what's going on in Fiarway right now, but the only news I've seen since they locked us in was that official statement Alban made yesterday. Did you see it?*

Yeah, I figured out how to call up a replay after you told me about it. They're obviously prepping everyone to expect Molly to take over. You told her she could pretend she's afraid of you. Then there was all the stuff you said to her Sunday while they had the place bugged. Maybe you were a little too convincing?

You heard what Alban said when he came here yesterday, right? Apparently I played right into their hands. I guess threatening her wasn't my best idea, even if she knew I didn't mean it.

He's quiet for a second or two, then says, *Even without the bugs, Connor heard it all, which would've made it easy to use it against you afterward. If they took Molly at her word that she really does want you out of the way... I'm scared for you, M. You're a sitting duck locked up in that house!*

I still have Cormac, I remind him. *They took his weapon, of course, but his training included—*

Wait! he interrupts. *They've just started that protocol I mentioned. I think Devyn's about to leave! Gotta go. I'll touch base...after.*

He breaks off our mental connection so he can focus fully on exactly what he needs to do, in what order, to take over Devyn's stronghold.

I pray with all my might he can escape without getting hurt—or worse. Unfortunately that's the only thing I can do...other than wait.

ACHRAHN

(AHK-rahn): confrontation; dispute

Molly

When I come down to breakfast the next morning, I'm unpleasantly surprised to find Devyn already sitting at the dining room table with Tristan and Connor.

"Good morning," I greet him, pretending to be pleasantly surprised, instead. "If I'd known you planned to be here so early, I'd have come down sooner."

"Not to worry, Excellency," Devyn replies, rising to bow to me. "I only arrived a few minutes ago. Tristan was just telling me how pleased he is that you're finally recognizing your true worth."

Tristan nods. "It's taken her a while, after living her whole life thinking she was an Ag. I love how much her confidence has increased since we arrived here. You and my father have been a great help there. Mayor Alban, too."

"Yes, I believe she's now ready to take her rightful place as a leader to our people," Devyn agrees as I move to the chair next to Tristan. "Though of course she'll still need guidance."

"Definitely!" I assure him. "Fortunately, I have the best counselors I could ask for, between you, Connor and Mayor Alban. Not to mention my parents and the whole *Echtran* Council. It's not like I'll be trying to lead all on my own."

While we're talking, Sorcha and Gilda go through the rigamarole of tasting my eggs and hash browns. As soon as my breakfast is on my plate, I start eating—so I can talk silently with Tristan without being obvious.

Is that really all you talked about before I came down?

Mostly. Father did ask for confirmation that M's not in any danger. Seems like he still doesn't totally trust Devyn, probably a good thing. Devyn basically repeated that as long as you follow his advice, M and Rigel will stay perfectly safe. In other words, it's conditional.

I think about that for a moment. *So I have no choice but to play this awful role to the hilt. I sure hope when I see M in person we can come up with a way to keep her from being drugged and shipped off to Dun Cloch without Rigel.*

You two are pretty darned clever when you put your heads together, Tristan reminds me. *I'm sure you'll come up with something. Even if you can't, the worst that'll happen is you become Acting Sovereign until Devyn lets down his guard and Rigel can be rescued. Then you can spring M from Dun Cloch, too.*

What if that takes months? I ask worriedly.

I'm sure it won't. But if it does, our people will be okay with you as Acting Sovereign. You really would be good at it, you know.

Though I appreciate his faith in me, I wonder again if he secretly hopes that'll become necessary.

Devyn stands up as soon as we all finish breakfast. "If you wish to see your sister today, Princess, I suggest we leave soon. My men have confirmed that a chartered plane is already waiting at the private air strip, ready to convey the Sovereign to Dun Cloch. Your Kyna is most efficient."

"She really is," I agree with a smile, wishing I could call in her strike force *now* without risking Rigel's and probably M's lives. "I'll be ready to go in a few minutes."

Upstairs, I excuse myself from Sorcha, again using the bathroom excuse so I can give Kyna the latest on Devyn's plans. I pull out my omni...and see a waiting text from Kyna asking for an update. Quickly engaging my silencing app, I call her.

"I can only talk for a second," I say when she answers. "Devyn's waiting downstairs to finally take me to see M." I go on to tell her about that awful statement he made me record last night, and that he apparently has at least one Mind Healer in Dun Cloch willing to go along with his plot.

"Hm. Clearly security there isn't as tight as we'd like," she observes.

"That being the case, I'll have her flown to Jewel instead, where we can fully ensure her safety."

I let out a cautiously relieved breath at such an easy solution. Except — "What about Rigel, once Devyn realizes M didn't really fly to Dun Cloch? I know M would never willingly sacrifice Rigel's life for her own, or forgive either of us if we let that happen."

"Possibly true," she concedes, "but I *must* put the Sovereign's safety first. If we can neutralize Devyn quickly once the Sovereign is in the air, Rigel's rescue should be a relatively simple matter."

Though I doubt it'll be quite that easy, her confidence is comforting.

"Thanks, Kyna. I'll let you know right away when they take M to the airport."

Emerging from the bathroom, I have Sorcha dress me in an outfit similar to the one I wore yesterday to give my talk to the school. The others are waiting in the foyer when I come back down.

"Connor, why don't you remain here?" Devyn suggests. "From what you've told me, you and the Sovereign did not part on the best of terms."

Clearly relieved, Connor nods. "True. I certainly wouldn't want my presence to aggravate her condition."

"My thoughts exactly. Princess, I believe it would also be best if your *Costanta* and *Chomseireach* stay behind. Too many people arriving unexpectedly at her residence might overly agitate your sister. Tristan can provide any protection you may need, while I will ensure sufficient chaperonage."

Gilda starts to protest, but I give her a little shake of my head and she subsides, frowning.

Devyn turns to Tristan and me with a smile. "Shall we go, then?"

We accompany him outside, where a white SUV with tinted windows is parked at the curb with a burly-looking driver standing next to it. Part of his security team, I'm sure. I wonder if the car is armored.

When we pull up in front of the VIP guesthouse a few minutes later, I see Mayor Alban waiting out front. We all get out, including the driver, and as we approach the door, Alban palms it open without ringing the bell. Not that there'd be much point, if M is locked in.

The five of us have barely stepped inside when Cormac appears at the top of the stairs, followed a second later by M and her temporary Handmaid.

"Good morning, Excellency." Devyn's bow is more perfunctory than respectful. "Princess Malena asked me to bring her here. She wished to confirm for herself that you are unharmed before you leave Fiarway. She would also like to speak with you briefly, if you are willing to grant her an interview."

"I suspected you were behind this, Devyn, though Mayor Alban denied it," M replies, looking at one, then the other. Then she shifts her gaze to me, her eyes holding a question. But even if I knew how to answer it, I wouldn't dare with Devyn and Alban standing right here.

Devyn bows again, this time mockingly. "No one has ever questioned your intelligence, Excellency. Only your sanity."

She glares at him for a long moment, then shrugs. "Very well. Come on up, Malena. We can talk in my sitting room."

I take her use of my real name as a signal she's still willing to play along with whatever my plan is—not that I have one! Just a desperate hope that the two of us can somehow stop Devyn from knocking her out, without getting her or Rigel killed.

I start toward the stairs, but Devyn stops me.

"A moment, Princess. To ensure privacy, Excellency, I would prefer that your *Costanta* and *Chomseireach* wait down here for the duration of our visit."

Cormac stiffens, but M nods to him. "You may as well do what he says. I'm sure he and his guard are armed, and you're not. You, too, Morag."

With obvious reluctance, Cormac comes downstairs, M's terrified-looking Handmaid trailing behind. Devyn's goon ushers them both into the ground floor office and shuts them inside.

Devyn smiles up at M. "A wise decision, Excellency." Then, to me, "Perhaps your sister is not quite so irrational as you led us to believe."

"Apparently she still has her lucid moments," I reply, then look at Alban. "Your local Healers agree that Emileia should be committed to a proper Mind Healing facility, correct? You said yourself there's a risk she could become violent."

The mayor nods jerkily, darting a nervous glance up at M. "I, er, yes."

I'm dying to reassure M this is still an act, but for now I need to be as convincing as possible. That may be our—her—only chance.

Still smiling, Devyn turns back to M. "Before we come up, Excellency, you should know that should I feel at all threatened, I can instantly give the order to have Rigel Stuart terminated." He holds up one arm to display an ornate metal wristband. "Merely a precaution, of course."

His tone is conversational, even pleasant, making the threat that much more chilling. So much for M and me somehow getting the drop on Devyn while I'm here!

"Tristan," Devyn continues, "I'd like you to help my man stand guard here while we conduct our interview."

I glance at Tristan, fighting down a stab of panic. "Um, shouldn't he come with us in case the mayor's right and I need protection from my sister?"

"As the Sovereign correctly guessed, I am armed." Devyn pats his front breast pocket. "Should it become necessary, I'm confident I will be able to subdue her. Alban, would you care to join us upstairs?"

"I...ah..." He looks up at M again, then back at Tristan. "I'd prefer to remain here, actually. It will give Tristan and me a chance to, er, catch up."

Devyn's smile becomes sardonic. "Very well. Should I require your assistance, I'll let you know."

Alban swallows, then nods, looking almost sick with relief. I wonder what M has said to him, that he's so afraid of her?

Devyn extends an elbow to me and we proceed up the stairs as M watches us approach impassively, giving no hint of her thoughts. When I'm within a few feet of her, I try reaching out telepathically.

Can you hear me?

She frowns but doesn't answer—and then I notice how pale she is. After two days apart from Rigel, she's probably not feeling great, which is bound to make telepathy even harder for her. I'm trying to think of a plausible reason to touch her when she turns away to lead us down the hall to her suite.

"Devyn let me talk to Rigel last night," I say as we enter her sitting room, hoping to at least cheer her up. "He...he sounded good."

She darts a quick glance at Devyn, then focuses on me. "Good? Alive, you mean? I get why you'd want me to believe that, since you're using Rigel as leverage, but why should I take your word? For all I know, you already had him killed! Mayor Alban told me *you're* the one who ordered Rigel kidnapped and me locked up here."

"What? That's not true!" I respond, aghast. No wonder Alban didn't want to come up here! A frown from Devyn reminds me of my role and I quickly add, "Though maybe I should have, after the way you threatened me. At least without Rigel here, you can't suddenly decide to fry me with a lightning bolt. You've been totally unpredictable ever since you messed around in Faxon's memories."

"I won't let you get away with this, Malena." Her glare looks disturbingly real. "When I tell the Council what you've done, they'll—"

"Why would I let you do that?" I retort. "There's a reason you can't call out of this place."

Beside me, Devyn smirks at M. "You were quite smug, Excellency, when placing *me* under house arrest. Now that the shoe is on the other foot, you know what it feels like. I must thank you for the idea, however."

She turns her glare on him. "I let you off easy, after what you did to Rigel and then *lying* to me about it!"

His smirk still in place, he replies, "You do have a regrettable tendency to put his welfare above that of your people. Just one more way you've proved yourself unfit for leadership. Your sister has now come to realize that as well, though unfortunately not in time to prevent the death caused by your most recent lapse in judgment."

M flinches visibly at the reminder, but rallies quickly—though I can see it's costing her an effort. Without Rigel, she's definitely not at the top of her game.

"Am I supposed to believe you two only started plotting against me a few days ago?" she demands, as though this whole thing wasn't her idea.

In keeping with how I've been spinning things, I assume a sorrowful expression and take a step forward, hoping to get close enough to touch her.

"Up until Faxon escaped, you were a great Sovereign—and a wonderful sister," I assure her. "But spending all that time in his memories affected your sanity more than you realize. You insisted the Mind Healers cured you, but you're not the same person you used to be. It's obvious to me and everyone else you need more time under their care if you're ever again going to be the leader our people require. I'm just trying to make sure you get that help."

"As you can see, Excellency, your sister has only your welfare in mind," Devyn smoothly interjects, stepping between us. "You should be grateful to her for her willingness to assume your duties while you undergo further treatment."

M laughs in his face—a surprisingly genuine-sounding laugh. "Grateful? That she's agreed to help you finally get rid of me, Devyn? It's what you've wanted all along. Why else did you work so hard to keep me from being Acclaimed in the first place?"

"It was clear to me from the start that you were far too young to take on the responsibility of Sovereignship," he replies. "I withdrew my bid for Acclamation to safeguard Nuath from the Grentl, no other reason. My original objections to leaving our leadership in the hands of an Earth-raised teenaged girl still stand. Your sister, at least, is willing to be guided by those older and wiser than she. Nor is she hampered by an inappropriate attachment to a non-Royal. Her presumptive Consort will provoke none of the animosity among our people you've expended so much energy combating. She will therefore be able to devote all of her energies toward leading Martians everywhere into that best future you always claimed to want for them."

M's eyes go unfocused for a second, then she pins her gaze back on Devyn. "Their best future will *never* be achieved under a power-hungry would-be petty tyrant like you!" she declares. "You only want my sister to take my place so you can direct everything yourself, through her. Do you think I don't realize that? I suspected your hand in this thing as soon as Alban tried to separate Rigel and me the night we arrived in Fiarway. Malena, you can't trust him!"

I hesitate. Does this mean she's giving up on the plan? Surely not, when Devyn still holds Rigel's life in his hands? No matter how much I want to drop this terrible pretense, I'm not going to be the one who signs his death warrant!

"Maybe you can't trust him, Emileia," I finally reply, "but Tristan and Connor both believe I can—and I have complete faith in Tristan's judgment. If he thinks I should let Devyn be one of my advisors, I'm more than willing to do that. Just because you've always been prejudiced against him—"

"Now you sound like Connor!" she exclaims. "What have he and Tristan done to you? You say I'm not the same person I used to be, but you're acting *nothing* like the sister I thought I knew! Is Molly O'Gara gone forever, replaced by Sovereign-wannabe Malena? Have you totally forgotten Devyn tried to have you killed just a few months ago, then nearly killed both of us plus the whole Council the very next month? You've obviously been brainwashed!"

I shake my head, though that's exactly what I've allowed Devyn to think. "No, Devyn explained all that! The guy who tried to kill me was crazy, you know that. Devyn didn't send him. And he was never going to kill us with that Ossian Sphere—though he's sorry now he tried to take over by force."

"Sorry? And you believe him, just because he told you so? I thought you were smarter than that." Her tone is so scathing it hurts, even though I'm *almost* sure she's faking it. "The last thing our people need is a stupid Sovereign!"

"That's enough," Devyn snaps. "Princess, it's time to do what we came for."

I look at him in confusion. "What do you mean?"

"You agreed your sister should be sedated for her transfer to Dun Cloch, did you not? Nor did your Council leader object when you told her last night that would be done."

A stab of alarm goes through me. "Now? Here? I thought a Healer—"

"We can't risk her repeating any of what she's just said to anyone else." He pulls a tiny ampule out of an inner pocket of his jacket. "I also see no point in allowing her to hurl more insults our way. She's given us ample proof of how irrational she's become, all of which I've been recording, should any questions later arise." He glances over at the vidscreen on the wall and I see a red light blinking in one corner of it.

Swallowing, I send M a frightened glance. Crap! This charade of ours could be the very thing that proves to the Council she really *should* be committed! Oddly, she doesn't look nearly as worried as I am. In fact, she looks like she's suppressing a smile.

Then Devyn says, "Princess, I believe you should be the one to administer the sedative."

"Me?" I gasp.

He nods. "She may despise you now, but apparently did care for you in the past. That has never been the case with me."

M looks alarmed for a half-second, then defiantly lifts her chin. "If one of you is going to touch me, I'd definitely rather it be Malena—but I guarantee you'll both be sorry for this."

Devyn chuckles. "I rather doubt that, Excellency. Here." He hands me the ampule. "You need only touch the needle to her skin. The effect should be nearly instantaneous, though I recommend you quickly move away from her afterward, to be safe."

I gingerly take the tiny glass phial with its almost microscopic needle at one end—disturbingly like the ampule my would-be assassin tried to use on Tristan in November. Though this one contains a sedative rather than poison, it still represents what Devyn intends to be a one-way trip for M. If he prevails, she'll never be allowed to return to Jewel or her true position.

For one crazy moment, I'm tempted to whirl around and stick Devyn with it instead...before remembering what he said about Rigel. Swallowing, hating what I'm about to do, I hesitatingly approach M.

She just stands there, not even trying to avoid me when I reach for her arm, though with her Taekwondo training, I'm sure she could knock this nasty thing out of my hand if she wanted to. I wish she would! Instead, she remains passive as I grasp her wrist with my left hand.

I'm so sorry, M, I tell her silently as I prepare to stick her with the ampule in my right.

31

CLOIGH

(kloy): to overpower or overthrow; defeat; subdue

M

The moment Molly touches me and silently apologizes, but before she can bring that ampule to bear under Devyn's watchful eye, I mentally send her one, urgent word: *Stall!*

Clearly startled, she blinks—and hesitates. *What?*

Stall! Play for time. Rigel just needs a couple more minutes to get free.

For real? How—?

I'll explain later, or he will. For now, we just need to distract Devyn in case someone tries to contact him before Rigel's completely out of that fortress.

"Princess?" Devyn says from behind Molly. "I realize you weren't expecting to do this yourself, but delaying won't change anything. You may as well get it over with."

Still holding my wrist, she turns to face him. "Are you *sure* this is the only way?" she pleads. "Emileia has proved herself a true hero in the past, several times over, risking herself for the good of our people. What she did to find Faxon was only the most recent example. It's not her fault it ended up breaking her mind."

A flash of impatience crosses Devyn's face before he assumes a sympathetic expression. "All true, Princess. However, you and I have agreed that our people deserve better than a Sovereign with a broken mind. You yourself have repeatedly said you believe she will need additional treatment by Mind Healers to fully recover. As Dun Cloch possesses our best facility for such care, it only makes sense to send her there. The sedative is to ensure her safety, as much as that of everyone else, during transport."

"I know, but...this just feels so sudden. I'd really like a chance to repair my relationship with her first, since it sounds like I might not see her again for a long time. What if her treatment takes years?"

Devyn hesitates—Molly must be using some "push"—but then he frowns, his impatience now more pronounced. "A reconciliation will be far more likely after the Mind Healers repair at least some of the damage to her mind, don't you agree? This last-minute vacillating is keeping her from the very treatment that could restore her sanity."

Molly manages a convincing little sob. "I know. But look! She's seems almost normal right now. Can't I just—?"

"She could turn on you at any moment," Devyn insists. "Have you forgotten how she threatened you only two days ago?"

He's still talking when I finally, *finally* get the update from Rigel I've been so desperate to hear.

I'm out! All of Devyn's men are now locked in their quarters, though that last one was trickier than I expected. I'm hoofing it up the road now, in case he's set a self-destruct or something I didn't find. Feel free to send in reinforcements as soon as you and Molly are both safe at your end.

Because we're touching, Molly hears everything he says. Her hand on my wrist twitches slightly, but she manages not to react otherwise.

"I...I guess you're right," she admits to Devyn, hanging her head. "There's no guarantee she'll be like this for long."

"Precisely. Now, proceed." His voice holds so much "push," anyone but Molly would be forced to obey.

With another little sob, she nods, then thinks to me, *Pretend it hurts a little, okay?*

She brings the hand with the ampule close to my arm, then pinches me with her fingernails, forcing me to flinch for real.

"Ow!" I exclaim.

A satisfied smile spreads across Devyn's face as Molly backs away from me.

"Now, *Emileia*—" He makes my name an insult— "you reap the result of forcing me into the shadows. You will soon be consigned to the trash heap of history, while I am free to help your sister bring our people into a glorious future."

I blink rapidly, as if confused, then sway a little. "What—?"

His smile broadens. "Not to worry. In a moment you won't feel anything at all."

Since I've supposedly been injected with a powerful sedative—or maybe something lethal?—I pretend to stumble, then sink to the floor, afraid Devyn might retaliate against Molly if he realizes she faked it. As I watch through half-closed eyes, she shrinks against his side as though dismayed by what she's done.

Devyn places a proprietary hand on her shoulder. "Well done, Princess. I know that took courage, but you've just proven your loyalty to our people—and to me."

Smiling up at him, she puts a hand over the one he has on her shoulder. "No worries, Devyn. I've always known exactly where my loyalty lies —with my true Sovereign." With a slight shift of her hand on his, she sticks him with the ampule she's still holding.

Devyn's eyes go wide and horrified. "What...what have you—?" His gaze swings to me and I quickly scramble to my feet. A fierce grimace overtakes his features as he looks wildly from me, back to Molly, then frantically taps his wristband. "At least I'll have my revenge. Rigel Stuart —" He breaks off, choking. A shudder convulses his body, then he collapses in a heap.

Molly rushes over to me. "Are you okay? Is Rigel?"

"Yes! Thanks to you."

"Finally!" Pulling up her sleeve, Molly taps out the emergency sequence on her tracker implant. "I had Kyna keep her troops on standby until one of us signaled."

I smile my admiration at her ingenuity. "It may not get through this comm block, but if it does they'll probably come straight here.

"Where's Rigel?"

"Heading away from Devyn's fortress on foot until we send someone to pick him up. And in case it's set to blow up or something, though I hope it's not. The whole point of this was to prevent unnecessary loss of life. We need to get out of this house so we can call Kyna."

Molly nods, then frowns. "First we'll have to deal with Devyn's security guy, and the mayor. I've just told Tristan what happened. He can probably take them both, but...I have an idea. Wait here."

I watch curiously from the doorway as Molly goes to the head of the stairs.

"Mayor Alban?" she calls down. "Can you come up here? We could use your help."

There's a startled silence, then I hear his tread on the stairs. "It's... it's done, then?"

"Yes," Molly tells him tonelessly. "It's done."

I duck back into the sitting room before Alban can see me and a moment later Molly comes in, Alban a few paces behind her. He stops cold on the threshold when he sees me standing next to Molly...and Devyn crumpled on the floor.

"What—? How—?" He's suddenly gone white as a sheet.

"I take it you expected to help Devyn carry *me* down the stairs?" I pleasantly inquire. "As you can see, there's been a slight change of plans."

Swallowing convulsively, he stares at Devyn's inert form. "What... what did you do to him?"

"Exactly what he intended to do to me," I reply. "Fitting, don't you think? I'm curious to know why you told me it was on my sister's orders that Rigel was kidnapped and I was imprisoned here?"

Swinging his gaze back to me, he opens and closes his mouth a few times before bursting out, "It was! She asked Devyn and me to help her take your place as Sovereign. Didn't you, Princess?" He smiles ingratiatingly at Molly. "We may have improvised a bit on the details, but—"

"A bit?" Molly's brows go up. "Meanwhile, you told *me* my sister was dangerously insane, even violent. That she'd threatened to kill me."

"But...but she did threaten you, you know she did! Perhaps not *specifically* with violence, but on Sunday she said—"

I allow myself an ironic smile. "Everything you overheard during our luncheon Sunday was staged for the benefit of the listening device you'd planted that morning."

Molly nods. "And everything I told you and Devyn about wanting to take my sister's place was only to expose you both as the traitors you are —which we've now done."

"It...it was all Devyn's idea!" Alban's pallor has taken on a greenish tinge. "His and Connor's. And Tristan's. They all told me—"

"Told you what?" Tristan asks, coming up behind him, weapon in hand.

Alban flinches away from the doorway, then turns to face him. "That...that Malena would be a more effective Sovereign than her sister, particularly with you as Consort. That she—"

He breaks off at the sound of more feet coming up the stairs.

"That'll be Cormac and your Handmaid," Tristan tells me. Then, to Molly, "Your distraction gave me a chance to stun Devyn's guy and release the others."

Cormac appears in the doorway then, Morag hovering fearfully behind him in the hallway. Quickly sizing up the situation, Cormac steps forward and places what must be Devyn's security guy's weapon against Alban's side. "I can cover this traitor now."

"What? You can't do this!" Alban blusters. "I'm the mayor of this town."

"Not anymore," I inform him. "As Sovereign, I hereby relieve you of your position, which you apparently only achieved with Devyn's help."

We all look down at Devyn, still motionless on the floor.

"How long do you think he'll be out?" Molly asks. "That must have been a pretty strong sedative if it was supposed to knock you out until you got to Dun Cloch."

Motioning Tristan to cover Alban again, Cormac kneels next to Devyn and touches the side of his neck—then presses more firmly. Then, frowning, he puts an ear to Devyn's chest. Finally, he straightens.

"I find no sign of a heartbeat. He appears to be dead."

Molly's mouth falls open and we stare at each other in horror—though hers is greater than mine.

"I...I killed him?" she gasps, staring at Devyn's body. As the full import sinks in, her shocked gaze swings back to me. "That means he planned for me to kill *you!*"

Swallowing, I nod. "Looks like."

"Oh, M!" Molly wraps me in a fierce hug. "I really thought it was a sedative! What if I'd—?"

"But you didn't." Returning her hug, I pat her back comfortingly. "Instead you saved my life! Rigel's, too, by stalling until he escaped."

Keeping his weapon trained on Alban, who now looks ready to faint, Tristan stares at us in confusion. "Rigel got out of Devyn's stronghold?"

"Yes, partly thanks to Molly right at the end. He managed to hack into the fortress's systems, though the timing was apparently a little tricky. We need to send someone to pick him up and bring him back. Nope, that won't work," I add when Tristan pulls out his omni. "We'll have to get outside first. Unless you can deactivate the comm block right now?" I ask Alban, who stupidly shakes his head. "Oh, and we should tie up that security guy before he comes to."

"Already done, Excellency," Cormac assures me. He then makes a quick search of Devyn's body to retrieve his omni and energy weapon before getting to his feet and again taking custody of Alban.

Tristan immediately crosses the room in two steps to give Molly and me both a relieved hug before kissing Molly. "You did it," he whispers to her. "I knew you could!"

I'm almost limp with relief myself that it's really over and we're all finally safe. "Come on," I say to everyone with a shaky smile. "Let's get out of here so we can call Kyna."

⁺₊

Leaving Devyn's body where it is, the rest of us go downstairs. Alban, appearing completely deflated by Devyn's death, obligingly palms the front door open for us. Under Cormac's watchful eye, he then reprograms the front door lock and security system for my palm instead of his and contacts his tech guy to remove the comm block on the house.

While that's going on, Molly calls Kyna, then hands me her omni-phone.

"Excellency?" Kyna's clearly startled to hear my voice. "Dare I hope this means you are free and unharmed?"

"Yes, I'm fine. So is Rigel, other than being stranded near Devyn's fortress until your people pick him up and bring him here. Please send at least some of them to do that right away. You still have those coordinates, right?"

She assures me she does. "But how—?"

I quickly explain that Devyn is dead and Cormac has Alban in custody. "So I guess send a few from your force here, too. There's also Devyn's security guy to deal with, though he's stunned and tied up, so no threat at the moment."

"Very well. You're *certain* you're all right?" Kyna sounds as though she's barely suppressing strong emotion.

I repeat that I am. "At least, as all right as I can be without Rigel. The sooner he can be brought here, the better."

"I'll make that call now, and will handle all the other necessary arrangements, as well—after which I would very much appreciate a more thorough recounting of exactly what transpired."

Promising to explain everything soon, I disconnect the call and hand Molly's omni back. "Connor needs to be told what's happened, too, though maybe you should tell him in person. He and Devyn used to be good friends."

Alban gives a little moan and sinks down on the front doorstep to put his head in his hands. Close as he and Devyn obviously were, I can't summon a lot of sympathy after the way he tried to play Molly and me against each other.

A few seconds later, a van drives up. Four men from Kyna's security detail get out and I quickly explain the situation. "If you can, download the recording from the vidscreen upstairs," I add before they go inside. "Devyn recorded everything that happened."

My words produce one of Cormac's rare smiles. "That will come in handy when *this*—" he looks down his nose at Alban— "is brought to trial."

Alban whimpers.

Kyna's security guys are so efficient, it takes them less than twenty minutes to remove Devyn's body, take custody of both Alban and Devyn's driver, and bundle them all into the van.

As they drive off, Tristan pulls out his omni again. "Oops, Father messaged me half an hour ago, asking me to call him. Guess I should do that?"

I motion him to go ahead.

"Father? I just saw your message," he tells Connor a moment later. "No, everything is fine. That is…" Tristan glances at me, then continues. "Can you come to the VIP residence? There's kind of a lot we need to tell you, and Molly and I will need a ride back."

At the other end, I can hear Connor's voice urgently asking if he's sure the Sovereign and Molly are both safe.

"Yes, they're right here with me. We'll see you soon. Thanks."

By now, I'm more impatient than ever to see Rigel. *Are you almost here?* I think to him.

Yep, already in Fiarway, should be there in just a minute.

Can't wait! we both send at once.

Sure enough, a moment later a car comes around the corner, stops in front of the VIP guesthouse and Rigel jumps out. "Thanks," he says to someone inside, before turning to face me.

I'm already racing down the front walk, heedless of how undignified I look to anyone watching. He opens his arms as I reach him and then we're hugging and kissing like we were apart for months instead of two days.

I was so worried— we think to each other at the same time, then stop kissing long enough to laugh.

Glancing over my shoulder, I see Molly and Tristan on the doorstep, grinning at us. Behind them in the doorway, Cormac and Morag also watch our reunion, Cormac smiling almost as widely as the others. Even Morag looks more pleased than disapproving.

After a few more kisses, Rigel and I go up the front walk hand in hand, pausing for one more wonderful kiss along the way. As soon as we reach them, Molly and Tristan pull us both into a group hug.

"We were both so worried!" Molly tells him.

Tristan nods. "I want to hear exactly how you managed to escape without Devyn—" He breaks off, swallowing. "Anyway, well done!"

"Yep. You really are a superhero." I smile up at Rigel, which earns me another kiss.

"I'd say we all are!" he says then.

Tristan and Molly both laugh.

"Let's wait inside until Connor gets here," I suggest. "Hopefully that comm block's been lifted by now."

Cormac and Morag step aside and we all join them in the entrance hall. Then Rigel reaches into his pocket and pulls out not one, but *three* omnis—mine and Cormac's, along with his own. "On my way out, I broke into Devyn's lab and grabbed these," he explains. "It looked like they'd been trying to hack into your omni, M, but couldn't get past all its security."

"That's good," Molly says. "If they'd called up all your texts and holos and stuff, it would have revealed our whole plan!"

I shudder, realizing that almost certainly would've gotten Rigel killed before he could escape.

"We don't have to leave as soon as your dad gets here, do we?" Molly asks Tristan then. "M and I need to catch each other up on everything that happened after that weird lunch Sunday."

"Why don't we do that over lunch?" I suggest. Now that Rigel's back, I'm suddenly ravenous.

As we turn toward the breakfast room, the doorbell rings. Cormac opens the door and Connor steps inside, looking confused and startled to see all four of us together in the entryway.

"You were right!" he exclaims to Tristan. "I hardly dared to believe—"

"Why don't you join us for lunch?" I interrupt, tamping down my resentment for the passive role he played in everything that happened. "We have a lot to tell you—and each other."

ATHMUNTHERAS

(ad-HWARD-this): redemption; reconciliation

Molly

Connor looks uncertainly at M, then at Cormac, hovering protectively behind her. "Are you sure—?"

"Yes, I'm sure." M's face relaxes into a smile, though I can tell she has to work at it. No wonder, considering how readily Connor went along with Devyn's treasonous plot, even if he wasn't an active participant.

Still clearly nervous, Connor accompanies us all into the same breakfast room where M and I staged our fake fight two days ago. I imagine Alban's bugs have all been removed or deactivated by now—not that there's anyone left to listen.

"Morag, we'll let everyone order what they like this time," M tells her Handmaid, who goes into the kitchen as we all take the same seats as before around the square table

M and Rigel again sit directly across from Tristan and me, with Connor on my right. Of course there are no silly finger bowls today. Then M takes the informality further by asking Cormac to sit down, too.

Morag returns with little menu tablets and we all make our selections. Then, when she returns with our food a couple minutes later, M motions her to the seat next to Cormac.

"Now that we're all comfortable, I suppose it's time for explanations.

Molly, can you start? Because I'm starving," M says, picking up her fork with a grin.

I smile back, then sober, remembering Connor still doesn't know about Devyn. *Maybe you should tell him that part?* I silently suggest to Tristan.

With a little nod, he turns to his father. "Actually, I'll start. Father, there's no easy way to tell you this, but...Devyn is dead."

Connor had just picked up his own fork, but now he sets it down, his eyes wide and shocked. "Dead? I...I assumed he'd been arrested, since —" He glances at M and Rigel. "But dead?"

Tristan and I both nod.

"I know you two were close for a long time," I tell him. "I'm...I'm sorry. Especially since...since I—" I break off, my appetite abruptly gone.

You didn't know! M thinks to me, clearly sensing my sudden distress.

At the same time, Tristan squeezes my hand under the table. *You had no choice,* he silently reminds me. *It was him or M.*

Then, to his father, who's looking understandably confused, Tristan says, "Devyn had planned to kill the Sovereign, not sedate her, though Molly didn't know that. He handed her the syringe to use on M, probably so he could blackmail Molly later if she refused to go along with his plans. But she was too clever for him. She only pretended to stick M with it, then injected Devyn instead—still thinking it was just a sedative."

I blink at Tristan. "I hadn't even thought of the blackmail angle! But...you're probably right. He even made a point of saying he was recording the whole thing." Realizing that helps...a little.

Connor still appears to be struggling to absorb the news. "Then... Council leader Kyna had nothing to do with it? I messaged her, you see, shortly after the two of you left with Devyn this morning. I...should have tried much, much sooner to warn you that Devyn was not necessarily to be trusted. Finally, afraid of what he might intend, I messaged Kyna myself to warn her. I understand better than anyone how very trustworthy Devyn can—could—seem. It was always a special ability of his, one that served him extremely well throughout his political career." He still looks slightly stunned.

"You and he were friends for a very long time, weren't you?" M asks gently.

He nods. "More than thirty years, yes. And acquaintances for another thirty, before that."

"I'm sorry for your loss." She sounds like she means it, in spite of everything.

"Thank you—though he and I weren't nearly as close these last few months. After I told him I no longer wished to be part of his plan for dominance, he understandably kept me at a distance. Recently, however, he attempted to mend fences, likely realizing I was still his easiest path to influence with the Council—and with you," he adds to me. "I...I wished to believe he had truly abandoned his earlier plans, but I now realize my own ambition partially blinded me to his motives. When he pointed out the potential advantages to my family, should you become Sovereign—"

"I guess that was pretty hard to ignore, huh?" Tristan says. "I get it. I won't say the same thought didn't occur to me—though more along the lines of Molly sharing M's role, not taking it over completely. She always shut me down in a hurry if I even brought that up, though."

Connor's frowning again. "So you'd told me. It's why I felt sure Devyn, and perhaps Alban, had used unethical means to effect your change of heart," he says to me.

"They certainly tried," I reply. "And I let them believe it worked. The thing is, since bonding with Tristan, I seem to be much more resistant to Royal 'push.'" No need for him to know I'm totally immune. "That's why M suggested this strategy when I told her what Alban and Devyn were planning."

"You...you told—?"

I nod. "I called her as soon as we got back to your house on Saturday, after that lunch where Alban tried to bring me on board." With occasional help from M, I describe her plan, which seems safe enough, now that Alban's been arrested and Devyn can never threaten anyone again.

Connor's eyes get wider and wider as I share everything that was really going on, including how thoroughly Alban incriminated himself upstairs. By the end, he's shaking his head in disbelief.

"I must say, Princess, you were *very* convincing. I truly believed you'd been persuaded to fall in with Devyn and Alban's plans to install you as Sovereign—and that you had good reason to doubt your sister's sanity." He sends an apologetic glance at M.

She smiles back. "Molly can be awfully convincing when she wants to be. Of course, I also did my best to act kind of crazy during our lunch on Sunday. Sorry if I scared you a little."

"And I'm sorry we didn't let you in on the plan," Tristan tells his father. "Even though we were pretty sure you weren't in cahoots with Devyn and Alban, the stakes—"

"No, you were wise not to," Connor interrupts. "I want to believe I'd have kept your ruse secret, but I might well have said or done something to raise Devyn's suspicions, if only by accident. He was very clever."

Surprised and gratified by his father's admission, Tristan smiles. "I'm glad you understand—and that you were never an active part of their plot."

"Yes, well." Connor shrugs. "I can't take much credit for that. As I said, Devyn no longer trusted me to keep such things to myself, after I betrayed him to the Council." He pauses, then asks, "Was Council Leader Kyna aware of the Sovereign's plan?"

Tristan and I both nod.

"Ah. That explains her reaction when I messaged her this morning. I expected her to ask questions, but she merely thanked me."

"She probably didn't want to risk saying anything that could tip Devyn off," I tell him. "Especially after the call I had with her last night, when he was listening—which she knew, by the way. She and I both knew it might be tricky to rescue M from the web he'd woven without getting her and Rigel both—"

My throat constricts and I break off, realizing again how close we came to a very different result. What if Devyn had given M that injection himself? Then she'd be—

"Fortunately, Rigel's an even better hacker than I thought," M says, apparently picking up on my sudden distress.

She goes on to tell Connor how Rigel took control of Devyn's whole complex from what was basically a prison cell.

By the time she finishes, I have my emotions back under control. "Now that they're both safe," I comment, "the hardest part left will be convincing everyone M is perfectly fine to continue as Sovereign."

Connor smiles, his first real smile since hearing about Devyn. "Relieved as I am to hear those rumors about the Sovereign's sanity were completely false, I can't help but feel that you, Princess, have also amply demonstrated excellent leadership abilities. Our people are exceedingly fortunate to have both you *and* your sister to guide them into the future."

He's right, Tristan silently tells me as I try to come to terms with the idea that I might actually have leadership skills. *You get a whole lot of the credit for how well things turned out.*

Then M echoes them both aloud. "I agree. *I'm* exceedingly fortunate to have Molly to help me lead from now on! She wasn't a fan of my idea to trap Devyn, but—" Her omni pings, interrupting her. "Oh, it's Kyna."

On answering, M immediately asks Kyna if it's okay to let us all listen in. "Molly and Tristan will want to hear your updates, and they can help fill in any details I forget when I explain how things went down at this end. Oh, but you should know Connor's here having lunch with us. Is it okay if he hears what you have to say, too?"

She must've said yes, because M sets her omni on the table and we all hear Kyna say, "As you're there, Connor, I'll begin with an apology for the terseness of my response to your warning earlier."

"Not to worry, Council Leader," he tells her. "I now understand why you feared to say more. Thankfully, all is well now and I've been briefed on the deception the Sovereign and Princess carried off so brilliantly."

As he's speaking, M silently confirms to me he's every bit as relieved as he claims. *The news about Devyn shook him, but he was even more upset about what Devyn tried to do. I think maybe we really can trust him now.*

Tristan's relief at hearing M's thought comes through loud and clear. *I was hoping he—* he starts to send back, but breaks off when Kyna responds.

"So it seems. I would very much like to hear *how* brilliantly, Excellency, if you would care to share the details you promised me earlier?"

"Oh, right." M proceeds to explain how everything unfolded, starting with the night of our formal dinner. Rigel, Tristan and I fill in a few blanks along the way, until Kyna's brought up to the present.

There's a pause at her end before she says, "It sounds as though all of you contributed to bringing about this happy conclusion. Particularly given your youth, I'm extremely impressed by the ingenuity and courage you and Princess Malena displayed when the original plan was upended. Indeed, things might easily have ended disastrously without the Princess's quick thinking right at the end. A valuable leadership skill, I must say."

M grins at me. "We keep telling her that. Maybe she'll finally believe it coming from you."

I feel my face going red. To change the subject, I ask, "So, um, what did your security team end up doing about Devyn's fortress?"

"Ah, yes," Kyna says. "The search of Devyn's stronghold turned up several items of note. While he did not, in fact, possess another intact Ossian Sphere, he did have most of the parts for one. More concerning was the discovery of nearly sixty picograms of antimatter, along with a dozen drones that were apparently designed to deploy it at some future time."

"Then Connor was right that Devyn still planned to take over, even before we came here," M says.

Kyna agrees that antimatter-equipped drones would have posed a significant threat. "I'll write up a MARSTAR Bulletin to refute the claims Alban made in that broadcast yesterday morning," she continues, "and have it sent tonight or early tomorrow. First, however, I'll see to a complete clearing out of Devyn's residence and the disposition of his security team...and Alban. I'll report back once everything is in order. Meanwhile, I'd say you've all earned a well-deserved break. Well done. Again."

✦

"So, now what?" I ask the others as we all get up from the table a few minutes later.

"How about we try to enjoy what's left of spring break, like Kyna said?" Tristan suggests.

Rigel smiles at M. "I like that idea. You're way overdue for a real break, even if Molly's started sharing some of the load."

"Only a little," I protest. "But I agree about her needing a break. What do you say, M? What sounds fun to you?"

She blinks. "Fun? I...hadn't even thought about it. Any ideas?"

"How about a hike this afternoon?" Tristan suggests. "Weather's pretty nice, and I think it's supposed to turn colder tomorrow."

M and Rigel agree to that, so we arrange to pick them up in an hour or so. Then Connor drives us back to his house so we can change.

We're on the way there when Connor clears his throat. "Princess, I apologized to your sister, but must also apologize to you—and to my son

—for not trying sooner to warn you both about Devyn's possible motives. I know now you weren't nearly so fooled as I believed, but—"

"Actually," I interrupt, "it would have been kind of awkward if you had, because then we'd have felt like we had to explain M's plan."

"Ah. Yes. I see your point." Frowning, Connor lapses into silence, apparently still struggling with all the ramifications.

The first thing I do when we get back to Connor's is reassure Gilda and Sorcha that I'm fine, and so is M. "None of that stuff Mayor Alban said about her yesterday was true," I assure them. "It was all part of a plot. But...it's kind of a long story. I'll tell you the whole thing later, or you can read the next MARSTAR when it goes out. Right now, I need to change out of this fancy outfit into something I can hike in."

Ten minutes later, now dressed in jeans, sweatshirt and my sturdiest shoes, I leave the bedroom and find Tristan waiting for me in the hall.

"Father says we can borrow his car, so I messaged Rigel we'd pick them up at two-thirty." Then he silently adds, *I actually told Rigel three o'clock, so we'd have some extra time—*

To go parking somewhere? I finish hopefully. He winks in response.

It takes a bit of effort to persuade Gilda and Sorcha—and Connor— to let us leave without my attendants, but I point out that M and I can act as chaperones for each other and Tristan and Rigel are both trained Bodyguards.

"So we'll only be alone together for the five minutes it takes to get to the guest house. Besides, we drive around Jewel just the two of us all the time, since it would look weird if we didn't." Though I probably shouldn't, I add a teensy bit of "push" to stave off further argument, I'm so eager for the alone time with Tristan we both need.

Promising to be back before dark, we go out to the car. "Where—?" I start to ask but break off at Tristan's grin.

"I've already thought of the perfect place. Don't worry, it's not far." He's as hungry for this interlude as I am. A few minutes later, he turns up a little side street heading up into the mountains. "The hiking trail I have in mind is a little ways further up here, but for now..."

Pulling off the road at a wider spot clearly intended as a scenic over-look, he parks the car and turns to me with a smile that sends a delicious shiver through me. I quickly unbuckle my seatbelt and an instant later we're hungrily kissing, something we've both been starving for since last week.

After a solid fifteen minutes of bliss, I straighten up with a happy sigh. "Let's try to never—"

"Go this long without making out again?" His chocolate brown eyes twinkle at me.

I nod. "Yes. That."

But then his expression turns serious. "A few times over these past few days, I could tell you were a little worried I was too into the idea of you becoming Sovereign—and not just the time you accused me of it after that formal dinner. Am I right?"

"Um...maybe a little, once or twice," I admit. "Some of the stuff M said during that awful lunch reminded me—"

"That I really did move to Jewel hoping to become her Royal Consort. I can't blame you for doubting, Molly, especially when things got so crazy and stressful and I kept telling you to stay the course. But I swear what matters more to me than *anything* else is for you to be happy. Sure, I think you sometimes underestimate yourself, but you'd never be happy if you were forced to be Sovereign—especially because of something happening to M. I never, ever wanted that, I promise!"

His sincerity comes through clearly, not just in his intense expression, but through his touch, still holding both of my hands in his. That last, tiny niggling doubt disappears and I lean toward him for one more incredibly sweet kiss before we go meet M and Rigel.

NASCH DHIRFURACHA

(Nash dji-FUR-uh-sha): bonds of sisterhood

M

"Ready to go hiking?" Tristan asks when Cormac opens the door to him and Molly, right at 3pm.

They're both so relaxed and happy as they step inside, I can instantly tell they didn't come straight here—not that I blame them! They might not have been kept completely apart since we all arrived in Fiarway, but staying with Connor, they can't have had any more opportunities for a proper makeout session than Rigel and I did. I hope we can squeeze one in today, too!

"Yep, just let us get our jackets," I reply. "Or are we staying in Fiarway? If so, we can use our omnis to stay warm instead."

"The trail head's in Fiarway," Tristan tells me, "but the trail itself winds all over the mountains. There's still some snow up there, so maybe bring jackets for show, on the off chance we encounter any *Duchas*."

As Rigel and I grab jackets, I again insist to Cormac and Morag that their services won't be required for this outing. Cormac's clearly a bit disgruntled, but Morag's just as clearly relieved to be excused from a mountain hike.

Half an hour later, the four of us are enjoying the spectacular scenery along what Tristan says was always one of his favorite paths. Walking hand in hand with Rigel feels wonderful—though we still promise each other some serious kissing later on.

Tristan points out a few things as we go, every vista a new beauty. Then, a mile or so along, Molly suddenly says, "Hey, guys, do you mind if M and I talk a little without you, um, listening in?"

Though they both look a little surprised, they don't object, so Molly drops back to walk with me while Rigel and Tristan continue on a dozen yards ahead.

"What's up?" I ask, though I suspect I know.

In response, she takes my hand and thinks, *We haven't had a chance to talk, just us, since, well...you know.*

Good point, I agree. *We both said some pretty awful stuff to and about each other—*

—especially at lunch Sunday, she finishes my thought.

I nod. *We both knew we didn't really mean any of it, but—*

Again, she completes my mental sentence. *But some of it still bothers me a little. Maybe you, too?*

Yeah, a little, I admit. *The stuff we said about each other's guys... I felt awful saying what I did about Tristan. It totally wasn't true! Shoot, I guessed before you did he was falling for you, way before we found out—*

I know. He and I got past that stupid gossip a long time ago. But the stuff I said about Rigel was every bit as mean, maybe more. You could tell from my emotions I didn't really think any of that, right?

I squeeze her hand. *You just repeated some of the crap Gwendolyn Gannett and others have been saying all along. I still hate hearing it, but I never thought for a minute you feel that way. Definitely not now.*

Sure, when she and Sean first got to Jewel, they both resented the heck out of Rigel and never missed a chance to point out how inappropriate our relationship was, but hasn't been true for a long time now.

Molly smiles over at me mistily, her love and support coming through loud and clear. *Good. Because I don't. You two are perfect together.*

My eyes are a little misty, too. *So are you and Tristan,* I respond. *I love the way you've made each other blossom. It's beautiful.*

And then we're hugging, right there on the path. Up ahead, the guys turn to watch us, both of them grinning.

"I guess you two cleared the air about that super awkward lunch you staged?" Tristan asks, looking back and forth between Molly and me. We both nod. "I have to say, my father was seriously freaked out by it."

I chuckle. "I could tell. So were Gilda, Sorcha and Morag. Cormac at least knew to expect it, though he was still uncomfortable. Considering what happened afterward, though, faking that fight might not have been one of my better ideas."

Molly shrugs. "Devyn claimed that was the reason he changed his plan, but I'm pretty sure he would have done that anyway. He didn't want to risk you escaping his control before I was actually declared Sovereign."

I realize she's probably right—which makes me feel a little better.

Resuming our original positions next to our partners, we continue our leisurely hike until Tristan warns us we need to turn around if we want to get back to the car before dark. By mutual agreement, we separate into couples shortly before reaching the little parking area and step into the woods on opposite sides of the trail for a bit of privacy. The second we're out of sight of the path, Rigel and I indulge in a few minutes of proper making out. Then, feeling totally at peace with the world, we rejoin Molly and Tristan for the drive back.

That evening is blessedly uneventful. There's not even anything distressing on the news. Not till we're finishing breakfast the next morning does my omni ping.

"Kyna's MARSTAR is out," I tell Rigel, as well as Cormac and Morag, who are again at the table with us. "Let's see what she said." I prop my omni on the table and bring up the holo screen so we can all read it together.

MARSTAR Bulletin
For immediate distribution

By now, many of you are no doubt aware of the broadcast Mayor Alban of Fiarway made on Monday, concerning Sovereign Emileia's mental health. The *Echtran* Council has now confirmed that broadcast was part of a treasonous plot by Devyn Kane and Fiarway's mayor to discredit our Sovereign. Apparently believing Princess Malena would be easier to influence, they conspired to install her in Emileia's place, intending to direct her actions going forward. Fortunately, our Sovereign and her sister both possess far more intelligence and strength of will than the traitors anticipated, and successfully overthrew the traitors' scheme.

A full investigation is now underway to determine how widespread this plot was and to root out any others who might have been working to undermine our Sovereign and the Martian government. It is now believed that certain information, previously published and broadcast by *Echtran Enquirer* reporter Gwendolyn Gannett, was given to her by Devyn Kane himself in order to lay the groundwork for his plot. While we presume Ms. Gannett was an unwitting accomplice in those efforts, we strongly recommend she more thoroughly verify her sources going forward.

As for the two primary traitors, Alban has been removed as Mayor of Fiarway and will face an inquest in Dun Cloch, after which formal charges are expected. Devyn Kane, however, will face neither a trial nor our ultimate punishment, as he was inadvertently killed while attempting to assassinate Sovereign Emileia. Our condolences go out to anyone who still held him in affection.

Expect further updates as our investigation unfolds. Our Sovereign and Princess will remain in Fiarway for the remainder of their school spring break, after which they will return to Jewel to continue guiding us all toward our best possible future.

"Not bad," Rigel comments. "You okay with staying here another couple of days?"

I nod. "I messaged Kyna late yesterday that it might be a good idea for Molly and me to make a few joint visits and appearances while we're still here, to show we're a unified team. Also—"

"To prove you're perfectly sane?" he suggests with a grin.

"That, too." I grin back. "After the rumors Alban and Devyn spread here for months, my credibility in Fiarway definitely needs shoring up."

Twenty minutes later, I give Molly a call. She and Tristan are fine with us all sticking around until Friday, so Molly and I plan out which visits and appearances we should do together. Tristan and Rigel make sure we also build in plenty of time to relax, hike and sightsee.

One of our first joint visits is to Fiarway's Healing Center, where I'm pleased to pick up noticeably less uneasiness than on my tour here Saturday.

"I must say, Excellency, I was very relieved to receive this morning's MARSTAR Bulletin," the head Healer tells me as soon as we arrive. "Even before the *Echtran* Council's explanation, I thought the mayor's explanation odd, as I knew none of my Healers had been to see you."

I almost ask why she didn't mention her suspicion to anyone. Then I realize if she had, Devyn likely would have moved even more quickly to shut me up—permanently.

On Thursday, Molly and I make a joint appearance in the town square, more or less reprising our last broadcast before leaving Jewel. When people come up to us afterward, nearly as many seem eager to speak with me as with Molly, a nice change. Some even apologize for believing the earlier gossip about me. Of course, I assure each one their concerns were understandable, though privately I'm a little ticked they were so ready to believe the worst of me.

With the loyalty of Fiarway's Town Council still in question, I appoint Connor Acting Mayor until an election can be held to replace Alban. Given Connor's existing popularity here, and Molly's and my tacit endorsements, I suspect he'll have no trouble winning that election if he decides to run.

Between various other meetings in Fiarway, we go on two more hikes and do a little sightseeing in and around Denver, with Tristan as tour guide. And then it's time to go home.

Morag is touchingly sad to say goodbye, hinting that should I need the services of a Handmaid in the future, she'd like to be considered for the job. On the way to the airport, Molly tells me Sorcha actually broke down in tears when they said their farewells.

Instead of ordering another flashy limo, Connor himself drives us to the airport in one of the Town Hall's vans. Then, when we arrive, he actually gets out to help Cormac and Gilda unload our luggage.

"I very much hope you'll come visit me again this summer," he tells Tristan and Molly at the curb. "I promise to make your next visit far less stressful than this one turned out to be."

We all chuckle a little at that.

After hugging Tristan goodbye, Connor takes a tentative step toward Molly, then halts uncertainly. Smiling, she steps forward and gives him a quick hug herself.

"Thanks for everything, Connor. I'm sure we'll see you again soon."

The flight back is uneventful. We spend most of it talking over the week just past, though of course we've already discussed it to death over the last few days. At one point Tristan mentions the MARSTAR Bulletin, and how much it seemed to help.

"I'm glad they didn't go into detail about how Devyn died," Molly comments, her lingering guilt still perceptible—to me, anyway.

I reach over to put a hand on her shoulder. "It was him or me," I remind her—again.

She nods. "I know. I can't regret what I did, not really. I just—"

"I understand," I assure her. "Trust me."

What I did a month ago was far worse, even if the guy I killed deserved it every bit as much. Unlike me, Molly didn't have a choice, nor did she realize her actions would result in a death. I hope that means she'll get over it much sooner than I will...if I ever do.

But maybe neither of us *should* completely get over the idea of killing someone, no matter how necessary? I'm still pondering that concept when the flight attendant comes to take our drink orders.

⁺₊⁺

Saturday afternoon finds the four of us seated with the *Echtran* Council around the big conference table at NuAgra to relate everything that transpired in Fiarway. Tristan and Rigel were invited to attend in case any Council members have questions for them, too.

Because we keep getting interrupted to clarify practically every detail, up to and including exactly how Devyn died, the debriefing takes nearly two hours. Finally, all the Council members seem satisfied they've pried every bit of info out of us they can.

"It's as well you insisted on sending that MARSTAR Bulletin on Wednesday, Kyna," Teara Roark comments after we finish. "I trust it finally put to rest any remaining concerns about our Sovereign's fitness to lead?"

"Let's hope so," Kyna responds. "Particularly as we have much cause to be grateful to her—to you all," she continues, including Rigel and Tristan in her thanks. "Of the fourteen men captured, twelve were already wanted for crimes committed in Nuath during Faxon's reign—brutalities and even murders carried out at his behest. Now, with their arrest, nearly all of those who disappeared after their Orientations are now accounted for."

An approving murmur goes around the table.

Kyna then clears her throat. "Excellency, I didn't wish to tell you this immediately after the trauma you endured in Fiarway, but our team there did make one other discovery. Traces of a lethal gas were detected in the room where Rigel was imprisoned. Based on the logs they downloaded, it was released approximately at the moment of Devyn Kane's death."

I turn to Rigel with a horrified gasp. "So if Molly and I hadn't continued playing along that morning, he'd have—" I break off with a shudder.

Rigel squeezes my hand reassuringly. "The two of you made sure that didn't happen. Much as I argued against it, your plan worked—though with a few more bumps along the way than we expected."

His understatement draws a chuckle from everyone.

Then Breann speaks up. "I must say, I'm impressed as well as grateful to all of you. Given the ingenuity displayed by Princess Malena, it's clear our people's future is in doubly good hands now."

"Most of the ingenuity was M's," Molly protests. "She's the one who came up with the plan to lure Devyn out of his fortress."

"The original plan, maybe," I concede, "but you're the one who implemented it, almost completely on your own. When you had to take charge, you did it brilliantly. Like it or not, Molly, you're excellent Sovereign material yourself—even if it looks like I get to keep my job a while longer." I wink at her.

Obviously shaken, she looks around the table like she expects someone to contradict me, but only respect is reflected in the eyes of the Council members as they nod their agreement. Mrs. O positively beams at her, both admiring and proud.

"Um, thanks," Molly finally says, "but I hope it won't matter again for a really, *really* long time!"

That gets another general chuckle, and a few minutes later Kyna adjourns the meeting.

"Well done," Mrs. O congratulates Molly as we exit the conference room with our boyfriends. "Without your quick thinking, it sounds as though things would have turned out far, far worse."

But though her actual words convey satisfaction with the outcome, I sense a small trace of disappointment. That Molly missed her chance to become Sovereign once and for all? Probably, but I'm not about to call her on it.

Muttering an embarrassed thanks to her mom, Molly turns to me. "Tristan asked if we can go to Dream Cream on the way home. What do you say?"

"Sounds good to us," I reply, receiving Rigel's mental agreement.

A short time later, the four of us are sitting in a back booth of Jewel's ice cream shop with our milkshakes, which Molly insisted only count as drinks, so won't spoil our dinners.

"You know, the more I've thought about it, the more sure I am that Devyn totally intended all along to have you and Rigel nabbed at Alban's formal dinner. In fact, I think that was the main point of that dinner. He—"

Molly breaks off, looking over my shoulder, and I realize a *Duchas* family just sat down in the booth behind me.

He said from the start it would be easier to have me replace you with us both in Fiarway, where most of the people plus the whole security force were on their side, she continues silently.

Because she and I are touching our boyfriends, communicating this way is as easy as talking out loud. Maybe easier?

That makes sense, I mentally agree. *If Rigel and I left town, he couldn't use our safety as leverage to force you to go along—though you obviously convinced him it was voluntary.*

The four of us continue silently dissecting a few details about the past week that came up for the first time during the Council meeting— like Rigel using Devyn's security software to track where every guard was at any given moment.

Wow, you really took over the whole place, didn't you? Tristan comments. *Could you have taken out Devyn yourself the night before everything went down? Gassed him like he planned to gas you?*

Even if I could have, I wouldn't have, Rigel responds. *Not while they still had M prisoner. What if he'd rigged something at her end, too?*

As we're leaving, Molly comments—aloud— "Did you guys notice how much easier it was to talk like that just now? *Way* easier than on the plane to Denver. I wonder what our range is now?"

"I guess we never tried to test it, did we?" I glance around at the others. "Why don't we do that on the way home? We'll give you guys a head start."

Now we're all curious, so Molly and Tristan drive off in his Porsche while Rigel and I take our time getting into his Audi and buckling our seatbelts. As he's starting the car, I put my hand on his arm and think, *Molly? Can you still hear me?*

I can! she sends back excitedly. *And we're already coming up on Opal Street, nearly half a mile away!*

Should I keep driving? Tristan asks. *You guys are still in front of Dream Cream, right?*

Rigel confirms that, though he makes sure nobody's waiting for our parking space. *We'll sit tight while you go another half mile, then try again.*

We sneak in a few kisses while no one's watching, until a couple of minutes later I hear Molly's voice in my head. *How about now? We're over a mile from Dream Cream now, I think.*

Yes! I think back. *Loud and clear!*

Then Molly sends the same thought that just occurred to me. *Maybe if we'd tried this in Fiarway, we could have skipped hiding in bathrooms to communicate, and even that awful lunch M staged. Too bad we didn't think to test it then.*

Next time, Tristan silently comments.

After a startled moment, we all start laughing.

Then, by mutual agreement, we abandon our four-way mental link so each couple can have some real private time before Molly and I go home for dinner.

"Arboretum?" Rigel asks, finally pulling away from Dream Cream.

"Absolutely." I happen to know Molly and Tristan's favorite makeout spot is somewhere else.

Half an hour later, after the best session of kissing we've enjoyed since leaving Jewel more than a week ago, I feel recharged enough to take on the world—though I hope that won't be necessary anytime soon.

If it is, we'll conquer whatever it is together, Rigel thinks to me, leaning in for one last kiss.

Together, I agree. *Always.*

⋆

"Thank you, Excellencies." Our last Monday afternoon petitioner bows to Molly and me. "I appreciate the opportunity to make my case. You'll notify me of your decision?"

I nod to the statuesque brunette. "We expect to finalize the slate of candidates within a few days. As impressive as your credentials are, I'm fairly certain you'll be on it."

Smiling her appreciation, she thanks us again and bows her way out of the NuAgra audience chamber.

Molly waits till she's gone to say, "Did you notice? Even though we had more petitioners than usual after missing last week, not one of them acted afraid of you today. Last week's MARSTAR combined with that Mind Healing report reconfirming you're totally sane obviously did the trick."

"Apparently so," I agree. "I didn't even sense any fear today, and I focused on every single person."

"The guys are already here," Molly comments as we head for the door of the audience chamber—noticeably spiffed up since we last used it. "Guess we should join them."

Take your time if you need it, Rigel sends, to my surprise. Then I realize why.

Turning to Molly, I take both of her hands. "Remember what I said three weeks ago when we were leaving here, about how great it is we get along so well? Now I'm even more grateful to have you as my sister. Not only are you just generally awesome, you've saved my life twice now."

Though obviously touched, Molly grins. "Seems only fair, considering you've saved everyone on Earth *and* Mars a few times over. But I'm the lucky one, having you as *my* sister."

"It's scary," I say, still holding her hands. "Everything we went through last week could so easily have torn us apart—"

"—but instead it only strengthened our bond as sisters," Molly finishes before I can, throwing her arms around me in a tight hug. "I love you, M!"

I hug her back just as hard. "Ditto. You know, growing up, I used to wish I had a sister. Now... Not only are you my best friend, Molly, you're a better sister than even *my* imagination could have conjured!"

"Best sisters ever," Molly agrees. "Forever!"

A MARTIAN GLOSSARY

Acclamation: Nuathan electoral process whereby citizens indicate approval or disapproval of a proposed Sovereign.

achrahn (AHK-rahn): confrontation; dispute.

aetigh har (AY-teeg-ur): convince; persuade.

agoid (AH-gyoyd): organized protest; opposition.

aitlean (ayt-lee-AN): airplane; primitive aircraft used extensively by Duchas; Earth's primary means of intercontinental travel.

Arregaith (ah-ree-GAYTH) (pop. 1,413): town in southeastern Nuath containing spaceport and supporting industries.

ateamh rioga (ah-TEV ree-OH-gah): a persuasive ability shared by some of Royal blood.

athmuntheras (ad-HWARD-this): redemption; reconciliation.

athshondis (ath-SHON-dis): resonance.

avhras (AHV-ruhs): suspicion; doubt; misgiving.

Bailerealta (BAY-luh-ree-AL-tuh) (pop. 412): village on the western coast of Ireland, est. circa 1575, populated entirely by Echtrans.

Ballytadhg (BAH-lee-teeg) (pop. 1,106): east-central Nuathan village known for Arts fine and industry.

beidan (BID-den): gossip; scandal.

brath: Martian "vibe" detectable by other Martians.

breag fionn (brag fin): discovery of a lie; detection of falsehood.

bru (BROO): pressure; insistence.

caidpel (KAYD-pel): predominant sport in Nuath combining elements of the Irish sports of hurling and Gaelic football.

camastall (KAM-uh-stahl): deception; deceit; falsification.

cannarc (KAN-ark): rebellion; mutiny; resistance.

chabhil (KAB-vil): negotiation; debate; (occ.) ultimatum.

chas pell (CHASS-pel): a ball game played by Nuathan children, nearly identical to the Earth sport of basketball.

Cheile Rioga (KEE-luh ree-OH-gah): Royal Consort.

chomhaerle (KOM-ahr-lee): advice; counsel.

Chomseireach (kom-SAY-rik): Handmaid; lady's maid, chaperone and companion to Princess or (female) Sovereign.

choridigh (KOR-digh): search; seek; investigate.

Cinnwund Rioga (KIN-wund ree-OH-gah): Royal Destiny.

cloigh (kloy): to overpower or overthrow; defeat; subdue.

comblacht (KOHM-vlakt): fight; conflict.

chomhaerle (KOM-ahr-lee): advice; counsel.

combriteach (KOM-ree-teek): compromise.

cosc damaste (kosk DAHM-uh-stay): damage control.

coslacht (ko-SLACT): appearance; impression; influence.

Costanta (ko-STAHN-tuh): Bodyguard assigned to protect the Sovereign or other members of the Royal family.

cruinhu (KRIN-hyu): meeting; gathering, as of a committee.

dabhal (DOB-uhl) (*slang*): damn, damned.

danghan (DANG-un): fortress; stronghold.

dhualgis cumann (doo-AHL-gus koo-MAHN): benevolent duty; royal obligation.

dilsacht (DIL-sok): loyalty; allegiance.

dhirfuracha (dji-FUR-uh-sha): sisters.

doolegar (DOO-luh-gahr): despondency; depression.

Duchas (doo-kas): normal Earth humans.

Dun Cloch (Dun Klok) (pop. 1,247+): largest *Echtran* compound on Earth, founded 1933 in north-central Montana. Main production hub for Martian technology.

ealu (AY-loo): to break free, escape, or elope.

Echtran (ek-tran): person of Martian birth or descent living on Earth; expatriate.

Echtran Council: governing body for expatriate Martians living on Earth.

Echtran Enquirer: unofficial news source for expatriate Martians on Earth. Tends toward the sensationalistic.

edhmiu (FEY-mew): implementation; application.

efrin (EF-rin): Hell; used as a mild curse (var. *hefrin*).

eginntacht (egg-EEN-tok): confusion; uncertainty.

Emileia (em-i-LAY-ah): current *Thiarna* (Sovereign), granddaughter to Sovereign Leontine; sole heir to the Nuathan monarchy.

fasneis (FAHSH-ness): information; intelligence.

fellbheiart (FALL-bahrt): conspiracy; treachery.

Fiarway (fee-AHR-way) (pop. 1,032): *Echtran* compound near Denver, Colorado, founded 1948.

fine (feen): genetically related subsets of the Martian population, each with certain attributes.

flach (flok) (*slang*): socially unacceptable swear word.

foare rioga (fair ree-OH-gah): ancient, traditional syringe used for blood draw to verify Sovereign lineage.

gaiscigh (GAH-sheeg): heroism; act of extreme bravery.

giola uresal (gee-OH-la OO-ree-sal): menial servant.

Glenamuir (GLEN-uh-mer) (pop. 898): largely Agricultural village in northwest Nuath; longtime home of O'Gara family during Faxon's reign.

graell (grayl): intense emotional and physical bond believed mythical by most Martians.

grechain (gree-SHAYN): Nuathan information network, both personal and mass-media; news channels within the greater *grechain*.

Grentl (GREN-tuhl): advanced non-human alien race from an unknown part of the galaxy; likely founders of underground human colony on Mars.

hiarmarti (hee-ehr-MAHR-tee): consequences; results; price to be paid.

Hollydoon (HOL-ly doon) (pop. 1,677): largely Agricultural village in northwest Nuath; suffered particularly harsh ravages by Faxon's forces.

Horizon: one of four Nuathan transport ships traveling between Mars and Earth during biennial launch windows.

Insealbau (in-SALL-baw): Installation, as of Nuathan Sovereign.

Installation: Nuathan ceremony signifying a new Sovereign's ascension to power.

Jewel (pop. 5,013): town in north-central Indiana noted for corn, artisan jewelry and annual Jewel Jewelry Festival.

Launch window: period occurring approximately every 26 Earth months and lasting approximately four months, when the distance between Earth and Mars is small enough to allow travel between the two planets.

MARSTAR: official channel for communication from Echtran Council to expatriate Martians living on Earth, generally in the form of MARSTAR Bulletins.

mhinhu (MIN-hyu): explanation; clarification.

mihuinas (mee-HOY-nus): discomfort; embarrassment; apprehension.

Miochan (mee-OH-kan): healing; curing; a major fine.

moill (mahl): delay; postponement.

naesc geaniteach (nesh gan-it-EEK) genetic affinity.

nasch dhirfuracha (dji-FUR-uh-sha): bonds of sisterhood.

nimhic (NIV-ik): antidote; cure.

Nuath (NOO-ath): underground human colony on Mars.

omni: a small, multifunctional device developed on Mars.

orinacht (OR-in-ott): propriety; seemliness.

phaeraid (parr-OYD): procession; parade; display.

pleanal (plenn-UHL): advance planning; scheming.

Populists: a minority movement among Nuathans advocating equal rights and representation for all *fines*. (Sometimes referred to as "Anti-Royals.")

probalreith (pro-BAHL-reth): opinion poll; public opinion.

probleid (pruh-BLAYD): privilege; status.

Quintessence (kwin-TESS-ens): one of four passenger vessels used to transport Nuathans between Earth and Mars.

Rigel (RY-jel): a blue supergiant star, approximately 860 light years from Earth, located in the constellation Orion; 7th brightest star visible from Earth, its brightness (or apparent magnitude) making it an important navigational star; Rigel Stuart, son of Ariel and Van Stuart.

rundacht (ROON-dahct): extreme secrecy; classified information.

scar a cheila (scar ah KAY-lah): separated; torn asunder; ripped apart.

Scriosath: memory erasure, the most complete being the tabula rasa or "blank slate," the highest form of official punishment.

Sean O'Gara (shawn oh-GAYR-uh): son of Quinn and Lily O'Gara; destined Cheile Rioga (Royal Consort) to Princess Emileia.

shilcloas (shil-CLO-ahs): hearing another's thoughts; telepathy.

sochar (SO-kar): Nuathan credits, used to purchase anything beyond provided necessities.

sohnnihe (SON-ye): trapped; held captive.

spiare (spee-AH-ray): spy; snoop.

stochail (sto-KAYL): preparation, as for a battle or journey.

streach suas (stretch SOO-ahs): resist oppression; underground resistance.

taghal ardus (TAHG-ul ar-DOOS): first touch causing a "tingle" between opposite sex teens, rarely repeated on second touch.

taigde (TAG-duh): research; records.

thrais (thrās): treason.

Teachneaglis (TAK-nee-glish): small minority of Nuathans and Echtrans who prefer to do without most modern advancements, primarily found in the villages of Bailerealta on Earth, and Keary and Eriu on Mars.

teachneoc (TEEK-nee-ok): technology; gadgetry.

teachtok (TEEK-tok) (*slang*): non-omni phone.

threoirach (TRO-rok): instruction; orientation; guidance.

tinneas (TIN-es): physical illness. Rare among Martians except in the very elderly.

toachai (TO-uh-kay): future; destiny.

triail (tree-AYL): test or audition; ordeal by trial.

Tullymayne (TULL-ee-mayn) (pop. 1,993): town in southeastern Nuath containing main transportation hub and supporting industries.

twilly: obnoxious person; jerk.

ulmuchan (UHL-muh-khan): preparation.

udaris thusmithoir (oo-DARE-is thoos-MITH-er): parental authority.

unbaen: dictator

ABOUT THE AUTHOR

New York Times and USA Today bestselling author Brenda Hiatt writes novels of sparkling romantic adventure spanning Regency England, Americana, contemporary teen science fiction and more. Which ever you pick up, you'll find excitement, romance and, always, an uplifting happy ending. In addition to writing, Brenda is passionate about embracing life to the fullest. She enjoys scuba diving (she has over 60 dives to her credit), Taekwondo (where she's currently working toward her 4th degree black belt), hiking, traveling...and reading, of course!

For a free Starstruck short story and the earliest news about Brenda Hiatt's books, subscribe to her newsletter at:

brendahiatt.com/RJsubscribe

Connect with Brenda at:
brendahiatt.com

www.ingramcontent.com/pod-product-compliance
Lightning Source LLC
Chambersburg PA
CBHW060657190726
48289CB00002B/443